"Having read books from every region of the world except the Middle East, *Escape to Aswan* opened up a whole new world of intrigue for me."

—Jim McDermott, U.S. Congressman (ret)

"The character of Salma is the main strength of this novel, showing a bicultural woman caught between the superficiality of American life and the richness and rigidity of Egyptian culture, "seeing both sides and belonging to neither." An international adventure tale that effectively works as a study of the contrast between Western and Arabic cultures."

—*Kirkus Reviews*

"A tour de force! A suspense thriller, an action movie, a travelogue, a social commentary. A complex love affair, and for me, a remembrance of things past."

—Carol Ruth Clark, Egypt Tours

"You know you have stepped into a different world from the first page. As the pages turn you can't put it down, and then you are gripping the book and starting to wonder who the good guys are and who are the bad ones. When the book ends your first question is "Where is the sequel?"

—Margaret McCormack, Geography and Middle East Lecturer, Butte College. California

"This culturally complex thriller features multilayered characters and tense action... The characters are complex, and Sedky-Winter avoids genre stereotypes by rendering messy but relatable relationships torn between any number of options..."

—*Booklife Review*

ESCAPE

- TO -

ASWAN

A NOVEL

Amal Sedky Winter

Escape to Aswan
A Novel
© 2023 Amal Sedky Winter
Cune Press, Seattle 2023
First Edition

Hardback   ISBN 9781951082741
Paperback   ISBN 9781951082581
EPUB   ISBN 9781614574408
Kindle   ISBN 9781614579816

Library of Congress Cataloging-in-Publication Data Names: Sedky Winter, Amal, author.
Title: Escape to Aswan : a novel / Amal Sedky Winter.
Description: [Seattle] : Cune, [2023] | Identifiers: LCCN 2022017831 (print) | LCCN 202201 (ebook) | ISBN
   9781951082581 (trade paperback) | ISBN 9781614574408 (epub)
Subjects:
Classification: LCC PS3619.E3444 E83 2023 (print) | LCC PS3619.E3444
   (ebook) | DDC 813/.6--dc23/eng/20220523
LC record available at https://lccn.loc.gov/2022017831
LC ebook record available at https://lccn.loc.gov/2022017832

Bridge Between the Cultures (a series from Cune Press)

Afghanistan & Beyond	Linda Sartor
Congo Prophet	Frederic Hunter
Confessions of a Knight Errant	Gretchen McCullough
Empower a Refugee	Patricia Martin Holt
Nietzsche Awakens!	Farid Younes
Stories My Father Told Me	Helen Zughaib, Elia Zughaib
Apartheid is a Crime	Mats Svensson
Arab Boy Delivered	Paul Aziz Zarou
Finding Melody Sullivan	Alice Rothchild

Syria Crossroads (a series from Cune Press)

The Dusk Visitor	Musa Al-Halool
White Carnations	Musa Rahum Abbas
East of the Grand Umayyad	Sami Moubayed
The Road from Damascus	Scott C. Davis
A Pen of Damascus Steel	Ali Ferzat
Jinwar and Other Stories	Alex Poppe

Cune Press: www.cunepress.com | www.cunepress.net

DEDICATION

This novel is dedicated to my late husband,
my muse and mentor,
William David Winter
and to the
Egyptian women we both admired

Alexandria

Cairo

Suez

Sinai Peninsula

FAYOUM

MINYA

SIDI OSMAN ★

Luxor

ASWAN

★ Fictitious Place

Part I

They [the Egyptians] were a joyous folk, and it seemed their faces were the first rays of the dawning sun. So let the journey end here, let it end with those four verses. Remember them, and them alone, when they're throwing you into Cairo Airport's "detention room."

—Najwan Darwish (Palestinian poet) (1978–)
   Exhausted on the Cross

Chapter 1

"**A**TTENTION." THE WORD POPPED ACROSS THE AIRPLANE movie screen. Salma pulled out her ear buds. This was her first trip to Cairo since bringing her two recalcitrant teenage daughters to visit her family three years ago.

"Ladies and gentlemen, this is your pilot," a disembodied voice filled the cabin. "Cairo air traffic control has redirected us to the old terminal." That got Salma's attention. Things would be messy. Who would handle her passport if her cousin didn't know of the change?

"You may collect your luggage there." She really didn't want to handle luggage alone. Not in the old terminal. "Air France ground personnel will meet you to answer questions after you disembark," the pilot continued. "We apologize for the inconvenience. Thank you for flying Air France."

Salma had delayed the start of the sociology classes she taught at the University of California, Santa Cruz, and came up with a way to join her fiancé, Paul, in Cairo without scandalizing her family by appearing to accompany him. She submitted a paper based on a sociological study she'd directed: *The effects of Islamophobia on American children of Arab heritage*. The research paper had little to do with the theme of the Conference on Counterterrorism, but the conference panel chair had been Salma's schoolmate at the Cairo British Academy twenty years ago, so naturally, she invited Salma to present it. Things worked that way in Egypt.

She steadied herself against the arm rest to look out the window at the Nile flowing south to north from Aswan to Alexandria, the length of the country, slicing through the largest non-Arctic expanse of desert in the world. Twenty years ago, her high school class took a trip to the ancient temples of Aswan, but because of her up-coming marriage to ex-president Mubarak's nephew, Salma's parents had not allowed her to join. In fact, except for airplane trips to the condo in Sharm el Sheikh, she'd never been south of Cairo. Perhaps she and Paul could go to Upper Egypt. Not this time. Maybe next. She watched the desert's colors transform from indistinguishable grey to gradations of ochre yellow sand as the plane descended, struck once more by the dramatic demarcation between the arid yellow sand and the deep-green strip of irrigated land that spread into the lotus-shaped delta anchored at Cairo, on its way to the Mediterranean Sea. She felt the plane circling and looked out at a forest of satellite dishes mounted on rooftops covered with debris—fortifications meant to hold her at bay as they prepared to land.

Pausing at the top of the airplane's metal stairway, she slipped on her sunglasses to fend off the harsh glare of the Egyptian sun. Thick air wrapped itself around her body and seeped into her pores as she surveyed the familiar landscape. This moment of return insisted on being absorbed: air sodden with industrial effluence, field manure, carbon monoxide, the boil of heat from the tarmac, the bleached-white sky. This wasn't her favorite time of day, here. Cairo was at its best at night. She loved the short route to the art classes she took in her teens with neon strips outlining the facades of stalls she walked past awash in fluorescent lights. Yellow phosphorescent lights in apartment windows. Strings of colored bulbs across the alleys off the main road. Adjusting her carry-on shoulder strap, Salma started down the stairs.

Something was wrong.

She felt it—like static activating the tiny hairs on her arms.

Humvees on the tarmac? Machine guns atop Jeeps? Soldiers at the airport?

There were always soldiers at the airport though never this many. Some on the rooftops in desert camouflage fatigues. More lined up in the building's thin shade.

Had the Muslim Brotherhood moved against Egypt's president, the Rayyis? Perhaps a radical Islamist had assassinated him. Couldn't be. It would have been all over CNN. So, what kind of disaster was she walking into?

She headed across the tarmac to the terminal, worried the oven hot asphalt would melt the soles of her sandals, her father's voice in her head, "Why aren't you wearing decent shoes?" After twenty years of growing into adulthood in California, visits to her upper-class family in Egypt had become challenging. She found the social structure oppressive, family obligations were weighty, and her father was maddeningly controlling. She didn't want her family to know she and Paul planned to marry until she'd felt them out.

Still brooding, she reached the entrance of the one-story terminal building where two rows of soldiers stood guard with shouldered machine guns. So much for a better Egypt after Tahrir. Once inside the old arrival hall, whose air conditioner had already succumbed to the heat, she looked around for her cousin, Mokhtar. He had to be here soon. He'd never stood her up before. Always escorted her to the VIP lounge, took her passport, and handled her visa while she sipped from the water-bottle he'd brought. But he wasn't here today. No matter how awkward it felt to stand in line with non-Egyptian citizen passengers, that's what she'd have to do.

Salma wasn't a foreign passenger. She'd been born in Cairo, lived there until she was seventeen when she married and went to college in the States. Yes, her mother was American, but her father was Egyptian, and she thought of herself as half and half. Now her Egyptian half screamed, "What about me? You should be embarrassed standing in a line for foreigners." But Salma had never taken out an Egyptian passport. She'd always travelled on an American one for which many countries didn't insist on visas.

Concentrating on the line she stood in, she looked beyond the passport control kiosk for her cousin, again, until she reached the head of the queue. Still, no sign of him. She stood behind the yellow line on the floor wondering how going through Egyptian immigration on her own would work. The man behind her cleared his throat to hurry her along. Half a dozen butterflies trembled in her stomach as she stepped up to the control booth to hand her passport to its agent.

"*Amrikeya?*" The tone jolted her. Coming from this uniformed official, it was more an accusation than a question. "Step to the side," the jowly man ordered. "Let the others pass." A bad sign. His contempt was palpable; she smelled his spite—the odor that small people in positions of impotent authority exude. Salma knew her father could terrify this man with a single word, but she wasn't about to call him. He couldn't tolerate her choosing to be American. As far as Hani Hamdi was concerned, Salma's choice meant she was siding with her mother against him, betraying him and his country—Salma's real country. The one where she was born. He didn't care how much she appreciated having the right to free speech and assembly and that the American embassy quickly replaced the passports she'd lost when she traveled to the Middle East to train Arab women in political empowerment. None of this made a difference to her father.

She leaned against the thick chain corralling the kiosk and waited for the officer to call her back. Maybe she could reach Paul. Scheduled to be the keynote speaker at the Conference on Counterterrorism in two days, he'd gotten into Cairo last night. Salma shifted uncomfortably at the thought of the article he'd agreed to write for *Harper's* Magazine while he was in Egypt. He was good at picking up the details that others missed. She fished her cell phone from her handbag and activated its call function.

"What's the matter, sweetheart?" he answered with the comforting composure Salma relied on.

"Something's up. The passport officer is giving me trouble."

"Yeah? What kind?"

"Haven't figured it out."

"Why don't you give your dad a call?"

"Are you nuts? It's about my passport. He blows sky high at the merest hint I'm American."

"Got it. They issued a terror alert this morning. It's a *Hala Geem* emergency maybe it has something to do with that."

"Do you know what it's about?"

"Not really. The only danger this president faces is from Islamists, so it must have something to do with the Brotherhood or one of its cohorts."

Paul knew the Middle East. Before meeting Salma, he'd been a foreign correspondent in Egypt for two years, wrote a book about ISIS while he was there. A month ago, *Harper's* offered him an eighteen-thousand-word assignment to investigate the *Jie Shun* incident and its relationship with corrupt arm sales.

The Egyptian coast guard had seized a North Korean freighter by that name preparing to enter the Suez Canal. Manned by North Koreans, flying Cambodian colors, it carried over thirty thousand rocket-propelled grenades concealed under bins of iron ore. When the United Nations condemned the clandestine purchase for violating international sanctions against the Kim Jong Un regime, only the Egyptian coast guard purported to be surprised. As to the Egyptian munitions' community? It knew exactly which businessmen and military officers were complicit in the scheme.

For five decades, Egypt's military had gulped down, some would say been force fed, American equipment ranging from supersonic jets to hammers and nails. The billions of dollars Egypt guzzled every year served the American economy. Assault rifles, hand grenades and launchers, bombs and tear gas flowed through a pipeline filthy with corruption and backed up with bribes. The *Harper's* editor was counting on Paul's journalistic acumen to expose the illegal deals, and banking on his reputation to increase the story's credibility. The assignment was an important feather in Paul's cap at a time in his career when he was shifting focus. So, she'd come to Egypt to help him by tapping into her family's contacts.

She heard his voice grow soft and brought her attention back to the phone call. "How was your flight?" he asked. "Any trouble with your asthma? I worry when we're far away from each other." Salma felt the invisible filament connecting them tug at her heart reminding her how much Paul loved her.

"Don't worry. I have inhalers." Turning to check the kiosk, she realized she hadn't acknowledged Paul's expression of concern and quickly added, "Thank you for asking, sweetheart."

This time she'd caught herself. When they first started dating, it never dawned on her that Paul might care how she felt or how she managed. She'd kept going on as she'd always done—alone. One time, she didn't mention how upset she'd been when her daughters' friend was killed, dragged under the wheels of a lumber truck.

"I didn't want to intrude on your life," she explained.

"You are my life," Paul had said, and Salma forgot to breathe.

Once, after one of their early fights, when she'd hurled hurtful words at him in anger, "You only think of yourself," that cut him deeply, he'd asked, "Would you have said that if you knew how much I loved you?" Put that way, of course, she wouldn't have, but she'd grown up without the steady, unconvoluted, love he offered. She hadn't learned that healthy love came with expectations as well as privileges.

"I love you, Paul," she whispered into her cell phone, staring at the ceiling to create the illusion of private space. Then she checked on the immigration officer again. Although most of the passengers were already at the baggage carousel, he was still stamping visas into foreign passports.

She didn't realize she'd been distracted again until Paul asked, with his usual optimism as though she'd already gone through customs, "When are we getting together?" Salma hadn't made a plan. Paul knew planning didn't work well in Egypt, where a date with friends to watch a movie might or might not happen before its run was up. Or half of the group would decide to meet at a coffee shop instead.

"I'll call you as soon as I know how the evening's stacking up with the family." A heavy weight landed on her chest when she thought about her family and Paul. "Have you touched base with Abu Taleb?" Even as she asked about his friend, the editor of the *Ahram News*, she knew her attempt to sound neutral wasn't likely to fool Paul.

"I was about to when you phoned." He sounded annoyed—as though she were nagging. "I'm also waiting for *Haaretz News* to call back from Tel Aviv." American publishers were reluctant to release books about the Middle East without Israeli vetting, and *Haaretz* had been generous in reviewing Paul's.

"Your friend, Abu Taleb, is a government mouthpiece." Salma pushed the issue. The editor had never strayed from the former president's side and now was in lockstep with the current one.

"A government man, for sure. Makes him a wonderful authority on who has his hand in the cookie jar."

Salma didn't miss the challenge in Paul's voice.

"My father's a better source," she shot back. "Particularly when it comes to Ahmed Omar." Egyptians had once hoped the 2011 Tahrir uprising would rid the country of men like Omar and Walid, both friends of her father, both corrupt to their core. Omar, a deposed president, Mubarak, cohort, skimmed millions from arms sales, bribed and blackmailed officials to garner preferential access to other lucrative contracts. One of the most depraved of the Egyptian oligarchs, the shadowy, secretive man with an off-kilter eye, was cozy with every president and everyone in the presidential orb—including Salma's father. So, her first order of business would be convincing Hani to arrange a meeting between this sleazy character and Paul. Yet, it frightened her to know Mubarak cronies like them were back in power after the 2011 Tahrir uprising—angry, more dangerous than ever.

Ordinarily, there would be no reason for Salma to be concerned for Paul's safety. But these were far from ordinary times. Islamists had spooked the government once more, and the two of them seemed to be in Egypt in the middle of a terror alert. The more she thought about that, the more concerned Salma became. True, Paul wasn't an American household name, but he was a well-known journalist connected to people in important circles. He'd make a perfect hostage. Jihadists had taken journalists with lesser reputations—murdering some to make a point. Every muscle in her body felt tight, even her face. But before she could share her concerns with Paul, the same ones she'd shared before, the passport control officer rapped on his booth's Plexiglas.

"Gotta go," she signed off with her fiancé. "His Excellency, the bureaucrat, summons." Signaling she was on her way, Salma slipped her phone into her bag and returned to his kiosk where the taciturn official pulled her U.S. passport through its document slot.

"Your name is Salma Ibrahim, right?" He glared at her, then at her passport, then at his computer screen. This wasn't good. There'd be hell to pay if her passport caused a problem. Her father would blow his stack if he had to deal with that.

"What is your father's full name?" the officer demanded.

"My father's name?" Salma repeated, not sure how to respond, hoping to deflect the question. Her mouth was dry. She swallowed, hard. The officer slammed the passport face up on the desk. From her side of the partition, she could see her picture: the olive of her skin, the darkness of her curls, and, thanks to laser surgery, no glasses. The photo made her look younger than her thirty-eight years.

"Your national identity card?" The officer thrust his rough-skinned hand through the slot.

"I don't have one," Salma replied in English. She'd never even applied for one. He raised a thin black eyebrow in disdain. "*Anna assfa*," she apologized, switching to Arabic like the native she'd once been. There was nothing more exasperating than an Egyptian bureaucrat with a smidgen of power and all the time in the world to abuse it. She'd be here forever if he thought she was too uppity to speak his language.

"You were born in Egypt, right?" The officer lowered his head and, this time, raised both eyebrows to glare at her.

"Correct. My father is Egyptian."

"If your father is Egyptian, you are Egyptian. Where is your card?" Salma didn't answer. At least he wasn't asking for her father's name, again.

"Your card." Pointing to the bag at her feet, the officer scowled.

"I told you, I don't have one." Salma raised a defiant chin. The stony-faced man, thin and stringy, rose from his seat.

"You are Egyptian. You must have an identity card." He slammed his fist against the kiosk's ledge. Salma fell back as though the man had punched her solar plexus, crushed her chest, and stopped her breath. She glanced over her shoulder automatically as though she could call for Paul even though she knew he wouldn't be nearby. Just imagining his presence calmed her.

"I'm also American," she said, straightening her shoulders, pulling herself to her full five feet six height. "Why are you doing this? You have my passport in front of you." Salma thought of adding, "Do you have any idea who I am?" Instead, she ran her tongue around her mouth to moisten it, swallowed again and told herself not to challenge this over-stuffed uniform if she hoped to manage the situation on her own. A man in his position could trump-up charges: smuggling currency, transporting drugs, or any other infraction he thought up. Still, if this officious visa stamping bozo actually detained her, she would pull rank. Risky as it was, she'd invoke her father's name even though doing so meant paying an unacceptable price. Hani would combust at the public disclosure his daughter was an American citizen and that would destroy any chance of establishing a delicate detente between him and Paul. Salma's chest tightened, she started to wheeze.

She peeked around the kiosk. Perhaps her cousin had sent someone for her when he couldn't come himself. Various guides and drivers stood in line along the passenger exit route. A man in a black and gold uniform held up a sign for Ramses Tours. A female limousine attendant, in blue skirt and blazer, had a sign with the name of: "Fraulein Ulrich." Nothing with Salma's name. Her face itched as though covered with heat-rash. She worried a pearl earring round and round—a habit she fell back on when anxious—then searched for Mokhtar's number in her phone's contact list and gave a premature sigh of relief. It was an old number, no longer in service, no referral to a new one.

She'd been back to Cairo to visit her family at least ten times in the past twenty years, each time using her American passport. But her cousin had always dealt with the technicalities. No problems. Nothing. The Egyptian government welcomed foreigners—and their money—with open arms. Officials only glanced at their passports before waving them through Customs. No one inspected their bags. Porters were gracious, not pushy. Soldiers ignored them. Police watched over them. Without even knowing it, foreigners moved in a benign bubble that excluded Egyptians. Something had changed. Whatever it was wasn't good.

The officer spit another question through his smoke-stained teeth. "It is written here. Born in Egypt, yes?" He pounded his finger at her passport.

"That's correct. I was born in Cairo."

"*Muslima?*" Once identified as Egyptian, it was a standard question, but one seldom used in this context.

"I'm Muslim, God be praised." Salma had gone agnostic over the years, yet the traditional acknowledgment still tasted sweet on her tongue. She examined the warrant officer's face for a clue to how he had taken her response. He stared, expressionless. She looked down the hall at the Egyptian nationals' kiosk. A sullen crowd waited while that officer scrutinized every page in every passport. He shouted at a young man and then, to emphasize his authority, called for two soldiers standing in line behind him. One of them stepped out of line wielding a baton to wallop the unfortunate youth. No one budged. No one uttered a word. Salma felt faint and sick to her stomach. The dignity and self-respect of the Tahrir Square insurrection seemed nothing but a mass delusion today.

"It is written in your passport you were born in Egypt," repeated the officer she was being forced to deal with.

"We've established that." She struggled to breathe.

He rose and stretched; his chair's metal legs scraped against the marble floor. He checked behind him, spun back, and lowered his head to better peer at her over his black-framed glasses.

"Are you accompanied?"

"I expect my—" Salma's face turned crimson with resentment; her stomach bound itself up in a knot. She was tired. Hungry. Hot. Her American confidence had evaporated, abandoned her. Helpless before a junior-grade officer who hadn't bothered to sift the disdain from his voice, she was about to spiral down into a muddled, mushy, mess. What made her think she could steer Paul through the nuances of his investigation when she couldn't even navigate passport control?

Again, she scoured the area beyond the booth for Mokhtar. There was a message flashing on an electronic board overhead. *Hala Geem, Hala Geem.* Emergency. Her chest cramped. She checked her purse to reassure herself; her asthma inhaler was where it belonged.

"You are not in the computer." The man leaned forward, close enough to spray spit. Salma pulled her head back. "You have no identity card." As he talked, both sides of his fleshy mouth filled with white specks of froth. He snapped her passport against the shelf between them and pointed to two guards behind her. "You go to Security with them."

A guard grabbed her bag. Salma felt her heart clench. The other seized her arm. Her body went rigid. She marched between them through the terminal, recoiling each time one of their hip pistols bumped against her own hip.

Chapter 2

Monday
September 29, 2014
3:15 pm

THE TWO GUARDS IN KHAKI LED SALMA INTO A CORRIDOR THAT reeked of vinegar and ammonia and was lined with metal doors. The eye-level rectangles of wired-glass windows looked like those one would expect in psychiatric hospitals or jails. Unearthly fluorescent bulbs buzzed and flickered overhead, as if ready to explode. The light striking from the ceiling glanced off the marble floor. The dull sound of thuds pummeling against flesh and an agonized scream escaped into the hall. Salma's head spun. She shrank into herself. Sinister things happened on the dark side of clanging doors: waterboarding, rubber hoses, forced virginity tests.

Instinctively, she pressed her hands against the door jambs and stiffened her arms, but the two soldiers easily pushed her into a windowless office with walls of mottled beige in need of paint. Paper-stuffed folders were stacked high against one of them. There were no file cabinets.

An indeterminate-aged official with traces of brown bristle on his chin and along his mustache line sat at a battleship-grey desk. Salma's heartbeats thrashed in her ears. Is this where they'd work her over? She had to pull herself together. Focus. Get out of here. And if this guy started anything, she'd call in her father's protection, whatever the cost. Then, one of the soldiers shoved her forward, and she decided not to wait for what seemed inevitable.

"Please call my father," she told the officer in a tone of authority she wished she possessed.

"Hala Geem emergency. No telephone calls." He brushed his forefinger up and down his chin then exhaled through his fingers.

"I'll call." She started towards her bag on the floor by the door.

"No," the officer shouted. Salma turned back to his desk. "What is your name?" the man asked roughly, opening her passport to the front page, and holding it up as though to compare her responses to the data it contained. "How long have you lived in the United States?"

"Over twenty years." Although, she counseled herself to be patient, Salma felt stupid humoring the man.

"Did you emigrate?"

She ran her tongue over her upper lip. Too complicated to explain. Egypt only honored patrilineal citizenship. Let him think she'd emigrated. She resented his inquisition. Her head ached and the room seemed to be orbiting around her, whirling her towards undoing her caution.

"What is the year of your birth?" Again, she didn't answer. The date was in the passport.

"I see," the officer continued, letting out a vexed breath through pursed lips. "Before the Six October War." Like most Egyptians, he was marking the passage of time by political events: after the Suez War, before the rout of 1967, after Sadat's assassination, and now, before the Tahrir uprising.

"What is your occupation?" he asked, reaching for his glasses as he gave Salma a long, considering look.

"I'm a sociologist. I'm giving a lecture at the Conference on Counterterrorism, the day after tomorrow."

"Can you prove that?" The note of hesitation in his question held the promise of at least a sliver of hope. If Salma didn't defy the man, perhaps he'd let her go.

"I have a letter from the head of the committee." She pointed to her bag propped against the wall.

The officer motioned to a soldier, who brought it to the desk where Salma shoved her toiletry bag and inhaler aside to dig through house keys, dark glasses, crumpled bills, and old receipts.

"Here it is," she said with sweat seeping from her armpits as she handed it to him. Apparently struggling with its English, the officer read it slowly.

"This letter is to Doctor Salma Hamdi. Not to you, madam. Not to Salma Ibrahim."

"In America, I use my ex-husband's name. The chair of the committee is a friend and used the name I grew up with. I am Salma Hani Hamdi." So, that's why the kiosk officer had been upset. In Egypt, she didn't exist—not by that name, at least.

Keying in her maiden's name, the officer checked his computer database. Salma watched as anxiety replaced the look of irritation on his face. He hit the side of his head with an open palm and grimaced. Then, he took a deep breath and pointed to his screen with exaggerated restraint. "Salma Hani Ahmed Hamdi." He read the names off aloud, pausing between each one for emphasis. "Not Salma Ibrahim." Hearing both of her names together made her feel disassociated. One was the daughter of an eminence of the country. The other was the divorced wife of a president's nephew. And neither name was related to who she felt she was. She watched the man press his lips together and swallow. She heard him say, "Please, *ya doctora*. Please. I did not know your father was Dr. Hani Hamdi."

Salma wasn't prepared for the fear in the man's voice. It focused her. Avoiding his eyes, she glanced at the soldiers by the door. Their eyes seemed to have sunk into their chalky faces. She clicked the clasp of her bag back and forth waiting for the apprehensive silence to end.

"Please, *ya doctora*." The officer's dark face paled as he pleaded. "I did not know, *ya doctora*—I did not recognize your father's name." Beads of sweat broke out on his nose. "Please, excuse. Please, forgive." Most of the time, Salma hated the groveling her father's name elicited. This time she savored the pleasure of seeing the visa stamp shake in this bureaucrat's hand.

The door flew open and banged against the wall. The officer leaped from his chair and Salma swung around to face the commotion. Her father's friend, Colonel Rashid, and two of his henchmen, swaggered into the room.

"You honor us, Excellency," the poor immigration officer stammered. "The entire airport is bright with your presence. I hope we have met your expectations for *Hala Geem.*" The colonel ignored him, pushed aside his retinue, made a beeline to Salma and took her hand. She noticed he now sported three stars on his epaulets and four rows of medals over his pocket. But his eyes hadn't changed. Still cold, sharp, corrosively black.

"Your father called me. He's in the car. Your cousin could not come. I wish you had called me." Rashid hesitated for a fraction of a second but maintained the steady pressure of his fingers on her skin. "If I'd known you were coming, I'd have met you at the airplane myself. There is much tension today." Releasing her hand, he snapped his fingers in the officer's face. "Give me the passport. I will escort the *doctora* to her father myself."

Wrapped in angry silence at Rashid's presumptuous interference, Salma had to accompany him through the terminal, his hand too familiar on her arm. Waves of revulsion washed over her at the thought the colonel had once asked to marry her. No way. She couldn't stand him then. She couldn't stand him now.

They passed the usual complement of laptop-toting businessmen trailing behind "fixers" who herded them first to the currency exchange then to the visa desk. More soldiers. A row of them, eyes alert, hands clasped behind their backs, standing beneath a large red, white, and black Egyptian flag. She told herself to relax. The worst was over. She looked around the hall to take her bearings.

The people surrounding her were dressed differently from when she was young—especially the women. No fashionable Calvin Klein miniskirts for these teens. And their mothers weren't done up in Gucci outfits. No Hermes scarves, no stylishly coiffed hair. Today, there were waist length *hijab* scarfs everywhere and way too many ominous black *abayas*—even some like Saudi women wore, with netting instead of slits for the eyes. How would a lost child recognize his or her mother when all the women in sight were shrouded in black? The country had become more religious over the past thirty years, and that pained Salma. Muslims prayed five times a day, halting work to do so. Christians wore large crosses on their chests and kept to their own.

Threading her way through the melee of the terminal, she felt half naked in her knee-length skirt and short-sleeved blouse. A flush of shame crept along her exposed skin. Again, she'd acted like a foreigner—more worried about Egypt's heat than its puritanical dress code.

Halfway to the arrival hall's exit, Rashid stopped to talk to a young security officer and Salma used the time to look around once more. A middle-aged man straddling a boxed microwave oven must have once dreamed of escaping Egypt's poverty by emigrating to Europe. But he and his fellow Muslims were no longer welcome there. Salma had seen the signs plastered on buses, scrawled on overpasses, stamped on walls. They sent a clear message: Muslims go home. She figured his knock-off Cartier wristwatch might salve the man's ego for a while, but Egypt's lower class would soon reabsorb him. His dusky, plump, wife would exchange the flowered green dress she was wearing for a plain dark one and take up the *hijab*. Salma watched as the woman tried to catch her daughter's eye but the girl who was standing several slouched adolescent steps away, had her mind attached to an iPhone anchored across the Mediterranean Sea. This connection would break, too. Salma wondered if the girl would continue to listen to pop songs and podcasts, or if soon only the Quran would pour forth from her headphones. Her spirits sank even further. But for her lucky stars, the country's upsurge of religiosity might have swallowed up her and her daughters.

While the Hani family wasn't observant, she recognized the challenge she presented in planning to marry Paul. He was not only American, he was also Jewish—although more agnostic even than she. She could predict the reactions. With typical Egyptian avoidance, her uncle would be silent. Her cousins, Farida, and Mokhtar would be distant, formal, and correct. Her father? The nose in his red, blotchy face would turn white with anger and he'd explode with something like:

"Never! I'll disown you if you go through with this."

So, she wouldn't be breaking the news of her plans to marry Paul on this trip. His investigation for *Harper's* was enough for now. But she had to bring him and her father together, not only for Paul to get her father's contacts, but also for the protection her father could provide him. Willing to do whatever it required to make this happen, she braced herself to comply with Egypt's conservative social rules as though she still lived here. She wouldn't disagree with anyone or offer information or add anything new to a conversation. She was here to help Paul. And as a good daughter should, she'd stay at the family home, instead of with him at the conference hotel. She'd humor her father no matter how much he provoked her.

Chapter 3

Monday
September 29, 2014
4:00 pm

FLANKED BY COLONEL RASHID AND HIS TWO GOONS, Salma stood in the shade of the terminal overhang, her hair clinging to her forehead from the heat. Traffic officers blew their whistles. Tourist police shouted at porters who shouted "*yalla, yalla, 'alatool*" at other porters reluctant to leave the companionship of their small groups. Perhaps because nearly a billion people were crowded into a narrow strip along the Nile, proximity was embedded in Egyptians' DNA. As her mother, Ann, once told her, "There are never fewer than three workers for every job in this country: a man to do the work, a sidekick to keep him company and a guy to bring them tea." Everyone was glued to someone. No one stood alone.

Soldiers—heads capped with red berets; their rifles topped with bayonets—saluted when three black Cadillac limousines drew up to the sidewalk. The window of the middle one slid halfway down, and Salma saw her father seated, ramrod stiff, in the backseat. With a nod in her direction to acknowledge her presence rather than greet her, he reached over the tinted glass to shake the colonel's hand. Although her body and brain went numb for a second at this unexpected affront, Salma quickly regained her normal vigilance to observe her father more carefully. Only just arrived and already in his debt.

As fastidiously dressed as ever, Hani wore elegant dark brown pants and the expensive rough-weave jacket Salma and he had bought in San Francisco last year. He'd gained a few pounds. The way his face had filled out attracted attention to the cleft in his chin and the sharp angry lines at the edges of his lips still dominated his countenance. Salma stood by the car, her blouse sticking to her in odd places, searching the nuances of his every expression for a sign of a real greeting. Her father's attention remained on Rashid.

"I will not stand for it." Hani was firm. "Dock both officers three months' pay." Salma guessed Rashid gave the matter his own spin when he reported on the trouble her married name caused. Did that explain the extra chill in her father's reception? Without thinking, she reached for his arm, resting on the frame of the now fully opened window.

"Dad, it wasn't their fault. It was because I didn't—" Hani brushed her hand away.

"You have caused enough trouble, Mrs. Ibrahim."

She plucked the back of her cotton blouse from her skin. There was no mistaking the emphasis on her married name. A terrible start to this trip. To preserve their patrimony, Egyptian women keep their fathers' names after they marry, and her father never forgave her for taking her ex-husband, Atif's. He certainly didn't understand why she'd kept it after the divorce.

"*Alph shukr, ya habibi,*" Hani thanked Rashid. "And my best regards to your parents. You will lunch with us while Salma is here."

"It would be my pleasure, sir." The colonel guided Salma to the car, a firm hand cupping her elbow. "Welcome back," he said. "Here's your passport, *doctora*. I hope you'll stay a while longer this time."

This oily opportunist tempted Salma to call a cab and go straight to Paul's hotel. Instead, she stiffened her spine and plunked herself in the backseat next to her father. Part of managing him meant resigning herself to behaving like the good Egyptian daughter he expected her to be.

She leaned into the luxury of the leather seat to let its coolness soothe her skin. No harm in her appreciating one of Hani's perks. Waiting for him to reach out to her, she watched him from the corner of her eye as she pretended to stare out her window. He pushed the button that rolled it up.

"You are fortunate," Hani said. Salma turned to face him, with a silent body language question. "Rashid was promoted last year."

"Really?" she asked to be polite, hoping he'd appreciate her reaching out to him.

"Yes. He is now chief of the Egyptian General Command for Counterterrorism. At the airport for the Hala Geem alert," he replied and that had to serve as a "Welcome home."

"It must be serious. The airport was full of soldiers." At least Salma could encourage the conversation her father started. "I saw the notice of the *Hala Geem* emergency, but I don't know what happened."

"Two days ago, the Brotherhood bastards set off a car bomb at the Presidential Palace. Now there are check-points and blockades all over the city. Mokhtar asked me to pick you up because he couldn't leave Heliopolis. The police blocked the area in at least five places. For one thing, it's too close to the airport. There are riots in Tahrir Square right now. You don't understand the danger. People killed. There's a fire at the Mogamma'a building."

Salma froze imagining Paul rushing to the explosion. He'd do that, no matter the danger. Something about being in the middle of the action. Images roiled in her head. The crowd discovering that he was American. Men tearing at his clothes. Women spitting in his face. Feeling as though a hole had opened below her, she grabbed the window strap to steady herself as they drove in silence down Salah Salem Street. Then, determined to reach out to her father, she took a deep breath and said, "I'm touched you came to the airport, Dad. Sorry I didn't figure out the passport thing." That's when she should have stopped. Instead, she added, "It doesn't seem right to punish those men."

"Are you telling me what's right and wrong in my own country, Mrs. Ibrahim?" Her father raised his bushy eyebrows in contempt and Salma knew she'd blown it. "Egypt is not a theme park for your holidays. Temples, pyramids, palm trees and photogenic poverty. People here must be handled firmly. Authority is essential." He straightened the sharp creases of his trousers.

She was more than familiar with her dad's authoritarian style, but in large and small ways, he'd become colder during the past several years, less tolerant than ever. He treated his family as though it existed only to serve him. He'd fired three gardeners in a row, and it looked like he'd replaced Abdou, the family chauffeur for twenty years with today's sour-looking driver who kept a square-handled pistol on the passenger seat.

What Salma was about to say was best left unsaid but, as usual, the words rushed up her throat. "I respect your authority, Dad—not this streak of cruelty. You didn't used to be like that. Last year you hurt Mom's feelings, again. The American Medical Association Convention in San Francisco was two blocks from her condo. You didn't bother to visit her—not even for ten minutes. And you never called her, although I begged you to. I don't care if you're separated. It's still not right."

The air in the car felt like cracked ice but her cotton blouse had plastered itself to her back, again. A long moment slid by before she added, "I guess your job has changed you."

"What would you know about my job? I'm responsible for the health of our soldiers, our sailors and coast guards. And I'm accountable for the health of all prisoners in military detention." Human rights groups reported Egypt held sixty thousand political prisoners in military prisons filled three times over capacity. The filth, the sodomy, the torture would harden any heart. She tried to push away the thought that hammered at her head: perhaps it was the hard heart that created the foul conditions. So, she couldn't stop going at her father.

"Why don't you do something to improve prison conditions?"

Hani's dark eyes turned an arctic-ice black, the edges of his mouth turned downward. "Supporting Amnesty International doesn't make you an authority on prison conditions," he said, leaning back and spreading his legs wide, as if giving his arrogance room to stretch. "I don't care who you think you are in America. I will not allow you to talk to me this way. *Ayb, ya* Salma. You will respect me."

Salma wanted to scream. *Ayb, Ayb, Ayb.* Shame, Shame, Shame. The most overused injunction in the Arabic language. One that smothered life itself. "*Ayb*, your skirt is too short. *Ayb*, your voice is too loud. *Ayb*, young lady, don't you ever cross your elders." Social rules like this had buried any sense of personhood in this country and the weight of adhering to suffocating mores to protect family honor pressed like a granite block on her chest. She'd have already died of it if she'd had to live here, but there was too much at stake for her to lash out now. Although her heart was beating fast, she dropped her hands to her lap, laced and unlaced her fingers, and composed herself.

She watched her father pull a newspaper from the car door's leather pocket. He shook it open and held it up between them so the three red pyramids on the *Ahram News* masthead formed a barrier between them as effective as the limestone of the physical ones. Salma had lost count of how many times her father had hidden behind a newspaper, but she'd never forgotten one incident in particular. He was in his armchair, her young eyes level with his hand. She'd just sounded-out the Arabic headline and was proud of her accomplishment. Arabic was a difficult language and she'd waited for the praise she was surely due. Glaring at the shiny aquamarine in his University of California ring, she'd waited for what seemed like forever. Then she bit his finger and ran.

Now, she itched to blast this paper from his grip. Rip it to shreds, toss the scraps out the window. Instead, she crossed her knees and smoothed out a non-existent wrinkle in her skirt. But try as she might, she couldn't stop the words toppling from her mouth, "For God's sake, Dad. Put down the paper." Hani brought the paper's pages together, ran his thumb and forefinger along their midline crease and set it on the seat between them.

"So, how do you like Egypt, Dr. Ibrahim?" He gave out one of the contemptuous laughs she hated. Again the Mrs. Ibrahim.

"Dad, that's not fair." She raised her hands palms forward, in a plea for understanding. "After the divorce, the girls insisted I keep Atif's name. It's their father's name, after all."

"You live in America like an American, don't you, *habibti*? No one knows what people you belong to or who your father is." Hani's contempt was everywhere—in the corners of his eyes, in the curl of his lips.

"For heaven's sake. My mother, your wife, is American."

"Is that why she hasn't lived with me for the past five years?" Salma felt the sadness beneath his anger. "And you?" Hani continued. "Have you forgotten the life you enjoyed here? The mansion full of servants? The finest private schools. Vacations in Europe and America, every year. Have you forgotten your wedding? A thousand and one guests." His voice trailed off; his shoulders slumped. He refolded his handkerchief and returned it to his suit pocket with the monogrammed "H" facing out.

Salma hadn't had much to say about her wedding, more an exposition of her father's wealth than a celebration of her marriage. Not that she'd expected anything different. She was thinking of how much she'd changed since then when her father asked, "How do I explain to myself and my family that my wife and my only child—my only grandchildren—don't live in my home like regular people?" She couldn't answer him, so she didn't. Salma knew what would follow the so-called question. "I don't know why you take your mother's side against me."

It was a familiar accusation. She could only console her father by taking his side. Which she couldn't. It was fruitless to take either of her parents' sides. Her mother could never survive today's Egypt; her father would never surrender his homeland. She drew a deep breath. Her dad wouldn't take her side on anything if she couldn't keep this angry scolding from trespassing in her brain.

"I was out of line, Dad. I'm sorry. Stressed out. The incident at the airport scared me," she said, knowing he'd never acknowledge her apology should he deign to accept it. She created a mindless gray of lifeless space inside her and focused on that. It was something she'd done since she was nine. Something she'd kept doing when she was married to Atif. That's how a thinking woman survived.

"How is your mother, anyway?" Her father asked the question she knew was coming, the one she dreaded.

"She's staying with the girls while I'm here. Oh, and she's starting to play bridge again," Salma answered warily.

"What kind of an answer is that?"

"Okay. What do you want to know?

"How's she responding to the electric shock treatment?"

"I think it's working. She's made a few friends in the condo complex and at least I'm not speeding up the freeway when she swallows a bottle of pills. She'd obviously been scamming her doctors." Fleetingly, she wished her mother was not her mother and felt a blend of guilt and sadness. From the time she was ten years old, every time her mother overdosed on her sodium pentothal, she'd summon Salma to her bedside for her to go bring her father there. It was wrong. Why was Salma in the middle? Hani should have been the one caring for his wife.

"Why didn't you bring her with you?" her father persisted, putting it on Salma, again.

"You know perfectly well there's no way to make her come," she answered, as steadily as she could. "She's stubborn, like you." She immediately regretted the last phrase when her father's nose turned its angry white.

"You have no right to think that," he scolded. "You were stubborn as a child and you're stubborn now. You haven't grown up. Life hasn't taught you a thing."

"Dad, how could you say that? I'm trying to make a life. I'm raising two daughters. I have a career. I wish you could be proud of me." She felt a headache starting at her temples, faint for the moment, but coming on strong.

"Without a father? Is that raising them?" Hani asked in contempt. Salma forced a flat, even, tone to her voice before she replied.

"I'm raising my daughters alone because Atif ran off to Kuwait after the divorce you insisted upon."

"No one slaps my daughter. No one insults a Hamdi. Not even Mubarak's nephew," Hani replied fiercely. "Of course, you had to divorce him in America where it is easy to get one. But I told you to come back to Egypt after that. I told you I would take care of you and your children. You could have married Colonel Rashid."

Salma clamped her hands against her head. Lord. If he said another word, she'd pull out her hair. She'd vowed never to marry another Arab. And if she did, it would have been Murad, the Egyptian graduate student she'd loved in California seven years ago. She could see his face now. The color of fine sandalwood, set off by a widow's peak of black hair that was straighter than hers or Paul's. And there was his smile. A smile that zapped her chest like an electric shock and made her body tingle. She could see his deep-set, ocean-green eyes, his hand reaching to steady her across the moss-covered rocks in the mountain stream behind her cottage or holding a pen to calculate statistical co-variances for her doctoral dissertation. He enthralled her daughters with complex cat's cradle games and turning her knees soft when he set them on her shoulders. If he hadn't let tradition triumph over his love, they might have made a good life together. And if Paul hadn't come into hers, she'd still be wishing things had worked out with Murad.

"You can still marry him." Hani's voice was softer. Salma spun to face him. Had she been thinking aloud? Had she even uttered Murad's name? "Rashid's still asking for your hand. He's a wonderful, dedicated, mature man who wants to---"

"That's never going to happen." Salma almost laughed.

She used the ensuing silence to center herself then hauled out her smartphone to check her social media dashboard. A tweet from Paul. *1000s in Tahrir. Tense.* Relief. He was tweeting. He must be safe.

"Can't you get along without that thing?" her father sneered.

"I'm checking on the girls," she lied. "High school starts this week."

She peeked at her watch. A half past six. They were still on the wide, extravagant, Salah Salem Street lined with fancy patisseries and designer clothing stores that screened the ugly realities behind them and welcomed foreigners and dignitaries on their way downtown. It was as good a time as any to engage with her father about Paul's mission. She picked up the newspaper, rifled through its pages without unfolding them. There. Page three. A photo of Ali Walid, with his tight, pursed lips and the genteelly tousled, unnaturally black hair.

"Dad." She cleared her throat. "What has Walid been doing since the courts exonerated him of—"

"Money laundering," her father completed her question. "The court fined him three billion dollars and sentenced him to seven years in prison. That was during the hysteria of the Tahrir uprising. Fortunately, once the country came to its senses, he only served two years and most of his money was refunded." Salma didn't point out Walid's high-class incarceration—catered meals, cell phones, unlimited visits with friends and coconspirators in the exercise yard.

"So, no one went after the Walid Cement Company's monopoly?" As long as she could remember, folks had complained of the parliamentary ban on the purchase of the significantly cheaper Chinese cement.

"They didn't have anything on him," her father replied. "Why punish a guy who worked day and night? God cleared the path for him. So, he got rich. No crime in that." Possibly her father had reason to defend his friend. At the height of his power, there was no crossing Ali Walid. He'd been head of the then president Mubarak's National Democratic Party—a bunch of neo-liberal financial interests masquerading as an organization—and a front for Gamal Mubarak, heir apparent to his father's presidency. With that kind of financial and political power, Walid was bound to be a lightening-rod.

It would be up to Paul to discover what the suave, sixty-year-old man in his Italian suits was doing dealing in arms. Had he stolen hand in glove with Ahmed Omar? As early as 1984, a U.S. District Court convicted

Omar of felony charges for overcharging the Pentagon millions of dollars. Undeterred, he continued to skim millions more from other U.S. military contracts. Paul would have to track not only his more recent transactions but also what role he'd played in the *Jie Shun* shipment from North Korea.

And Salma had to pick the right time to talk to her father about Paul. This wasn't one—he was upset; the driver was tense. On the road for less than an hour and already her muscles were jerking under her skin. To drive in Cairo was precarious in ordinary circumstances. Lanes were nonexistent. Vendors spread mats on the street in front of cars parked in rows on the sidewalks; bicyclists cycled in and out around pedestrians and vehicles, traffic police motioned drivers to cross against red lights and, except in a few squares like Tahrir, crosswalks did not exist. Egyptian streets were theater. A matter of humans and nonhumans swarmed through them like a single organism. Salma found herself scowling at the ubiquitous white taxis moving like a herd of cows hemming-in the Hamdi limo.

Too anxious to wait for Paul's next tweet, Salma texted him. No reply. She tried to convince herself he was all right. Riots were nothing new to him. He'd been in worse trouble spots. She was making herself anxious when what she should do was concentrate on the here and now. One of the things she needed to do was call her daughters, tell them she'd arrived safely and see how school registration had gone. Nawal's phone went to voicemail after four rings, so Salma left a message. At least they'd know she was now in Cairo. Hoda's mailbox was full, she only binge listened to her messages every couple of weeks. Calling her mother while sitting with her father was awkward at best.

"Everything seems okay at home," she told him and switched subjects before he could drag her into one about her mother.

"Where are the protesters?" she asked him although she knew.

"Tahrir Square—Liberation Square—as always."

"I thought the *rayyis* outlawed all public gatherings, especially demonstrations?"

"Today is different. After the Brotherhood attacked his palace, the president called for the spoiled kids of the bourgeoisie to show their support. Students from fancy colleges: the American University, the German one. They're in love with him." Her father was probably right.

The economy was on an upswing. China's state-capitalism model, with the military directing investments and sharing profits, was working where Mubarak's American neo-liberal style had failed. But, while Asian money was pouring into the country, satisfying the elites and the contractors who could now buy the cheaper Chinese cement, profits never trickled down to the average Egyptian.

Salma's father surprised her by continuing his diatribe. "I don't trust the man who's advising the president. Why is he encouraging demonstrations like this? Everyone knows that as soon as the president's coddled supporters get tired, they'll dash into McDonald's to slurp McFlurries and mess around in KFC's air conditioning. At that point, as it does every time, the Brotherhood will take over the square. Then the army shoots, everything goes to hell, and the Islamists come out ahead."

"How?"

"They show the people they are still strong even though the authorities have been arresting them by the thousands."

"So, who's advising the president to do this?" Salma asked when Hani paused to unbutton his jacket.

"You don't know him. The man is ten years younger than I am, but he was only a class behind me in the Military Academy. He has powerful friends. A bunch of officers got him to the top of the pyramid fast. Now, he's a presidential adviser. But the man is stupid. He doesn't look more than one move ahead so he's only helping the damned Brotherhood." Hani looked as though he could spit.

Salma assumed her father knew the military's inner machinations. All she knew was that a short year after optimists called the 2011 uprising a revolution, a rigged election, supported by the military, allowed the incompetent Morsi to become president and his Muslim Brotherhood to take over. Votes were cheap: a bottle of cooking oil, a sack of rice, a blanket. Polling place inspectors who belonged to the Brotherhood, stood over the shoulders of bribed voters to make sure they checked the Morsi symbol on their ballots. As for those who didn't feel like standing in line, someone cast a ballot for them. Although Salma hadn't voted in the sham elections, even at a distance she felt as powerless as the army wanted her to feel.

The blast of fresh air that had blown through the country in the Arab Spring, had left havoc in its wake and Egyptians were willing to support a fascist religious power grab. Then, disaffected, they changed their minds and clamored for a fascist secular military to overthrow it. So, after only one year, a military coup overthrew the Brotherhood's pseudo-legitimate government as the generals had always planned to.

Could democracy work where people were abjectly poor, uneducated, illiterate? The Arab women she trained to participate in politics had all been from the upper classes, some were even members of royal families. Their countries' political soil, depleted by centuries of colonialism and corruption, didn't support grass roots activism. Most Arabs lived in generally authoritarian families, almost always patriarchal. It was natural for them to look to a strong man. She was remembering the frosted cupcakes topped with the president's image she saw street vendors selling the last time she was in Cairo when her father asked, "What do these internet dandies know about the real Egypt, anyway? They're all graduating from private colleges and heading to Europe or the States." Salma couldn't believe what she'd just heard. Her father was referring to people like the kind he'd raised her to be. The kind her own daughters would have been if they'd grown up here. Rich, powerful, and disconnected from eighty-five percent of the country. There had to be a way in which the privileges she received didn't alienate her from those who weren't as lucky. The rigid social-class structure she grew up in was disgusting. Thank God she lived in America with its refreshing anonymity.

Again, she checked her social media feed. Found Paul's tweet: *Water cannons. Machine guns. Army? Police?* A prickling ran up and down her arms. What would she do if something happened to him? Paul was different from Murad. He wasn't as serious, not as easily disheartened and he had a fantastic sense of humor—the smart, witty kind. Himself a father of teenagers, he was sensitive to the boundaries her almost adult daughters needed—probably wouldn't have been that close to them, anyway. He wasn't interested in creating another family. Perhaps it was selfish, but Salma loved that Paul concentrated his attention on her. When they were part of a gathering, he kept track of where she was, smiling, winking, raising his glass of wine towards her. He liked being physically close, not just in bed but in public. He'd put an arm across her shoulders, reach for her hand, kiss her on their walks in the park. Salma couldn't imagine Murad being demonstrative in public.

"How many people in Tahrir today?" she asked, fiddling an earring in a reddening earlobe.

"Depends on who's reporting," Hani answered. "The government stations say several thousand. *Al Jazeera News* claims they're only in the hundreds. But who trusts it?" His response didn't surprise Salma. The Kingdom of Qatar had financed the Brotherhood regime and owned the *Al Jazeera* satellite station. In other words, it wasn't on the government's payroll. She looked down at her phone.

"It's going to take forever to get home," she said, ducking the *Al Jazeera* bait, not mentioning that Egypt had lost what little freedom of the press it had had under Mubarak.

"Every day we deal with traffic blockades. You should be glad I got to the airport. It was only courtesy of the Presidential Guards. The ones you disdain. The ones that come with my authority."

Salma pictured the man in the terminal shuffling his microwave oven. He'd never have what her father called authority. He'd be lucky paying off the police to keep a cigarette and soda-pop stall open. How would folks like him adjust to Egypt after life in Europe?

Hani drew a monogrammed handkerchief from his breast pocket to mop the top of his bald head. The gesture was so familiar it tugged at Salma's heart, reminding her of how he used to be. Slipping off her sandals, she stretched her legs and listened to him fume.

"The Brotherhood is blowing up things here. Their Islamist friends are blowing them up in Sinai. Every day, there is more and more violence."

Salma appreciated her father's concern. She was concerned, too. But at this moment she was consumed with just getting out of the car. She leaned over the chauffeur's shoulder, reeking of stale cigarette smoke, to check the speedometer. Their speed had increased from ten to a rousing twenty miles an hour and it was already five thirty in the afternoon. It would be another hour before they reached the Hamdi villa. How did anyone get anywhere in this coagulated mess? Twenty-two million Cairenes with years of their lives lost to dust and pollution. If streets are a city's arteries, Cairo was poised for a major heart attack.

They passed the City of the Dead, a four-mile area supplied with municipal sparse water and electricity. Half a million permanent squatters, including those in the Hamdi mausoleum, were permanently settled in with the deceased. As one of the thousand slums in Cairo, this one was better than most, Salma recalled as she watched the cemetery's low crypts recede. Only the carved domes of the Turkish Mameluke mausoleums, towering over the tombs of those they'd once ruled, caught the last of the evening light at the foot of the sandstone outcroppings of the Muqqattam Hills. Just the thought of being interred in the Hamdi mausoleum with endless generations of dead Hamdis—bone upon bone forever—made Salma cringe.

She'd been ten years old when she made her first visit to commemorate the passing of forty days—the *arba'een*—of her grandmother's death. The ancient Egyptian ritual celebrated the embarkation of the spirit on its journey to the netherworld where it would live the life it had enjoyed on Earth. Salma shut her eyes to summon up what a maid had told her about a parallel realm where djinn spirits walked right through people's bodies as they went on with their daily business, cooking meals, sweeping floors, washing their shrouds. It became her favorite childhood daydream.

The afternoon of the *arba'een* in the cemetery had been hot, heavy with the odor of dung and burning garbage. The fine sand blowing off the Muqqattam Hills, settled in Cairo's every nook and cranny. That same sand prickled Salma's skin as she skipped along in her father's shadow, sheltered from the sun.

The squatters who maintained the mausoleum had left for the day. Informed by the Hamdi family that it planned to pay its private respects, they'd shoved their meager furnishings against the flaking walls and cleared out the three antechambers. They'd swept the marble plaques of Salma's oldest uncle and watered the clay pots of succulents. Hani didn't seem to notice the household goods—dented aluminum pots, battered primus burners, piles of worn rugs and heaps of laundry. But Salma took in every detail, transfixed. She tried to make sense of the small television set. She never imagined these invisible people watching the same T.V. shows she watched. The poor in Egypt, like the spirits of the dead, simply inhabited a parallel realm. Ninety million people, wretched in their poverty, simply did not exist for the other ten.

Suddenly, her smartphone vibrated. Paul's text: *Gotta go. Trble. Serious.* A rush of adrenaline surged through her body. What kind of trouble was he in? She felt her saliva thicken in her throat but pulled herself together to text back: *What's up? Leave now.* Paul answered: *Can't. Talk later.* Why couldn't he talk now? And how long was "later?" Salma's brain filled with static. She felt like throwing up.

"Look," her father grumbled, pointing at his phone. "Just as I said. The Brotherhood's taken over the square. Their men crawl out from tunnels under rocks in the sand."

Salma was too anxious to respond. Her breath was caught in her chest. She closed her eyes to keep from getting dizzy and to ward off an asthma attack as they drove in silence for ten minutes before her father spoke again.

"I hear you're going to the conference at the Shams hotel. What do you know about terrorism?"

Salma turned to face him, expressionless.

"I hope you're coming, Dad. I'm actually presenting, I'd love to have you there," she said. Her father had to know by the saccharine sweetness of her tone that she'd heard him insult her. She watched him rub a smudge of dust off his high-polished shoes and move a not-so-subtle inch away. Another ten silent minutes passed before she pasted a thin smile on her face and took the plunge. "The keynote speaker is a friend of mine. I'd like you to meet him."

"Why?" Hani's tone was as short as his monosyllabic response.

"He's writing an article on the relationship between America and the Egyptian military. There must be good and not so good people for him to meet. It's important you steer him to the right people."

"Why would I do that?" Her father was still on the offensive, but Salma stayed calm.

"You'd want to be certain his assessment is fair. That he writes a balanced article. It would be better for everyone if you took him under your wing." Hani's face tightened.

"Are you insinuating I have a reason to do that?" The ensuing silence was too solid to penetrate. She hadn't been prepared for him to take her on so bluntly. "Is he worth the trouble?" Before she could reply to him, he leaned towards the driver, whispered. The driver muttered. What had disturbed the men? She looked out the back window, checked on the black Cadillac behind them then checked on the one in front. The two limos still had Hani's limo sandwiched between them.

"What's the matter, Dad?"

"Nothing."

"Something is wrong."

"I said: nothing." Salma felt scolded like a child.

Usually, the traffic opened up past the cemetery and the Muqqattam Hills. This evening, police-manned barricades blocked the five-way intersection with razor wire coiled around steel cross bars and recast concrete t-walls and sandbags to either side of them. Salma despaired of ever getting through, praying Paul was safely out of Tahrir Square.

A bullhorn in the front car hawked, scratchy and monotonous, "Make way for the Presidential Guards."

"Be careful," a policeman told the driver as Hani's convoy inched through the cordon. "Demonstrators marching to the presidential palace, again. It is safer to detour."

"I worry when we have to slow down, sir," the driver told Hani, scanning the shadows along the road, steadying his Glock against the dashboard. Salma's scalp tingled as though it had electrodes attached. She twisted in her seat to stare at her father who kept staring, forward shoulders squared.

"Turn off at the Le Baron mansion. Take the parallel street." When the driver turned at the next corner, Salma caught a glimpse down a side street. A forbidding mass of women, wrapped in black *abayas*, was spreading toward them as though a huge bottle of ink had tipped over. The demonstration was silent, peaceful, tightly organized, and terrifying. Who could stand up to this kind of power, over and over, again? By the very nature of its silence the throng of women seemed ominous. She wrapped her hands around her legs and buried her head between her knees, feeling like her insides were about to leave her body.

The women, young and old, many with children on hip or shoulder, marched in disciplined lines, brandishing yellow placards stamped with the Brotherhood's four-fingered emblem of the Rab'a el-Adaweya mosque massacre. For six weeks, Brotherhood members and sympathizers had encamped in the fortified mosque to protest the military coup against them. Human Rights Watch reported Egypt's security forces had set a world record for the slaughter of demonstrators in a single day. Two thousand killed. One thousand wounded. No ambulances. No medics. No help. And no whitewashing the incident. Given that her father headed the military's medical division, it was likely he would have had a hand in withholding medical assistance.

What if he was linked to the Raba'a disaster? Salma forced herself not to go down that rabbit hole. If he was involved in the massacre, she didn't want to know. Still, she couldn't keep herself from asking, "Dad, why did the police attack the Raba'a Mosque?"

"The bastards wanted to die—martyr themselves so they'd go to heaven." Hani's voice seemed to be caught in his throat. "The government negotiated with them for weeks. Set up safe corridors for them to leave through. But they're fanatics. All of them. Insisting on their precious martyrdom. Refused every offer to disperse. Shot at the police. What did you expect the government to do?"

"At least send ambulances," Salma protested. Hani gazed down at the car mat.

"You shouldn't have come now. It's dangerous. Death threats. Assassinations. Riots. Massacres. Go back to your mother. I don't want you killed." Salma was surprised by her father's distress. Something else was going on.

"What about you? Are you safe?" she asked.

"There's a new group of extremists: Taj al Islam."

"Are they serious?"

"Twice last month, their thugs tried to kill me."

"Good God! Why didn't you tell me when it happened?" For her father to exclude her from such important information seemed like a betrayal of their relationship, rocky as it was. She felt it in her chest. Then it came to her that he might have felt betrayed, himself. What if he believed she'd read about the attempts and hadn't bothered to reach out to him? He couldn't know she'd been too wrapped up in Paul's assignment to keep current with news from Egypt.

"In fact, you're making things worse for me being here at this time." Salma glanced down at the phone in her lap, once more. Her father didn't know the half of it. Paul's investigation could create another front of danger. She clenched her hands until her fingers ached. She had to stop worrying about the future, she had enough to worry about right now. Again, she texted Paul: *r u ok?* No reply. A shudder ran down her spine. Was he hurt? Was he . . .? She didn't dare complete the thought.

Paul was the best thing that had ever happened to Salma. He completed her; filled the empty pit in her soul, made her whole. She could lean on his steadfast love when she needed to be brave. His calm smile reassured her and the kiss he blew from the back of the room when she stood behind a podium made her feel she could do no wrong. It was Paul who supported her defense of political rights for Arab American. "It's as a Jew that I believe in an even playing field," he'd explained when he was accused of being a self-hating Jew. It was short and sweet and true. Salma admired his elegance; carried his voice with her, like a song in her heart. What would life be without him?

But there was still no message from him. She braved her father's raised brows to check her phone, again. No texts. No tweets. Nothing. God knew where the phone charger had disappeared to. The battery had reached its red line and they hadn't even reached the Salah el Din citadel and the Mohammed Ali Mosque. Its four, thin, Turkish-style minarets dominated the Cairo skyline. Last time she was in Egypt, she'd taken her daughters to the mosque to see its garnet-red carpets, the green and gold calligraphy of its ceiling friezes, the complex carvings of the dome, and its enormous chandelier. When they pointed out how everything was covered with a thick film of dust, Salma feel defensive, even angry at them. Why hadn't they learned to do what she did: look beyond the dust, appreciate the beauty it obscured? Why hadn't she taught them to do so?

The limo approached Azhar Park as the evening's darkness descended. Salma didn't need light to recall its large open spaces, marble walkways and its restaurant's Arabesque motifs—its maintenance guaranteed by a foreign trust and worthy of her daughters' approval. Across from the park, tall streetlamps accented the shadows they created on the pavements and a thousand lights sparkled in apartment house windows.

The shriek of tires shocked her out of her musing. She smelled the scorching of rubber on the asphalt. Heard cars scatter, horns howl. Her body went rigid. She looked in the side mirror. Headlights were barreling towards them. She screamed. A white pickup truck crashed into the front Cadillac, thrusting its back fender into Hani's shatterproof windshield. Salma felt its impact in her chest cavity like a subsonic vibration from huge amplifiers. For a moment, she thought the car had exploded. Her father pulled her down and leaned over her. Panic came at her in waves. Her breathing sounded loud to her and jagged, but she had to know what had happened.

Still in her father's protective grasp, she lifted her head to peek into the headlight-illuminated dark. The driver was already positioned outside Hani's car door, pistol drawn and pointed at the people screaming on the sidewalk. Beyond the ripped-out section of the front car, one of the Presidential Guards was in his seat, his head smashed against a bulletproof window while blood streamed from his temple. The rest of the guards were crouched in shooting stances behind the open doors of that vehicle. *Bratatat. Bratatat.* Bullets perforated the pickup.

Finally, two crouching guards crept up to the cab door to pull it open. A man crumpled lifeless to the ground and Salma's stomach heaved at the sight of the first death she'd witnessed. A lump from inside her body pressed hard against her sternum. The muscles of her belly contracted and convulsed, shooting up a bitter liquid. She swallowed it, suppressed it. It was horrible. She'd never had to swallow vomit before.

As she pulled away from her father, she discovered the pickup had crashed through the front limo, taking out its backseat and trunk. It forced the limo onto the sidewalk into a soda pop and cigarette stall that collapsed on its owner.

"Call his father," someone hollered.

"Grab a car. Get him to a hospital," another voice rang out, "Call an ambulance," Salma begged her father.

"Keep your head down. He'll be dead before one gets here. Better a private car."

Meanwhile, Hani's guards formed a traffic-stopping line across the road so the driver could back out the Cadillac.

"What happened?" Salma wheezed out the question.

"An accident. Stupid driver. High on hashish."

"No," she insisted, scrambling in her bag for an inhaler. "It was deliberate. I saw him speed up before he hit the front limo. Could the Taj be—?"

"If the Taj meant to hit us, they wouldn't have missed." Evading her eyes, Hani folded his jacket lapel back in place. "And don't mention this to the family. Nobody needs to know."

Salma took two puffs from her inhaler. One in. One out. Repeat. If it was only an accident, why had her father's guards shot to kill? She wasn't naive. The only accident tonight was the pickup crashing into the wrong limo. Her father knew that. Why was he pretending they were safe? She stole another glance at him. Loving him was a form of torture.

Chapter 4

Monday
September 29, 2014
1:00 pm

I
N THE EARLY AFTERNOON OF THE DAY SALMA ARRIVED, Paul woke to the sight of pharaohs walking sideways on the wallpaper behind his hotel's television console. It seemed only a minute since four in the morning when he'd fallen into bed. He was jet-lagged. How had the fierce shaft of sunlight made its way between the curtains he'd pulled shut?

The top-notch Shams Hotel he'd checked into had once been Princess Diva's riverside palace and thus decadent beyond belief. Gold-leafed Greek columns wrapped in Arabesque designs held up its vestibule's Romanesque dome. The peach-colored walls were real alabaster as was the gold in the mosaics embedded in the floor. Paul could imagine the princess preening on her balcony, the moon glinting off the waters of the mighty Nile beyond and eunuchs swirling peacock-feather fans. What had possessed the Egyptian government to host an international conference in a venue that could serve as a backdrop to the opera, *Aida*? Egypt's Ottoman, Khedive Ismail, had bankrupted the country building this and other edifices to impress Princess Eugenie of France when she attended the celebrations for the opening of the Suez Canal. Like the khedive, perhaps the *rayyis* also wanted to impress the foreigners—the conference delegates—with how European and civilized Egypt was under his regime.

Seated at the window desk, towel-drying his hair, Paul called Benyamin at the Tel Aviv *Haaretz News*. The paper had followed Ali Walid's shenanigans since the late seventies. Paul would save himself countless hours of research if he could convince someone there to dig out information from its archives.

"Hey, bro." Faking enthusiasm, Paul greeted the techie who answered the phone. "I wonder if you guys put together the information on Walid I asked for before I left the States?"

"Not my department." Benyamin avoided confrontations. Paul could almost see the short man blinking behind his thick glasses, staring at electronic smart boards, computer screens and the newsroom's instant coffee machine.

"This guy's gas deals with your country cost Egypt billions of dollars. I don't know how he got away with it. I do know Mubarak let Walid sell natural gas to Israel at the subsidized domestic price. As though Egypt could afford enriching you guys. That was only a side deal. Walid has made several fortunes off the arms business."

Four sharp knocks on Paul's hotel door—followed by insistent rapping. "Stupid room service," he muttered into the phone. "I put out a 'do not disturb' sign before I went to bed. I'll call you later, Ben. I have to get that."

He opened it to a tight-faced man in his mid-fifties he'd never met before but looked like he could have been a *Haaretz News* journalist. "Good morning, Mr. Hays. My name is Aaron Schwartz," the man said, shouldering his way in. "Please sit down," he ordered rather than invited Paul. Then, securing his perch on the hotel desk with thick-muscled legs to the floor, he seemed satisfied that he'd positioned his head three feet higher than Paul's. "You're surprised," he concluded, with a smug look on his face. "An understatement." Paul wondered how the stranger had managed to seize control of the room. "I asked for information on Ali Walid," he said, regaining equilibrium. "I didn't expect *Haaretz* to deliver it by hand."

"I'm not from that news rag," Aaron replied, his voice thick with disregard. "And it's the other way around."

"Meaning?" Paul felt he had every right to be curt.

"We want information from you."

"Who the hell are "we"?"

"An inappropriate question." Aaron pulled away from the desk and stood with strongman arms across his chest. "Suffice it to say, while I don't work for *Haaretz*, I work with the CIA, FBI, Interpol and the Mukhabarat. My job is essential to Israel's security." He stepped to the window view and looked out. "We're happy with the this regime. Call it a popular mandate or military coup—it's all the same to us. We work together well."

Paul rubbed the back of his neck. "I take it you're Mossad." It wasn't the first time Israel's secret service had approached him. Once they'd wanted him to smear the international movement to boycott goods manufactured in the Palestinian territories occupied by Israel. He'd declined. Another time, to write an article accusing several Congressmen of anti-Semitism for deviating from the Israeli hardline against Iran. Again, declined. Given how conflicted he was about that country, it would be a cold winter in hell before he'd cooperate with the Mossad. Aaron's voice cut through his concerns.

"We have a lead to Sheikh Nabulsi, head of the Taj."

"What the hell is the Taj?"

"Short for Taj al Islam. In English that would be the Crown of Islam." The gratuitous translation was insulting. The Mossad had to know Paul's mastery of Arabic was more than adequate.

"Another offshoot of the Muslim Brotherhood?"

"Yes. The latest one. Butchers in the name of Allah. Like ISIS in Iraq." Paul rubbed his hand back and forth across his beard stubble and stared out at the Nile. The more international support the Israelis lost over their brutal occupation, the more paranoid they became about terrorism. Not that he blamed them, but they'd keep making enemies until they made peace with the Palestinians. This was not the time to go down that dead-end road. It was time to get firm with this man. Paul spun around in his chair.

"I'm not following the Brotherhood's latest off-shoots. I'm gathering information on arms deals in Egypt. Folks have made fortunes—"

"Who cares who's making money off guns?" Aaron interrupted. "We need to concentrate on Taj al Islam."

"Okay, so they're new on the scene. Don't know them. Don't care. Every news anchor has suddenly become an expert on Muslim extremism. I'm moving on." The back of Paul's neck burned.

"We aren't concerned with your career plans," Aaron said, dismissively. "Don't tell me you're addressing the Conference on Counterterrorism but don't know the Taj?" Aaron's tone was one of scorn not disbelief as he continued, "The Taj is in cahoots with Hamas to take over Egypt—beginning with the Sinai Peninsula."

"Egypt has a scorched earth policy. It's evacuated all civilians from Sinai," Paul said, drumming his fingers on the desk edge.

"Hasn't done much good." The Mossad guy was relentless. "The Army's losing to ISIS. The Taj and its co-Jihadists have base camps in caves. Tunnels under hills. Sixty thousand men, twice as many RPGs and Kalashnikovs. They'll be tougher to rout out than the Taliban."

"A quantum leap in the Middle East disaster index." The fact that Paul's voice was heavy with sarcasm didn't stop Aaron.

"In spite of American arms and our assistance, the Egyptian army is quagmired in its deserts. Ambushed in its mountain passes and blown up in its bunkers. Enough of this." Aaron arched his back, linked his fingers, and stretched his arms above his head. Paul heard his knuckles crack. "I'm here about your editor friend, Mr. Abu Taleb."

"What about him?" Paul asked, surprised. Why was the Mossad involved with Abu?

"An operative in our Cairo Embassy contacted him when he returned from Yemen. That was almost exactly three months ago. What was the domestic editor of the *Ahram News* doing in Yemen, anyway?"

"How would I know?" Paul collected the loose papers on the desk and thumped them into a neat pile. This guy was exacerbating his annoyance.

"Whatever," Aaron shrugged. "He probably didn't know the man he met there had founded the Taj and was its chief terrorist."

"Did Abu Taleb run a story about his trip to Yemen?" Paul asked, facetious.

"Of course, not. Your friend doesn't stick out his neck."

"What about him and this Taj guy?" Paul asked, curious how Abu Taleb fit in Aaron's plans. It wasn't like his friend to deal with the Mossad.

"According to our informant—now deceased—Abu Taleb returned with a scan disk we must have."

"Why the hell should I get involved? Why don't you ask him for the disk yourselves?"

"We did."

"And?"

"He was reluctant. We had to tighten the screws we'd attached to him before he agreed to give it up—but only if you're the courier. He knew you were coming to the conference, and he trusts you."

Paul felt an instant throbbing in his carotid artery. The stakes had increased. Why had Abu Taleb dragged him into this dangerous mission? It felt as though ants were crawling along the inside of his collar. Abu Taleb was no secret agent. What sword was the Mossad holding over his friend's head?

"How did he get his hands on it in the first place?" he asked.

"On that, our informant was not clear. We suspect a disgruntled Yemeni slipped it to him. Apparently, it's Nabulsi's private disk with information that's vital to Israel and Egypt. Perhaps even to the Hamdi family. It may reveal the identity of a high placed mole in in the government. We suspect there has been one in place for the past year."

"I assume you tortured your informant," Paul said. "You know you can't trust what people say under "enhanced interrogation."" Paul made quote marks in the air around the last two words. Whatever Israelis did, they did with a vengeance—and with expertise. They'd trained half the Western world in their gruesome methods, including the American police they'd helped militarize.

"What makes you think there's a mole? Who's he betraying the country to? Russia? China? Iran? And what do you know about this mastermind Taj leader? What did you say his name was?"

"Nabulsi. Tall man, close to seventy. Visible limp."

"Not much to go on." Paul shook his head.

"True. And we don't know where the rat's dug his hole or where his fellow rats are hiding. But not for long, Paul. Not if you help." So, that's what Aaron wanted.

"Help? With Nabulsi? Are you serious?" Paul played for time, braced himself against the pressure he knew Aaron would exert. He stood up to lean across the desk and slide open the window. The fragrance of green palm fronds and pink jacaranda blossoms that struggled through the dusty air cleared his head. He focused on the Nile's dull brown water rather than look at the man from the Mossad. "Since when do journalists work for Israel's secret police?"

"It's Israel." Aaron huffed a laugh and pulled a smartphone from his blazer pocket. "I'm texting you a copy of Nabulsi's picture."

So, the spooks already had Paul's contact information.

"Why would I mess with the Mossad?" He hesitated. "It's a breach of professional ethics and hardly light work." He didn't add that working for them wasn't in line with his views of Israel.

Not in the slightest.

He'd resisted Israeli policy for the past thirty years; ever since graduating from high school and going on the annual trip to the country sponsored by the Jewish Agency to make true believers of young Jews.

The trip backfired with Paul. His curiosity—so natural to the journalist he'd later become—led him off the beaten path of the Agency's controlled tours. He cultivated a relationship with an Arab hotel waiter who took him to a Palestinian refugee camp on the outskirts of Bethlehem. Since then, every time he thought of Israel, he remembered the tattered cloth tents. The battered tin shacks. The stench of raw sewage. Animals in the zoo lived better than the seven-year-old Palestinian girl who stared at him through a chain link fence, her face streaked with mud, her eyes squinting in the sun that highlighted the gold strands in her matted hair.

Paul's cell phone dinged. A text message appeared. A photo of Abu Taleb and two other men in front of a building with the white brick geometric patterns unique to Yemen's capital, Sana. He recognized Abu Taleb. The tall man in cleric garb had to be Nabulsi. The third wore a checkered cloth *keffiyeh* on his head and had a Kalashnikov slung across his chest, likely a bodyguard.

"You're assuming I'll work for you," Paul said, wanting to add, "with your typical Israeli arrogance."

"I'm assuming I'll convince you."

"I doubt it."

"I think…Actually, I'm sure I will." Aaron all but smirked. "Think back to three months ago. Remember the "heads up" that landed in your lap—or rather, your email inbox? The one about my boss's boss, head of the Mossad, flying to Qatar to meet with a prince?"

"What about it?"

"You even got a copy of the agenda: Israel urging Qatar to continue supporting Hamas in Gaza with billions of dollars."

"Doesn't make sense. Hamas is Israel's sworn enemy. It makes a big deal about the Palestinian resistance group's haphazard missile strikes."

"Behind the scenes, Israel encourages Qatar to mollify the Palestinians trapped in Gaza by subsidizing Hamas."

"Still doesn't make sense. Why would Israel want Qatar to mollify the Gazans?"

"To ward off another rebellion, another *intifada* we'd be forced to crush. Makes for bad press when we do that, you know."

"So, what about the email you claim, "dropped in my lap?" It came from a think tank in the Netherlands. My article made it into the *New*

York Times and *Der Spiegel* all on its own." Paul's shoulders ached; he stiffened his back against his chair. That article came out three months ago. Something about the time frame was suspicious. Hadn't Aaron said that was when the Mossad heard of the disk?

"The think tank in Amsterdam is ours. You wouldn't want it known the Mossad gave you the information, would you, Paul? We have an electronic paper trail to you." Aaron stared him in the eye. "We could undercut your cherished reputation for neutrality. Spin it into a scandal. Innuendos. Embellishments. Hypotheticals. All sorts of trouble for you if your public came to believe you were one of us."

"You set me up! God damn it," Paul practically shouted. "Why me?"

"You're the keynote speaker at this Counterterrorism Conference. That came to our attention three months ago. The timing was perfect." Aaron stood up, stretched his leg, and stood in front of Paul. "We know you have a relationship with Salma Ibrahim," he said, evenly. "And by extension, her father. A man highly placed in Egypt."

"Why bring her up?" Paul asked, and now felt as though the ants had been replaced by a porcupine in the space between his collar and his neck.

"Another reason for you to cooperate." A threat lurked in Aaron's words. "She and her family, particularly her father, are in danger. Twice the Taj has tried to assassinate Dr. Hamdi."

"Why the Hamdi's?" Paul asked, his voice mirroring the stress he felt.

"We don't know. Perhaps you can find out. In any case, once you get the disk from your friend, we will decommission the sheikh. Meanwhile, your fiancée is an easy, opportunistic target for him to get to her father." Paul would go mad it he thought of Salma in the hands of the Taj. He shook his head to clear it. Drumming his fingers, this time on the armrest, he asked Aaron, "Why doesn't Abu Taleb just give the disk to the Egyptian authorities?"

"You know better than that. Leaks, deceits, betrayals. He has good reason to fear for his life." More of Aaron's arrogance. "As long as the disk is in his possession, your friend's life is in danger. He's probably only alive because of its password protection. Sheikh Nabulsi would have already had the man killed if he thought he could access its information."

"You're telling me my friend is willing to hand off a primed grenade and have the Taj kill me instead?"

"You won't be at risk of anything like that. Just hand off the disk to us at once." Aaron interrupted Paul before his resistance turned into a rant. "Mr. Hays, it's important for you, and for us, to eliminate Nabulsi," he continued in a more conciliatory tone. "So—" he dragged the word out. "When your lady gets here–we know she arrives this afternoon—she's likely to be an attractive target for the Taj. And—" he paused for effect, "we can always arrange that she become one. The Taj need only discover she's with you and you, of course, are with us. It could be fatal for Salma if Nabulsi ever linked her to the Mossad."

Paul's heart skipped several beats. The Mossad was capable of anything. There was nothing left to ponder. He would have to work for this disgusting man.

Chapter 5

Monday
September 29, 2014
11:00 am

ON THE MORNING OF THE SAME MONDAY PAUL AND SALMA had flown separately into Cairo, Murad Ragab sat at a glass-topped table surrounded by the interminable crackle of a television set, its volume turned up loud enough to mask the headquarters' activities: moving assault rifles and grenades in and out, discretely. The city was full of mixed-use buildings, residential apartments interlaced with law offices, sales offices, heating and refrigeration services, marriage ma'azouns, tourist agencies, and full-fledged medical and dental clinics. It was natural for this building's occupants to assume the Taj safe house was the import-export agency it purported to be.

Murad ran the little finger of his right hand between the laptop keys in a futile attempt to wipe off Cairo's ubiquitous dust. It had been a week since Sheikh Nabulsi agreed to consider assigning

Amin, Murad's insubordinate malcontent to another unit before the frequent skirmishes between the two men escalated. He'd hoped to talk to the sheikh this morning before the Taj Council convened. But it was already late, and the sheikh hadn't arrived. Murad reflected on the strange fate that brought him to this table. It was seven years since Salma refused to marry him and he left America heart-broken, and humiliated. Counting on Sheikh Nabulsi's support and guidance in Egypt, he'd abandoned his studies in California not knowing his mentor had split from the Muslim Brotherhood to form the more radical Taj al Islam. Murad would likely not have joined the extremist group if he'd had a real choice, but it was impossible to get a job without highly placed "influence" of which from a village south of Minya, he had none. The sheikh would only secure him a part-time job teaching electronic equipment repair at a vocational institute there. In exchange, he put him in charge of a local Taj cell in the agricultural area surrounding it. In fact, Murad was meeting with his men tonight. He wasn't looking forward to dealing with Amin.

Stifling a frustrated sigh, Murad stared at his smartphone. It was eleven in the morning; four of the five Council members had taken their seats. With his hands resting lightly on the keyboard, Murad studied the four men at the table who were waiting for the sheikh to arrive. He'd known the Admiral, the General, and the head of the Syndicate of Journalists for some time now. The doctor, Mohamed Mazen, he knew less well—only that he was a neurologist from the Department of Military Medicine whom Murad suspected of heading a secret network of Taj sympathizers in the Egyptian army.

He drummed his thumb against his thigh, used his shirt-cuff to wipe the laptop's screen, then, as though it would somehow summon the sheikh, turned to look at the door behind him. If the meeting didn't start in the next few minutes, he'd miss the two o'clock train, the day's last one to Minya, from where he had to take a ferry to his grandparents' village of Sidi Osman.

At the whiff of rich coffee wafting into the chamber, he glanced over his shoulder again. The sound of Nabulsi's cane tapping on the hallway's wood floor preceded him. Murad jumped to his feet, raised his right hand to his heart, and bowed his head to acknowledge his mentor. In his early seventies, the sheikh was tall for an Egyptian. A white, turban-like cloth coiled around his red clerical skullcap made him look taller than his six feet; the wire-framed glasses hanging over his beige cleric coat added to his gravitas.

And finally, the Council convened, Murad recording the minutes with thick but nimble fingers on the keyboard. Admiral Ahmed Tarazi, stocky, and square-chinned, summed up the naval support for a Taj operation when he clicked to the last frame of his PowerPoint presentation. "It's time, brothers," he concluded, resuming his seat.

The imperious General Fawzi with a thick, black, mustache on his narrow upper lip, rose to his feet in a manner slow enough to capture everyone's attention. Fawzi enjoyed an impressive level of support in the military. Yet Murad had heard it rumored that the president had fired him in an uncharacteristic fit of temper. He'd canceled the general's pension, confiscated his villa and luxury car. So, in a rush of vengeance Fawzi defected to the Taj where he was probably as important as Nabulsi, himself. It mattered that the general agreed they had to act now. For months, Murad had sensed a kind of internal fury fomenting in the streets.

Nothing about the Taj coup d'état plans was unique. For three thousand years, from the age of the pharaohs until today, an unbroken chain of foreign powers had occupied Egypt and controlled the military that regulated the country. The Taj's plan to overthrow the current regime relied on the same well-tested elements used by previous coups: massive, widespread civil disruption and simultaneous explosions in cities, followed by the breaking out of political prisoners. As in similar actions, networks of university, college and vocational school students would disburse to the streets. Since the Brotherhood had been secretly taking over the country's professional associations or syndicates, its members would strike. Those in other syndicates that hadn't been purged would also strike. Its members would close hospitals, judicial courts, schools, and colleges. Paralyze the state. Incapacitate the government. In other words, unleash a civil war and then in the wake of predictable upheaval, a small group of Army officers allied with the Taj would establish an interim government headed by Nabulsi. This president did it, so would the sheikh. That was what Nabulsi, and his council expected.

Murad was not so sure. The *rayyis* was in great standing with the Americans who had aircraft carriers in the Mediterranean and Red Seas. The Taj couldn't easily dislodge him. And if they did, Murad doubted anything would change. For seven years, he'd devoted himself to the Taj call for social justice, believed in the slogan "Islam is the Answer" although he couldn't see how it answered the questions he had. The Islam of the crazy Taliban was anathema to him. His was the Islam of the Prophet Mohammed and his caliphs: Abu Bakr, who held the *ummah*, the Muslim community, together, and Omar, whose rule was so just, he could sleep unguarded in the shade of his palm trees.

The Taj had stopped serving the people and grown into an army preparing for war. Now, Murad believed he was following Nabulsi's orders only because he dared not defy him. There was a vicious side to the man to whom he'd once been loyal. Nabulsi had become more autocratic and as ruthless as he was righteous. When the Taj Dark Wings Brigade bungled the initial attempt on Hani Hamdi's life, the sheikh waited until the next scheduled Council session to have his guards escort the brigade leader from the place. Murad heard the first gun go off. Then two *coups de graces* shots, and the council chamber going totally silent.

General Fawzi reached the end of his presentation and Murad refocused his attention on his laptop. "The *rayyis* is consolidating power," the general announced as though the men in the room didn't know. "He's bound to pounce again as soon the counterterrorism conference concludes and the delegates leave."

"I appreciate I can count on you to mobilize our army cells," Nabulsi said, fiddling a string of crystal prayer beads. "That is, of course, if you agree." The general was the only man to whom the Sheikh deferred. "God willing, we will soon announce the exact date and time when we bring down this Godless ruler."

The sunlight was softening when Murad reached his village of Sidi Osman. Sandstone hills guarded the river valley surrounding it and fields of emerald-green alfalfa alternated with wide swaths of yellowing sugarcane. He leaped off the bow of the fluted-sail *felucca* that had ferried him from Minya as soon as it hit the shore. Once off the boat, he crossed the mud road along the river to the alleys behind its riverfront shops—three dried-goods shops, two cafes, a butcher shop, and a barber. Then he followed the familiar tentacles of narrow, dirt-packed roads to the village where he was born.

There is no twilight in Upper Egypt. The temperature drops the moment the sun goes down letting the heavy breeze drawing the heat off the land ruffle Murad's skin. The wind hurled scraps of garbage and tattered sheets of newspaper against the wooden doors. Metal lampshades on corner lampposts creaked, shadows lurched up and down the squat ocher walls and the darkness quickly purpled.

At the first corner, he leaned into a sudden gust to zip up his already sand-caked jacket. He circled past the Hoodhood Café, where his grandfathers were certain to be playing backgammon as they did every evening. Then, in the final hundred feet, he sprinted to a construction site between two huts where the men of his cell would be.

The graffiti-scrawled wall surrounding the site that was covered with construction debris had not protected it from indiscriminate dumping. The ground was strewn with the detritus of many meals: discarded water bottles, plastic spoons, foil plates, plastic bags. The trench at the foot of the wall smelled of sewage. Murad startled when two stiff-tailed cats emerged from the dark and a baby goat skittered from the rotting chicken carcass it had been chewing. With a hand over his nose, he checked the surrounding dark before entering the enclosure, then stepped over the low wall to weave his way around looming hulks of cement bags.

At the far end of the site, ten men were squatted, balanced on their haunches, around a meager fire, their speckled blue enamel teapot nestled in glowing embers of dung. Kadri, at eighteen, was the newest and youngest recruit. With tight red curls encircling his fair face, he was the first to greet Murad. "Praise God for your safe arrival," he called out, reaching for the pot to fill a shot-sized glass with tea as dark as Assyuti amber and sweeter than Murad liked. "We were afraid the soldiers stopped you."

Mustapha, a village fixture with an onyx-black Nubian face resembled a coarse-grained woodcarving. Murad had often watched him steer his *felucca* with toes curled around the rudder and marveled at how his thick neck muscles disappeared into his huge shoulders when he hauled in the ropes. Now, they stood side by side with freshly filled tea glasses in hand. "I'm nervous," Mustapha said in a voice meant only for Murad's ears. "For days, men and women, their animals and goods, had to wait on shore while I ferried at least five army platoons across the river."

"Do the soldiers suspect any of us?" Murad asked.

"Of course, they suspect us." Amin's scornful voice rose from the dark and almost drowned out the question. The faint gray light stressed his wiry thinness and sharp shoulders and emphasized the unnatural blue-black of his slick, oiled hair. "They're not stupid." He spat at the ground in disgust. "They've already arrested Zacharia."

"That's serious." Murad scrutinized the rock-strewn ground. It was a perfect time and place for the scorpions that reminded him of Amin. "But why Zacharia?"

"They caught him with leaflets in his schoolbag," Amin replied with insolent nonchalance

"He's only thirteen. Who told him to carry leaflets?"

"I did." Amin glowered in Murad's direction, lobbed his orange-tipped cigarette into the fire and smashed a lizard with his heel, leaving a moist spot in the dust. Amin was a sadist. He'd poked out one of his sister's eyes for looking at a man and insisted she was lucky he hadn't stoned her to death. He was an ignorant thug who'd never studied the Quran and listened to no one—not his parents or uncles. He'd even ignored the village sheikh's warning: no one could accuse anyone of illicit sex unless four separate people witnessed the act. Only then could the alleged culprits be punished…the woman often by death. "Meeting tonight is dangerous," Amin persisted. "Government squads bulldozed nine more houses in Mahatib yesterday. Their dogs are sniffing for explosives. The Special Forces are right behind us, blowing up first one place then the other to find our stuff. You can't hide dynamite forever. And they're bound to find the stash of nitrogen. No one uses that much fertilizer for sugarcane."

The Taj Council's concern about the army mobilization was appropriate. If the army was closing in on Sidi Osman, Murad and his men were in danger. A giant hand squeezed his ribcage. Would he be able to protect his men?

As though to prove Amin's point, something exploded in the nearby cane field. A dozen soldiers emerged from the stalks with flashlights in their hands and assault rifles slung across their chests. Murad gestured to his men to wait and headed to the troops, straight-backed, squared-shoul-dered, projecting authority.

"I'm from the Vocational Institute," he declared to a young man who appeared to be in charge. He'd seen this youngster before—a conscript fresh from the next village, newly minted. Although he had his rifle pointed at Murad's chest, it was hard to take the dark-haired man seriously. With his pale-yellow complexion and honey-colored eyes set in a round puffy face, he looked like the cornhusk doll his sisters used to play with—puckered at the neck, two slits for eyes, a slash for a mouth, its strands of hair in every direction. "The director personally sent me to tutor these men," Murad said, stiffly formal and firm.

"Since when do peasants get a tutor, sir?" the soldier asked.

"Germany gave the Institute a grant. Have you heard of the GTZ?"

Murad was not surprised when the soldier scowled, looked down at the ground and shook his head. He likely had no idea what a grant was and had certainly never heard of the German NGO with its country-wide projects.

"Wasting your time," the young soldier scoffed. "You can't teach peasants anything except how to plant sugarcane." Murad sighed. Not too long ago, this self-loathing youngster had been a peasant, himself. "And why outdoors in the dark when it's cold?" The soldier launched a short volley of bullets into the air to assert his power.

Murad didn't flinch. "Just finishing," he said. "Would you join us for tea?" The cornhusk man lowered his rifle and squinted at the group of men around the dying embers.

"Do your men have weapons?"

"Only walking sticks," Mustapha called from the shadows. "To chase off dogs."

The soldier spun to signal his recruits who slipped back into the cane field with their rifles balanced on their shoulders, like the spades they used when they were peasants, too.

"Go back to your homes," their young leader called out as he joined them. "Curfew," he shouted. "Everyone indoors."

Murad's men scattered; he allowed himself a deep breath. The recruits were kids, only dangerous if cornered, but he had to activate his men in case more seasoned troops arrived. He'd stashed gasoline cans and detonators in the dovecote emptied of birds after his grandmother's death. At dawn, he'd tell Kadri where to find the materials if they had to use them. Murad knew by rights he should deputize Amin, but he'd never be able to keep the power-hungry hog from blowing up everything in sight.

Satisfied with his solution, he retraced his steps to the Hoodhood Café and past the Ehssan Clinic where his sister worked and where she and her family lived in its upstairs apartment. The curfew seemed not to extend to the café, where the place, semi-darkened, was as crowded as usual, heavy with sheesha smoke, noisy with the click-clack of backgammon tiles. He wondered if the patrons had heard the explosion above the television noise of a Manchester United soccer game, opium of Egypt's men. It took Murad several minutes to wind his way around tables and chairs to where his mother's father, the village chief, was playing backgammon with Murad's paternal grandfather who once had been the village scribe.

"*Shish-bish, ya satar. Shish-bish*, I need a five and six," the *omda* called out, slamming dice against the wooden sides of the worn game set. Even before the dice stopped spinning, Murad was certain his grandfather would win. "There they are—a five and six." The old man laughed. "My game. Praise God." Many in Sidi Osman suspected the chief of pinching the dice, but no one ever questioned his extraordinary luck.

"*Salamu 'aleikum*," Murad rested one hand on his maternal grandfather's shoulder and held the other over his own heart.

"*Ahlan wa sahlan*." The old man spread welcoming arms. "What brings you here, son? Your mother is well?"

"She is well, praise Allah. She said to tell you her heart is heavy with missing you."

"A glass of tea—extra sugar—for my grandson," the *omda*, his prosperous roundness stuffed in a cane-bottomed chair, hollered into the dark hole of the kitchen. Not even his own grandfather respected Murad's distaste of sugar.

"Did you hear the explosions, *guidu*?"

"They've been going off all week," his paternal grandfather said.

"It's as bad as it was in the eighties when Sadat was president," an old man at the adjoining table, his gray-haired head wreathed in smoke, joined in. "City folks think every inch of land beyond where they live is crawling with terrorists."

"The government treats us like we're Sinai Bedouins." A younger man in a conspicuously white galabia, also needed to have his say. "We'd be better off if they hand us over to the Sudan." Murad understood the sentiment behind these exaggerated laments. The fault lines between urban and rural populations and the haves and have-nots had grown from cracks to chasms.

"Be cautious." He felt his paternal grandfather tugging at the cuff of his windbreaker. "I don't know what you and your guys are doing," the *omda* said. "And don't want to. I just want you to be safe."

"God is our Protector, sir," Murad reassured him. "And you know what I'm doing. Tutoring. The land can't support the village anymore. One day, God willing, some of the men I help will find work."

"Hmmm. Ever the optimist, my son." His maternal grandfather shook his head. "As I once used to be."

His grandfather seldom mentioned it, but Murad knew what he meant. Neither of them would forget the night soldiers pulled up in an Army Jeep and flung Murad's father's mutilated body to the ground. The village men fired rusty rifles in the air, women wailed. His mother howled like the wolves in the sandstone hills beyond. He remembered staring at the dislocated arms across his father's back, the smashed limbs, the mangled ears, and the darkened blood oozing from his crushed fingertips. Streams of warm urine ran down his young legs and Murad found himself floating above his own body, watching the seven-year-old child he was then. A kid who sucked his thumb, wet himself, and worried about disappointing his father by acting like a baby.

It had taken days to realize the man he adored would never make cat's cradles again, pull shiny coins from behind a "lucky" ear, or read to him from the Bukhari. "The army killed your father, a scribe, an innocent man, for no reason. He had done nothing," his mother had screamed but Murad's sorrow metastasized into fury only gradually.

His tea untouched, he turned to leave, to spend the night at his grandfather's house. He shook hands, patted shoulders, and made sure he missed no one before he reached the door. About to push it open, he caught sight of a newspaper on a narrow side table and stopped to skim the front page. Another pro-government demonstration. Good. It meant the *rayyis* was feeling pressured and appealing to his base.

Murad shook out the paper and ran his eyes down a column about Syrian refugees. A small, black outlined box announced a movie star had died. A larger one announced an antiterrorism conference with a list of Egyptian presenters attending from abroad. Something nagging at him to be discovered, he scanned the list of names. Salma Ibrahim. The pain, like shrapnel buried in his body, burst out. When he could think again, his first thought was: Why was she still using her ex-husband's name?

He felt more regret than ever. Bitter regret. He'd been a fool. Too proud. Too easily hurt. And too impulsive. He'd lost everything. He should have stayed in America with Salma where they could be together. In Egypt, the path of an upper-class woman like her would never cross his. But the only one he'd ever loved refused to sanctify their relationship, refused to obey the word of Allah though she was a Muslim—at least by birth. How could a decent woman like her give him her body and refuse to be his wife? Murad was a deeply religious man. He left her. Yet, no matter how hard he prayed to be released from his enthrallment, his faith in the All Mighty had not replaced his love for Salma; had not flowed through his body, had not healed his heart. He grabbed the doorjamb for support until he could pull himself together, then stumbled into the dark night.

Down the Clinic's alley, past the mosque to which it was attached, to the corner where he turned with his breath racing ahead of him in the gathering chill. He rushed past what was optimistically referred to as the village's elementary school where two or three kids shared a desk chair and where the two toilets were so disgusting, girls refused to attend. By the time Murad reached his grandfather's house, he was in a foul mood.

A narrow façade of baked brick separated the house's dirt courtyard from the packed dirt lane. As he opened the gate, he looked up at the empty whitewashed dovecote above the roofline and felt a soft pang of sadness at the loss of his grandmother and the pigeons she'd always raised. Inside the house where his grandfather held court, the bare-walled reception room was furnished with four rattan chairs pulled around an ottoman topped by a large brass tray. A calendar with a photograph of pilgrims circling the Ka'aba. A table with a big ashtray before the overstuffed, slipcovered couches lining the wall.

Too upset to use the room set aside for him, Murad rolled out a thin mattress in the still midnight on the roof, where the tile beneath him and the air above him were cold. The moon had not yet risen; the sky as densely strewn with stars at the horizon as it was overhead. On his back, his head resting on his arms, he stared at them until his strained eyes closed. Still, he couldn't sleep. The memories Salma evoked kept him awake, his body charged with a kind of energy he hadn't felt for years. Twisted in confusion, he tried weaving the day's events together. Specters of explosions and soldiers. Nabulsi, the Council. And Salma. He tossed from one side to the other on the pallet and, flooded with dreams of her, wound the cotton blanket into knots.

Chapter 6

Monday
September 29, 2014
1:00 pm

AFTER AARON LEFT THE HOTEL ROOM, A THOUSAND QUESTIONS bored through Paul's brain. The deeper the probe, the more sludge was dumped. He went back and forth between possibilities, got confused, felt crazy. Was Aaron telling the truth? Was Nabulsi real? And dangerous? If so, why hadn't he been arrested? Did Abu Taleb have information or had Aaron invented a threat to Salma to hook Paul in? It didn't matter. He had to follow Aaron's orders if there was the slightest chance of her being harmed.

Paul had met Salma at the University of California Santa Cruz campus when he interviewed her for an article about the experience of Arab Americans in the reign of Donald Trump. Barely hiding her annoyance at his barging into her office late for their appointment, she rose from her chair and knocked the air out of his lungs with her dramatic presence even before. Suddenly, all he wanted was to wake up early in the morning sleeping beside her, an image he couldn't shake while he switched on the recorder and rushed through the interview, ending it as soon as he could so he could invite her out. He felt ridiculous not being able to remember what he'd ordered for dinner. All he knew was, the more she tried to focus him on her intellect, the more sensual she became. Sexist as it might have been, he'd been swept away by that, completely out of his control.

Since then, wherever he was—just going on with his life—an intense spotlight seemed to be concentrated on her. His other relationships became vague and blurry fixtures of the past. He didn't need to hold onto his failed marriage to Ellyn, the acrimony of its dissolution, and the distance she'd created between him and his kids. He could let go of his hurt and wounds and resentments. One day he realized he was not afraid of anything—except losing Salma as he had once almost done.

They were in a Pajaro Dunes condo on a foggy afternoon, discovering each other as new lovers do. Salma asked him to name an image that affected how he thought of himself. He should have known better than to lead with the one of Israeli soldiers at the Wailing Wall, their boots planted firmly on freshly liberated land, protecting the Jewish state so there could never be another Holocaust. It was far too early for that. They'd only been dating for two months. Still, he didn't expect her to be so bitter when she said, "Your Jewish state is just another occupying power in the Middle East. Those boots are crushing Arab necks." His mouth hung open, his lips slightly parted; totally stunned, unable to speak. His mind swirled desperately, scrambling to make sense of it all as Salma jumped off the couch, grabbed her tennis racket and left. He remembered how terrified he'd been, afraid she'd call a cab and never come back until she finally returned.

Staring at the pharaohs on the wallpaper he no longer noticed, he crossed the room for his cell phone. The damn thing was as dead at the outlet he'd plugged it into before he went to bed. He fumbled picking up the hotel phone and took a deep breath as he dialed nine for an' outside line. When a male receptionist at the *Ahram News* put him on hold, Paul perched on the edge of his bed, prepared for the interminable wait.

Patience was religion in Egypt, and Abu Taleb was worth waiting for. Always straight. At least as straight as a reputed mouthpiece for the government ever was. Abu Taleb followed the internal machinations of corrupt officials the way other men followed football teams. Despite Salma's faultfinding, he'd be a terrific source of information on military deals. Propping his feet on the desk, Paul leaned back in his chair, remembering his friend as he waited.

It was hard to believe it had been five years since his two-year stint in Cairo. The two men spent many a Thursday night at the Green Garden Café, a legendary watering hole for journalists. With a scotch and water for Paul and a nonalcoholic Birell beer for Abu Taleb, they lounged in cushioned armchairs on its terrace surrounded by the tang of trees and mulch and earth. The upright fans rattling at full speed did nothing to dispel the humidity or blow away the mosquitoes they had to swat. Paul loved the evening view from there. To his right, the Giza Bridge crossed to Rhoda Island—its yellowish lights spread across the night black river like a sheet of gold foil. To his left the Six of October Bridge—the water beneath it silvered by its bright white lights—lead to the Mohandessin district.

Even in their silences, the two men became close. Although Egyptians avoided sensitive issues except with close intimates, Abu Taleb had been candid with Paul. He'd shared his worry over the future of his three teen-aged sons whom he wanted to send to college abroad. And he'd talked fondly of his wife although mentioning a spouse, except to acknowledge he was married, was a taboo not lightly broken by an Egyptian man.

They had grown comfortable enough with each other that Paul risked broaching the subject of Abu Taleb's relationship to the Jews who'd once lived in Egypt. "I'm not religious," Paul had old his friend, "but I've wondered about the life my Sephardic Jewish grandfather would have had if he'd lived here."

"It is a mystery to me. How can you be a non-religious Jew? There's no such thing in Islam," Abu Taleb said. "You are either Jewish or not Jewish—you are a Buddhist, a Christian, a Muslim, even an Atheist or not." Paul sidestepped the confounding issue of religion versus ethnicity to ask about the prominent Jewish families: the Suarez's, Mosseris, and Cattouis whom Abu Taleb described as special kinds of Egyptians. With foreign passports or *laissez faire* passes they circumvented Egyptian laws, civil, commercial, and criminal in a unique institution known as the Mixed Court. There, they submitted only to the laws of their countries of origin—actual or titular—even when some of their forbears had been born in Egypt before the time of Alexander the Great.

Still, Egyptian Jews were generous and civic-minded members of society who served in parliament, published newspapers, owned huge factories and nation-wide department stores. There was also a lot of cotton-trading and whatever else. Paul wondered if "whatever else" were a code word for arms.

Paul realized he'd touched a sensitive nerve when he mentioned ghettos. Abu Taleb sounded personally insulted to be tainted by what he referred to as a European thing. "Yes, they lived in their own neighborhoods. So did the Greeks, Armenians, and Italians. It was a matter of exclusivity not exclusion."

"So, what changed?"

"Arab nationalism. Bloody revolutions in the fifties: Algeria, Iraq, Libya, Syria. Wars of liberation from British and French colonization." Abu Taleb stopped talking and sighed, reluctant to continue. When he did, his voice was undercut with heaviness. "Meanwhile, Israel had been established by the British and supported by your country. It is colonizing the Palestinians with its cruel occupation. You can't expect Arabs to tolerate that."

"Many say Egypt expelled the Jews." Paul had left the most controversial issue until last.

"Nasser nationalized the Suez Canal in July 1955. Soon after, England and France joined Israel in an unprovoked surprise military attack on us. At that point, all British and French nationals were deported, their property seized. The many Jews who had secured the advantages of coveted French citizenship were also deported. Not only the Jews, but Egypt's Greeks, Italians, and Armenians panicked. Xenophobia ruled."

"Yes, but were they expelled?"

"In contrast to the deportation of those with foreign passports, a handful were expelled: spies, violent provocateurs, and material supporters of Israel. Many Jews also chose to leave, their livelihoods squeezed out after President Nasser nationalized businesses—Jewish and not." Of course, they left, Paul thought. He would have joined them. The Holocaust was still fresh in Jewish minds and the handwriting on the wall was in Arabic.

Abu Taleb talked about the modern exodus that affected his early teens. "My best friends left. Icarus, the son of the Greek *khawaga* Girgis, who owned a bunch of taxis. Mario, the oldest son of the Italian family that lived across the hall. Rebecca, a Jewish girl I had a crush on. They all left. No goodbyes, no *ma'al salamas*. Gone. And the country changed, completely."

Paul knew that people of Abu Taleb's generation distinguished between Jews and Israel. Their children and grandchildren did not. To the younger generations, the enemy was clear: Israel in particular and increasingly, "the Jews." Soon, Salma's family would have to face the fact she was marrying one. Presumably, the Hamdis were worldly enough to accept that.

At the window of his hotel room, still on the phone, still on hold, he stood musing until his arm went numb and he set the receiver, speaker up, on the desk. Abu Taleb might not be at work yet. Like everyone else, he probably coped with the heat by starting late in the morning then taking an afternoon siesta, waking around seven in the evening, and staying up for hours after midnight.

Paul gazed out at the palm trees growing down to the river's edge, their overlapping fronds patterning the cloudless sky and their fire-red *zaghloul* dates ready for harvest. A damn disk had put him and Abu Taleb in danger of being killed by the Taj and the Mossad had essentially threatened to have the Taj harm Salma. A band of steel tightened around his insides.

Aaron had shaken him to the core. He opened the small refrigerator before he remembered drinking the lone bottle of local Stella when he first arrived. Last time he was in one of Cairo's swanky hotels like this one, it was stocked with Courvoisier and Johnnie Walker Black.

Waiting to connect with Abu Taleb was taking too long, even for Egypt. Exasperated, Paul crossed to a side window for a change of view. Below him, in the inner courtyard, slabs of black, white, and brown marble measured off the square. A scattering of raw canvas umbrellas floated over dark round tables, emphasizing the bold geometric motif.

Past the courtyard and beyond the palm trees, the Nile was the color of creamed coffee and flanked by tall buildings with eddies dotted along its shores turning green with algae. Here, where it flowed through a wide urban strip before it branched off to form the delta, it was bustling with tour boats, yachts, powerboats, and ferries. On the far bank of the river, Paul could make out the Gezira Club. Three blocks south of it, the Green Garden Café was squeezed between two luxury apartments with rooftop helicopter pads and indoor swimming pools—built and owned by Saudis with their petrol dollars and taste for ostentation. The swath of water was as deceptively serene as the country had been before the Tahrir uprising in the Arab Spring.

He held the receiver to his ear, again. There was a dial tone. He clicked the button on the phone's cradle, and the front desk assured him the line was connected although still on hold. Then it went dead. Paul cursed as he hit Redial.

"Operator," a soft-voiced female receptionist answered. "Are you trying to place an outside call?"

"Yes. You've disconnected me."

"Please accept our apologies, sir. There may be something wrong with the line. I would be happy to reach your party for you."

"Thanks," Paul said, giving her the name and number. Let the *Ahram News* leave her on hold, he thought, but almost immediately, the telephone rang.

"*Mabruk,* my friend," Abu Taleb congratulated him. "Even here, in Egypt, we are reading your new book. How are you doing?"

"*El hamdu lillah,*" Paul thanked God in reply and prepared for the inevitable exchange of social niceties, hallmark of Egyptian interactions. "I am doing well. How is your health? Recovered from your bypass surgery, I trust?" He doubted Abu Taleb had stopped smoking or lost any of his three hundred pounds.

"I am still alive, praise Allah. How are your children?"

Paul smiled. There it was again. Abu Taleb ignoring Paul's divorce of ten years and the fact that his children lived with their mother. His friend didn't approve of this arrangement. Muslim fathers assumed primary care of their teenagers after a divorce.

"They're well, thank you. Talia is finishing high school. David is in the second year of college." Paul dragged a legal-sized pad toward him from the far side of the desk. "You probably already know I'm here for the counterterrorism conference. I'm also writing an article for *Harper's* magazine about the military arms deals between Egypt and the States." Paul had no intention of wasting his time on that article now. He was going to retrieve the disk and its information, discover why the Taj had targeted Salma through her father, and protect her from Nabulsi. It didn't matter what excuse he used to arrange a meeting. Both men knew Abu Taleb would be giving Paul the sheikh's disk to pass on to Aaron. Neither knew the nature of the sword the Mossad held over the other's neck.

Paul tipped back in his chair to grab the *Ahram* newspaper off the bed. Its front page led with news that the president's supporters would demonstrate in Tahrir Square today. There was no point in raising that subject. Nothing new Abu Taleb could add. Paul had something else with which to kick-start a conversation. He folded the newspaper to the fifth page where he'd circled an article on Sheikh Maarouf.

"I need your help, my friend," he said, clamping the receiver between his chin and shoulder and flipping through the pad's scribbled pages to find a blank one for taking notes. "I need a local angle for my conference talk. Can you fill me in on Sheikh Ma'aroof's *fatwa*? It's here, on page five of your paper." He stabbed at the article with his pen. "This guy says: the conference is "non-Islamic." Who is he? What does he mean? My Arabic is not good enough to read the nuances between the lines." Abu Taleb chuckled. Paul's accent was atrocious, but his Arabic was good enough to read the daily news.

"He's just a minor cleric. Who knows what he means?" Abu Taleb said. "Hundreds of self-proclaimed sheikhs with bullhorns but no religious authority, preach worthless injunctions all day. Only fanatics listen to them. Now, to silence the Brotherhood's hateful messages, the authorities had issued Friday sermons for every mosque to use." Paul heard Abu Taleb light a cigarette and inhale. When he spoke again, his voice was grave. "Things are volatile, my friend. You know the Islamists? The ones who assassinated Sadat? They are underground again."

"What did the government expect after the coup toppled the Brotherhood's president?"

"That's not the problem. A sheikh Nabulsi leads a new group of Islamist Jihadists who call themselves Taj al Islam. They plan to make Egypt part of *Daesh*—you know *Daesh*? You call it ISIS." Abu Taleb spoke faster with greater agitation as though re-experiencing his fear. "Last month, they set fire to the Mena House Hotel, where you used to swim. They burned the Coptic Church in Qena. Attacked a checkpoint in Damietta, the police academy in Tanta. They're killing our soldiers in Sinai and—"

"They'd blow up the pyramids if they could just to keep tourists out of Egypt," Paul interjected. "Didn't some terrorists murder a bunch of them? Cut their throats and disembowel them?"

"I don't think they were behind that, Paul. Islam forbids desecrating bodies."

"It doesn't mean they didn't do it. ISIS—I mean, *Daesh*—chops off heads on prime-time television." Paul was glad Abu Taleb couldn't see him roll his eyes in disbelief. "If they didn't, who did?"

"There are rumors."

"What rumors? Must be another Middle Eastern paranoid conspiracy theory." Silence on the phone as Abu Taleb ignored the comment.

"I think the Israelis did it," Abu Taleb said, and Paul sighed. An international investigation had implicated a gang of terrorists connected to an Islamist group based in London. If a man as reasonable as Abu Taleb believed junk like this, what did the average Egyptian think?

"Next, you'll be telling me the CIA murdered Arafat, and Bin Laden didn't mastermind the 9/11 attacks."

"There are many who believe that." Abu Taleb was quiet for a moment, as though wondering whether to proceed. Paul heard him flick his lighter, again, before he did. "The situation is dangerous."

"Worse than usual?"

"Much worse, my friend. More kidnappings, more assassinations."

"We don't get that news in the States."

"Because this is different, Paul. They're not attacking people with international reputations like Naguib Mahfouz or Ala'a Aswani. They're killing government leaders, and anyone related to them. And journalists. Especially foreign ones." True. Paul knew the Islamists knocked off journalists they hated while the government jailed or killed the rest. "These are times of danger," Abu Taleb said. There was a long pause before he asked, "Have you been contacted, Paul?"

"This morning." Paul noticed he'd unconsciously lowered his voice.

"I had no choice but to ask for your assistance. I'm sorry to bother you." Being bothered was the understatement of the day. "If the Taj hears the Israelis are involve—" Abu Taleb stopped mid-sentence and lowered his voice. "Did you hear that?"

"What?"

"A click. Something wrong with our connection? Anyway, I have talked too long." Paul hadn't heard a click, but he winced at the suggestion. Abu Taleb possessed a healthy level of suspiciousness.

"Well, let's get together," he said with almost too much enthusiasm. "I'd love to catch up with your news. And I've got news for you. I'm getting married. You'll be surprised to learn to whom, my friend. I'll show you her picture. Why don't you bring some of yours?"

"I have nothing worthwhile." Abu Taleb forced a small laugh. "But I have some cigarettes for you. A gift from Turkey. I think you will enjoy them. Much richer than the ones you smoke."

"Cigarettes?"

Abu Taleb cut Paul off. "Meet me at the Semiramis Hotel at half-past four. The Ibis Café for coffee. And" he added before hanging up, "be careful, Paul."

An apprehensive shiver chilled Paul's body. Cigarettes? Why cigarettes? Abu Taleb knew he didn't smoke. Why the mystery? What if meeting Abu Taleb led the Taj to Salma through him? He couldn't see how, but neither could he rid himself of the TV image—the haggard face, the sunken eyes of an Irish aid worker pleading with Islamic terrorists for her life. If they could murder a woman who'd done their people nothing but good, what would they do to a woman whose father had done nothing but harm them? Perhaps the Taj didn't know Salma was coming to Cairo. It did, an inner voice insisted. Don't be a fool. She'd arrive this afternoon.

It was only one o'clock and he wasn't meeting Abu Taleb until after four. He'd go crazy cooped up for the next three hours. He had to do something. He could go to Tahrir Square early, check in with Gabber, one of the "everyman" shopkeepers Paul had cultivated when he reported from Cairo. Gabber's television repair shop was close to the Semiramis Hotel.

Chapter 7

AFTER STEPPING THROUGH THE SHAMS HOTEL'S REVOLVING doors into Cairo's autumn sunshine, Paul took a quick look around. He could see why the conference committee had selected this venue. Built on a reinforced Nile promontory with only one side approachable by land, its grounds were large enough to accommodate the three army tanks already positioned among its banyan trees. More security than normal. The government was nervous. Nervous was an understatement for how Paul felt. Aaron threatening Salma's safety had shaken him to the core. If he didn't walk off his anxiety, he'd go off like a hand grenade.

The hotel was convenient to downtown, less than a mile from Tahrir Square—a site now featured on Cairo's tourist lists. Though it was off limits to demonstrations, the morning's *Ahram News* suggested the president had made exceptions for his supporters. There was plenty of time to check out the square before meeting Abu Taleb.

On his way down the driveway to the riverfront Corniche, an officious policeman with a battered notepad asked for Paul's destination.

"For your safety and security, sir," the officer said, holding his nub-sized pencil above his pad. Paul didn't know why today this guy's thin-grinned self-importance grated on his nerves. Thousands of Egyptian tourist policemen seemed to have no purpose other than to loaf around.

"For a walk," he answered curtly.

"When will you return, sir?" the policeman persisted.

Paul wanted to say, "When I damn well feel like it," but looked at his watch and settled for "in five hours." A respectable amount of time.

Heading north along the Nile Boulevard, he imagined Salma strolling with him. He could almost hear her wry comments and the laugh she had that sounded like singing. "Strolling isn't the right word," she'd have said, stepping over and around blocks of broken pavement on the unpredictable sidewalks. "More like class-three hiking in Yosemite." He missed her sardonic wit. At the thought of her, a rock seemed to have lodged in his breastbone. What if Aaron set her up like he'd threatened to? Drew a target on her back for the Taj? What if Paul couldn't protect her?

He tried to concentrate on the moment. Cars were inching past one another, forming seven lanes in a street designed for four, their incessant horns honking in the coded language of greetings and warnings. Pedestrians were jostling their way around the vehicles, but something was different. There were more people than normal for this time of day, and they were all heading north. Paul noticed more women than usual abroad, their hijab scarves a garden of blooming colors. The ever-present host of young men—the unemployed generation, wellspring of unrest in the Arab world—were hanging out thigh-to-thigh on the river balustrade smoking cigarettes, as usual. But today they weren't ogling every girl who passed. They seemed as serious as their elders, the men walking arm in arm with cell phones and cigarette packs in one hand and prayer beads in the other. Things might get interesting in Tahrir Square even before he met Abu Taleb.

At the thought of his friend, Paul's breath caught in his chest. What about the click in the middle of their phone call? All at once his mouth was dry. Was someone monitoring the call.? Clearly, the Mossad had been monitoring him for years. How else could they have linked Abu Taleb to him and set up the two at the same time? When his friend, who knew Paul didn't smoke, said he was bringing Turkish cigarettes, he figured he'd come through. This didn't make him happy. Having the flash drive was like having a stick of dynamite in the pocket of his pants. His mind raced through possibilities, each making him feel more paranoid and vulnerable. How long had the Mossad been spying on him? Had they been monitoring Salma, too?

The crowd he was part of was getting thicker as he got closer to the square. Street vendors multiplied. Mothers with infants at their breast squatted by trays of homemade biscuits for sale. Children crouched like crickets by small mounds of chewing gum to ostensibly sell; outright beggars stretched their arms for alms. A young man in a striped *gallabiyah* hawked ice cream from a rusty bicycle that might once have been blue. A peanut seller beseeched God's mercy in a reedy voice with words that echoed the verses from the Quran painted on his pushcart.

The aroma of charcoal-broiled kebab from across the street filled Paul's nostrils, but the smell of grilled corn rising from a makeshift sidewalk brazier appealed to him more. He bought a cob from a woman with watery eyes and waved away the change. She covered her mouth to hide her toothless smile and he felt the familiar fury at the government's abuse of the Egyptian poor.

The flow of people carried Paul to the square's southern entrance where he rounded the corner of the Omar Makram Mosque and passed the entrance to the Semiramis Hotel. Could Abu Taleb, anxious to get rid of the disk, be there already? On the other hand, what if he didn't show? Damn him for dragging Paul into this mess. And damn Aaron for forcing Paul to do his dirty business.

Paul looked diagonally across the street, barely registering the Soviet-style Mogamma'a building—home to Egypt's corrupt bureaucracy—that threw its shadow upon the American University's first campus. Passing the campus' filigreed wood *mashrabeya* façade, his route took him along a row of once stylish eight-story apartments with *fin-de-siècle* wrought-iron balconies that creaked with age and dust, overwhelmed by the looming high-rise hotels replacing them.

Folks crowding their windows and balconies cheered the ones pouring from side streets into Tahrir Square. The area was peaceful, even anticipatory. Unlike other demonstrations Paul had seen in Egypt with glum protesters and bored police, this one felt celebratory. People with Egyptian flags painted on their faces like football fans converged on popcorn booths, pink cotton candy barrels, and soft drinks stands. A large contingent of young ones, a cadre of the president's upper-class elites—men in designer shirts, women in Western clothing and no headscarves—were demonstrating, dominating the space.

Demonstrations demand popular music—so, ad hoc bands drummed jaunty rhythms from makeshift wooden platforms. Spokespeople, male and female, shouted in voices made harsh by hissing microphones and scratchy speakers. The slogans people yelled back to them were clear.

"Allah sent us our president. We will defend him with our blood. Down with the Brotherhood. It knows not God."

Making his way through the crowd, Paul excused himself with "*ma'aa iznak*" to slip past someone, pivoted in *Aikido*-like moves to let others pass. His progress stalled suddenly. A wedding engulfed him. Three and four people deep, the circle of celebrants clapped to the rhythm of the "*Ali ya Ali*" song packed with sexual double *entendres* blaring from giant speakers set ten yards apart. In the space between them, two young men, one in jeans the other in a traditional *gallabiyah*, stick-danced together, twirling eight-foot bamboo poles, catching them in midair to mock fence with each other. Then, each holding his phallic stick to his crotch, they thrust their hips back and forth while the bridegroom, in dark suit and bowtie, laughed sheepishly.

A belly dancer emerged accompanied by a long drum-roll and the men pulled back from the center of the circle and into the crowd. Now in center-stage, she flourished her arms, swayed her hips, fluttered her stomach and quivered her breasts for an exhausting five minutes. A woman handed Paul a bottle of warm Coke.

Then it was the bride's turn to shine. Dressed in a white wedding dress, wearing thick blue mascara and bright red lipstick, she joined the belly dancer. At first it was just the two women reflecting each other's sensuous gyrations, but soon the bride and groom's mothers, their aunts, and sisters, began belly dancing, too. Eventually, it seemed as though every female and young child who could fit into the space had joined them.

The music paused for a moment. Shrill ululations filled the early afternoon air as the bride took a seat in a wicker armchair hoisted by four young men who snaked it above the crowd to display her beauty. Four other men hoisted the bridegroom overhead in a matching chair and a man pulled Paul into what was becoming a procession. No one was ever left out of an Egyptian celebration.

In some ways this wedding was like his and his ex-wife, Ellyn's. Of course, the setting was different. Theirs has been as luxurious as she'd wanted it to be: Thirty tables set with white orchids drowning in glass vases. Lox, roast beef, and salads of every kind. Ten multi-leveled dessert trays and gallons of champagne. But it was the same clapping, the same dancing and loud music, and the same raised chairs—except people at their wedding sang *Hava Nagila* instead of ululating. He doubted Salma would countenance an elaborate wedding, Muslim, Jewish or atheist.

Salma. Paul froze where he stood. His knees locked. Beads of sweat erupted at his hairline. Had her plane landed yet? Would someone grab her from the terminal as soon as it did? He would have worried about the love of his life for hours, but he heard shouting and screaming from the direction of the Mogamma'a building he'd just left. Telling himself, for now, his fear for Salma's safety was irrational, he headed back to the heart of the action where slogans, leftover from Tahrir's Arab Spring, were followed by chants: "*Eish, horreya, adalah ejtemaei*"—bread, freedom, social justice. "*El thawra mustamira*"—the revolution continues. Apparently, some folks out there still had hope.

He stopped in front of a group of boys in T-shirts and jeans beating drums at ever-higher decibel levels and rapping, in Arabic, a language well suited to percussive rhythms: "A kilo of beans costs fifty pounds! A kilo of meat two hundred. Egyptians are eating bricks." Women in the crowd chanted, "*Labseen akher moda, sakneen 'ashra fi oda.*" You wear the latest fashions. We live ten to a room. It looked to Paul; a mini demonstration was emerging from the sanctioned one.

He'd flown in on assignment the day after protesters "captured" Tahrir Square in January 2011. Those were heady days. Arteries of people flowed into the heart of the uprising. Middle-class, college-aged, men and women paraded through slum alleys and side streets, exhorting residents to join them. Join they did. Magnetized, they came first in the hundreds, then the thousands and tens of thousands. Estimates varied. Most agreed twenty million Egyptians rallied at one time or another in the streets of Egypt. Laborers and housewives, peasants, and professors. Small business owners, vendors, college students, and housemaids defied social class divisions to share tents and blankets in city squares throughout the country. Mom-and-Pop shops trundled in bottled water, apartment residents brought food, and several couples celebrated the protest with their weddings. Today's demonstration was not like the spontaneous uprising of 2011. This one felt staged.

There was also an ugly side to the 2011 uprising. The police fired until they ran out of ammunition. Lung-searing teargas rose like fog from the square to the Giza Bridge. Bolstered by the military's vow not to shoot, the people called for the army to protect them. Fortunately for the protestors, the military had been planning its own coup to keep Mubarak's son from "inheriting" the presidency. So, protect them it did. Game over. Military wins. Now, except for the Muslim Brotherhood's reign that the generals had brought to power for a year, the military ruled, openly, and still did.

Paul stopped to check his smartphone and tweeted: *Undercurrent of discontent in otherwise peaceful Tahrir demonstrations.* It was ten past four. A fifteen-minute walk retracing his way through the crowd would bring him to Abu Taleb at the Ibis coffee shop. His erstwhile friend better be there with the cursed disk. Paul's feet felt rooted to the ground at the thought of the Taj.

He brought his panic under control and followed a woman with a wicker basket full of plastic brushes on her head and rubber flip-flops, twisted and crushed with overuse, on her feet. Short but heavy, her large rear end and big thighs filled her black gown, and her wide-hipped sway cleared a path through the crowd.

The ground shuddered. The woman pitched forward. Paul stopped obsessing about Aaron and the disk when a roar reverberated in his skull, exploded in his eardrums like a mortar round. A sound like thunder crackled as though inside him. Something had blown up. Exploded.

The roaring receded, Paul's reporter's mind clicked in. He joined the heaving mass of pushing, screaming people. Boys swarming over buses. Women dragging children towards the river. Young men shimmying up lamp poles, clinging like locusts. Dark smoke rose from the Mogamma'a building. He thrust ahead, past upended newsstands, package-sized shops, and a smoke-filled KFC. His breath was jagged. Flames were shooting out of the Mogamma'a's first-floor windows.

Taking refuge against a wall, he pulled out his press card. He could be mistaken for an Arab in the Middle East when he toned down his body language and let the card speak for itself. "*Sahafa, Sahafa*"—Press, Press, he shouted, waving the card in the air until it worked its magic. Three young workmen elbowed people out of his way to guide him around pools of burning oil and wrecks of hot metal as close to the building as they could get.

Caustic waves of smoke blew off scorched metal. Paul recognized the distinctive roast-pork odor of cooked flesh and the stench burning rubber. Just like the Gulf War. Chunks of concrete. Charred body parts. An arm severed at the elbow. A hand with fingers still attached, its wedding band seared into blackened skin. Years covering guerrilla attacks had inured him to carnage, but not dampened his need to do a job well. Reporting this to the *Mercury News* would remind his editor he still worked there. If he ended up blowing the *Harper's* assignment, Paul would need that job.

He looked for a uniform and found a police sergeant—a short man in a black jacket with a white sash across his chest. "What happened?" Paul asked. Despite or because of Paul's press card, the policeman was taciturn, bordering on rude. He stood with his feet apart and his hands clasped in front of him.

"Building crash. Fire." He tapped the forefinger of one hand and on the other hand at his waist, eager to be done.

"Yes, but how did it happen?"

"Maybe, car-bomb." The man's arched black eyebrows sent furrows up his forehead to his receding hairline.

"Do you know who did it?" Dumb question. Paul wasn't thinking straight.

"No one knows." The answer didn't surprise him.

"How many victims?"

"About thirty-five killed, fifty injured." The policeman turned as though planning to leave.

"Last question," Paul said, clearing his head. "Were there American casualties?"

"One." Another hapless soul in the wrong place at the wrong time.

Paul knew the police made up information on the spot. He also knew how the official investigation would go. The police would arrest hundreds of young men. Torture them—electrocute, water-board, burn them—and accuse the Brotherhood of plotting against the government, which it did. But no one would invent an American victim.

He was asking about the supposed American victim, when a double line of two hundred well-disciplined men cut through the crowd—full-bearded, party-crashing, radical Jihadists in *gallabiyas* hemmed to a foot from the ground like the Prophet Mohammed had worn his. They marched in ominous formation, waving copies of the Qur'an and chanting with a stubborn streak of menace, "*Allahu Akbar*" God is greatest. "*Al Islam huwa al hal*" Islam is the solution.

Four police squads burst out from behind the Mogamma'a building; shields raised, anti-riot visors lowered, machine guns aimed. All purchased with American military aid, thought Paul, and courtesy of whoever delivered them after skimming off a cut. The police confronted the religious extremists with an offensive line. Conscripts in front, officers behind them, every 47K poised. Teargas canisters exploded. The air, thick with poison, seared Paul's lungs and made his eyes water. He was rubbing them with his fists when a fire truck, three Humvees, and several water cannons rolled into the square. Steel-treaded armored tanks thundered out of Bab el Louk Street to add to the excessive show of strength. The government was powerful. The military was in control. The protesters fell silent but did not disperse. Men linked arms to stare down the police. A huge truck fired water jets. Protestors tumbled over one another, fell down, got back up. A bottomless well of defiance seemed to have gathered today.

Lines of policemen with locked shields surrounded the men. A squad of police culled the spontaneous demonstrators, leaving men with their beards and *gallabiyas* in the circle. Then, with brutal efficiency, they pummeled their heads with batons to clear the way for a canine unit. Six snarling German Shepherds. A screaming child bolted. A woman dashed out to rescue him; a policeman spun around and shot her. She stood still for a moment, vomited blood, and fell. Paul gasped. Jerked back his head. His hand flew to his throat. Every part of his body felt disconnected from the other.

The crowd turned furious, their anger now visceral. Men tossed teargas canisters back at the police. Voices, rough from yelling, swelled in the afternoon heat. "*Kifaya!*" Enough! Enough brutality. Enough corruption. Enough murder. We want liberty! We want life! Down with military rule."

Paul covered his nose with his arm and ducked into a storefront entrance where three young men were using tire irons to break up the pavement. In a well-practiced rhythm, two of them crushed cement into fist-sized chunks that they flung to a third, to hurl at the police. Paul scanned the area. He was only a block from the Semiramis Hotel. He could file his story.

Suddenly, someone grabbed the back of his shirt so tightly it blocked Paul's breath before his collar ripped away. He turned, ducked a blow, then landed a solid punch against his assailant's jaw. Thankful for years of martial arts training, he gripped the man's arm, flipped him to the ground and heard a satisfying, bone-crushing sound. The guy who'd assaulted him was strong-muscled, broad-shouldered and shorter than him; the lower half of his face hidden by a black and white, checkered *kiffeya*. He was on his feet quicker than Paul expected, leaping backward and kicking out to catch him in the chest. Paul landed awkwardly, the air knocked out of him. For some reason the man didn't move but stood there waiting, wiping saliva from the corner of his mouth with the back of his hand. Paul got to his feet and approached him slowly, feinting left and right working an opening that never came. Instead, a jab caught his chin, rocked his head back. The man slammed into Paul who threw out his arms and spun into the fall, the momentum smashing him into the storefront window. Glass shards cut into his scalp. Blood ran into his eyes and dripped down his chin. He grasped the window frame, hauled himself to his feet and regained his balance. Shoulders first, he launched into his assailant, breaking his nose, splattering blood on his shirt. The man reeled backward down the sidewalk. Grabbed a chunk of broken cement and hurled it one-handed. Paul stumbled into the storefront wall, blinded. He blinked rapidly to clear his eyes in time to see the man look beyond him and flee around the corner. Shaken and unnerved, Paul sat on the ground, clutching his aching ribs. The man was probably ten years younger. Too fast, too strong, and out to get him. A professional, for sure.

He turned to look behind him for another possible source of danger and caught sight of the squad of National Guardsmen who must have spooked the man who'd attacked him.

"Help me," he yelled. "Help me. I'm an American." A guard broke formation to reach him. "I'm American," Paul repeated, his heart pounding, blood roaring in his ears. The young guard grabbed his arm. "We go now. Hotel Semiramis. We protect." While Paul couldn't tell if the guard was referring to protecting him or the hotel, his heart swelled with gratitude as he merged into the squadron that was saving his life. Recalling this morning's policeman with his notebook on the hotel's driveway he silently thanked the hyper-vigilant Egyptian authorities for watching over Americans like him.

Protected, Paul stayed in the middle of the squad's formation as it cut through the square—emptying, devolving into subsections of the original crowd. With each step he took, the swelling knuckles of his right hand throbbed. His head throbbed even more. When he pulled his shirt away from his chest, its fabric stiffened where the blood it soaked up had dried.

The Semiramis Hotel's staircase at the back entrance was blocked by a line of policemen and a navy-blue van discharging more of them into the square. A small mob jammed the area, quiet and intense. The people closest were pointing to a spot on the staircase past the police. Paul craned his neck to look over their heads. Abu Taleb's huge body was sprawled across the steps.

Jabbing with his elbows, pushing with his hands, and kicking when he had to, he dodged the police and their rifle butts and forced his way up the stairs. Black flies had collected at the corners of his friend's eyes. Some buzzing in and out his open mouth. The slash across his throat was so deep, his trachea was visible, a flash of ivory. The pool of blood around his corpulent body had already congealed, some caked in his combed-over hair. The sour contents of Paul's stomach surged into his throat and suddenly his legs felt boneless.

Someone had ripped off the outer pockets of Abu Taleb's brown herringbone suit. Two police officers were going through the inside ones. The one in charge, a man with an untrimmed mustache, motioned Paul to leave "I'm an American journalist," Paul barked, his shoes skidding in a rivulet of blood until he found a dry spot on which to stand. "Mr. Abu Taleb is the editor of the *Ahram News*. He is also my close friend." The policeman at Abu Taleb's side slipped his hand into his uniform pocket and rose to his feet.

"*El ba'eya fi hayatak, ya bey*," he offered the short, traditional, condolence: may Paul's own life continue. "But this is a police investigation. You must stand away."

"Who did this?" Paul asked. "And when?" The officer fastened a button and straightened his jacket.

"It happened at the time of the explosion, sir. Who is responsible? It could be anyone." He glared at the people milling behind the police cordon as though suggesting their existence explained everything. "This is not the first assassination. It will not be the last. You must leave."

Paul did not leave. He stood by Abu Taleb's corpse and the circling flies, staring at three plastic bags of evidence on the ground, near it: the editor's car keys, his leather wallet, and the silver cigarette lighter Paul had given him before returning to the States. But the set's silver cigarette case was missing. The officer who'd stood up must have palmed it. Paul pointed to the lighter in the smaller plastic bag.

"I gave my friend this lighter. I'm sorry to see it in such sad circumstances. It was part of a gift." He lowered his voice so only the officer could hear him. "I also gave him a matching cigarette case. The one in your pocket." The officer glanced back at his companion for support. "Open it," Paul insisted. "I had my name inscribed inside it. A name well known to people in the highest places. I can identify it to Dr. Hani Hamdi when I inform him of your theft." He pulled out his smartphone and hit numbers at random. With the phone to his ear, he raised questioning eyebrows as he asked the officer's for his full name and badge number. The hapless man's face blanched. His hand reached into his pocket.

"I was saving it for evidence," he protested in a voice edged with worry.

"You were not. Your companion is collecting the evidence in bags. Just give me the case," Paul said, slipping bank notes into the man's hand. "I will tell no one. Offer me a cigarette, and I will keep the case."

With the case in his pocket, Paul climbed the stairs to the hotel. His bones ached. He still felt like throwing up. The hotel's back door opened onto the Semiramis shopping mall where he picked up bandages at the pharmacy and charged an overpriced pair of jeans to his credit card at a Ralph Lauren store. Its solicitous clerk shook his head in sympathy when he escorted Paul to a fitting room where he bandaged the cuts to keep them from oozing and refused to accept a gratuity.

By the time Paul was presentable again, it was six in the evening. The shock of the afternoon had worn off, but he was so tense his face felt as though it had been sprayed with starch. And he was hungry. Fortunately, the hotel's *Birdcage* Thai restaurant was serving foreigners who ate much earlier than the locals.

Waiting for his order of pad thai and green beans, Paul snapped open the cigarette case. As he'd expected, no Turkish cigarettes—only a row of Abu Taleb's Marlboros with a thin square memory disk squeezed behind them. He had a small mound of pad thai in his chopsticks when his phone rang. He lowered the chopsticks to his plate and answered an unknown caller.

"Do you have the disk?" It was Aaron. In his habitual arrogance, assuming Paul would recognize his voice.

"No."

"That won't do." Aaron's voice was steely cold.

"I know where it is," Paul said. "Abu Taleb said he'd locked it in his desk. He had a small apartment in Garden City he used as a personal office. I'm sure your sources have informed you he was murdered before I could meet him."

"What's the address?"

"I can't risk your people being spotted. I'll go myself. The building's *bawab* knows me."

"You're a journalist, not a spy, Paul. And you're out of your depth here. If you try to back out of our deal…"

"Don't worry, you'll get it." Paul shut down his phone.

Well, Aaron wasn't going to get the disk until Paul discovered what was on it. He needed to get out from under the guy's thumb. And, more crucial than his own safety, he needed to be able to protect Salma from the Mossad as well as the Taj. He propped his elbows on the table and pressed his hands against his temples to contain his raw nerves. The Mossad was on his back and someone was willing to murder a public figure to make sure the man couldn't talk. After combining what Aaron and Abu Taleb had told him there was no avoiding the fact: whoever killed his friend—most likely Nabulsi—would be willing to murder Salma and Paul.

Chapter 8

September 29, 2014
7:00 pm

A FEW MILES SOUTH OF TAHRIR SQUARE, HANI'S DRIVER eased the Hamdi Cadillac through the dusty streets of the once elegant district of Rhoda where Salah Salem Street petered out into the old residential district. Nothing in the neighborhood had changed. Nothing ever seemed to. Cars still rubbed sides with horses. Horns honked at pedestrians and bleated warnings at donkey carts before nudging them aside. The few old villas that remained in what had once been a Mammaluk orchard sat nestled and decaying behind high stucco walls embedded with glass shards. Apartment buildings, with satellite TV antennas sprouting from their roofs, had taken over the rest of the land. The urban island was choking.

The driver turned right at the roundabout in front of Sabri's old gelato shop where her father used to let Salma have a crispy cone with two scoops of lemon sherbet—defying her mother, who allowed only one. Salma would lick the top scoop on the way home, stopping to let her father wipe off her chin with one of his monogrammed handkerchiefs. Where had his old sweetness gone?

The three limousines drew up to the Hamdi mansion's wrought iron gate flanked by police-manned sentry boxes. Salma jumped out without waiting for the driver to open the door and circled around the back of the car. An old barefooted woman, hawking paper cones of peanuts, was sitting against the wall not far from the front gate, her thin bare ankles against the concrete sidewalk. Salma hesitated for a moment before she walked past her. It wasn't the first time she'd been in this predicament. If she bought anything, the woman would hound her whenever she left the house. Humiliating as it was, she resorted to the necessary skill, too-easily acquired in Egypt, of ignoring the poor. Somehow, in America she could deal with poverty; help ameliorate the oppressive conditions that created it. Here the problem was too big to get her head around. There were simply too many poor people to deal with.

A silent sentry opened the gate so Salma could wait in the garden where she couldn't stop fretting about what her father insisted was an accident. It wasn't. She could still see the white pickup truck careening towards them, hear people screaming. Her shoulders rose to her ears again as the crack-crack of the Presidential Guards' machine guns still ringing in her ears. Now, she jumped at the sound of a young man's voice greeting her. The gardener's son on the way to the car to help with the luggage.

Finally, she recognized the jasmine fragrance of the frangipani tree that dwarfed the broad-leafed loquat by the water fountain. Vines of bougainvillea, red blood-of-the-gazelle, frothed over the garden walls dropping blossoms that somersaulted in the spray of the gardener's hose. This was the Egypt she knew best—on the outside dry and dusty, on the inside glowing, lush. Surrounded by the musky scent of water meeting dry earth at the end of the day, she put the car "accident" behind her.

She was about to lean into a deep, relaxing breath, when her cousin, Farida, her red slippers scurrying like roosters underfoot, shattered the brief calm.

"*Ahlan wa sahlan ya habibti, nawarti elbalad*," Farida trilled, fluttering her pudgy, diamond-ringed fingers around her full-moon face. Salma's heart warmed at the expression: her presence lit up the country. She loved Arabic phrases like this one even if they were "over the top." Farida planted two kisses on each of Salma's cheeks as she continued in the mix of English and Arabic the family used when Salma was around.

"How's Tante Ann? And your girls? Why didn't they come? You should bring them every year. We have *wilad nass,* good men from good families. Don't you dare let them marry American boys." There was no point in getting worked up about her girls' marriage issue; it was only Farida's way of saying the family would always love Hoda and Nawal, who, no matter where they lived, would always be Hamdis. The sentiment confused and comforted Salma at the same time.

The thumping sound of a rolled-up newspaper against a tree trunk reached Salma and her cousin at the front door. Hani, who'd lagged, was ordering the gardener to trim an offending branch.

"I see you have already angered him, *habibti*." Farida laughed. "You're in his face, already."

"He's been worse since my mother left him," Salma said, not laughing but rather swallowing the emptiness that stuffed her throat. "I don't know—I don't know what to do."

"Don't aggravate him, *habibti*." Farida's voice softened with understanding. "He's had some difficult times this year, but he'd give his two eyes for you. Don't worry about anything. We all love you," she said as she ushered Salma through the front door.

Salma's eyes adjusted to the shuttered light in the entryway, a mosque-like whispering space between the inner and the outer worlds. The foyer's deep honey-colored parquet floor bore testament to years of wax and polish. The light from the tall windows had faded the rich red and burgundy of the carpets a little.

They climbed the curved oak stairway to the mezzanine. The same arabesque couches of dark wood inlaid with mother-of-pearl. The same muted television set turned on and her uncle Abdel Magid's library still overflowing with bookcases lining every wall but one. Books he'd set aside for her when she was a young teen stood where they'd been for twenty years, probably untouched. *Lady Chatterley's Lover, Vanity Fair, The Pilgrim's Progress.* Salma smiled when she thought of the scraps of paper stuck between pages he'd singled out with passages "your mother wouldn't want you to read."

She was thinking of her uncle when he burst out of his study as though summoned. His wild hair and bushy eyebrows were whiter than before—a better match to his white linen shirt, white pants, and the white jacket with a white frangipani blossom in its lapel. "I am a poet. All poets dress in white," he'd told her when she was seven years old. Her mother scoffed at what she called his affectation, but Salma had believed him.

She was half lost in those memories when cello music, the kind that signaled death—rumbled from the television and Farida screamed. A grim-faced announcer intoned: "Nile TV regrets to report the Honorable Mohamed Abu Taleb, the respected editor of *Ahram News* was murdered this afternoon. Fifteen Egyptians and one American also died in the Mogamma'a bombing. The *Rayyis* calls on . . ." Salma stared at the screen, stunned. A picture of the El-Hussein Mosque. *One American. One American.* Her throat closed itself around a scream.

"Animals! Monsters!" Farida pounded the set. "Abu Taleb's been our friend forever. God have mercy on his soul."

*One American. One Americ*an. Salma's face felt Novocain-numb, her ears felt stuffed with cotton and the chill in her bones was leaching into her veins as the room turned grey

She didn't see Farida come to her side, but she heard her uncle say, "You're pale" and found herself with a glass of water that trembled when she brought it to her lips. "This is terrible news," she said with no emotion while the words repeated in her head: *One American.* It couldn't be Paul. It just couldn't be Paul. She grabbed her purse for her cell phone. Its battery was dead, and if she hadn't lost it, its charger probably buried in her suitcase. She'd use the phone in her father's study. "I need to wash my face," she said, shaking as she stood.

Her father's study was dark and private—reflecting who he was—with drapes drawn across its shuttered windows. The pendulum of the grandfather clock behind his mahogany desk had been stilled. She sat at the desk facing at least twenty photographs of Hani with someone important. Secretaries of State John Kerry, Hilary Clinton, Condoleezza Rice, King Abdullah of Jordan, Kofi Annan. Hani with the president, of course. There was one of her mother, in the background of a photo, looking vague and confused. There were no pictures of Salma or her daughters.

Paul's phone message box was full, so she called Cairo *El Dalil* information for the Shams Hotel number and phoned. According to its guest log Paul had been due back an hour ago. The receptionist tried to reassure her, "Often people tell us one thing and then change their plans." But Salma heard the concern behind the promise he'd given her that he'd have Paul call the moment he returned. Afraid she wouldn't find her cell phone charger in time, she left the Hamdi home phone number with him.

Sick to her stomach, she retired to the bedroom she always used. The maids had already hung her clothes in the armoire, folded her lingerie in the bureau, and stowed her suitcases. *One American. One American.* Salma threw herself on the bed and rocked back and forth like a child. Curled up waiting to hear from Paul, she made herself focus on the mindless dead space inside her. A half hour passed before she could rouse herself to fret through the obligatory high tea and fruitcake in the family room. The television station was running what it always ran in emergencies: archival footage of the Nile flowing under Cairo's bridges. Always calming, always a sign something was wrong.

The front door opened. Slammed shut. "*Allo*? Who?" Hani climbed the stairs to the mezzanine with the phone to his ear. "It's for you," he told Salma, his eyebrows arched in disbelief. No one in Egypt ever called her at this number. Light-headed, dizzy, she gripped the bannister on her way down the stairs where she might have some privacy. What if it was the hotel receptionist on the line? What if he had horrible news? Her throat convulsed; the receiver shook in her hand.

"Paul? Are you alright?" she whispered, the words almost refusing to come out.

"I'm okay."

"They said an American died. I thought—" Salma sank to a stair step, her legs folding as she subsided.

"It's about Abu Taleb." There was a nervous break in Paul's voice.

"I heard. I'm sorry. I know he was your friend."

"People are out to get you and your dad." Paul's tight vocal cords made his voice sound strident.

"What?" A line of fear wove down Salma's spine. "What makes you think that?"

"It's serious." Paul's voice rose.

"You're safe. Right? Back at the hotel. I'll be there right away."

"Don't leave your house. It's not safe. There are people out there set on harming you. Maybe worse."

"Who's set on harming me? Why? Who'd even care? "

"Apparently it's got to do with your dad." Salma bit her tongue to keep from mentioning the pickup crashing into the limousine. "An extremist Islamist group wants him dead." She knew who that group was. Her father had called it Taj al Islam.

"Okay. I'm going to check something with him and call you back," she said, pulling herself up by the handrail to climb back up to the mezzanine.

Slumped on the family room couch, his eyes fixed on the television screen, Hani's face was colorless. "That was Mr. Hays," Salma said, standing behind him, too tentative to rest her hands on his shoulders. "An American journalist. He has information about Mr. Abu Taleb."

"What would he know?" Hani asked, his sarcasm undiminished by shock at his friend's death. Salma took a step back.

"He's a journalist, Dad. Journalists tell each other things they don't tell ordinary people. I think it's a good idea to find out what he knows."

"Who's this Mr. Hays of yours? How do you know him?" Her father seemed to be targeting her to mobilize his strength, but Salma held her ground.

"We know each other from work," she responded. A lie of omission but technically correct. "He's the keynote speaker I told you about. He and Mr. Abu Taleb were friends."

"Invite the man for lunch tomorrow. We'll have Rashid over, too," her father said, reestablishing his authority.

"I'll be glad to." She came around the sofa so she could look at the three people in the room at once. "I'm sure he'll be honored. But—just so no one's surprised or embarrassed—you should know, Paul Hays is Jewish." The room went silent.

"*Ayb, ya* ya, Salma, shame," her uncle admonished. "The American ambassador, Ernie Reichert, is Jewish. He lunched here last month. It's where he meets Rashid when they need to be discreet. Please don't insult us by—" He straightened the Bedouin rug with the tip of his white shoe and swallowed the rest of his sentence. "We're civilized, you know. The food won't be kosher, but there will be no shellfish."

Smarting at the rebuke; her face breaking out in splotches, Salma went back to her bedroom. She'd lived in America and with its black and white thinking too long. Things were so much more nuanced—more complicated—in Egypt.

Chapter 9

September 30, 2014
11:30 am

NEXT MORNING, AFTER A LATE BREAKFAST, SALMA JOINED her father and uncle who were sitting in matching rattan armchairs near the garden fountain, reading their newspapers, drinking Turkish coffee, and smoking mid-morning cigars. The odor of tobacco pierced the coffee's aroma and wafted up to mingle in the leaves of the loquat tree. For the fifth time, she glanced at the gate. She was supposed to pick up Paul from his hotel to bring him to lunch with her family. The chauffeur still hadn't arrived.

"What time is it?" she asked, neither man.

"Eleven," her uncle answered from behind his paper.

Her father's paper rustled as he lowered it to peer at her. "You don't have a watch?" he asked, ruffled and annoyed. He stiffened his back against his chair. "Where's the one I gave you when you got engaged? You should wear it if you're going out."

"It's in my jewelry bag."

"And where's your jewelry bag?" he asked, exaggerating each word as though questioning a child.

"In my bedroom," Salma said, a quiver of resistance running through her. What right did her father have to tell her what to wear? "I'm only going to pick up Mr. Hays at his hotel." The protest wavered on her lips, yet she refused to surrender to the maze of tradition her father was leading her into.

"It doesn't matter where you're going. You are going out. Please go to your bedroom and retrieve your watch from the jewelry bag. Wear it or stay home." The blank gaze in his determined face chilled her. She turned to her uncle, opening her arms in a questioning gesture of stunned incredulity. Her heart sank as she watched his face fall abruptly into stern lines. He folded his newspaper on his lap, pulled in his chin and shook his head at her. How she appeared to the outside world seemed as important to him as to her father. The way women dressed in public and what accessories they wore were indicators of a family's social status. The world had to be advised that Hani Hamdi had bought his daughter a diamond watch.

Overtaken by a wave of despairing acquiescence, Salma went to her bedroom as instructed, crossing through three flowerbeds rather than following the pathways. Her head throbbed dangerously. What if she'd forgotten to bring the damn watch?

She rummaged through tee shirts and underwear all the way to the back of the dresser's top drawer until her fingers felt the watch's solid band in the velvet pouch. She didn't realize she'd been holding her breath until she let it out. A pair of diamond earrings tumbled out of the jewelry bag and onto the dresser when Salma withdrew the watch. Might as well go for the whole shebang, she told herself, exchanging them with the pearl earrings, with which she'd started out the day.

Her father registered her return with a glacial stare, then retreated behind his newspaper while Salma took her place on the bench with a flame of scarlet spreading across her cheeks. Her uncle rose from his chair, brushed the creases from the front of his white linen trousers and plucked a blossom from the frangipani tree to give her.

"I gave the driver a call. He'll be outside in less than a minute," he said as though nothing untoward had occurred. If nothing is said, then nothing happened is the way things worked in this culture.

"An Egyptian minute could be an hour—or more," she muttered, pulling open the wrought iron gate.

The chauffeur surprised her by being outside, chatting with the guards in the sentry boxes. Catching sight of Salma, he ground out his cigarette with the heel of his shoe and followed her to the first of two limousines. She noticed for the first time how deep-set his eyes were and how his brows bulged as though swollen. The man seemed cross to her, but she gave him the benefit of the doubt thinking it might just be his natural look.

"*Shukran,*" she thanked him as she got into the limo where two armed guards were already positioned—one in the front seat, one in the back.

"Many roads in that area are closed, madam," the chauffeur grumbled when she asked him to drive to the Shams Hotel.

"Then take me as close as you can. If I need to, I'll walk the rest of the way."

"Your wish is my command." The reluctant driver nodded but Salma thought she saw, beneath his meekness, the suppressed challenge that lurked in his eyes.

Followed by a second limo with three more guards, they drove north along the Nile, past riverfront restaurants, coffeehouses, and a multiplex movie theater. The driver was right. They couldn't cross the Kasr el Eini Bridge because there was a double line of policemen stretched between the pair of bronze lions that had been guarding it since the time of the Khedive Ismail.

"You see, madam?" the driver said, pointing to a cordon of police struggling to hold back several hundred flag-waving pedestrians.

"You're right, *ya usta*," Salma placated him. "We'll have to circle. Let's take the next bridge and double back."

"It will not work," the driver scolded under his breath, turning north at the Kasr el Eini hospital. Salma ignored this old master-slave game. It was one of the few ways with which people in his position tried to preserve their self-respect.

Another blockade. This time across the entrance to the Six October Bridge. Here, the driver flashed an official card at the officers, who saluted and waved the two limos through.

"You could have done that at the first bridge," Salma said archly. The driver shrugged, drove a quarter mile, and stopped.

"You'll have to walk from here, madam."

Walk Salma did, with guards at her side, her senses sharpened at the threat of danger from a source she couldn't identify. Sunlight glittered on the hotel's beveled glass doors and glinted off the polished fenders of limousines parked along its driveway. The marble stairs gleamed. With the guards at her heels, Salma dashed up them, past the liveried attendants and into the hotel lobby.

Europeans huddled on sofas in the hotel's magnificent peach and gold lobby. The air pulsed with agitated references to Tahrir Square. Egyptian police officers described their heightened security precautions. Embassy aides rustled tickets and schedules for chartered planes. Salma felt the familiar mix of sadness and anger at the sight of foreigners preparing to flee.

Ordering the guards to wait in the foyer, she headed to the reception desk, where an attendant gave her the number of Paul's room. Salma wasn't sure whether it was in the name of security or propriety, but he prevented her from going up to it. She was a single woman meeting a man in a hotel. Dialing the room from the lobby phone, she thought of the twenty-five million residents of Cairo, each one into the other's business—any one of whom might shake a disapproving finger at her—

Smoothing down the sides of her pants, straightening her blouse, she stood before a bank of elevators watching numbers light up as one of them descended. The three minutes of waiting felt like an hour until the steel doors dinged opened and Paul stepped out.

The familiar citrus odor of his shaving lotion grew stronger as she approached and could look more closely at his face. Handsome as ever but exhausted, distraught, and unusually hard. Salma longed to throw herself into his arms, but this was Egypt, so she grasped only one of them. Paul would understand her restraint.

He was wearing the olive-colored shirt she'd given him on his forty-fifth birthday a few months ago. She'd chosen it because it accentuated the hazel color of his eyes—brown and green and gold all at the same time. Today they were blood-shot, a stain of tiredness brushed under them.

"I've had time to think," he said, leading her up a broad flight of marble stairs to the balcony rather than into the elevator and up to his room. "I'll tell you outside," he added, as though expecting her to object.

In fact, it made little sense to her. The corridor was empty and quiet. Outside, the world would be thundering with interminable noise: the drone of cars crawling across the bridges, the whine of speedboats zipping up and down the river, the seemingly endless pleasure boats blaring songs of unrequited love. Still, she followed him onto the hotel's narrow balcony from where royalty once waved to its subjects. Today, an old Umm Kulthum song drifted up from one of the boats to tremble in the air like fragments of crystal. Its lyrics spoke to Salma—to the confusion love created for her.

The sunlight they stood in was so bright it turned the potted red geraniums a strange orange color. After checking out the balcony, Paul guided her to an alcove of comparative shade and privacy, his hand at the small of her back. In the relative dark, they stood against the stucco wall where he leaned his head towards Salma's to whisper, "I think my room's bugged."

"Bugged?" Salma pushed off the wall and turned to face him. "I can't imagine anyone risking doing that to you."

"Someone did," Paul insisted. She noticed that shadows were intensifying the worry lines around his eyes and making the hollows beneath his high cheekbones look bruised. "Someone bugged my room or phone."

Salma stepped forward to place reassuring palms on his chest. Beneath the soft fabric of the shirt, she could feel his heart beating too fast.

"Why do you think so?"

"No one but Abu Taleb knew where and when we'd meet. I told no one. And he had every reason not to say a single word."

Salma felt Paul's heartbeat thump harder and faster. "You're probably right." Her hands continued tracing circles on his chest. "Your friend is known—was known," she corrected herself, "as a cautious man."

"Yet, someone found out where he'd be. And someone slit his throat. Blood everywhere; flies all over his face." Paul shook his head as though to rid himself of the image.

"Horrible," Salma said. In fact, it was unspeakable. There were no words for it. "I'm sorry. I know you two were close. Could his murder and the Mogamma'a bombing be related?"

"Perhaps. These folks are heartless." Paul looked wounded.

"Who are they? Who'd kill thirty people to get at one?"

"Taj al-Islam."

Salma raised her eyebrows as he spit out the word. "My dad said they tried to assassinate him."

"I'd heard something like that."

"Really? When? Who told you?" Salma had heard him hesitate before responding and each question she asked was more dagger-like than the one before it.

"A journalist here in Cairo emailed me about a month ago." Salma tried to puzzle out what that meant.

"I'm supposed to believe you knew my father was almost killed and didn't tell me?" Her strong accent of reproach was as bitter as it sounded. Her eyes squinted, her frown deepened, she twisted an earring around and around until her earlobe burned.

"I checked every news source I knew." Paul hadn't had time to slip on a mask of neutrality. "Nothing. Nada. Zilch. No assassination attempts on anyone."

"Still, you should have told me." Salma gritted her teeth and pursed indignant lips.

"I didn't want to alarm you. I chalked it up to rumor. You know Egypt has more rumors than grains of desert sand." Salma knew Paul was trying to mollify her, still his forced smile felt condescending. "Listen," he continued, with a measuring eye the length of the balcony. "I've actually learned something about the assassination attempts."

"What?" Still guarded, Salma unfolded the arms she'd crossed against her breasts.

"I know who's behind them."

"Taj al Islam?"

"Specifically, it's leader, Sheikh Nabulsi."

"Why would he want to kill my dad?" There was an acute note of distress in Salma's voice "Why would a military doctor pose a threat to him?" She stared at Paul, appraising him.

"I don't know. Perhaps he's a symbol. After all, he is the department's head honcho."

"That doesn't make sense." She frowned, perplexed. "It might be something unconnected to his position."

"Dr. Hamdi leading a conspiracy to poison the sheikh?" Beneath Paul's half laugh lay a sober undertone.

"Now who's spreading rumors like grains of sand?" A faint tremor of amusement appeared on Salma's lips. "For heaven's sake, with whom would my father be conspiring?"

"With people connected to the president, perhaps. Your father would only be dealing with a powerful ally." Salma sensed Paul's sudden stillness was one of forced composure waiting for her reaction. A sort of tenderness towards him returned, remembering that he always cared about her feelings.

"Who'd be more powerful than the *rayyis*?" she asked.

"I can think of at least two: the CIA and the Mossad."

A formless dread ran through Salma's body. Compared to her father, these were high-stakes players in a game too dangerous for the man she thought she knew.

"You can rule out the Mossad. My father would never have anything to do with them."

"I wouldn't be so sure. The Mukhabarat is hand in glove with the Mossad. Together, they're the best intelligence service on the planet. There's no reason for him not to help them rein in the Taj."

"Forget it. My father would never, ever, work with the Mossad," Salma insisted with a hostile challenge in her voice. "The Mossad is a red line for us.

"Okay. For the purpose of argument let's say he's conspiring with the CIA. Is there some way that makes sense to you?"

"If he's conspiring with anyone, it would be with them. But I just don't see him taking that on."

"Well, to protect your father—to protect you—we need to know what that is."

Salma watched waves of heat rise off the tiled balcony. Her mind began to freeze as Paul let out a weary sigh and the silence between them grew stolid.

"Look," he said, pulling out his smartphone, "I have a photo of Abu Taleb in Yemen." He swiped his finger across its screen and held the phone out to Salma. "Nabulsi's the tall man. The one who wants your father dead," he said, pointing at the screen. "The man to his left is Abu Taleb. You probably recognize him, but I don't know who the third man is. He's got an assault rifle, so he might be a bodyguard." Paul rubbed the phone up and down his pant leg, which he did when he was anxious.

Salma felt as though the balcony lurched, as though her legs would detach from her body. Trembling, she made it across to hold on to the bannister, her knuckles turning white.

"What's wrong?" Paul wrapped an arm around her shoulders.

"I know the man on the right," she said, her throat tightening around the words.

"Who is it?" Paul pulled her towards him with his reassuring grasp.

"It's Murad," Salma said.

"Whoa. The graduate student you knew before we met?" Paul pulled away to face her. "Are you telling me your ex-boyfriend's an armed terrorist?"

"I wasn't telling you anything." Salma stared through the hotel's palm grove to the Nile without seeing the trees.

"Unbelievable." Paul's face flushed red. "What am I supposed to make of him?"

"I can't think of him as a terrorist, but…" Salma couldn't think of what to make of Murad herself. She made another half-turn toward Paul but didn't lift her gaze from the middle button of his shirt. "It doesn't matter, anyway. He's in Yemen," she said, surprised to find despite the sick roiling in her stomach she sounded calm.

"You don't know that."

"You said Nabulsi was the problem," Salma continued as though she hadn't heard him. "We need to warn my father." Again, she thought better of mentioning the "accident." There was already too much to worry about.

"Nabulsi's just as likely to come after you," Paul said.

"Me?"

"Kidnap you. Blackmail your dad. Lure him into a trap."

"That seems farfetched. Who thought that one up?"

"A reliable source."

"A journalist?"

"The Mossad. And they didn't just think that one up. They knew what they were talking about." Paul drew a quick breath, released it, and rubbed the back of his neck.

"You've got sources in the Mossad?" Salma's voice, strident and accusatory, masked her visceral revulsion and fear.

"No, I don't have sources in the Mossad." The vein that pulsed in his neck when he was angry, twitched as he paced along the balcony. When he stopped, the distance he created between them, while not large, was deliberate. "One of them came to see me," he continued. "The Taj scenario—abducting you—was his. Nevertheless, the guy was convinced it wasn't just about your dad. You're in danger. Go back to the States. Go home to your girls."

Salma looked behind her to be sure they were alone before she headed back to the protective alcove. "Go home? Are you kidding? I'm safer than you are," she said to Paul when he joined her. "Besides, I am home," she insisted, surprised at how vehement she felt. "Where the Big Brute protects us with his Presidential Guards."

"He may be protecting your father," Paul objected. "He's not protecting you."

"That's not true. My father's guards came with me tonight." Salma hardened her stance, put her hands on her hips. "What do you want me to do? Hire my own private army? Really, Paul. The *rayyis* may be an ass, but one thing he can do is protect me and my father. He's already jailed over thirty-five thousand Brotherhood militants."

"Don't call them militants. Every one of them is a terrorist like your boyfriend. Abu Taleb drowned in his own blood because of people like him."

Salma pulled her head back and tensed her body to keep from shaking. Flashes of red filled her narrowing range of vision as she focused on the light sconces above Paul's head.

"Hitting below the belt is nasty. You're better than that," she said.

"I'm sorry. I didn't mean to say that. But I'm terrified about the danger you're in. The whole country is on the edge of something scary."

"It's complicated."

"Not complicated. Dangerous. Lots of conference delegates have already left."

"It's different for me." Salma's voice lowered; her eyes threatened to fill with tears. "I'm not a foreigner. Not a turncoat. My family would think I'm a traitor."

"It's not about your family, for God's sake. Go home."

"But you...you'll stay. Right? You're not in any danger even though your room is bugged?" Once Salma's sarcasm chased away her tearfulness, she glared at Paul and kicked the wall. "You're probably fine without my father's help, but I'm not leaving until you and he are working together. Otherwise, one or both of you will get hurt."

"I don't need protection and I've plenty of my own sources." Paul's frustration was evident in the hard set of his shoulders. "In my own way,

I know this country better than you do and I'm telling you to go home. Now."

Salma's eyebrows shot up. An angry throb in her head spread through her body. It wasn't like Paul to frighten her. Something was wrong. He was dealing with Israelis and acting like a full-blown American. She was about to challenge him when he pivoted and looked away from her.

"My friend..." Paul stared into the distance and hesitated before completing his sentence. "Abu Taleb had a disk the Israelis wanted. But he refused to hand it over to the Mossad and insisted I be a go-between— something of a courier."

Salma stood frozen, her mouth half open, her elbows pressed into her sides. "Don't tell me you're going to work for the Mossad. Do you know what that means to me? What would it do to my father?" A crimson flush spread across her face and into her ears. "Don't tell me you crossed that line."

Paul stopped pacing to lock eyes with her, ready to defend himself. "I had to. They wanted the disk so badly, they blackmailed me." The blood drained from Salma's face. What secrets did Paul have? Which so scandalous they could use against him?

"Blackmailed you with what?" She held her breath; stared at a geranium-filled terra-cotta urn on a nearby pedestal.

"Letting it be known that I work for them and that you and I are together. Not good. Word travels fast. More reason for the Taj to harm or ..." He didn't complete the sentence and there was a catch in his throat when he continued, "I'd have agreed to absolutely anything to keep you safe."

"Why did they want the disk so badly?" Salma asked, softening a little.

"All I know is, it must be important enough for the Taj to murder my friend to get it."

"What's on it that's so important?"

"I tried to download it," Paul said. "It's protected with a super-long password. A warning came up as soon as I stuck the disk into my laptop that it would self-destruct at the first incorrect entry. I'll have to find a good hacker."

"Now you have me worried," Salma said, frustrated enough to almost cry. "You're the one with the disk. You're the one in danger. It's you who should go home."

"You're not the only one who wants me to. *Harper's* called the American ambassador here after the Mogamma'a bombing. Together they decided the situation is"—Paul made quote marks in the air—"critical" so they want me on the first plane out. The editor doesn't want another murdered journalist, like Giulio Regeni, tortured to death on his watch."

"I assume you didn't tell either about the disk." Salma didn't mean for her voice to sound so acid-soaked.

"Of course, I didn't," Paul replied, ignoring her hostility. "But I had to agree to bodyguards or cancel the conference keynote speech. I'll go to the opening ceremonies. I don't care what *Harper's* thinks, I'm off the investigation for now. The most important, the most urgent thing I need to do, is to figure out the disk. I hope to God I can use what's on it to protect you."

"Worry about yourself. How do you plan to keep from becoming another dead journalist?" Salma didn't try to disguise her sarcasm.

"Sources."

"What sources?"

"Sources from streets you don't even know exist. Where the *bult-ageya* congregate—the thugs who protect or kill you, depending on who pays." Salma blew out an exasperated breath of air and concentrated on a zigzagging crack along the balustrade. "Talk to your dad. I'm sure he'll agree you should go back to the States. You might even find out why the Taj wants him dead."

"Okay. I'll talk to him," she conceded, shoving her hands into her pant pockets and dropping her tone a notch, not wanting to continue sounding so sharp. "And if you drop the *Harper's* thing so you don't get my father in trouble while I'm gone, I'll consider going home after my conference presentation. No guarantee," she added, to be fair. She rubbed a rough leaf of a potted geranium between her fingers and took the time to calm down. "So, let's stop arguing. We need to leave soon. The traffic's still bad."

"I've been looking forward to meeting your family for months." The air around them seemed to warm up a notch as Paul's arm slipped companionably around Salma's waist.

"I doubt any one of them is half as interesting as you." To avoid another argument, Salma didn't ask what he meant by 'interesting.'

"My father loves to entertain visiting dignitaries," she said, instead. He's invited Colonel Rashid to meet you. A man who'd be good for you to know for later when you start working on your article again."

"Speaking of good, it was kind of you to come get me instead of having me call an Uber. I'm sorry we clashed."

Salma looked around. They were the only people on the balcony. She wrapped her arms around him and pressed her body against his. She felt his arousal.

"Would you come up to my room?" Paul asked in a warm, creamy caramel voice. "A gentle interlude before we go?"

On the way to the lobby, they comforted each other, holding hands with tightly intertwined fingers. In front of the elevator, they stood an awkward foot apart but once its door swished shut Paul pulled Salma's head to his chest and she settled against his shoulder. She was tired. Shifting back and forth from one culture to the other for two days had been a constant strain. No matter what culture she was in, the other came with her. She was never able to live in only one. Yet, she couldn't live only in an American world. It was too shallow—all in pastels. And she'd suffocate if she lived only in an Egyptian world now dense and rigid, and frozen in time. Still, seeing both sides and belonging to neither, was lonely. And she'd just had a fight with her lover.

"It's a crazy country," was all she could say, pulling in closer to Paul. "The city goes on as though nothing important has happened. Cars honk, music blares, people crowd the streets. Who'd believe there were riots in Tahrir? That Abu Taleb was murdered? I doubt people even know how many people the police suffocated with their tear gas. Do you think it's all about riot fatigue?"

"I think millions of Cairenes are just trying to get on with their lives," Paul said. "They've adjusted. Egyptians always adjust."

"I never will," Salma objected. "It's impossible to get from one place to the other." Even the elevator, ascending in a series of disconcerting jerks, seemed stuck and took forever to reach the eleventh floor.

The table lamp was on in Paul's room and the drapes were drawn. Salma sank into a velvet covered chair and crossed her legs and Paul perched on the edge of the bed. They looked at each other in silence until Salma undressed, then helped him unbutton his shirt and unzip his pants. A familiar shiver ran through her body at the zipper's sound.

The bed sheets felt cool against her body as her finger traced his, lingering on his belly, flitting to his groin. She ran a hand along his lean muscles to where the smooth skin of his stomach ended and its thick, coarse hair began, and he turned to pull her to his chest. He parted her thighs. She arched her back to meet him. His breathing grew faster; her hand reached to bring him into her. When his muffled groans set loose stomach-fluttering waves inside, the rest of the world became an unimportant blur. A quiver, a shiver, a thrill erupted from her toes; throbbed in her groin with his every thrust. When the thrall finally released her, she lay next to her lover, quiet, yet plagued with concerns.

To her surprise, Salma was tempted to leave the country. Life was too complicated in Egypt. The highest level of terror alert hadn't prevented the Mogamma'a from being bombed nor kept Abu Taleb from being murdered, and the streets were roiling with demonstrators. If Paul dropped his *Harper's* investigation, at least for now—so she didn't have to protect her father from it—she'd gladly go back to the States. The entire country was on tenterhooks and her relatives had leaned so far back to welcome her that she'd discounted how the tension was affecting them. Her father was more angry and cross than usual—perhaps because some sheikh was sending terrorists to assassinate him; perhaps even threatening to harm Salma. To top it all, her fiancé believed he was protecting her by working with the hated Mossad. Now, telling the Hamdis she was marrying Paul would be like dropping a bomb on the family.

Salma pressed her lips against her teeth and took a gulp of air. It wasn't that simple, and she wasn't that clear. She turned on her side, put her hands between her knees and clamped her legs together. A drop of sweat, then another, slipped under her breast and over her waist to disappear into the bed sheet. She felt her mind starting to fail, like an engine turning over and over, but never kicking in, and couldn't formulate another thought.

Chapter 10

September 30, 2014
4:30 pm

THE RAYYIS WAS TAKING NO CHANCES. WITHIN TWO HOURS of the Mogamma'a bombing, his forces had occupied every square in Cairo—the city of squares. Police had blocked the roads into the Sayedna Hussein Square, but Murad had anticipated the closures and made his way through side streets to the Farag's outdoor café to keep the appointment with his mentor.

There were half a dozen older men hunched over backgammon games puffing at their water pipes. A thick layer of sheesha smoke, its tobacco infused with molasses, hung in the air. Gathered at a far table, a group of younger men puffed cheap Cleopatra cigarettes, punctuating their banter with laughter while waiters wielding gravity-defying trays angled over-head wound their way around customers, the tea glasses hanging on, somehow.

Murad pushed back his chair and stood to look around the square for his boss. Having missed talking to him at the Taj Council meeting, he hoped today Nabulsi would say he'd agree to transfer Amin—get him out of Murad's hair before they came to blows. Amin treated his sisters insufferably, but the way he was around young men whose facial hair was still downy, creeped Murad out. And his jealousy of Murad's closeness to the sheikh bordered on the pathological. Nabulsi simply had to reassign the brute.

A waiter cleared his throat to encourage Murad's attention to order the two cups of Turkish coffee, one without sugar, and a glass of sheikh Nabulsi's favorite mango juice. Stiff-backed yet restive, Murad ran his hand over the worn surface of the wood table, swung at the sheesha smoke and jiggled his knee. He heard the call to prayer ring out from the Azhar nearby. Fortunately, it wasn't Friday, the Muslim sabbath and no coarse-voiced muezzin, like the one near his uncle's house where Murad stayed in Cairo, was threatening fire and brimstone. He hated sermons like that; preferred ones that honored the Quran's poetic melody.

As he assessed the Sayedna Hussein Square once more, a commotion caught his eye. City buses, delayed by the car bombing at Tahrir Square, were discharging passengers at the Hussein mosque's southwest corner and men were rushing to the mosque for the fourth of five scheduled daily prayers. Women weren't stopping to buy vegetables for lunch and homebound office workers slipped past one another without exchanging greetings. Shop girls stared at the ground; mothers pulled frightened children to their skirts. The line circling the Imam Hussein mausoleum praying for his blessing thinned out and people stood stunned as a dozen soldiers heaved sandbags against a metal fence to barricade themselves behind coiled concertina wire.

The tension in the air matched Murad's own. The muscles in his forehead constricted, his eyebrows knit below his frown lines. He lifted his shoulders, then let them drop and laced his fingers under his chin. Yesterday, in Tahrir Square, Paul Hays had gotten away from him. Nabulsi didn't tolerate setbacks; there'd be no way to get through today's meeting with Murad left unscathed. Why was the journalist suddenly so important, anyhow? He'd never factored into the Taj Council's plans.

Murad jumped to his feet when Nabulsi rapped his ebony-handled cane on the café's table and propped it against one of three chairs surrounding just as the waiter set down the juice and coffee orders on the scraps of paper that served as both napkins and placemats. At the adjoining table, Lipton tea bags were already steeping in the glasses of sweetened tea the three Taj bodyguards had ordered. The sheikh looked shaken. His gaunt face was paler than usual, the lines above his gray beard deeper and the liver spots on his slender hands darker than usual. Pulling a string of amber prayer beads from his caftan pocket, he winced as he sat down, coughed into his armpit and reached for a glass of water.

His first ice-cold words were: "Amin succeeded. Abu Taleb is dead. You failed to capture Hays."

"Sir." Murad started to respond but Nabulsi raised his hand like a traffic cop.

"Hays is with the Mossad. You heard the recording of the phone call he made to Abu Taleb this morning. I'm sure the editor planned to give him something. If it is my disk, the one that disappeared in Yemen when Abu Taleb was there, the Taj will be destroyed." There was fear in the harsh whisper and a flash of it in Nabulsi's obsidian black eyes. Murad reached across the table for his mentor's hand but the older man dropped it to his lap.

Murad's first response was to retract his own hand and ask himself how such a dangerous disk could exist, unsecured, in the first place? Who would have betrayed the Taj in this way? But he only asked, "What's on the disk, sir?"

"This is not the time for you to ask such a question. It is obvious that I cannot trust you when I need you."

"But…" Murad started to object, again. Nabulsi ignored him.

"Hays must have seen your face. Now, he will recognize you. You have put me in danger."

"Hays will never trace you to Taj al-Islam, sir," Murad reassured him. "We will do everything—Insha'allah, we . . ." The sheikh shook his head with a note of finality.

"I ordered you to deliver the American journalist to me but you failed, Murad."

"It was bad luck, sir—only bad luck. The National Guard arrived before I could drag him out of the square." Murad clamped his right hand around his left biceps and ran his thumb along the knotted scar courtesy of the Yemeni war. "And we prevented the journalist from receiving anything from Abu Taleb, sir, although Amin should have handled things more intelligently. As it is, sir, he killed the man but didn't search his body before the police arrived." Deciding this was probably the best time to raise his concerns to Nabulsi, Murad added, "Amin is a problem. He will not listen. He does not follow instructions. I have given up trying to deal with him. I beg you to transfer him to someone who might manage him better." Murad held his breath while Nabulsi stared at the square, his prayer beads clicking as each bead landed on the one below it.

"It is not the time or place to discuss this," Nabulsi said, when he finally turned back to him. "Our man in the American embassy's garage informed us their Marines will take Hays directly from the conference to the airport after he gives his speech. That means he must be captured at the opening reception tomorrow night." He slid his coffee cup to the middle of the table.

"Sir—" Murad started to protest, but Nabulsi raised a hand, palm forward, for silence.

"No excuses." His prayer beads crunched in his other hand.

"Sir," Murad pleaded. "Cairo is under siege. There are three Army tanks and and a dozen soldiers positioned at the Shams Hotel." He pushed his knees further under the table and clenched his fingers around them to hold himself in check.

"The government has moved the reception to the *Nile Bride*," Nabulsi said. "It believes its guests will be safe on a cruise boat in the middle of a river. As I told you before, I want this journalist, this Mossad agent, alive. We must discover what he has and what he knows. As to the daughter of Hani Hamdi. Praise Allah for delivering her to me." Murad's heart lurched, starting to pound in his ears.

"What does Hani Hamdi's daughter have to do with the journalist?" he asked, a telling catch in his voice. A look of suspicion crossed the sheikh's face before it turned mask-like. Murad shifted uncomfortably under the continued scrutiny. Had Nabulsi discovered Murad and Salma's relationship? He had the feeling that something between him and his mentor had changed.

"She is with him," Nabulsi said, his dark eyes dead at the very center. The world around Murad briefly tilted to one side. The vein over his right eye bulged as it pulsed. She was with him? Salma was with Paul Hays? As if rising from deep water he heard the sheikh say, "You will instruct Amin to lead the operation."

It seemed almost impossible. Murad tensed his legs. His chair grated on the sidewalk cement as he pushed it back. He crossed his arms across his chest, uncrossed them, and set them under the table again. Salma was with Paul Hays and Nabulsi had just demoted him.

"Amin is a hothead, sir. I should be the lead." He tried to regain his footing.

"No." Nabulsi stared at him, his eyes black stones.

"Sir, I have always—"

"I wasted my money sending you to America. You should have gone to Saudi Arabia like most of the other indentured servants do. You could have returned with enough money for an apartment, married a cousin—remained the *fallah* you are—nothing but the peasant you'll always be." Nabulsi's insult was honed for maximum pain.

"I qualified for Cairo University," Murad countered, but his heart was still thudding. "I endured," he persisted. "I got a graduate scholarship to America. I know I couldn't have accepted it without your help," he added, forcing himself to sound appropriately beholden.

"Do not mistake me." The sheikh's lips barely moved. "I loved your father; may God have mercy on him. Before the army tortured him to death, I promised I would take care of your family which you know I have done for thirty years. You became like the son I never had." Murad took a sharp breath. Nabulsi had used the past tense. "But no man is indispensable." The sheikh fixed his eyes on Murad and stirred his mango juice with a misshapen spoon. "Who but Allah the All-Knowing can tell what lies in store for anyone?" He threw back his head to down the last mouthful then, slowly, deliberately, tapped the bottom of his glass against the top of Murad's. Murad fanned his fingers on the table, forcing them not to tremble. Drops of sweat collected along the black widow's peak of his hairline. *Sheikh matte.* Nabulsi had checkmated him. "You will immediately convey my order to Amin to lead tomorrow night's operation and that you will assist him." Nabulsi's voice was as dry as parchment. Signaling his guards, the sheikh grabbed his cane, rose from his chair, and limped to the curb where he submerged into the crowd like a swamp crocodile.

Murad ran his tongue over his dry lips and gulped down one of the untouched glasses of water. Shoving his hands into his armpits, he closed his eyes and tried to calm his breathing. Nabulsi had deliberately humiliated him. Called him a peasant. Assuming Nabulsi had caught wind of Murad's past relationship with Salma, did he know how he'd felt when it ended? For seven years, the pulse of his heart increased with indignation every time he thought of her turning him down. Yes, he was still enthralled to loving her, but he could feel the anger that lurked beneath his memories.

Today, his emotions were waylaying him once more. He needed to concentrate on what had happened between him and the sheikh. It couldn't only be about Salma. Had Nabulsi sensed Murad's innards churning at the Taj's increased militancy? Did he suspect the turmoil he was in? A fresh stab of fear accompanied every answer he conjured up. Many sharp knives awaited his back should he fall from Nabulsi's favor. He swirled the coffee dregs in his cup, covered it with its saucer, and flipped it over to examine the dark tracery of grounds. His aunt often read the future in coffee grounds like these, ignoring that fortunetelling was forbidden in Islam.

Ten years ago, two weeks before he was to leave for America, he sat in front of his grandfather's house tossing a smooth pebble from one hand to the other as she spread her worn playing cards on a grass mat. When it was time for him to choose a card, he drew the diamond queen, and he saw his aunt flash her gold-toothed smile at him before she spread the other cards. She foresaw a long trip. No surprise. She said he'd receive several messages by mail—also no surprise.

Suddenly, a darkening shadow crossed her face. She swept the cards into a heap. "The cards make no sense," she protested. "How could a woman have two hearts? One who will . . .? No, they mean nothing. Don't listen to me. This is nothing but a silly game." He remembered how agitated she'd been straightening the cards, wrapping them in a scrap of cloth and stuffing them into a crudely stitched bag. She should have warned him not to fall in love with Salma.

Murad was not superstitious, but walking this tightrope between Nabulsi's trust and distrust, he was willing to clutch at a straw. He wished he could feel the loyalty he'd once felt toward the man. He wished he felt safe in the Taj. If only his aunt were here to read his fortune. Actually, it was better not to know. Whatever it predicted was bound to be bad for Salma and him.

Chapter 11

September 30, 2014
6:00 pm

THE CROWD IN SAYEDNA HUSSEIN CONTINUED MILLING after Nabulsi left the Farag Cafe. Sheesha boys slipped between the café's tables twirling long-handled metal scoops full of red-hot embers with which to refresh their customers' water pipes. Meanwhile, Murad sat glued to his chair overwhelmed by the pervasive wave of shame sweeping over him. He felt an infinite sadness, a void in the sense of who he was—of who he'd been since his return from the States. For over a year, he'd wanted to leave the Taj but, to betray the sheikh, meant instant death. No one left the Taj and lived.

An angry rumble filled the square. A siren sounded. Warning shots exploded in the air. "*Allah hu Akbar.*" Voices swelled. "God is watching!" The crowd had blocked a paddy wagon so the police couldn't drag a young Azhari cleric into it. More gunfire. Egyptian Maadi assault rifles. The firecracker sounds of Yemen.

The war in Yemen that Nabulsi joined had been hopeless from the start but Murad's job had been simple: make illiterate young insurgents at least literate enough to read instructions. He'd carried a Russian Kalashnikov which he'd never had to fire although he would have if forced to. He was no pacifist. But shooting unfamiliar looking men in a distant land was different from what was happening today.

Today, the *rayyis'* police were preparing to turn guns on their own people. The *irkasous* vendor, his brass decorated goatskin bulging with iced licorice water; the girl fingering glass beads strung across a stall; the child whimpering against his mother's thigh. Murad's stomach clenched as he looked away. He, too, could have been shoved into a paddy wagon like the hapless cleric the crowd had failed to protect, but when Murad returned from Yemen, he'd continued to obey Nabulsi. Shaved off his beard. Wore T-shirts and jeans instead of caftans. Kept his distance from militant Islamists and kept a low profile teaching electronic equipment repair in his part-time position at the vocational institute. The Mukhabarat had no reason to keep track of him.

He'd lived quietly in a small apartment in Minya above the Blue Rose barbershop. There, his mother used the bedroom with the television set, and he slept in the front room, its closet crammed with cardboard boxes full of fuses, tobacco tins packed with Semtex plastique, and canisters of sulfuric acid. The place was a hovel compared to the California dormitory of his graduate student days. He regretted coming back with nothing to come back to, but Salma's rejection left him feeling he'd had no other choice.

The clamor in the Sayedna Hussein Square escalated. Police shot a barrage of tear gas canisters into the crowd. One rolled close to Murad's feet. His lungs seared. His nose and throat burned, and his eyes watered until they swelled closed. He buried his face in the crook of his arm to block the worst of the gas fumes in the air and cleared his eyes enough to find a shadowy path across the square to the Khan Khalil bazaar. If he didn't reach Amin today, he was as good as dead. Nabulsi would make sure of that.

Bazaar stalls were still open despite the chaos. Glass prayer beads from China—orange-red, turquoise blue—sparkled in the overhead lights. Further in, where guides would have been directing tourists, the stores with kitschy leather camels and brass pyramids made in China, were air-conditioned. MasterCard, Visa, American Express logos were plastered on double-glass doors. It was not until deeper into the serpentine area that the bazaar receded into the safety of a gloom Murad welcomed.

Rounding the corner of a disheveled alley, he heard footsteps faintly echoing his own. He stopped. They stopped. He turned. Saw only a young boy sprinkling water from a can to quiet the omnipresent dust. Murad scooped a handful of water to wash teargas from his eyes and studied his surroundings. For sure, there was someone shadowing him. He watched reflections in the shop windows, saw nothing suspicious, but slipped into a narrow passage and then waited. Still no tell-tale sign. Not that it mattered, Nabulsi's man—it had to be Nabulsi's man following him—would have nothing to report but that Murad had obeyed the sheikh's orders and was looking for Amin.

Soon he entered the historic residential area. The light seemed softer, older, the air sharp with the smell of varnish. A century ago, the narrow road had been lined with fashionable homes. Now they'd been reduced to storerooms although, cheek to jowl, filigreed wood *mashrabeya* balconies, still arched across the passageways, blocking the sky. Imagining his great-grandmother peeking out one of the latticed harems overhead, Murad kept to their shadows until he found himself surrounded by fragrant mounds of spices in burlap sacks. With the familiar odor of coriander and cardamom, his footsteps grew faster. He'd reached the quarter where the locals shopped.

Past the spice market was a row of tiny stalls, once the stables of a giant caravanserai, a rest stop for camel caravans. Today, there were no silk Chinese rugs or Indian gold goblets, only baskets of oranges and small cans of tomato paste. Complacent shopkeepers sipped tea and smoked cigarettes where once wealthy, vibrant Arab merchants had held court.

The air was heavy with chest-crushing humidity and Murad was thirsty. But the ancient stone drinking fountain built into the wall of the caliphate aqueduct merely taunted him. Its brass faucet was missing, its carved basin filled with empty plastic bottles and piled with candy wrappers. He walked deeper into the narrow alley, past his cousin Safwat's perfume and fragrant oils stall. Anxious to find Amin as soon as possible, he rushed past it.

At Amin's butcher shop, bare light bulbs struggled through the evening shadow to suggest welcome. "*Al salaamu aleikum*, my friend," he called to a white-aproned man listlessly swatting flies off a camel's butchered hindquarter. "May God smooth your path."

"May Allah hear your prayers," the butcher responded. His skin was like brown roasted cumin, his greying hair matted, his odor pungent.

"How's your family? Murad asked. "Where's your brother?"

"Which one?"

"Amin."

"At the slaughterhouse. Back soon. What are you doing these days?"

"Still tutoring village boys who can't keep up in school. How's business?"

"Customers buy only bones to flavor their rice. And my wife is sick." The butcher let out a long sigh. From the next stall, the grocer brought over a tray of dark tea in shot-sized glasses. "*El-hamdu lillah*." Praise be to God," he said with faithful certainty. "*Il sabr gameel*." Patience was beautiful.

Murad knew how this conversation would proceed: complaints, more pleas for heavenly assistance, then total resignation to a dismal fate. These were men who had mobilized for the Tahrir uprising but who'd been crushed when the aspirations they'd mustered brought no change, whatsoever.

Seven o'clock. Amin had to come soon. He listened with one ear while he scanned the alleyway. A boy on a bicycle, its tires strained to flatness by the load of lumber he balanced on his head, turned at the corner of the kushari stall. A girl about eight years old in a yellow ruffled dress and blue flip flops, worn down at the edges, balanced a child sucking a pacifier on her hip.

Finally, there was Amin in a blood-soaked apron and with a sheep carcass slung across his back. Only four hours ago, his hands had been covered not in animal blood but that of Abu Taleb. Murad repeated his silent vow: never would Amin's murdering hands touch Salma.

"Abu Taleb was big as a buffalo." Amin grunted, not bothering with a greeting. "It took two swipes to slaughter him. Only one for this animal."

"I have a message for you," Murad said, ignoring the crude comment. "Let's talk outside." Amin flung the freshly flayed meat on a butcher block and glowered at Murad who led him to the tiled stoop where Nabulsi's man would be sure to observe the two of them together.

"The sheikh is pleased with your work this afternoon," Murad said. "And wants you for another important assignment."

"What? When?"

"Tomorrow night." Although no one was within hearing distance, Murad lowered his voice. "The *Nile Bride* boat. You must kidnap an American and the woman who is with him."

"*Allahu Akbar.* It is my honor to do God's bidding." If Amin hadn't been a moral ignoramus, Murad would've reminded him it was Nabulsi's bidding not God's he was about to obey. "Exactly what's the plan?" Amin's question was loaded with sarcasm, bordering on impertinence. Murad had to actively resist challenging the haughtiness with which the arrogant man asked, "And what is it that you're going to do?"

"Nabulsi assigned me a different task."

"There'll be hordes of soldiers guarding the foreigners. Are you expecting me to take them on, alone? You'd better have a good plan," Amin grumbled.

"Of course, we have a plan." Amin was a moron. "Gather the ten men of our 'family' and get hold of the *Nile Bride's* head cook. He must insist on extra waiters to accommodate the conference. That way, we can get our men through security—no one knows he's one of us. Have Mustapha, the Nubian, draw a map of the upper deck. He worked on the boat a few years ago; I doubt it's changed much. And contact the guy with the wooden leg." Amin rolled his eyes, insolent even in his puzzlement. "You know him." Murad ignored the disrespect, again. "He can put together a band of musicians. That's another five men. We'll work out the details."

"When do I ...?" Amin asked.

"Take as many men as you can with you and board from the water. I'll be waiting on the street with a getaway car for you and the journalist and the woman." With that, he linked his arm through Amin's and turned back to the shop. Murad hoped his shadow—the man Nabulsi had sent to follow him—noticed how close the two men appeared.

In the butcher shop, Amin's brother was still gazing into space and whisking away huge black flies. "I'll take a kilo of meat for my cousin," Murad said. "His shop is on my way. Perhaps he'll invite me to dinner." Neither Amin nor his brother were polite enough to pretend to brush away Murad's money. Once he'd paid for a lamb shank, he folded it into a paper packet, tucked it under his arm and retraced his way to his cousin's stall.

Safwat was leaning a compromising inch from a young woman made-up in bright lipstick, two blotches of cheek-rouge, and heavy mascara. The long lavender colored dress that matched her hijab clung to every curve of her body and she didn't seem to be shopping. Women couldn't stay away from the man. Meanwhile, Murad who was here to borrow Safwat's car, needed to work around this would be assignation. Pulling his cousin away from this woman was no way to start asking for a favor and it was too risky to ask Safwat in front of her.

"*Salamat, ya* Safwat. I see you're busy," he called out, pointedly leaving the meat package on a stool outside the store as he passed it. "Your mother wants to talk to you. Call the pharmacy. Ten fifteen tonight." Safwat knew the code. In their teens, the cousins had used Haj Omar's pharmacy as a phone booth to elude their parents' vigilance. The place was like a telex center in the enormous Shubra district of Cairo. You could find out everything about anything or anyone there—deaths, scandals, glad tidings, catastrophes. Soccer scores, local news, terror attacks and arrests.

Murad squeezed in among rank-smelling laborers on the microbus trip to Shubra, long, hot, and jerky. By the time he reached Haj Omar's Pharmacy to wait for Safwat's call, circles of sweat had spread beneath his arms and across his shoulders.

Haj Omar, the blind pharmacist with a sclerotic back, was propped up in a white plastic chair engulfed in clouds of acrid exhaust, ceramic grit and industrial debris. "*Salama*t *ya* Haj," Murad said, his hand on the old man's shoulder. "It's Murad. I'm waiting for a call around ten o'clock. I came early to ask how you're doing."

"*Allah kareem.*" The haj praised God's generosity in the ragged rasp acrid as Shubra's. He coughed and put a bottle of syrup to his mouth. "Millions of lungs corroded with filth," he said, taking a swig. "Many children to feed. No money for medicine." Murad nodded, though he knew the haj couldn't see. The humble man would never mention the bottles he handed out for free.

"Come to Sidi Osman," he said, rubbing the old man's back as a son would a father. "We can still breathe there." Haj Omar would never leave this poverty-stricken neighborhood. Like many blind men of faith, he'd memorized the Quran and its melodious recitation and been teaching at a neighborhood mosque for the last forty years. He was a peaceful man, close to the Sufi mystics who brooked no violence. He was safe in his tight knit, defiantly proud Cairo dominion; safe from Mukhabarat informants infesting the community like the district's infamous rats.

"I'm stepping inside to check the clock," Murad touched the old man's knee.

The store's wall clock read the same as Murad's watch: seven minutes past ten. Tapping his fingers on the glass countertop, he willed the telephone to ring and searched the tiny store for insulin to replenish his mother's stock. He found a dozen general-purpose syringes, ten each of three kinds of antibiotics, a drawerful of aspirin, a score of light-blue notepads, a few ballpoint pens, two boxes of #2 pencils and finally, ten vials of Lente insulin.

Seven minutes until Safwat's call. Murad knew his cousin would be nerve wracked. He didn't sympathize with the Taj and was terrified of the Mukhabarat. With good reason. A year ago, the secret police had scooped him into one of their indiscriminate dragnets set up at least once a day to remind citizens who was in charge. Safwat was imprisoned for three months—rammed into an iron cage with thirty-five other young men who'd been in the wrong place at the wrong time—taking two-hour turns sitting on the concrete floor.

And yet, Safwat had been luckier than many. His sister had brought him feta cheese and flatbread to augment the prison's filthy slop. His mother sold her gold bracelets to bribe a guard, who honored it by beating Safwat with a rubber hose before letting him out. This sort of thing happened regularly to young men, Islamists or not. Safwat had a right to be terrified. But Safwat was family. He had to come through for Murad.

The phone rang.

"I thought I might miss you," Safwat said. Murad ignored the hesitation in his cousin's voice.

"I need your help," he whispered, his hand cupped around the receiver.

"I am at your service, of course." Safwat sounded cautious.

"I need you to leave your car behind the Salaam sandwich shop off the Fayoum to Cairo Road. Tomorrow at midnight." Safwat was silent. "I promise to make it up to you," Murad reassured him as though assuming his cousin's reluctance was about losing an evening's worth of fares driving an illegal taxi. "I really need it to—"

"Don't tell me why you want it. Take the car but leave me out of it. I know who you work for."

Safwat had never approved of the Taj; had often tried to convince Murad to break with Nabulsi. He'd insisted the sheikh was dangerous—even unstable. Murad didn't consider the man unstable—but he'd begun to see him as untrustworthy. There was no strategic purpose to abducting Hays, the sheikh was just having a paranoid reaction to a phone call overheard by a Taj sympathizer. As to kidnapping Salma, that was mean and devious, and not related to the Taj council's agenda. Nabulsi was draining off good men for his own purposes. He wanted his sworn enemy's daughter to get to the man. Both missions were dangerous. They conflicted with the Taj's planned coup and men would die for no reason.

A heavy weight settled in Murad's chest as he sat on the pharmacy's sole chair to consider his next move. Yes, Salma had wounded him deeply but that didn't mean he could let her fall into Nabulsi's hands. He had to protect her from Taj al Islam even though the sheikh would have him killed if he succeeded. No question about that. He leaned forward on the stool and pressed his thighs together until they twitched with pain. His heart pounded furiously, his throat tightened, and he had to swallow several times in a row.

Slowly, a plan unfolded as though on its own. If Nabulsi wanted Salma so he could blackmail Hani Hamdi, she could be Murad's ticket to safe passage out of Egypt. Rescuing her from the sheikh was a way he could leave the Taj alive. With a plan in place, he spent a sleepless night in his uncle's flat knowing Nabulsi's man was waiting outside.

Chapter 12

September 30, 2014
2:00 pm

P AUL AGREED WITH SALMA. HE'D MAINTAIN HIS role as an investigative journalist when he met her family even though he'd shelved the *Harper's* project to concentrate on unraveling Nabulsi's disk. He'd focus on deciphering its information to use as leverage against the

Taj and the Mossad to protect the woman he loved. He was surprised at the protection Salma's father had already supplied her, including the armed guards in a separate limo that followed her chauffeured car home. Traffic was manageable. Most demonstrators were either at home or in jail. The army had removed barricades, allowing streets to open by noon so Salma and he arrived at the villa at two in the afternoon, as planned.

The situation was ironic. Now that he'd shelved his investigation, Paul would be lunching with two men connected to the Egyptian president—one of them directly involved with Egypt's acquisition of military arms from the United States. But Salma had told her father about his *Harper's* article, so he'd still try to make sense of Egypt's recent arms deals. Hopefully, once Nabulsi was neutralized, he'd write the piece. What Paul really wanted was to make a good impression on the man who didn't yet know he was soon to be his father-in-law.

"Welcome to our home, Mr. Hays," Salma said, stepping ahead of him to open the front door of her family's mansion-home. Paul smiled at her correctness. The same formality she'd used when he first met her—minus the edge of hostility he'd sparked when he barged into her office.

"Thank you for inviting me, Dr. Ibrahim." Paul winked as he stepped into a darkened foyer right out of a Somerset Maugham novel. Mahogany fan blades spun overhead, the brass tips of their wooden blades throwing shards of light onto the walls. An electric version whirred before a shuttered window. The Persian carpet, worn elegant by the past, was smooth underfoot. Paul imagined a counsel of the British Crown descending the polished wood staircase, a cigar clenched between his teeth. The Hamdi mansion was as opulent as Salma's home was simple.

In the foothills of California's Santa Cruz Mountains, she lived in a log cottage. One large room served the fourfold purpose of kitchen, dining room, living room, and office and her daughters slept in tiny bedrooms on the first floor. Salma had a sleeping loft with a skylight open to a canopy of redwood trees.

"The family's in here," she announced at the door of a formal living room. "Please go in. I'm going to change for lunch." Feeling surprisingly abandoned, Paul stepped into the room and headed for the uncle whom Salma had described. Nearing eighty, an Egyptian-looking Albert Einstein with wild, white, leonine hair and bushy white eyebrow rose from a gold-leafed Louis XIV divan to greet him. Before Paul could reach him, a slightly rotund man, surrounded by a faint odor of cologne, crossed the room to take him by the elbow. A mauve colored silk hand-kerchief sprouted from its pocket, and the fringe of hair around his wide bald head was expertly dyed.

"Welcome, Mr. Hays, I'm Salma's cousin, Mokhtar. I'm pleased to meet you. I've heard many good things about your book." His middle-aged paunch curved in front of him and strained against the buttons of his expensive jacket as he steered Paul toward Salma's father, a man shorter and huskier than his older brother.

"Mr. Hays, it's a pleasure." Hani's charcoal Savile Row suit fit so well its sleeve slid along his arm without a wrinkle when he held out his hand. "May I introduce you to my friend, Colonel Rashid?" he said, his arm over Rashid's shoulder. "The two of you have much to talk about." Paul carefully considered the forty-something-year-old man with heavy-lidded, deceptively dull eyes who had nodded to Paul with a quick with-holding smile.

Suddenly, and with no warning, Salma's uncle swept Paul back towards the door. "Given you have to be at the conference in a few hours, we thought it would be more comfortable if we dined early, *en famille*. My daughter, Farida, supervised today's menu."

"I hope you'll excuse the informality," Hani added, as he opened the door to the dining room. "It's much friendlier than having the help hover around—more conducive to conversation, wouldn't you say?" Paul couldn't think of a thing to say; no one had asked him a question like this before.

The dining room felt smaller than, in fact, it was. A beveled glass hutch loomed over a large buffet, inlaid with colored wood. There was an oversized table covered with a cloth of Belgian lace. Indigo-blue dinner plates were set off by a dramatic centerpiece—a red-and-gold cloisonné bowl of white tuberoses, a color arrangement that shouted the American flag. The Hamdis probably owned table settings in the national colors of other luncheon guests. No wonder Salma wanted him to see the Egypt of cosmopolitan elegance in which she'd lived.

"Hays is not a Jewish name I recognize," Hani said, pulling out Paul's chair.

"It's derived from Hazan," Paul responded, reminded of how Abu Taleb had approached the subject. "My Sephardic great-grandfather anglicized it when he joined San Francisco's moneyed class."

"How interesting," Hani said. "Could be a variation on the Muslim name Hassan. We might be related."

"We might," Paul said, bemused at the thought of how Hani would respond when approached about marriage to his daughter.

As soon as Hani took his seat, he passed Paul a plate of wrapped grape leaves arranged in tight circles around a golden-skinned duckling stuffed with fragrant rice.

"Please help yourself," he said. Paul didn't know where to begin. There were artichoke bottoms stuffed with the pine nuts and ground meat he'd first tasted in Turkey. Matching bowls of *hummus* and *baba ghanouj*; sesame paste based dishes indigenous to the Arabs, reminded him of what was now considered Israeli cuisine. There were five silver bowls: two of yogurt flecked with green mint, two with olives, and one with *zaatar*, the medley of Seder-like spices he associated with Palestine.

Hani nudged Paul's arm and gestured to a carafe of wine, but Paul spread his fingers over his empty goblet and shook his head. Pork and alcohol were forbidden in Islam. No matter how urbane the Hamdi's seemed, he wasn't going to blow his chances with Salma's family over a glass of Egypt's Gianaclis wine.

The meal began with pleasantries. How did Paul like Cairo? Had he seen the sights?

Paul was trying to explain his familiarity with the city when Hani asked, "How did you meet my daughter, Mr. Hays?" The question didn't surprise him

"I was doing research for a news article on the effect of Islamophobia on Americans of Arab descent, and she was the perfect resource," Paul answered. To him, she was also perfect in another way. He remembered how Salma's classical Mediterranean face had struck him: her straight patrician nose, exquisitely etched lips; the look of a large-eyed, oval-faced Coptic icon—except for the stubbornness of her chin, he'd noticed even then. "She wore a black dress," he added. "Unusual for the University at Santa Cruz, where most faculty flaunt *de rigueur* blue jeans."

"She's an oppositional woman," Hani commented. "One day this will be her fall."

"Well, she was most annoyed with me," Paul said. "However, you raised a gracious daughter, sir. She served an excellent cup of tea." He recalled her graceful fingers—sans wedding ring, he'd noted—unfolding a foil-wrapped package of Harrod's Blend 42, measuring boiling water into a ceramic teapot as though she were filling a laboratory beaker. He'd looked around her office while Salma prepared the tea, stood before her bookcase—people's books hinted at their personalities and her eclectic collection intrigued him: *Three-Toed Sloths and Seven-League Boots*, Ibn Khaldun's *Muqaddimat*, *Trail-Walking on the Pacific Coast*, *Believing Women in Islam*, two copies of Naguib Mahfouz's *Children of Gebelawi*, one in Arabic and one in English, a book on the *Enneagram*, and an old, well-thumbed edition of *Carrots Love Tomatoes*, a manual on companion vegetable gardening. The range of interest the books represented made him even more determined to know this woman better, and not only for the article he was writing. "I don't know if she told you," Paul cut his recollection short. "In addition to her advocacy for Arab Americans, she volunteers with the Latino immigrant communities in Watsonville."

"She'd be more useful in her own country," Hani responded, caustically. Paul sidestepped the quicksand. He was here to ingratiate himself with Salma's father. It was a hard sell. Would offering Hani access to the disk to hold over Nabulsi soften him up? As to Salma, Hani was right. The woman Paul loved was a bundle of contradictions—well worth the effort but not easy to love. He glanced past Rashid where she sat between the colonel and her uncle. Her mouth tight, her neck rigid, with a frown tracing her brow.

Eventually, Rashid whisked his napkin from his lap, put it on the table, and turned to Paul. "Mr. Hays," he said, leaning forward, elbows planted beside his plate, fingers linked beneath his chin. "There's something I need to ask. It's about Mr. Abu Taleb, God rest his soul. The two of you knew each other?"

Paul wasn't prepared for this. He steadied his hand to reach for the silver bowl next to him, scooped out a spoonful of yoghurt to spread over his stuffed grape leaves, and deliberated his answer. He went for the truth, a guarded one perhaps, but nonetheless, the truth.

"We were good friends for more than five years," he said.

Hani laid his hand on Paul's forearm, but he couldn't tell whether the gesture was one of support or warning. "Mr. Hays," Hani said. "Salma tells me you knew the editor well."

"He must have told you something," Rashid pressed Paul who, peering past the vase of tuberoses, held the man's eyes for a second and then, not satisfied with the obstructed view, moved the bouquet aside.

"We were going to meet the afternoon he was murdered," Paul replied. "Ghastly. An atrocious act," he said in a tone of voice indicating he didn't see the point of Rashid's inquiry.

"Coincidences do not exist." Hani seemed to be controlling his anger. "Could your meeting have had something to do with his tragic death?"

"Why would someone kill him because of me?" Paul responded. This time he let his voice rise in incredulity. He should have changed the subject, but he couldn't resist a look across the table at Rashid. "Perhaps he was investigating something that might threaten powerful interests." Rashid threw a questioning glance at Hani who successfully intercepted any need for the younger man to react.

"Abu Taleb? He wouldn't have been investigating anything. He was chief editor forever and didn't write for years." Paul was getting impatient to broach the matter of military arms before lunch was over. He leaned back in his chair and turned to Hani.

"I hear the President is allowing—actually encouraging—people like Ali Walid and Ahmed Omar to buy their way back into power."

"You are right. The deals he's offering involve several billion dollars." He tightened his silk tie's knot and pushed it more snuggly to his neck. "It may look to you like guilty nobles buying papal absolution in the Middle Ages, but the court tried Ahmed Walid a second time and judged him innocent and released him from prison. The courts will exonerate Omar Ali, too." So much for the separation of powers, Paul thought. Egypt's judicial rulings were based on instructions from the Presidential Palace.

"Walid and Ali were in business partnerships with Mubarak; they're still partners with his sons," Paul kept fishing. Hani didn't respond, but Rashid dropped his fork onto his plate with such force that Mokhtar looked up from his artichokes.

"Mr. Hays," the colonel said, unfazed. "We have more important matters to worry about."

"I'm sure, sir." Paul exacerbated the colonel's annoyance by condescending with false innocence, but although clearly irritated, Rashid did not react.

"Our country is awash in illegal arms pouring in from Libya," he continued. "A huge black market we cannot control has developed since Gaddafi's fall. Nowadays, it seems everyone is armed. Taxi drivers pack handguns. Common thugs and thieves shoulder assault rifles. Islamic terrorists receive missiles and RPGs—even helicopters." Paul found himself respecting the man's self-control. "We have reliable information, several tons of ammunition, explosives, and Sarin-based toxins have been smuggled into Upper Egypt from Sudan."

"Sarin from Sudan?" Paul's eyebrows rose. "More likely from Syria. Both sides in that country claim the other side is deploying it."

"I think we know how things are here. Sudan harbors international terrorists." The edge to the man's voice was sharper now. "We are at war in Sinai. It's impossible to stop every camel in the sand, donkey in the sugar fields, boat on the river, and Cessna in the air. We need fifty helicopters."

"That's a problem, Colonel," Paul responded. "Our American Congress froze the last arms delivery to Egypt after the U.N. exposed the North Korea shipment to you. The *Jie Shun* freighter's cache of RPGs alone was worth twenty-three million dollars. Only last month, the U.N. commission reported secret arrangements between Egyptian business executives and North Korea to buy rockets for your military." Paul frowned at his plate and cut a thin strip of fat off his lamb chop while Hani took over from Rashid.

"Your Congress froze our arms shipments because of your country's pro-Israel lobby. The *Jie Shun* shipment was only an excuse," he said. "You are an important journalist, Mr. Hays. You could be helpful in this matter. You have contacts; your words have an impact. It helps that you are Jewish." The average Egyptian, deluged with anti-Semitic propaganda, believed Jews ran America, but these men were sophisticated. They knew better.

"It is not about journalism, Mr. Hays," Rashid interjected, even more annoyed than before. "We are hoping you will use your contacts. Congress must lift its freeze on the three hundred million dollars for military supplies they granted two years ago." Paul had been waiting for this opening.

"Colonel, my sources tell me the lack of transparency in contracts with your country are matters of concern to some members of Congress." Hani flashed his eyes at Rashid before pushing away from the table.

"This is a smokescreen, Mr. Hays. Spewed by the Zionists controlling your Congress. We are not the Axis of Evil. We have always been your friends. We supported you in the Gulf war, the Iraq war, and the one against Daesh. Now we need weapons to quash the Islamists before they take over our country. If they take Egypt," Hani touched his fingers to his lips, "you can kiss the Middle East goodbye."

"You're right." Paul tried to placate the man. "We do too little, too late. Or too much, too soon. Whatever we do seems to backfire, and we stand by, helpless, as American arms are turned on Americans."

"You sell arms to tribes in Syria, thinking you can buy their loyalty. A first-year anthropology student knows tribes are only loyal to their own." Rashid spoke slowly, for dramatic effect. "Someone comes along with more money—they switch, and with them go your military supplies. Egypt is not a collection of tribes. It has been a distinct country for seven thousand years." This time, Rashid slapped both his knife and fork onto his plate. "We have arms agreements with your country. Agreements you must honor. It is not for your country to question how we run our affairs."

"Respectfully, Colonel," Paul said, carefully, "before I put my reputation on the line, I need to know who controls whom and who gets what in the various transactions. It's important to know the stakeholders."

Paul looked to the far end of the table at Salma, again. The afternoon sun had moved and the thin shafts of light which streamed from the shutters haloed her hair and left her face shadowed. He knew she was tracking every beat of this conversation and hoped he was playing the role they'd agreed on well. He heard Hani clear his throat and turned back to him.

"We have said our piece, Mr. Hays. We hope you will use your good offices to influence the Israeli lobby in your Congress. Talk to congressmen. Write an article. Contact important people." Paul couldn't influence Congress, probably not even his own congresswoman, and these men were big ducks in a small puddle who could order their politicians around with a phone call. Somehow, they were missing the difference in scale between the two situations when they asked him to help.

"Let us not quibble," Hani said in a tone that telegraphed the subject was closed. "There are more than two sides to these transactions. None of them are straight. Everyone's making money, including your own defense contractors. As you say in your country, a pan cannot call a pot black."

"As I said, I might be able to help if I knew who's involved," Paul said with an emphasis on the word 'might', so he could tell himself he was almost being honest. "You're blessed with connections to important people, Dr. Hamdi. Perhaps you can put me in touch with someone who knows the players."

He paused. Hani and Rashid shifted in their seats. Paul looked Salma's father in the eye and went for it. "Not to change the subject, but I have information about a sheikh who knows you." Paul figured his timing was perfect. Hani's knife stalled mid-slice.

"What do you know about him?" Hani asked, setting the knife back on his plate and spearing a stuffed grape leaf with his fork.

"Enough to delight your Mukhabarat. Save your life, perhaps."

"My daughter tells me you have warned her of danger," Hani said. The statement was oblique. Paul wasn't sure whether its confidential tone was a sign of alliance.

"As you know, sir, the Taj considers you one of the most important men in Egypt," he said, appealing to the older man's pride. "You're a target."

"No gang of thugs will intimidate me," Hani said that loud enough for Salma to hear. Paul saw her cheeks flush in embarrassment. From out of the corner of his eye he saw Mokhtar take his time wiping his lips with his linen napkin. Hani's anger did not abate. "They're being arrested, even as we speak. Once in prison, every one of them will talk. We will protect our people. What does Amnesty International know about human rights?" He pounded his fist on the table. "They will not be here when the Islamists take over."

"Dr. Hamdi, I'm only concerned Salma may also be a target. My information comes from a reliable source. I worry if she's not near you and your protection she could be in danger. If she were my daughter, I'd keep her close to home."

"Paul! What do you think you're doing?" Salma gasped. Paul pulled back in his chair.

"Thank you for your concern, Mr. Hays," Hani said as he refilled Paul's glass from a pitcher of chilled water. "My family will consider your information after lunch." He glared at Paul as he raised his own glass to toast him. "L'Chaim."

"L'Chaim," Salma's uncle echoed, raising his glass of apricot juice and Paul raised his own glass in a halfhearted acknowledgement of the Hebrew toast to life.

The conversation was over. Paul worried but he saw no way to push further without exposing himself. Hani wouldn't tolerate the slightest interference in his family. He'd certainly do what he felt like doing, and Salma might be willing to do anything to keep in his good graces. She'd grown up in a social structure as tightly calibrated as any in a Jane Austen novel and when the strong woman Paul adored was thrown back in it, she lost her grit. Moreover, as far as ingratiating himself with her father, to be honest, he certainly hadn't found his way into Hani Hamdi's good graces.

Part II

If you want to move people, you look for a point of sensitivity, and in Egypt nothing moves people like religion.

—Naguib Mahfouz, *The Cairo Triology*
Egyptian author, Nobel Laureate, 1911-2006

Chapter 1

September 30, 2014
7:00 pm

THE SKY WAS GREY, THE AIR MUGGY. The boat to which the Egyptian authorities had moved the reception was moored between the Giza and Six October bridges where the red taillights of a steady stream of cars wavered in the humidity.

The authorities seemed serious about securing the safety of conference delegates. Paul checked it out. Police had routed traffic off the Corniche and blocked it to pedestrians. Two dozen Egyptian soldiers already manned the deck. Two dozen more were positioned on the shore. There were also the two American Marines in dress uniforms the embassy had assigned him, sitting at the table to his right while stone-faced Egyptian secret service men in dark glasses scanned the deck moving their heads back and forth like robots.

Still, something about the evening was off. The arrangement seemed haphazard. No one had factored-in yesterday's exodus of delegates and empty tables stood out like the empty spaces of missing teeth. The boat's green canvas awning had been rolled to the far side of the deck, but no one had tied it down. The only attempts at cheerfulness were strings of colored lights, trembling in the darkness, winding up the poles like festive lights festooning minarets in the month of Ramadan.

Paul did not feel festive, worried Salma would come to the reception despite his sober warning. Shifting in his uncomfortable chair, he stretched his back, and turned his head from one side to the other to release the knot in his neck. The minister tapped his arm to get his attention.

"Monsieur Hays, my colleague and I were discussing the risk of biological war." Although distracted, Paul pretended to listen as the man continued. "The threat is from outside but also from within. Thankfully, our government is in complete control," he added, dutifully. Words blowing out the same bubble in which the Hamdis and their elite compatriots lived.

He made himself sit up taller in his seat when the minister stood to introduce him to the TV cameramen. Soon, their cameras would roll, government-controlled stations would televise snippets of Paul's speech for CNN to transmit to the world as though Egypt were not on the verge of civil war. The government was using emergency rule's draconian responses to the situation while operating in flagrant denial of the conflict itself—denial seemed built into the Egyptian genetic structure. How else could over a hundred and two million Egyptians live on six million acres of land hemmed in by the desert?

The minister signaled to an obsequious old man who scurried over, his body bowed in humility. "Dr. Hani's daughter has not arrived," the minister said with an edge of irritation in his voice. "We cannot delay any longer. Tell the captain to prepare to leave." Paul looked at his watch: seven forty-five p.m. and Salma hadn't boarded. When the boat finally pulled away and the riverbank receded, he lowered his shoulders and leaned back in his chair. She'd decided not to come after all.

He looked around to reassure himself. No more than fifty delegates remained, most from Middle Eastern and African countries, all looking tense. Seated at tables set with gold-rimmed white plates on yellow tablecloths they scanned the deck, even as waiters in white caftans and red cummerbunds filled their water glasses.

Something about the five-man ensemble was off, too—the *qanoon* player messing up the simple syncopation on his zither-like instrument, the *oud* player's strumming coarse and clumsy. Paul heard ice cubes clinking and felt a strange sensation. Somehow, it seemed the narrow-faced waiter with the carafe had snuck up on him. Something about him was also off. Rather than being curved, the handle of the decorative dagger in his cummerbund was straight and looked entirely too real. Paul swung around in his chair to check in with the Marines scrutinizing the deck. There was a shift in the dark near the railing. A shadow took shape. Or were there two? Staring into the darkness, his apprehension grew.

Suddenly, a thud shocked the ship. Paul grabbed at the table edge. A second shock spun the boat around. The *Nile Bride* exploded. Its stern hung suspended for a moment then crashed into the shallow water with a series of muffled blasts. The night sky burned red, yellow, black. A wall of flames rushed across the deck. Paul cringed at the deafening sound of wooden beams crashing on to it. Windowpanes cracked and popped as they shattered. Gasoline detonated timber and melted epoxy. The fire spread. Pulled oxygen from the air. Iron shards flew through a mountain of yellowish smoke.

Paul sprang toward the stairs, coughing. A voice roared in Arabic, "Take him." Bullets whizzed past his ears. A Marine pushed off from the railing, dropped him to the deck and shielded him with his body. Another round of bullets splintered the wood near Paul's face. He heard the Marine say, "Shit" and groan before his body twitched and went still. The man's blood soaked into Paul's shirt and oozed between his fingers, viscous and cloying as he heaved the body off his and crawled under a table. An Egyptian secret service agent lay sprawled on his back, his eyelids singed, his pupils exploded. Paul lifted the tablecloth to orient himself. Around him lay dead and battered bodies covered in blood, blackened by heat. People moaned; some screamed. Through the noise of flames he heard the rattling sound of groans and sobbing.

Flames licked at small objects scattered on the deck. A Nigerian man beat the fire back with his dashi. An older woman sitting in a chair stared at a young woman who was slapping at her burning hair. Trails of smoke were still rising, and the air felt too thick to breathe. There was a whistling in Paul's nose. His nostrils filled with the smell of melting plastic and roasting human flesh. He gathered himself together to sort out what he was seeing.

The so-called musicians had traded instruments for AK-47s and controlled the deck forcing the soldiers to shoot high to miss the guests. He caught a glimpse of the thin-faced waiter with the dagger. He was barking out orders in a voice taut with pain but filled with authority. "I'll get the American. Find the damn woman, wherever she is. Throw her in the speedboat and wait for me." Paul's heart sank. The "woman" could only mean Salma. A tremor of dread throbbed through him. His blood, rushing and stinging, seemed to burn through his veins.

He lifted the tablecloth off the other side of the table; blood spreading from his left shoulder, the waiter was heading toward him, a Glock in his right hand. In a burst of adrenaline, Paul flipped the table onto its side, hoping it would at least deflect a shot. He was positioning himself behind it when the surviving Marine burst from behind another table, kicked the waiter's feet out from under him, and propelled Paul out of pistol range. Paul crawled around red-hot metal shards and burning scraps of wood, his breath bursting in and out as he grabbed a table edge to pull himself to his feet.

"Whoever he is, he wants you alive," the Marine yelled, tugging Paul toward the stairwell. "He was aiming at your knees." Machine guns were spraying the landing. Paul scrambled down the stairs to the lower deck where bullets were ricocheting off iron railings. Pulling him to a crouch, the Marine urged him forward. "Jump, sir," he shouted. "I'll cover you."

Paul hesitated—rooted to the deck. It was at least fifty feet into the murky water but there were guns at his back and flames lapped at his feet. He had no choice. He tore off his jacket and kicked off his shoes. His muscles tightening, he leaped into the smoky night as far from the ship as he could.

The water was colder than he thought it would be, but he stayed under, his sodden clothing weighing him down. Every stroke he made to fight the violence of the north flowing current required enormous effort, but he swam until he felt his thumping heart would burst, and he had to surface for air. Bullets whizzed past his head. He'd read somewhere they could only penetrate fourteen inches into the water before they shattered. He dove, again, his mind registering their sound as though through an anesthetic. He plunged deeper. Kicked harder. His ears rang when he surged up for another gulp of air; there were fewer bullets. The next time he surfaced, he was nearing the riverbank but still out of their range and the mud near the shore tugged at him like quicksand. A hand grabbed him—an Egyptian policeman. Two more policemen slid down the bank to help drag him up.

"Where's the American Marine?" Paul panted.

"God have mercy on his soul," an officer said, leading him to one of several SUVs. A muscle in Paul's injured leg erupted into spasms as he climbed into one of them. Seated in the back as it sped through dark streets cleared of all but military vehicles, he hunched his shoulders and shivered in the chill. The SUV drove the wrong way on one-way streets eerily silent except for the wail of sirens. In the headlight beams, the haunting shapes of banyan trees sprang up and disappeared. A dog with shining eyes darted across their path, startled by the violent clash of light with darkness. Slumped in the back seat in wet clothes, freezing in bursts of air-conditioning from an overhead vent, Paul obsessed over Salma. Had she been on the boat? Captured? Tortured? Shot?

Paul didn't need to ask where they were taking him. The SUV slowed down in the Garden City district where MPs ringed the floodlit American embassy complex. A row of khaki-clad, Egyptian riot police reinforced them, their assault weapons glinting with the light that was turning the trunks of palm trees black and the warm dark night a cold bright white. One after another, the cordons parted, and the guardhouse Marines waved the SUV in.

In under three minutes Paul found himself in a sparsely furnished windowless room with gray soundproof tiles on the walls and plastic light panels embedded in the ceiling that created an artificial brightness. An Egyptian staff-person brought a change of clothes—pants, short-sleeved shirt, shoes, socks, underwear—so Paul could change out of his wet ones. He checked his wallet. Almost everything in it was plastic and had survived and, fortunately, he'd upgraded his iPhone before he left the States to a waterproof one. Once dressed in dry clothes, he folded his arms on the table trying to find a position in which to rest his head. Just as he'd found one, Ernie Reichert in sweatpants and a baseball shirt erupted through the door.

"Goddamn it. You should've left when I told you to," he shouted in a voice distorted by his having been dragged from his bed. There were traces of brown bristle on his pale cheeks and along his mustache line and chin. "Two men died for you tonight." Paul swallowed a lump of guilt for the Marines who'd saved his life. Ambassador Reichert drew a chair to the table. "We've been informed the daughter of someone close to the Egyptian president has been kidnapped," Reichert continued, his foot thrumming on the cubicle's floor. "You're leaving tonight. I don't want your blood on my hands."

"I'm not leaving," Paul said in a hoarse whisper. "I know the woman. Her name is Salma. We're getting married in the spring."

Reichert's eyes opened wider. "I'm sorry. This must be very troubling for you." His tone was impassive, his words bland, insincere. "She's a dual citizen of Egypt and the United States. Both countries are committed to ensuring her safety. That's the official position. But between you and me, we consider it a matter for the Egyptians—an internal affair." There was nothing but a look of distant courtesy on the fellow's unshaven face.

"You have to do something," Paul protested. A frown formed between Reichert's black eyebrows.

"This is an official warning. You need to leave the country ASAP. The Embassy will not be answerable for your safety."

"No one's holding you answerable for me, but you are responsible for Salma."

"I'm not going to stonewall you, but if you quote me, I'll deny I ever said this: I don't intend to create an international incident over your girl-friend."

"What the hell—?" Paul blurted.

"She's not our problem; she's the Egyptian government's. Talk to her family. Her father and the Egyptian president are like this." Reichert brought two forefingers together to indicate how close. "I hope you understand," he said, leaning back in his chair, "it's not that we don't care what happens to Ms. Hamdi, but I must be honest, we have boundaries to respect and—" he slapped his hand on the table edge as he emphasized each word, "she isn't one of ours."

"Her mother's American!" Paul shouted. "Her grandparents and their grandparents before them were Americans: She could qualify for membership in the goddamn Daughters of the American Revolution."

"Your fiancée was born in Cairo to an Egyptian Muslim father. She's an Egyptian national by Egyptian law. And I don't mean to pry"—Reichert's sarcasm was clear—"but I suppose you're planning to convert? Muslim women can't marry outside the faith, you know."

"Neither can Jews."

The ambassador started for the door. "I'm afraid I have my instruc-tions. The matter is out of my control. Perhaps you should contact your congressman." He reached for the doorknob then pulled back. "I mean, your congressperson, of course." Paul wanted to strangle the man.

Chapter 2

September 30, 2014
8:30 pm

HUDDLED IN THE BLACKNESS OF A DARK CABIN on a floor sour with the smell of urine, Salma wrenched her mind out of a chloroform stupor. Her black evening dress was soaked, the duct tape plastered over her mouth was cutting into her skin, and plastic cuffs chaffed her wrists and ankles. A whirl of vertigo spun her in place, forcing her eyes closed until the walls stopped gyrating. When she opened them, she discovered her beaded purse and diamond watch were gone. Beyond the pounding of her heart and her own pulse throbbing in her ears, she could feel the rumble of a boat engine.

The Taj had kidnapped her—it could only be the Taj. Adrenaline surged through her body so fast she could taste saliva thickening in the back of her mouth. The truth hit her. She was going to die. Paul had tried to warn her. First, they were going to torture her, then they would kill her. Claws of panic scraped her lungs. Her brain was bursting. She saw Nawal's smile, Hoda's hands, Paul's eyes. What would he do when she died? What would her daughters do without her? Tears streamed down her face, over the duct tape, down her neck.

She heard ragged breathing. A man in a bulletproof vest over a blood-splotched T-shirt crouched on a narrow bench looking down at her with cockroach eyes. His other features were disproportionately large. Bold nose in a thin, pockmarked face. Wide mouth. Oversized teeth. He stretched out his legs and slowly ground his booted heels into her belly. Salma wretched and choked on her vomit. As she coughed, he aimed a long-nosed pistol at her forehead, unlatched its safety lock and squinted down its barrel. He smirked as he ran his fingers along the length of the barrel, over the pistol's trigger, and its curved handle. Then, as if savoring the thought of killing her, he stared into her face and rubbed the muzzle across her temple in a macabre caress. A small scar below his lower lip tightened.

The man was going to shoot. Salma heard herself moan. Her bladder emptied. She could already almost see her blood gushing onto the floor. Struggling to a kneeling position, she raised her bound hands over her head to cover her ears with her arms. Wondered what people thought when they knew their life was ending. She heard a loud metallic click.

"Look at me, stupid daughter of a bitch." Salma opened her eyes to the man's cruel grin. Her stomach turned to rock.

The engine stopped. Diesel fumes filled the cabin. The man thrust his pistol into his waistband, drew a long-bladed knife from the scabbard of his belt and waved it inches from her face. Salma jerked back, toppled over. Her head hit the floor. The man laughed as he dragged her to her feet, slashed off her flexi-cuffs, and threw a black cloth bundle in her face.

"Cover yourself," he shouted. Fighting off her dizziness, Salma untied what turned out to be a floor-length black *abaya*. Pulling the long, black robe over her black evening dress, she looked like a pious Muslim woman. "And this." The man threw a black veil for her face. "Now move." He forced her up four narrow steps with a gun nuzzle underscoring his command. "If you make a sound, I'll shoot."

With a pistol at her back, Salma stood, lock-kneed and pale, on the deck of what looked to be a small launch. Straining to see through the pencil-thin eye slit in the veil, she noted every detail. One of them might matter if she survived. The boat was docked on the west bank of the Nile at a spot she recognized. They'd traveled only three miles south, landing on the Giza side, across the river from her uncle's house. It couldn't be midnight, yet. Ordinary people doing ordinary things still crowded the riverbank storefronts.

"See the blue car at the curb?" her captor growled. "Walk. Don't look around. Others are also armed. Believe me, they will shoot." Salma stepped cautiously across a wood-slatted gangplank, her steps tentative, her vision restricted and amazed at how women dressed like this keep from tripping.

A policeman appeared in her limited view of the sidewalk. She lurched toward him. Her abductor kicked her feet out from under her, crashing her to the ground. The policeman didn't offer a hand to help her up. She was just another woman with a man by her side—husband or brother—protecting her honor, keeping her in line. Suddenly, she couldn't stop shaking.

With a painfully tight grip of her elbow, the armed man dragged her to the waiting car. "Get in," he hissed, climbing into the backseat beside her. The driver tipped the rearview mirror, hid his face as he pulled away from the curb.

Salma leaned against the door. It wasn't locked. Under the black veil, she was still gagged with duct tape, but her hands and legs were free. No matter how menacing the man beside her was, he wouldn't shoot her in public. Just as she'd managed to size up the situation, a convertible with three men perched on its open ledge crawled up beside them. Salma grabbed the door handle and pushed. Her captor pistol-whipped her to the floorboard before she could open the door. She landed on a tire-jack that crushed her ribs, inhaling more pain than she thought the entire world could hold. Everything dazzled before it went dark and she passed out for a second time that night.

When she came to, Salma remembered losing consciousness only a few hours earlier. She'd been standing at the top of the *Nile Bride* gangplank taking a precautionary puff from her prophylactic inhaler before handing her purse to an inspector. Something exploded—uncomfortably close. The boat rocked in place. Someone screamed, "Fire!" Then a cloth slapped over her face and the world went black.

Now, she was crumpled on the car floor, a solid lump on her temple, her left cheek throbbing. She must have cracked her ribs and she was sweaty—everywhere. Hair. Face. Armpits. The crooks of her knees. A sledgehammer was pounding, pounding, pounding in her head.

"You're an animal, Amin," she heard the driver shout. "Control yourself. The boss wants them alive." The timber of his voice surprised her. It seemed familiar. Familiar, but out of place, calling to her from a corner of the past.

"Forgive me, *ya basha*. I forgot you're the prince—the sheikh's only son," his accomplice snarled. Salma could picture his smirk. "No one ever makes you dirty your hands."

"Don't challenge me, ignorant son of a she-lion." The driver's threatening tone didn't match the voice Salma was trying to place.

"Don't tell me what to do," the man he'd called Amin said. "Stop the car. I want to ride up front." Salma felt the car pull to the right and stop; start up again after Amin slammed the door shut. She shifted her body to take the weight off her hip and screamed into the duct tape. When the pain receded a fragment of memory flickered to life. The memory solidified. The voice. The voice. She'd once loved that voice. Murad. The man she'd loved; the one Paul had called a terrorist. A terrorist with the Taj. A man who probably hated her for not marrying him.

A cell phone rang. Salma quieted her breathing to listen. "I don't know about the journalist, sir," she heard Murad say into the speaker. "I wasn't there." There was a short silence before he spoke again. "I'm sure Amin can explain." Another silence. "Yes, we have the woman. One moment, sir." He twisted in his seat to shake Salma's shoulder. She pulled away when he touched her. "She's unconscious, sir." Confused by his lie, she listened for what he'd say next. "Yes, you are right. The journalist must know something. Sir, I know it's important. But if he leaves tonight . . . " She heard the deference in his voice as it trailed off and, with silent thanks to a generic god, remained still. There was hope. They didn't have Paul. And, at least for now, the Taj wanted her alive. Why? Torture her to get to her father? Use her to trap Paul? Was that about the disk?

She tried to get her thoughts around this Murad—the Cairo Murad. Loose as the psychological profiles of people drawn to terrorism were, there was one that fit him. Early trauma: the murder of his father. A recent humiliation: her refusing to marry him. Had Murad been attracted to the Taj because of that? Guilt and anger could do that to a wounded man.

The car swerved, slamming her against the backs of the front seats. She closed her eyes, breathed evenly. One in, one out, one in, one out. Anything to avoid an asthma attack.

"We will cross the Giza Bridge," the Cairo Murad told his accomplice. "Past the Tewfik Sons supermarket, we'll pick up Dokki Street." They drove in stop and go traffic until what felt like past midnight when Murad, finally, hit the brakes. The jolt sent spears of pain through Salma's body wedged between the floorboard and the seats.

When Salma heard the ear-splitting sound of techno music blaring from too many discos, she figured they'd stopped somewhere on Gamat el Dawla Street in the upscale Mohandessin district.

"Why does *My Bride's* boutique need a twelve-foot-tall mannequin?" Murad grumbled at the floodlights lighting up the car's interior. "It's too bright here. We have to get the woman upstairs before anyone notices." Salma heard Amin open the car's front door. Before he could open its back door, Murad leaned over the passenger seat to poke Salma's shoulder. Again, she flinched. "That won't work," he said. "She's still unconscious," he lied, again. "It's your fault we can't walk her in. We'll have to carry her. Run upstairs before someone gets suspicious. Bring down a rug from the office. We'll roll her up—make it look like a late-night delivery."

"Slap her face. She'll come to. Let her climb the stairs on her own," Amin grouched.

"Her face is already bruised. The sheikh will think we roughed her up—maybe took something."

"What do you mean? I even brought her purse from the boat. She was on top of it. I'll take it up, give it to the sheikh." Amin opened the back door, once more, and reached for her evening bag. Salma didn't let herself breathe until the scuff of his feet on the sidewalk faded away.

The car took off immediately, tires screeching at every turn. Salma, slammed back and forth between the front and back seats was in too much pain to right herself. Abandoning the effort, she wrapped her arms around her chest and pushed her legs against one of the locked doors to keep from being so violently tossed around.

"We have an hour to get out of Cairo. Cooperate," Murad said, in English. Salma's heart pounded against her injured ribs. Her mouth went dry. What did he mean "cooperate?" Why would she cooperate with him? An hour ago, he'd helped truss her up in a smothering *abaya*, black like a garbage bag.

It seemed forever before the car finally slowed to a stop and Salma, clutching her ribcage, could sit up. They were in a dark alley, a dead end, at the front gate of a girls' elementary school its unpainted plastered walls with posters, their pictures ripped off, leaving jagged spaces above the print. Flyers and plastic bags swooped up and down in eddies of air. Not a soul, not a light, not a sound. A good murder location. She blinked rapidly. Her breath was coming in short bursts, and she didn't have an inhaler.

"Now get out," the driver said, opening her door. Salma rolled out but her feet refused to move. Terrified, her hands shot up to her veiled face, to block its eye slits. "Relax," he ordered, as though she could will herself to do so. "Turn around." Salma obeyed, taking in a huge breath of oxygen preparing herself for what would happen. "I'll explain later." She peeked out from between her parted fingers. What was he going to do to her? "Turn around. I'll cuff your wrists in front of you. It's less painful," he said, slashing through the plastic cuffs with a penknife. Salma's arms fell to her sides and the blood surged back to her shoulders. "Sit in the passenger seat. It'll look more natural. I'll replace the duct tape with a gag if you promise not to scream." She was surprised to see him grimace when she winced as he peeled the tape starting from her right cheek where a bruise was spreading.

Once in the passenger seat, Salma took a closer look at the man next to her. It really was Murad. There was an early sprinkle of gray at his temples and deep lines etched beneath the sharp planes of his cheeks that curved around the side of his lips. She tried to read his mood. Conflicted, perhaps, but determined. Now that her wrists were cuffed in front of her, she could reach the cloth gag which she wrestled off. She angled her body towards him to ask in a voice so hoarse it was barely audible

"Where are you taking me?" Murad was swerving through back roads, likely doubling back to the Giza Bridge. "Take me home," Salma shouted. "Take me to my father."

"Can't do that. A dangerous man is settling a score with him." Murad paused as though considering how much to divulge. "He'd hurt you—or worse. I couldn't let him do that. You have to trust me." The evenness of his voice sounded forced to Salma.

"Why should I trust you?" she asked. "You're holding me hostage."

"Better my hostage than Nabulsi's."

"So, you were on the phone with Sheikh Nabulsi. Are you with Taj al Islam?" Salma asked, suspecting she could anticipate his answer.

"I was." Murad's grip on the steering wheel tightened. "I've signed my death warrant to rescue you. To protect you." He dipped his chin and ran a hand over his hair. "Now, I need you to protect me." It wasn't at all what Salma expected him to say. What did this man, the one she now scarcely recognized, want from her? She had to get away from him.

"Take me home," she insisted. "My father will pay whatever you ask for."

"Shut up, Salma. You and your money." Murad struck the steering wheel with an open hand. "You don't know me. Don't think I still even care for you." His voice cracked. "But your daughters don't deserve to lose their mother."

Salma watched him stare through the windshield seemingly gathering his thoughts and regaining his self-control. When he spoke again, he said, half to her and half to himself, "We're going to take a *serveese* van from the Moneeb underpass."

"Where to?" Dumb question. She knew he wouldn't tell her.

Before reaching the underpass, Murad parked in the narrow side street behind the Metro Market to untie her wrists and dig into his pocket for a pair of black gloves. "Devout women wear these," he said. "Cover the plastic ties when you put them on." The gloves chaffed the sores on her abraded wrists when she pulled them on while Murad pulled a plastic bag from beneath the dashboard.

"I think these," he said, fishing out five flashy pairs of glasses with tinted lenses. And selecting a square, zebra-striped, frame. "The first thing people notice. Difficult to forget." Stuffing the other four into his vest pockets, he reached under the seat for a navy-blue baseball cap to pull low and backwards over his forehead like a badass high school kid. "Now get out," he barked at Salma. "Don't try to run."

Salma was in too much pain to even think of running—she barely managed to limp down the street, past road dust covered cars parked on the sidewalks. A young man pushed a handcart getting a jump and on the coming morning sales with late-season mangoes.. A red Pizza Plus delivery motorcycle whizzed past kicking gravel against her legs. Perhaps they'd run into an off-duty Hamdi guard. Even if they did, he wouldn't recognize her in this *abaya* and face veil, and Murad was wound so tight he could turn vindictive in a flash. A sharp sting of fear overtook her as she scanned the road.

The remnants of Ramadan celebrations—colored lights and cutout metal lanterns—had not been cleared. While the slight river breeze offered no relief, it fluttered the uneven loops of paper flags strung across the street. Salma felt as she'd felt as an eight-year-old child the Ramadan night she'd gone caroling "*haloo ya haloo*" with her friends, collecting nuts and dried fruit from the neighbors. The night she'd ended up alone and lost in the Sittena Aisha marketplace, too frightened to ask for help.

And now, she'd lost track of time although it had to be long past midnight. Smog had absorbed the urban lights and hung like a silver shroud over the city and Mars, Al Qahir, the Victorious—the namesake for Cairo—had disappeared into the polluted night air. Only a spot of sheen in the sky hinted the moon was up.

The staid residents of this end of Rhoda Island had turned in and all but one of the young couples, charged with repressed sexuality, who sought the scant privacy of the river balustrade had left. The man and woman who stayed were probably already engaged to be married but there was neither place nor permission to express the hunger their bodies felt for each other. No time to maneuver the transition from friend to lover before their wedding night. And yet, Murad had been a great friend, and—that one time—a graceful lover.

Salma's daughters had been on an afternoon bike with friends; she'd been working on her dissertation at the kitchen table and Murad was studying on the sofa under the bookcase. She'd had no conscious thought when she crossed the room to sit by him and rest her head against the sofa-back. In what must have been a fugue-like state, she waited for Murad to lay down his book. When he finally put it face-down on the coffee table he didn't look at her. When he reached over her shoulder to the bookcase, his arm brushed her breast. Neither of them moved. A not unwelcome warmth spread between Salma's thighs, her skin felt hot, pulsing, where he'd touched her. It had seemed natural to make her invitation clear when she led him to her bedroom and drew a condom from her bedside table.

Murad undressed her with understated elegance, even though he struggled with the zipper of her jeans. He shed his own clothes, quickly and they lay on the bed, she on her back, he on his side, his body perfectly contoured to hers. They took their time. He ran his hands from her shoulders to her groin, his fingers lingering to caress her breasts. When he brought his lips to hers, his breath brushed, soft, across her face. Finally, he slipped on the condom and straddled her hips. Then, to Salma's surprise, asked her permission before coming into her. There was no way she could have known making love would be the beginning of the end for them. She couldn't allow herself to wish this lingering couple a chance to do what she and Murad had done.

Now, the Cairo Murad grabbed her arm to keep her moving. Her every step felt like a new injury as they crossed the Giza bridge still bustling with people "taking the air." Vendors had set up their wooden carts and dark-green plastic chairs against the railings to serve families who couldn't afford the fancy coffee shops along the river. From here, they, too, could enjoy the lights reflected in the breeze-rippled water as they sipped sweetened tea instead of cappuccinos and nibbled on brined garbanzo beans instead of chocolate tortes. Not one of them greeted Salma with the "Welcome to Egypt" she used to elicit on her evening walks when she was dressed in pants and T-shirts. Not a single child tried out their English to ask, "What's your name?"

Salma's head spun from lack of food, but the odor of roasted peanuts drifting from a pushcart on the pavement nauseated her. She was dehydrated. Her side hurt and her sweat smelled sick. At the bridge's half-way point, she had to lean against the railing near the lupine vendor who used to chat with her. Tonight, he didn't look up from the paper he was rolling into cones for his beans. Why should he notice a woman who looked like so many others? Another black-robed member of a Muslim Klu Klux.

Would her father know she'd been abducted or think she'd died in the explosion? How many charred bodies would they have to sort through? Surely, he wouldn't wait for that before dispatching squads of soldiers and police to rescue her. And Paul? He'd been at the reception on the river boat. Her chest heaving with sobs, Salma couldn't stand to think of what might have happened to him. Pulling away, she tugged against Murad's grip.

"Don't even think of it," he threatened. "All I have to do is push you into this chair, stick a knife in your heart, and leave. Let you bleed to death. No one will wonder why you sit in quiet modesty. No one will see the blood until it puddles at your feet." He paused. His face and voice softened. "We help each other or Nabulsi will kill us both." At a distance, a sister restaurant boat to the *Nile Bride*, sparkled with colored lights as it plowed through a swath of dark water.

Chapter 3

October 1, 2014
5:00 am

A T FIVE IN THE MORNING, THE AMERICAN EMBASSY car that had brought Paul back to the Shams Hotel waited while he showered and changed, then dropped him off at the sprawling Ministry of Defense complex in the middle of downtown Cairo. Dawn was still an hour away, yet the building buzzed with activity—young men at computer stations, older ones at desks, small groups conferring in the halls. Paul's chin was covered with razor nicks, his red-lined eyes swollen and there seemed to be a paralysis rising from his legs. Only the jolts of pain, railroad spikes being driven between his wrist and shoulder, suggested he was alive.

He found Colonel Rashid at the center of an enormous room furnished with ostentatious gold-gilt furniture. Beneath the braid ribbons on his epaulets, the colonel's shoulders sagged, and his oblong face was gray.

"May I offer you a cigarette?" he asked, in the form of a greeting as he flipped open the silver box near the edge of his ornate desk. An image of Abu Taleb's cigarette case and its scan disk came to mind. He doubted Rashid knew about it. And if he did, he wouldn't summon Paul at dawn.

"Thank you, I don't smoke," he said as the colonel conducted him to a sofa under a huge portrait of the president. Paul adjusted the pillow behind his back then leaned forward and lowered his head. His eyes filled with tears. The patterns on the carpet swelled and ran together.

A buzzer on Rashid's desk went off. Before he could reach it, the office door banged open, and Salma's father barged in with Mokhtar. Hani's steps didn't match the bravura of his entrance. Crossing the red Bokhara carpet, they seemed hesitant. Although Paul's body felt heavy, water-logged, he remained standing until the older man took the armchair by the sofa. Hani seemed to take a moment to collect himself. Then he lifted his head, straightened his back, and thrust out his chin. When he spoke, his voice was deliberate and cold, but Paul noticed, above their dark circles, his eyes were moist. "Only Taj al-Islam would kidnap my daughter," he told Paul. "I will spare nothing or anyone to get her back. And our friend, Rashid, will spare no effort."

"You know my feelings for you and for Salma, sir," Rashid said, laying his hand on Hani's arm before turning to Paul. "Your government will send FBI investigators. It is a protocol for your citizens."

"I've met with Ambassador Reichert," Paul said. "He denies any responsibility for Salma. Claims the responsibility is yours, alone."

"That's impossible." Paul heard the disbelief underscoring Mokhtar's exclamation. "We are allies. The Americans must help. These subversives—these terrorists—are a danger to all of us. We need—"

"I will talk to the ambassador myself," Hani broke in. "And to our president," he added, his voice rising with his anger. Paul felt sick. No one had heeded his warning. Salma's father should have insisted she stay home with him.

"Will they ask for a ransom?" Paul asked, leaning forward with his hands on his knees. "Can they be bought?"

"No. They have more money than they can use," Rashid barked, pacing the room. "A year ago, they might have demanded we release prisoners. Now, they probably don't care." When he finally stopped pacing, he dropped into the chair behind his desk and said, "Meanwhile, it is likely you are also a target, Mr. Hays. Still in danger. The Taj has already tried to kidnap you twice. Perhaps, the next time they succeed, eh?"

"Of what use am I to them?"

Twisting side to side in his swivel chair, bringing his anger under control, Rashid stared at Paul. "Perhaps you know something the Taj does not want known. Something you may not think is important may pose a danger to them." Paul's shoulders rose to his ears. His instinct warned him not to react. "There is much at stake, Mr. Hays," Rashid continued. "Starting with the threat to Salma's life."

At that point, under different circumstances, Paul might have played the journalist card. Offer information about the disk in exchange for Hani's cooperating with him and the *Harper's* investigation. But he had no heart, no mind, no energy for that mission. Let the arms dealing scoundrels do their thing. He needed to find a hacker who could get into the disk and retrieve information to help rescue Salma before something terrible happened to her.

"How could you let someone like Nabulsi form a terrorist group right under your nose?" he asked, sounding even more upset than he was. "Why haven't you arrested him?" By the time he'd finished, Paul realized his voice shook, his face had reddened, and he was ready to body-slam Rashid. Instead, with his heartbeat throbbing in his throat, he clenched his fists and stepped back. He'd be a fool to alienate this man.

"Our army is policing the country. It is impossible to identify everybody," Rashid responded with equal restraint. "The Islamists are more secretive, more disciplined than ever and the Taj's core numbers are small." Paul understood why. The Taj didn't need a large, formal, organization. Deliberately small, it could be nimble, seize any opportunity that presented itself. Sixty percent of Egypt's population were poor, unemployed men under the age of thirty. All bored to death. And taking to the streets required no skills or training. The Taj could recruit workers for a pittance—for at most a few dollars a day.

The colonel stepped to his desk, grabbed a cigarette from its box and rummaged in his drawers for a lighter. "You need to return to your country, Mr. Hays." Rashid's casual demeanor stood in sharp contrast to his emphatic message. "Persuade your government to help rescue Salma. Apply pressure. Use newspapers, television, social media."

Neither Rashid nor the Hamdis could imagine Paul's torment. He was only Salma's colleague, after all. But he wasn't leaving Cairo without her. Period. He was going to find a way to get into the disk. Something on it was bound to help find her. Could he guess its algorithm generated password? Unlikely. He'd only erase the disk. But Ayman in the Ministry of Communications and Information Technology could. He was the best IT man in the country, if not the whole world. And he owed Paul a favor.

Meanwhile, the colonel had a point. Perhaps George Knowles in the US State Department would help. So could the *Merc* and *Washington Post*. Salma needed all the publicity Paul could muster—without Ambassador Richter's help. George Knowles, chief of the Department of State's Middle East desk was a longtime friend and Paul had his personal phone number. Despite Rashid's advice—or warning—Paul was not about to leave Cairo.

Chapter 4

October 1, 2014
8:00 am

A FTER LEAVING RASHID'S OFFICE, PAUL CRASHED for a nap and then packed the overnight bag he'd only half unpacked two days ago. The Shams Hotel was too public. Obviously compromised. How else could Nabulsi have had Paul's hotel phone tapped? Also, Hani and Rashid, who had practically commanded him to leave Egypt, had the power to enforce their order. Paul needed to move into a discreet place to organize his own search for Salma. He called his old landlord, a man he'd known for five years. Haj Tarek didn't have a vacant apartment but invited Paul to stay with him in the Zamalek district not far from the Shams hotel. He could have walked but took a cab. No need to telegraph his movements.

Although Paul had never visited, he'd seen the haj's residential building before. Like all Egyptian buildings, its exterior was deceptively drab, either to ward off the evil eye or in resignation to the hot sun's abuse. The building's *bawab*, a member of the Nubian brotherhood of Egyptian building custodians, took him up four flights of stairs where he opened the door to Haj Tarek's reassuring welcome.

The interior of his apartment was unusually modest for this upscale, Europeanized, district. Paul waited in the main room, long, narrow, and windowless, appointed in the Egyptian fashion with a lot of heavy hand-hewn wooden furniture, cotton rugs on the couches, an armoire and a full-size refrigerator at the far end of the room. The slipcovers of two wide, matching wooden-armed, chairs placed side by side, were worn. A framed photograph of white-robed pilgrims circling the Kaaba in Mecca hung on the wall and three framed passages from the Quran, in elegant Arabic calligraphy were displayed over the door to what Paul assumed was a bedroom. A copy of the Muslim Holy book stood open on a wooden pedestal. Offsetting the starkness of the spartan room were effusive plastic flowers in jarring chemical shades of red and yellow draped in swooping swags along the walls.

The muted sound of voices from behind the door stopped and Haj, a grey-haired man with a strong and well-defined chin, entered. There were deep laugh lines at the corners of his eyes although the strong cords in his neck pulled his somewhat rectangular face downward. The callus in the middle of the man's forehead was proud proof of prostrating in prayer for years. This was a pious household.

"*Ahlan wa sahlan*, Hays, *bey*. You light our home."

"It is lit by your light, ya Haj," Paul responded. "It is kind of you to offer this hospitality. I hope I will only inconvenience you for a few days."

"May you be my guest for many years. You are always welcome, here." With pleasantries dispensed with, the haj showed Paul to a bedroom that must once have been his son's. A bed with a cotton coverlet, a chair, a table, and a wardrobe adequate for a short stay away from the prying eyes of Hani, Rashid and Nabulsi's men. Paul set his bag on the table and sat on its accompanying chair to call the head of the U.S. Department of State's Middle East Section. If anyone could connect him to a member of the congress or senate who could pressure the FBI to join the search for Salma, it would be Harry.

"Knowles," his friend answered his personal cell phone.

"It's Paul Hays, Harry." Paul remembered the man's well-appointed room, furnished with good taste and the help of a wealthy wife. A series of David Roberts's original pen-and-ink lithographs of temples in Luxor and *feluccas* on the Nile balanced the window-view of the Potomac.

"Good to hear from you," Harry said. "I heard about the incident in Cairo. Too close for comfort. Thank God, you're safe." When Paul first met Knowles, he'd found his certain rightness of demeanor a little disconcerting, but he'd gotten used to it. Still, the less Harry knew of why Paul was in danger, the better.

"It's personal, Harry," Paul said, cutting to the chase. "The 'incident,' as you call it—the kidnapped woman—is my fiancée."

"I'm terribly sorry. I can't imagine how you must feel. She's American, isn't she?"

"She's a dual citizen," Paul replied. "Her family in Egypt doesn't know about our relationship."

"Let's hope the Islamists don't find out. A woman marrying outside the faith is a no-no. Some think it apostasy in Islam." Harry knew the culture of the Middle East. "What can I do to help?"

"As you know, when an American citizen is kidnapped the State Department is supposed to get involved and bring the FBI with it. But Ernie Reichert, your ambassador to Cairo, refuses to raise a finger." Paul massaged the bridge of his nose between his thumb and forefinger.

"Don't call him my ambassador, for God's sake. Reichert is one of his." Paul could almost see Harry single out his desk phone as he referred to the president. Every beltway insider knew Harry was the last Arabist at State, and every journalist knew "getting rid of Harry" was one of many payments the president was making on his campaign debt to the American Israeli Public Affairs Committee. A powerful group of pro-Israel political action committees referred to simply as "The Lobby" to whose machination no politician, no matter how small or hawkish, was immune.

"I'm sorry, Paul. There's nothing I can do. I'm afraid both your girl-friend and I are *personae nongratae*. They've asked me to retire early." He paused before he added, "As in next month." Paul sensed Harry backing away from the cliff edge of his bitterness and felt for his friend.

"Can you tell me who to contact?" he asked.

"There's no point going to your California representatives. You'll get the runaround. Not one of them will touch this with a ten-foot pole;

they're all in bed with the Lobby. Why should they risk their political careers over an Arab American who probably supports the Palestinians? That's really why Reichert wouldn't help."

"There must be someone who can at least get me to someone who can do something," Paul insisted.

"Doubtless, you know more people than I, but let's see what I can dig up."

Paul heard Knowles flip through the well-thumbed set of Rolodex cards he still used. "Ah, here's someone who might do. Lindsey, Congressman, Democrat, Wyoming. Unless it's smelling blood, AIPAC ignores smaller states like his. Give me ten minutes. It might help if I call him before you do."

Paul's phone call to the Wyoming congressman was answered immediately. "Mr. Hays? My name is Craig Ludlow, the Congressman's aide." He sounded like every other congressional aide with carefully coiffed hair and an orthodontically enhanced smile. Paul already felt vaguely irritated by this man.

"I don't think we've met, Craig."

"I'm sort of a floater for senators. I liaise with the National Security Council." Paul hated the word liaise. A French noun turned into an English verb that wasn't even grammatical. "Right now, I'm liaising with the senator," Ludlow continued. "And with Bill Sokol in the NSC. He's already briefed me on the matter. In turn, I will be briefing Congressman Lindsey after this call." Paul felt warned. Sokol was deeply involved with the Lobby. There was blood in the water. AIPAC was circling. Someone had already gotten to the honorable representative of the small state of Wyoming.

And every moment in the talons of the Taj put Salma in greater peril. She had to be terrified of Nabulsi. Would he negotiate with Hani without torturing her? A headache suddenly pulsed red and white behind Paul's right eye socket. He couldn't dwell on the images in his head. He had to do something, anything, before he exploded. If anything happened to her . . . He had to find her. He had to hope. First and foremost, he had to keep as calm as he could make himself be. He pressed his palm hard over his eye, but the blur and the pain remained.

Clenching his jaw against it, he unpacked his bag on the bedroom's twin bed, found the bathroom off the corridor, and planned his next steps as he shaved. It was only mid-afternoon. First, he'd go to Gabber, an "everyman" source from the lower class he'd cultivated for years, he might know someone connected to the Taj. Besides, the safe in his repair shop was a perfect place for Abu Taleb's disk. Paul headed out feeling better for having a plan.

The haj and his wife were waiting for him in the living room's reception area at the end of the short corridor. The wife, an overweight woman in a navy-blue housedress looked older than her husband who referred to her only as the *Hajja*, meaning she'd made the pilgrimage to Mecca, too. Her round face was lined with creases and dark with age spots, but her high cheekbones suggested an attractive face in her youth. Time takes a toll on Egyptian women. The *hajja* was old enough not to sequester herself from men, yet when she brought Paul a glass of *karkaday*, dark-red hibiscus tea, she averted her eyes, looked at the floor and didn't speak.

"Could you tell me where I'm likely to find a taxi near here?" Paul asked as he sipped the bitter-sweet hibiscus drink. "I need to meet a friend downtown."

"Not downtown, y*a bey*," the Haj reproached him. "It is Friday. Every Friday there are demonstrations after noon-time prayers. You must stay far from Tahrir."

"I'm a journalist, you know. I've been in demonstrations—even riots—before. I was at the last demonstration in Tahrir."

"I cannot let you be harmed, sir. Imagine what your country would do to us if, God forbid, anything happened to you."

"Don't worry. I won't be in the square itself, and I will be cautious."

It was a short cab ride to Gabber's place off Bab el-Louk Street, one of seven streets branching off Tahrir Square that was, indeed, packed with demonstrators. Townspeople had poured out of their apartments. Young people, old people, men, and women with children riding on their shoulders chanted, "*Salmiya. Salmiya.*" Peacefully. Peacefully. Some swore to protect their "savior," the president with their lives. While there seemed to be a healthy resistance to the Brotherhood—odd bedfellows to the secular liberals opposing military rule—there were plenty of its yellow placards stamped with four black fingers in view. United in the chant that mobilized the January 2011 uprising *"El sha'ab youreed esqat el nezam,"* they called for the government to fall. Wolves and sheep roaming the streets together, impossible to separate.

Some were attempting to do so anyway. Where the Corniche met the square, a security cordon of young men and women with white armbands stood shoulder to shoulder. A young man in a red, Ahly soccer team T-shirt, asked Paul for some form of identity. Paul flashed his press card. The man smiled and said in perfect English, "You're American. I hope you will tell your readers what you see today."

"May I pat you down, sir?" his dark-skinned comrade asked. "No offense, I assure you. Today, we'll keep both the Brotherhood and the thugs from taking over the square."

Once through the impromptu cordon, Paul stopped to take his bearings. A young man gave him a high five. A tabla player nodded without skipping a drumbeat and a shopkeeper, handing out bottled water, handed one to Paul. Meanwhile a woman pressed a plastic bag full of kushari into his hand and another ran alongside the demonstrators, passing cheese sandwiches to everyone within reach, including him.

"*Allah hu akbar,*" the call to prayer rang out from the main platform in the square. The chants, the drumming, the noise of feet scraping on cement and the din of voices swiftly evaporated. Men and women formed separate lines, crossed their arms at the waist, to start their noontime prayers. Toward the edge of the square, backing up to the Hardee's fast-food store, fifty men knelt on the Egyptian flag as though it were a prayer rug. They stood, knelt, and prostrated themselves as one while a hundred men, Orthodox Christian crosses around their necks, linked arms to form a protective human chain around them. Surprised, Paul once again reflected that the longer one was in Egypt, the less one knew and, that despite what he'd told Salma, he was no exception. Still, he didn't want to be in the square if the Islamists usurped this demonstration as they had the last one. Besides, he wasn't safe from Nabulsi or Hani, out here in plain sight.

He pushed through the crowd to Mohamed Mahmoud Street, cut across it to Bab el-Louk Street, entered a convoluted warren of ever-narrowing roads. All empty. Everything closed. Instead of twenty vendors on the sidewalk, there were only three, their keychains, rings and baubles were spread out on canvas squares. No repairmen in grimy workshops fixing motorbikes and scooters, carpenters chiseling wood for furniture, or metal workers smelting iron in red-hot furnaces. Paul figured people were either in Tahrir or avoiding it. It was Friday, the Muslim Sabbath. What if Gabber wasn't working today?

Paul had exhausted his other contacts, journalists, labor union activists, a cleric in the Azhar. Most never heard of the Taj and those that did had no idea how to reach any of its members. Ayman, his hacker genius, hadn't been able to get into the disk. Paul desperately needed a lead. Some way to reach sheikh Nabulsi. Gabber might be his last hope of saving Salma.

He skirted two grumbling *Butagaz* deliverymen unloading sky-blue cylinders from a beat-up pickup truck. He mulled over his limited options as he walked right through one of the hundreds of thousands of *ad hoc* cafés that pop up like weeds on Cairo sidewalks. Scarcely noticing the six old men smoking sheeshas and playing dominoes, his mind elsewhere when he reached Gabber's shop. A low-ceilinged hole-in-the wall squeezed in between a cobbler and a tinsmith's shop.

It was as dusty and dark as ever, with just enough light for Paul to see the man. A rural transplant worn down and looking older than his forty years, he sat on a low stool fenced-in by a tangle of cords in front of a television set. Gabber rose stiffly to his feet when Paul cleared his throat to make his presence known. Raising his right hand to his forehead, he lowered it to his heart in greeting.

"I thought—I hoped—to find you if I came early," Paul said, as the men shook hands and clapped each other's shoulders.

"I'm not usually here on Fridays but I have a rush-job for an important customer. Please forgive me. I must keep working." Gabber kicked some of the electric cords out of his way, refolded his lanky frame, and squatted back down on his wooden stool. No matter how pressured Paul felt to get to the point of his visit he went through the traditional formality of asking after Gabber's young family.

"Praise God, my family is well, sir. I am blessed with another child. Now I have five." Gabber switched his screwdriver to his left hand and kissed first the top of his right hand, then its palm, in gratitude. "God will provide. Thanks to your kindness—the money you gave me before you left—I was able to move out of my parents' apartment. I could even make a rent down payment on a small one in Imbaba for my family. Then, my mother, God have mercy on her soul, became ill. Cancer. May evil pass you by, sir. My brother and I spent all we had for her treatment before she died. Now, he and his wife and their four children live with us. We are in a two-bedroom apartment in Bulaq al Dukrur. All the children are happy together, but my wife doesn't get along with my sister-in-law."

"It's hard for two mothers to share a crowded space," Paul sympathized, then waited out a long silence before he said, "I have married."

"*Alph Mabruk*," Gabber pronounced a sort of *mazel tov* thousand blessings.

"But my wife has been kidnapped," Paul said. "It is a terrible thing. I need your help to find her."

"Sir?" Gabber asked, bewildered. "You know many important people, sir. Your embassy, sir?"

"She's Egyptian."

"The police?"

"They are searching, but I need your help. Do you know of Taj al-Islam, my friend?"

"I do not know them, Mr. Hays. Is the television I sold you still working well?" Gabber buried his head into the one in front of him.

"Don't change the subject. I need you to help me," Paul insisted. "What do you know about the Taj?"

Gabber leaned further into the chassis of his TV set, then flung the screwdriver on the bench and arched his back. "I trust you like my brother, Hays bey, but I do not speak of these things. I do not like killing."

"Is the Taj killing people?"

"Right now, many are desperate," Gabber said, side-stepping Paul's question. "The new Rayyis has betrayed us. It is a disaster." He stood up, painfully. "I cannot feed my children. They go to school for only three hours a day. Often, they don't go at all, which doesn't matter because their teachers do nothing. They only teach after school and I cannot pay for their private lessons, so they fail my children. It is blackmail. People are disgusted." Gabber's skinny body and drawn face undermined his attempt to sound forceful when he added, "But they are less afraid. They are out in the streets, once more."

"Hasn't the president prohibited antigovernment demonstrations?"

"Yes, but life for those like us is unbearable. Only our trust in Allah saves us from despair. We have no power. He gives us strength. Allah is the source of all strength. He will support us in this life and vindicate us in the next. But while we are on this earth, the government must do its part." Gabber started talking even more with his hands than his mouth and his neck turned an angry red. "We need money to feed our children; honest teachers to teach them, and protection, not brutality from the police."

"Yes." Paul acknowledged the complaint. "The president's harsh ways have shocked the world."

"It is not only poor people who are angry, Hays, bey. Would you believe this? Students and laborers, even professionals, marched with poor people like me. Not only in Cairo—also in the streets of cities like Tanta and Zagazig."

"What about the terrorists? What about the Taj?" Paul pressed Gabber who stood up to drag over an oscilloscope.

"The army has arrested thousands of men who are not terrorists, ya bey." He attached the oscilloscope probes to an electrical board. "You are American. America is a friend of the Egyptian president. It is not a friend of the Egyptian people." Paul groaned, inwardly. So much for McDonald's. So much for the internet and satellite TV. None of those soft power tools had fooled the average citizen.

"You know I do not agree with my country." The words sounded trite and irrelevant even to himself.

"Do not make temptation for Taj al-Islam. They will not ask what you believe, sir, before they chop off your head. God forbid Egypt should become like Syria and Iraq."

Paul kicked a knot of wire near his foot to tower over Gabber who'd returned to his stool. "They've kidnapped my wife. They will chop off her head." He took a deep breath and swallowed down his panic. "Help me find someone who knows what's happened to her. I need a thread. I need something. Anything." Gabber squirmed on his bench.

"I can do nothing, sir. I am father to my children and those of the Taj are dangerous."

"I am not asking you to put yourself in danger. I just want you to think of a friend, a neighbor, a customer who could deliver a message to the Taj. Tell their sheik I have something valuable to offer if he returns my wife." Paul took a firmer stance. "God willing, I'll be back tomorrow. If by then you have arranged a meeting, I will arrange another apartment for you."

Chapter 5

October 1, 2014
12:45 am

MURAD LED SALMA TO THE SMALL SQUARE UNDER THE Giza bridge's Moneeb overpass. It was hectic. Although well past midnight, families were herding children, wide-eyed with sleepiness, into serveese minivans. Mothers hurried the smaller ones while fathers threatened to leave without them. Customers thronged before neon-lit stands offering frothy glasses of sugar cane juice. All the while, drivers hawked their services, leading passengers to vehicles and collecting fares. Salma was perplexed. Less than half an hour ago, the man who'd once loved her had threatened to leave her to bleed-out on a green plastic chair. Now he was holding her up as she limped to a Fayoum oasis minivan. How could she trust him? Despite anything he might say, she was his hostage.

The van jerked; Salma fell forward onto a man sitting on the floor with his legs jack-knifed against the driver's seat. The van stopped, hiccupped, jerked again and finally got going. In twenty minutes, the car-clogged streets of the city released it onto the highway past the fork in the road to Alexandria where it veered west, setting off on a two-hour trip to the lush oasis of Fayoum, forty miles southwest of Cairo. They hurtled through darkness lit only by the blazing headlights of a seemingly endless line of transport trucks. The pot-holed road was oil splotched, and shops and houses were coated in greasy deposits of exhaust fumes. In the van, passengers were thrown against each other every time it hit a bump and although there was a no-smoking sign, several men smoked.

Salma stared out the window. The sensuous curves of sand dunes that once softened the view were gone. Overtaken by air-conditioned homes in gated communities so the rich could live where they no longer had to rub elbows with the poor. The crowded van drove through farmland where half-finished, red-brick buildings were invading alfalfa fields like medieval siege towers. She couldn't tell if the three and four-story illegal structures were going up or coming down. They all seemed on the brink of crumbling. Urban construction on fertile land had turned the country, once the world's breadbasket, to a net food importer.

Swinging on the edge of consciousness, she crossed her arms against her chest, braced her ribcage and propped her head against the rattling window frame. What if her ribs were broken? A bad jolt could puncture her lungs. She scrunched her eyes closed, pleading with the heavens: don't let me die in this van among these strangers. She was baffled when Murad drew her to him, lightly, as though he'd guessed what she'd been thinking. Hours of unrelenting pain had exhausted her. She was too tired to wonder if Murad was trying to comfort her before she fell into a fitful half-sleep and either dreamed or remembered the afternoon when she said she wouldn't marry him.

That time, her daughters were outside, bouncing a ball off the garage door, laughing, and shrieking as only preteens could. The odor of roast lamb permeated the kitchen; an autumn sun speckled the blue countertop. The short conversation she'd had with him ended with her saying: "I love you, Murad. I'd like to be your lover—for a long time. You're kind; you're gentle. But I'm not ready to marry anyone, again." The words had sounded rehearsed because they had been.

Salma would always remember the exact moment—the exact pattern of the scatter diagram she'd been studying when Murad came to tell her he was leaving. She'd been concentrating on the figures, tapping the table with the end of her pencil when she felt his hands on the back of her chair. It took a moment before she turned her head to him. Her heart sank. The pained grimace of his lips distorted his face whose ruddy colors had faded to a dull gray.

They'd stood side-by-side at the glass door to her cottage-garden, her body feeling only tenuously held together as they stared at clumps of hot-red dahlias he'd helped her plant the year before. Salma thought she saw his chin tremble a little when he said, "I'm leaving for London, tomorrow." A thin smile hid whatever explanation he was keeping from her.

"Because I don't want to get married?" Salma protested, hanging on to the doorframe to steady herself. "You're punishing us—hurting me—for making love you think is forbidden. You can only forgive yourself if we get married immediately." When Salma's hotheadedness took over, she couldn't keep herself from adding, "As though God grants convoluted, retroactive, absolution. Or did you want a Saudi-style 'pleasure marriage' to get around the rules?"

She'd stomped up the stairs to her bedroom expecting him to follow. He hadn't. If he had, would their love have been strong enough to overcome their religious disagreements? Their class differences? His resentment of her having been born into Egypt's upper-class. And when she'd said she didn't want to marry anyone, had she really meant she didn't want to marry him? Ever? Then, how was it that for five years, until Paul came into her life, she'd yearned for the California Murad?

Tonight, in the Fayoum serveese, with both pretending Salma wasn't resting against his body, she hoped he still felt something for her. Would he release her if she could regain his trust and . . .? The question trailed-off. The next thing she knew, he was patting her knee as though to wake her up.

"We're almost there," he said in Arabic. Salma figured he'd switched out of English to avoid raising anyone's suspicion. When she first looked out the window, she thought they were still leaving Cairo. In fact, in the breaking dawn, they were approaching the fertile oasis of Fayoum with its own red brick buildings of urban sprawl.

The bus stopped at a tilted kiosk missing most of its wooden planks. Salma prepared for an agonizing descent from the van, breathing so shallowly it was hard to move. She braced her hands against Murad's back but tripped on the *abaya* and fell against him.

"You'll be okay," he whispered through her veil. "I know you're exhausted. We'll stay at my friend Rami's house until daylight. Nabulsi doesn't know about him. No one in the Taj still has Christian friends."

"I need a doctor," Salma complained.

"My sister is a doctor. But we need to go to Rami before I take you to her," he said as he propelled her around the kiosk to where goats gorged themselves on heaps of turnip leaves and hens scrubbed through composting cabbage leaves covered with straw and pointed to a dilapidated Toyota. "We'll take this," he said, pocketing the key under the floor mat. "I'm trusting you. But I have eyes all over town," he warned. "We're in this together so don't try anything dumb."

"As though I could try anything—dumb or not," Salma muttered. "Your partner broke my ribs."

Driving over the rutted country road in a car without shock absorbers was only a shade more merciful than if they'd trudged on foot. By the time they knocked at Rami's gypsum brick house, Salma felt a burning in her chest covered with a sweat that smelled of sauerkraut.

A full-nosed, full-lipped beauty, her skin the deep brown of cocoa, opened the door. The young woman stood speechless for a moment, her nightgown covered with flour, her hands coated in dough.

"*Bism illah! Bism illah!*" In the name of God, you surprised me. "Rami's still asleep and I must take the bread to the public oven before the lines get too long."

"Maryam, I know I should have called. But this lady is sick. I had to bring her here."

"You are like our brother. Our house is your house and your guest ours," she said, wiping off her hands with the towel on her shoulder to point Salma toward an armchair. "Welcome, welcome, lady." Salma's legs were shaky, her nerves raw. Nauseated by exhaustion, she lowered herself into the chair too tired for anything to feel real.

An early ray of morning sunlight beamed from the room's only window, set close to the ceiling for privacy. A painted frieze, an arabesque motif of intersecting semicircles and diamond shapes, ran across the top of the wall. Murad put a comforting hand on her shoulder.

"Fadel's pharmacy is open twenty-four hours a day. I'll get penicillin."

"I'm allergic to penicillin. I developed asthma last year. Could you get inhalers? They're two kinds. One to ward off attacks, another to get through them."

"Tell Rami I'll be right back," Murad called out to Maryam before she disappeared behind flowered curtains separating the living from the sleeping area. Salma had just propped her head against the chair back and closed her eyes when Rami arrived, still in his nightshirt, his face puffy with sleep. Like Murad, Rami was in his late thirties, but although taller by at least six inches, ten pounds thinner. His skin was darker, too, his nose longer and his curly hair was brown, not the straight, raven-black of Murad's.

"A thousand blessings to your morning, Madam," he said with an almost imperceptible lisp of rolled 'Rs'. "I heard Murad leave."

"And I wish you a morning of jasmines," Salma replied with a favorite rejoinder. "Murad is bringing me antibiotics, but. . ." She couldn't stop the quaver when she tested Rami out. "He brought me here by force." Giving voice to reality made her eyes well up but didn't move her host. Rami blinked and took an astonished step back.

"You are not well, madam. I have known Murad since we were children. My wife said he brought you here because you are ill." Rami was humoring her because he thought she was delirious. As though to take her mind off her feverish delusions, he tried to entertain her with childhood memories. "Back in Sidi Osman, when each day was like the day before it, and like the one that would follow it, Murad and I spent every minute in little boats we hammered together. Four short planks of wood nailed to each other, one for each side, one for the back, and one for the bottom. Have you seen any?" Salma shook her head. In fact, she had seen boys selling shawls from tiny skiffs like those surrounding the cruise-boat she was on, but she was past responding. Her insides were tearing apart, her brain bursting out her ears, and Rami was prattling on about boats. "You kneel in the bottom and row with your arms. Your body is the ballast." He was enjoying his own tale. "My older brother painted huge eyes on the bows and told us this would let him keep track of what we did behind his back." Rami chuckled. "We chased ducks in the river and herons on the shore. Most of the time we did nothing. We lay with our boats side by side, our feet splashing in the shallows, waiting for the dates to turn red." Rami was still on his storytelling roll when Murad returned, his face looking tense enough to crack.

"*Al salamu aleikum*, Rami."

"*Aleikum al salaam*. You look like a nightmare." Christians also used the common Muslim greeting; peace be upon you. "What's the matter?" Murad handed Salma a box of Augmentin and one of Panadol without answering his friend.

"Fadel's concerned about pneumonia," he said while she checked the ingredients. Amoxicillin and clavulanate potassium sounded right. So did acetaminophen. "Fadel had only epinephrine inhalers," Murad continued, showing her the once familiar pale-blue boxes of inhalers, no longer sold in the States. "I bought all three of them. You don't have a pocket, so I'll keep them in mine." He turned to Rami. "We'll leave after the lady rests. She has eaten nothing."

A sudden surge of warmth rose in Salma's chest. A voice inside her whispered, "Beware the Stockholm syndrome." A louder one countered, "This is the man you could have loved." Guilty at even thinking of this, her mind turned to Paul. He had to be safe. He had to be looking for her. Why hadn't anyone rescued her, yet?

"What a terrible host I've been," Rami said, jumping to his feet. "Talking of our childhood, forgetting the tea. Forgive me. I'm still half asleep." He called his wife. "Maryam, take the bread to the oven later and bring tea and breakfast for our guests." He plunked back down to the floor, his nightshirt up to his kneecaps that protruded from his scrawny legs and propped his elbow on the wooden pallet covered with rounds of rising dough. "Now tell me what happened, Murad."

"What did you talk about while I was out?" Murad, muscular and taut, stood over his skinny friend.

"I didn't get to tell her about the fish we used to catch," Rami said, including Salma with a glance in her direction. "That was then. Things are very different now. Pesticides from the fields are poisoning the fish." Salma heard Rami's voice turn bitter. "And your people want to poison Copts like me."

Murad's face flushed; his cheeks puffed out. "Yes, things are different. I remember when we were not yet seven years old you ran up to my father, peace be upon him, with snot running into your mouth. 'The boys—the boys from Kafr el Nakhil, threw stones at me,' you wailed. 'The big boys, too. They were clapping their hands in a circle and chanting like women in the *zar*. Then they screamed *qubti, qubti*, shave your head. Copt, copt, go to bed.'"

"I remember what your father said when you asked what the words meant," Rami said, thoughtfully. 'The words mean nothing, but the lips are cruel.' I remember he pressed his own lips together so hard, I thought he'd swallowed them."

"I'll always remember that day," Rami said but Murad had more to say.

"Later, he told me you were right to be afraid," he continued. "He told me, we're all people of the Book and this must never happen again."

"This is the best part," Rami said to Salma, his voice softer now. "On the evening of the next day, the people of both villages gathered in Kafr el Nakhil's square. I'll never forget how the fathers of those boys made them go around in a circle seven times and each one of them caned his son when he passed in front of him." Salma couldn't imagine something like that happening in her world. She was trying to form the image when Rami said, soberly, "Now, there's trouble for Christians even here in Fayoum. Last week, a young Copt was accused of molesting a Muslim woman. The matter hadn't even been investigated before a crowd murdered him and burned down one of our churches. Religion has made people like you and your friends crazy," he said to Murad. His voice sounded like he was drowning in a sea of sadness.

"You know me better than that." Murad began to pace the room. "I'm crazed by fury not religion." His voice grew louder. "This president overthrew an elected president and released Mubarak and his friends from jail. Now the military is stealing the country from under our feet. They think it's their private estate. That you and I are serfs they keep alive to serve them." His voice filled the room. "Ever since college, I've been crazy with anger at the police. Can you blame me?" Salma knew that students had rioted to demand a real education—something better than classes of four thousand students and instructors who sold lecture tapes for profit to those who couldn't grab one of the auditorium's three hundred seats.

"At least you did something," Rami said.

"Speaking out earned me six months in Tora prison in an iron cage. Hung by my wrists against the wall; flogged with a cat-o-nine tails." Murad's voice shook. "I still have the scars."

"You're not the first one, nor will you be the last one to be brutalized," Rami said, his anger suppressed. "Not every Muslim who's tortured becomes an extremist like you."

"My people were not extremists when I joined them. They opened clinics where people like my sister still treat the poor. They fed the street children no one else cared about. Taught poor women how to tend to their kids and taught their kids how to read. Your churches do this. No one calls them extremists."

"That's because we don't want to topple the government like you do."

"It's the *rayyis* who's radicalized my people."

"That's not you, Murad. You don't hate people like me."

"And that's the trouble, isn't it? You think the government protects you from the Muslims, but it's driving a wedge between us. Burning churches and blaming it on extremists. They call it counterterrorism. It's the way they stay in power. You know it's evil. What are you doing about it?"

"Nothing. Slinking along the walls, keeping my head down, growing organic oranges for the Belgium market. But don't hide things from me, Murad. I'm sure your trouble is because of your sheikh. There's something wrong with that man." Murad stopped pacing to drop down next to his friend.

"The sheikh is just a man. Good? Bad? I don't know anymore," he said, angry and defensive in his confusion.

"Still, I'm sure your trouble is due to him."

"Yes, Nabulsi is going to have me killed," Murad interrupted, getting to his feet. "I don't have a choice. Last night, the sheikh seized this woman who was so kind to me in America." Murad pointed towards Salma. "He planned to torture her."

"Why did he want to do that?" Rami asked, raising baffled eyebrows as he stood up.

"Because she is Hani Hamdi's daughter." Murad gave his friend a somber look. "I can't let him torture her. She is innocent."

"Hani Hamdi?" Rami's mouth froze open, his shoulders came together as though to help him disappear. "The military doctor? God help us." Salma sat up in her chair. This wasn't groveling. This was utter fear.

"We have to hide, but as soon as he figures out that I'm involved, he will have me killed—assuming Nabulsi doesn't do so first." Murad's eyes pleaded with his friend to understand.

"How did you end up in such danger? You couldn't have made things any worse for yourself if you'd tried to."

"I'm sorry to drag you into my troubles," Murad apologized.

"Then don't."

"You're like my brother, Rami. You're stuck with me. There was nowhere else to hide until my mother arrived." Salma turned her head towards him. The room swam.

"Your mother?" she asked.

"Yes. We need her to tend to you."

"Or do we need a chaperone?" She was relieved she could still muster her sarcasm. "What about your sister's clinic?"

"It's a long way from—" Before Murad could complete his sentence, Rami interjected.

"You can't stay here. It's too dangerous. Too dangerous for us, too."

"I know. We need to disappear until I convince Salma's father I saved his daughter's life and he agrees to protect me. I have to leave the country."

"So, that's what's going on," Rami said, and Salma felt a swirl of anger at Murad for openly admitting he was using her.

"We must leave Fayoum." But now there was a hint of desperation she hadn't heard before. "Fadel told me the police received a fax in the middle of the night with orders to find a missing woman." Rami looked grave as he nodded for him to continue. "They are to arrest anyone with her—shoot to kill, if they resist." Salma's swirl of anger turned into fear.

"Fadel won't betray you," Rami reassured Murad. "He knows you're my friend and his brother is married to my wife's older sister. Did they identify the woman in the fax?"

"No. I don't think they'd want it known that Hamdi's daughter is missing. It's likely the people at the top think the Taj has kidnapped her, so we do have a narrow window of time to get away."

"Go where?" Rami asked, straightening his shoulders, and stretching his back.

"Some place where we will not be found by Hani Hamdi's soldiers or Sheikh Nabulsi's men. We need a safe place to hide."

"So, where is this wonderfully safe place?" Rami asked, sarcastically.

"Remember the caves in the hills where we played robbers and policemen?

"The ones near the monastery? That's halfway to Aswan. You'd have to take back roads. Is your car reliable? How many guns do you have?" Rami's words were sharp, his voice strained. "Even if you get past the police checkpoints, highway robbers control the roads between them."

"I was going to 'borrow' an armored SUV from the police station here." Salma saw a fleeting stiffening of Rami's face.

"So, that's your plan?"

"It's the best I could come up with." Murad shrugged his shoulders in surrender. "I never trained for this."

"You need a pistol."

"I have one in Sidi Osman."

"How could you get yourself into this mess without a real plan? I can't do anything about it." Rami clasped his head between his hands as Maryam parted the flowered curtains to join them.

"I was listening, Rami." Her almond shaped eyes glistened with tears. "You can't abandon your friend when he's in danger. How would you live with yourself if he gets killed? And on Judgment Day, how will you explain yourself to God? You must help these people."

"Okay. Okay. I'll handle it." Rami jumped up, angry and agitated, as though feeling trapped. "Murad. Stay inside. You can't go out again." He turned at the front door. "Maryam, when you bring breakfast bring something decent for this lady to wear; a pair of your blue jeans, a pair of running shoes and a tee-shirt—a bright one. She needs to dump this black sheet. The more she looks like a foreigner, the safer she'll be. No policeman wants to mess with foreigners. And, Murad, you'd better start making yourself look like her driver," he called out as he jerked open the door.

Chapter 6

October 1, 2014
8:00 am

Rami left Salma and Murad at a low table under a naked light bulb hanging from the ceiling. They neither looked at each other nor spoke until Maryam brought them the same breakfast with which practically every Egyptian—from prince to pauper—starts the day. The tomatoes were juicy, the feta cheese salty, the *fuul medammes* fava beans creamy and the *baladi* country flat bread yeasty and warm. Two toddlers ran into the room, laughing so exuberantly, the adults couldn't help but laugh, too. Salma pressed her hand to her ribs. It felt good to laugh. It didn't matter that she didn't know what she was laughing about. Once the laughter finally subsided, she watched Maryam chase her toddlers around the room to stuff their mouths with food the way solicitous mothers did—like force feeding geese for foie gras—and Salma almost started laughing again.

Meanwhile, Murad performed his ablutions in preparation for his morning prayers by washing his face, neck, hands, and feet three times at the sink outside the bathroom before spreading a clean towel on the floor. Facing east towards Mecca, he raised his hands to either side of his face, hooked his thumbs behind his ears, and recited the *Shahada*: "I bear witness there is no God but the one God." After lowering his hands to his waist and reciting a verse from the Quran under his breath, he knelt and pressed his forehead to the ground, repeating this twice more.

His prayers appeared not to have lifted his spirits; he was still brooding when he came back to the table. Had telling Rami who her father was so terrible? Had she demeaned him in the eyes of his friend? Whatever his problem was, Salma was too tired to try changing his mood.

"May your hands be blessed," she thanked Maryam for the meal before leaving to lie down on the couple's bed. The quacking of ducks and braying of donkeys pushed her into sleep, dreaming she was working in her vegetable beds with Nawal. Weeding between the tomato plants, feeling for the green beans hiding in the leaves, picking zucchinis when they were so small, she was reminded of Shakespeare's Caesar "being plucked untimely from his mother's womb."

She jolted out of the dream in the grip of an indefinable panic. It was already early in the afternoon. She was not in Maryam and Rami's bed. She was in the back seat of an SUV, covered by a scratchy woolen blanket that reeked of chloroform with her head cradled in the lap of a woman who smelled of fried onions. Obviously, Murad hadn't trusted her to accompany him out of Rami's house peacefully. Not a good omen. Suddenly, she felt a void at the center of her being that made her defenseless against her fear.

"Do you understand Arabic?" the old woman asked, stroking Salma's shoulder who nodded as she struggled to sit up. Beneath a black kerchief the woman's wrinkled visage was small and brown; her black eyes, lined with heavy kohl, were rheumy and filmed with age.

"I am Murad's mother. God heal you, my child. We are taking you to my daughter. She is a doctor." The woman pointed out her window. "Do you know where we are now?" Salma shook her head. Despite the pulse of pain that shot across her chest, she managed to right herself in the seat in time to see a sign: "300 Kilometers" north to Cairo. Once she oriented herself, she figured out Murad was heading south following the Nile.

Groggy from the chloroform, she wrapped her arms around herself and stared at the back of his head. Where were the caves in Upper Egypt he was going to take her? The one time she'd been in that area, she'd flown into Aswan with Farida to join a bunch of tourists on a Nile cruise. Salma had been to nine states in America, to seven European countries and five in the Middle East. Yet other than Cairo, she'd never been anywhere else in Egypt except to the family chalets and Alexandria on the Mediterranean and Sharm el Sheikh on the Red Sea.

Salma was digesting what that insularity, that distance from the "Egypt proper," said about who she was when Murad glanced at her in the rearview mirror. "By now, word of your disappearance has reached the checkpoints. We'll leave the highway again." They drove for another hour on the north-south highway before turning right on an unpaved road along an irrigation canal. Salma took a shallow breath and closed her eyes against the pain that shot through her chest every time the SUV hit a pothole. When she gasped after a particularly sharp jolt, she felt Murad's mother's hand on her knee, and without thinking, found herself covering the dark, blue-veined hand with her own.

The gesture had been spontaneous but, once she'd made it, Salma recognized its potential. Mothers were everything to Egyptian sons. Maybe she could gain Murad's trust by winning this woman over.

"Can you tell me your name?" she asked, stroking the woman's swollen knuckles with her thumb.

"Om Mohamed." The answer surprised Salma.

"Not mother of Murad?"

"My first son, may he rest in peace, was named Mohamed." Most first-born boys were named after the Prophet and because habits as deeply embedded as this didn't die, Salma almost added the requisite "peace be upon him" in her head. "But Allah took him early. Dysentery when he was four." Om Mohammed paused, looked out her window, before she continued. "After him, I had two girls and then Murad was born. But everyone still calls me Om Mohamed."

"What name did your parents give you?"

"My parents named me Aisha like the Prophet's—peace be upon him—youngest wife." The older woman's first name had been long buried by cherished motherhood and Salma would always be using the honorific: mother of Mohammed when she addressed her.

"What does Murad call you?" she asked.

"Amah or Om Mohamed, of course," Aisha replied with a huff of a laugh.

"My name is Salma. I knew your son in California. I didn't expect to meet him again like this." Salma tried to laugh, too.

"You have brought us much trouble, Salma," Aisha said, drawing away her hand.

"It was not I who brought trouble. Your son did that when he kidnapped me. I just want to go home."

"My son is a good man. God preserve him. He will not hurt you." It would take more than a mother's vouchsafing to reassure Salma. She stared ahead and noticed Murad trying to catch her eye in the mirror again.

"We'll soon be stopping for gas," he said over his shoulder. "Let's hope there's a bathroom." Had she heard a note of concern in his voice or only imagined it? Perhaps he was softening because she was cooperating. After all, he'd let her out of the shroud-like *abaya* now draped over the passenger seat. She glared at it, wishing she could rip the damn thing to shreds. Hijabs, headscarves, were one thing, but full faced Ku Klux Klan hoods *niqabs* were another. It was hard to remember that under those black sheets many women wore heavy lipstick and mascara, and T-shirts and jeans. Thank goodness, Rami told her to wear Maryam's clothes: blue jeans and a jean jacket over a red T-shirt with a yellow stripe across the breast. Dressed in clothes like those, Salma felt more like herself.

The sun was halfway to the horizon when they stopped at a Misr gas station; another company owned by the military. Once out of the Cherokee, Salma noticed the familiar CARE logo on its door: a circle of hands in alternating colors of brown and yellow with their palms on the circumference and spread fingers pointing inwards.

"What are we doing in this?" she asked.

"Rami must have stolen it. People in the countryside trust CARE. Heading to a clinic with a foreign aid worker will make perfect sense and make it easier to get through checkpoints. Plus, this one is bullet proof with run-flat tires and a self-sealing gas tank. By now, your father will have every soldier in the country on the lookout for you." Salma prayed, silently, for them not to shoot.

She stayed near the Jeep while she oriented herself once more. Fields of deep green alfalfa stretched behind a row of small shops, a pharmacy, and an automotive repair place fronting a collection of two-story brick apartments pushed against each other with laundry hanging from their balconies.

Small shiny-black flies swarmed up from the ground, buzzing around each other, each busily changing position but never straying beyond the boundary of the shape they made together. She watched them regroup and swarm off only to land a few feet away in a pool of their own blackness like animated Rorschach cards. Clouds of them wreathed the heads of local urchins standing in a semi-circle, oblivious to the ones crawling on their faces, in the snot of their noses, and the corners of their watery eyes. The youngsters stared at Salma as though they'd never seen a foreigner before. Swallowing her pride, she restrained herself from staring back at them because in Maryam's clothes she knew she looked like one.

The gas station consisted of three gas pumps, no building, and no bathroom. Salma followed Murad's mother to a faded blue privy. From a few feet behind her, she noticed the older woman was barefooted, the soles of her feet as thick as rhino hide, yellowish and full of gouges. Her heels were incised with deep cracks, and the calluses on her large toes had the soft, broken edges, of newly minted blisters. Salma wondered if Om Mohamed had ever worn shoes.

The privy's dirt floor had been swept clean, but the disgusting stench rising from the hole, over which she squatted, was sickening. There was a bucket full of water and no toilet paper. Salma splashed handfuls of water between her legs. There was a first time for everything.

"They think I'm a foreigner," she complained to Aisha when more village urchins in filthy caftans followed them back to the CARE Cherokee.

"Your accent is foreign." Aisha half snorted and half laughed. "You sound like a *khawagaya*. You walk like a Westerner. You're not really Egyptian, no matter what you think."

"I can't do anything about that." The rebuke had stung.

"So, you will be an Australian aid worker with CARE. One who speaks some Arabic so we can explain the way you talk." This goddess of contempt was going to live in Salma's mind forever.

Back at the SUV, she reached for the passenger door handle. "In back," Murad ordered, and she obeyed. A few miles past the gas station, they had to drive alongside a convoy of trucks splattering grime as its vehicles overtook them. Flipping on the wipers, Murad leaned forward with his forehead almost touching the windshield. An involuntary movement twitched near the corner of his right eye. Suddenly, he slammed on the brakes and screeched to a stop. A red and white striped pole blocked the road.

"Let's hope CARE gets us through this checkpoint," he said, gripping the steering wheel. "Hide the woman," he told his mother, who pulled Salma to her lap, covered her with the *abaya,* and held her down. "There don't seem to be any soldiers." He stuck his head out the window to check and Salma pushed against Aisha's arm, lifted her head and turned her face to see, too.

Murad waited with his left elbow resting on the windowsill as though relaxed, but he clutched the steering wheel so tightly, his knuckles turned white. Finally, a sleepy, middle-aged, guard with long earlobes and several missing teeth ambled out of a rundown lean-to.

"*Salamat, ya Haj*," he greeted the elderly man, handing him two identity cards. The guard poked his head into the vehicle.

"You have three people and only two cards. Where is hers?" he asked, pointing his chin at Salma. "Is something the matter with her?"

Om Mohammed clamped her hand over Salma's mouth all the while patting her back as though to comfort her. "My daughter is pregnant," she told the guard. "She cannot rest even in her mother's lap. CARE is sending us home."

"What did she say?" the old man asked Murad. "I don't hear well these days."

"My sister is pregnant. Her husband's an agricultural laborer, a *fallah*," Murad said, presenting the requisite bribe of a pack of Marlboros. "He got a contract to work in Chad—left last night."

"The man is lucky. There's no work here. Half of my village has emigrated."

"The women suffer most, brother." Murad handed him another pack of cigarettes and the guard raised the pole.

Salma couldn't believe what had happened. Two packs of cigarettes and the SUV was allowed to pass even though she didn't have a damned identity card. It was too bad she hadn't learned to navigate the labyrinth of bribery on her own. She might have cleared passport control with a carton of Marlboros.

After they passed through the primitive blockade, Aisha allowed Salma to sit up. She rolled the *abaya* into a pillow, tied it around her neck and soon nodded off. This was Salma's chance to get closer to Murad if she could. She needed to get and stay on his good side. How much had he changed since they were together? Who had he become? Yes, he was deeply religious, conservative and always observant, but a terrorist? She just couldn't believe that was possible

Salma was divorced, lonely, and too busy to date, when she met him at one of the bi-yearly picnics the Arab American Club organized for Middle Eastern students attending the surrounding colleges. She'd gone without her daughters that afternoon. The students, all young men, had not reached the halftime of the customary soccer game. One man, who appeared slightly older than the rest, was watching from a picnic table bench.

"How come you're not playing?" she'd asked, making polite conversation.

"I sprained my ankle yesterday. And hi, my name's Murad," he'd said with the broadest smile she'd ever seen. They sat at the table talking about food, describing their favorite dishes, and she'd invited him for dinner. It was as natural as that.

Of course, she'd been attracted to him, but she'd kept her emotional distance. At first. She couldn't help warming up to him when her then preteen daughters fell in love with his trickster, Goha, folk tales, the simple card games like *basra* and the soccer moves he'd taught them. Murad was the kindest man Salma had ever known, with a sense of humor that frequently broke through his serious façade. Today, what would it take for him to remember he'd once loved her?

She leaned over the SUV's front seat, her hand landing lightly on his shoulder. "Your mother's napping," she whispered near his ear. "She's worn out. We've been driving for almost four hours and I'm getting carsick. Do you think I could ride in front with you?" Murad pulled off the road so she could slide in beside him, her forearm pressed to her ribs. It took a moment for the searing pain to become just a steady ache so she could collect her thoughts. The most important thing she had to do was to reason out how far she could trust him and if she could get him to trust her.

Murad's startlingly white teeth were still wonderfully even and the lock of black hair on his brow was still as sharp as a bird's wing. Salma stared at him for so long, she felt awkward. He, on the other hand, paid no attention to her. He focused on the road and the roadsides with the blue-green eyes inherited from his father, a descendant of some Bonaparte sailor in the Battle of The Nile who'd decamped on the Mediterranean coast in 1798.

As they drove south, the low sandstone hills stretching along the riverbanks edged closer to the river, their caves trained sightlessly on each other like empty eye-sockets. Salma looked out at the blowing sand that smudged the passing landscape in its effort to reclaim the meager strip of irrigated fields. A village of mud brick homes emerged in the distance; squat huts wavering like mirages. Soon the sun would set, not with a warning twilight, but with a suddenness that would turn the hills purple for the briefest moment before they lost the light. This was undeniably Murad's territory. As unfamiliar to Salma as a foreign land.

"It looks like we're in sugar cane country," she commented, hoping to start a conversation.

"Cane is good for hiding from police," Murad said, and she wondered if he was referring to the long spat of terrorist activity in this area and if he'd once hidden in similar fields.

"Do you live around here?" She didn't ask if he had.

"I teach at the Vocational Institute in Aswan."

"What subjects?" she asked, maintaining her end of the hesitant conversation.

"Electronic equipment repair." There was bitterness in the brevity of Murad's retort. "Destiny." At his one-word conclusion, a twinge of disappointment crossed his face. Salma wondered if he was thinking—regretting—the fact he could be earning a hundred and fifty thousand dollars a year if he'd stayed in Silicon Valley.

"Do you like your work?" She kept her voice absolutely neutral, without a trace of emotion in it.

"No. It's impossible. No one can teach a thousand students with equipment for ten." He turned on the wipers to clear the dusty windshield again. "I tutor students in the villages around here."

Suddenly, the dirt road veered sharply to the right. Not an ordinary roadblock. This one was manned by a special military patrol. Over a dozen soldiers crouched with their assault rifle barrels resting on the hoods of two army Jeeps parked face to face behind scrolls of barbed concertina wire. These army squads—probably ones her father had mobilized by now—were going to kill Murad. When she automatically flung her arm across his chest as though that could save him, she realized she'd thrown in her lot with this so-called terrorist.

"We can't stop," Murad yelled, spinning the steering wheel, hand over hand, gunning the Jeep's engine and crashing through the barricade. Wood splintered. Bullets pinged off the bulletproof windows. Salma slammed her hands on the dashboard as he punched the gas pedal down. They slashed through jungle-dense cane stalks until the Jeep swerved out of control. It plowed across the bank of an irrigation gully. Tilted on its left wheels. Wavered. Tumbled. Plunged.

The airbag knocked Salma back and sideways. Her head snapped forward, crushing her nose against it. Pinned in her seat with her chest on fire, she heard Murad scramble out his window. It took longer than she'd expected for him to come to her aid.

"I got my mother out, all right," he said when he reached Salma's window. "Keep your head down." Puncturing the air bag with a pocketknife and severing her seatbelt he gave her room to move. She tightened her arms, braced her ribcage, and slid off the seat onto the ground. Murad raised a finger to his lips. "Not a sound. Those aren't soldiers. They're Nabulsi's men."

"Are you sure?"

"They're in stolen uniforms but I recognized two of them." He turned to examine the gully—up and down and along its ridges. "We'll walk through this." He pointed to the shallow water at the bottom of the ditch. "So, their dogs can't follow our scent." Then, with Salma struggling to keep her balance on the slick, wet rocks, he led the two women away from the crushed vehicle.

About a mile from where they'd crashed, Murad scaled the ditch bank and called down to where Salma and Aisha hunkered in the reeds. "They are going the other way. We're not far from the village. Let's go."

"That's crazy," Salma objected. "They're bound to be waiting for us there."

"My grandfather is the head man, the *omda*, of our village," Murad reassured her. "His men will protect us. Although they won't like confronting the Taj, they'll come through. They're like family. Besides, we won't be in the village long enough for Nabulsi to send more bastards after us." He gave Salma a wry smile. "I mean, send more after you. They're going to execute me."

"Do we keep following this?" Salma pointed down the gully, aware of how weak her knees had become.

"No. We go up this embankment and across some fields."

Aisha pulled the back hem of her dress between her thighs and raised it to clench between her teeth. Then sure-footed, despite her arthritis, she began her barefooted climb while Salma retied the laces of her sneakers and followed, her own balance shaky. She was clumsy. Slipping down one for every two steps up whenever the crumbly ground underfoot gave out. Handholds, like rocks or roots, were scarce, and when she did manage to grab something, she cringed in pain. Even in Maryam's running shoes, she lagged behind the older woman. Her temples throbbed with the effort to keep up. Loose dirt pelted her head and riddled her eyes and mouth with grit. She raised her head to gauge her progress then looked down to assure herself Murad was still with her. A rock went loose. Her back foot betrayed her and a poker-hot pain shot up from her left ankle. She grabbed at a bunch of dry reeds as she started to fall. They came out in her hand and she heard herself scream. Then, as suddenly as she started, she stopped, caught in Murad's arms.

She didn't know how it happened. She was gathered to his breast, her chin on his shoulder, his arms around her back. She felt his heart pounding. His sweat-drenched shirt rubbed against her face. When she felt his chest heave against her own, she imagined, for a fleeting second, he felt the same quiver and blushed. She was embarrassed at how quickly he lowered her to the ground.

"I'll go ahead of you," he said, starting uphill. "I'll point out what you can hold on to safely." Keeping her weight on her good right leg before she lowered her left to take a step, Salma hobbled behind him. Whenever she looked up to see her progress, she found the distance between them increasing. Finally, wheezing heavily, she gave up. Halfway up the steep incline, she stopped. Bent over with her hands on her knees, she didn't notice Murad slide down the embankment until he was by her side.

"Here," he said, shoving one of her inhalers into her hand. "I'll help you back down. My mother can take you by a different route. We'll meet up at my sister's."

On the bank of the canal, at the foot of the hill, Salma leaned against a rock, took two deep puffs from her inhaler, and tried to calm her breathing. Murad had brought her to an area in Egypt she didn't know existed. How would they get out of here? Where could they go? Even if the disk gave Paul leverage, how would he find her here—someplace south of Minya, north of the Valley of the Kings.

Chapter 7

SALMA FOLLOWED THE COURSE OVER THE ROUGH GROUND Aisha chose, her entire world compressed into two elements: the snapping of dry, razor-sharp, cane-stalks that snatched at her legs, and the wheezing of her lungs. She had reached a flat space to stand in when she saw a herd of scrawny, stubby-horned goats.

"Zainab's herd," Aisha said, grabbing the horn of a sinew-bodied goat with a pointed snout. "We'll go this way. It will be easier for your breathing," she said, egging on the smelly herd with a firm "*Herr, Herr,*" sound and pointing to a confluence of paths zigzagging like worm trails up a gentle slope. "We're near the waterwheel. The women washing in the river below it will wonder what a foreigner is doing so close to our village." Deciding the announcement required no response, Salma resumed the hike without making one.

The zigzagging trail ended at a wide canal where a dozen village women squatted, knees to shoulders, rumps to the ground. Some scrubbed pots, some washed clothes and some bathed their children in the algae green water. Most looked emaciated, their faces drawn, their eyes full of discharge, red and inflamed. It seemed trachoma was returning to the countryside.

Salma had seen photographs of scenes like these; old women garbed in black, younger ones in brilliant colors. Now, live human beings were singing as they beat their clothes against the river rocks in time to the tune of a folksong she'd never heard:

> *"I'll wear my yellow dress*
> *I'll take off my yellow dress*
> *There is no duress*
> *I only wear it for you."*

The group of women dissolved into peals of laughter at their suggestive song but stopped when she and Aisha approached. "*Salamat,* ya Om Mohamed," an old woman called out. "Who's the foreigner you've picked up?"

"This is Salma."

"That's an Egyptian name." This from a younger woman.

"I'm from Australia. I work for CARE," Salma responded, feeling oddly defensive.

"You speak Arabic?" the young woman half said, and half asked.

"I'm learning." She felt like a moron saying that and was perturbed by how estranged she felt from these women. As though picking up on how ill at ease Salma felt, Aisha told the women she was escorting the Australian medical-aid woman to the Sidi Osman Clinic. They rose from the ground like a cloud of grasshoppers. Salma took a step back. A tall, statuesque girl with a devastatingly tired face came forward with a baby on her hip and an offering of dates in her hand. Salma couldn't take her eyes off the baby's bloated belly. Limbs as thin as bird legs. Head, listless in the crook of his mother's arm. He could have been the custodian's infant—the one starving to death the day after Salma's tenth birthday while she and her mother shopped for flowers.

"My son's going blind," said a girl no older than Salma's youngest daughter, Hoda.

"My husband hasn't worked the fields for two years. His leg didn't heal," a woman with a pyramid of dots tattooed on her chin complained.

"We need penicillin, cough medicine, aspirin," several called at once. Salma found herself backing away. She hadn't meant to. Her reaction was visceral. Women begging for aspirin? How was that possible? Even as her indignation rose, her eyes brimmed with tears.

Perhaps sensing her distress, Aisha led her by the hand up the embankment on the other side of the canal. By the time they reached the top, sharp rocks and withered stalks had bloodied Salma's ankles, her ribs seemed to be goring her chest and a headache was near blinding her.

"Do people still use these?" Salma asked, referring to the waterwheel centered in a platform of earth tamped granite-hard by centuries of oxen in blinder-induced stupors circling around the structure all day.

"I don't know anyone who still does. Not too long ago, farmers who couldn't afford electric pumps and generators used them," Aisha explained as she slumped to the ground. "Life is harsh. But" Aisha pointed to the women beating clothes to the rhythm of another erotic love song, "everyone laughs; many people sing." Salma propped her elbows on her knees and held her head in her hands to listen.

"For fear your mother will come for you,
I'll hide you in my hair and knot my headscarf over you.
For fear your sister will come for you,
I'll hide you in my bosom and wear my pearl necklace over you."

"You told the women you were taking me to a clinic," Salma murmured, her eyes still fixed on the women. "Is that a government one?"

Aisha blew out an exasperated breath. "There's never been a government clinic in our province."

"But you said—"

"You know nothing about our Egypt. We have clinics, schools and food banks connected to our mosques."

"Who is 'we'? Do you mean, Islamists?"

"Islamists?" A slight smile of scorn curled Aisha's lips. "You really are an American," she said, scarcely containing her contempt. "We are all Muslims. It's everybody's obligation to provide for the poor as the Prophet, peace be upon him, instructed. Especially for widows and orphans." Salma lowered her eyes until they were thin slivers, but Aisha's tirade continued. "You could feed everyone in my village for a year with just one of your diamond earrings." The disgust in the woman's voice kept Salma staring at the ground, waiting for the signal to resume their trek.

Years of wear and tear had flattened the well-trodden path through alfalfa field that disappeared like the tail of a snake into a small village barnacled to the riverbank. But as they got closer, it became more of an extension of the village. White leghorn hens scratched in the dirt, red combs and wattles wobbling. Large, noisy flies buzzed around mounds of composting cauliflower mixed with straw and soil.

The clean-sweet smell of the compost was the same as the one in Salma's garden. She wanted to weep. If only she were in her backyard, weeding the raised redwood beds built into the hillside, tending their borders of marigolds. There was room to roam around her cottage. Here, whatever space existed, was crowded and dense and suffocating.

"Salma," Om Mohammed said. "I will pull down my face veil. You must put on the *abaya,* again. Many Taj men live in Sidi Osman. Murad thinks my father can protect us from them, but I worry the men from the Taj will be waiting. They must not recognize us." The logic was irrefutable. As she watched Aisha unknot the abaya she'd looped around her neck when she'd napped in the SUV, Salma felt an involuntary shudder but draped the black shroud over her T-shirt and jeans, anyway.

Sidi Osman village was a collection of mud-brick dwellings leaning against each other like drunkards or like the brown seals under the Santa Cruz pier. Enveloped in fields of luminous green, not an inch of ground was wasted in the skinny strip of soil supported by the country's declining supply of water.

"Are the homes close together to save land for farming?" Salma asked. The alley she and Aisha had entered was only wide enough to accommodate a single donkey with a bale of alfalfa.

"It saves land for growing, yes. But it is most necessary to make shade for each other." That made sense. Salma imagined the relief of reaching this respite after a long, hot day in the fields.

Several twists later, the track petered out at a nondescript hut insulated by sugarcane stalks stacked on the roof. The shutters of its two narrow windows—one on each side of a wooden door once painted green—were closed. The only sign of life were images painted on the whitewashed walls—most faded with time. Yet, Salma could still make out an airplane, a train, a camel, a duck, a donkey, the green fronds and red dates of palm trees, and a dozen blue handprints.

"This is Murad's house now, but it is empty." Aisha ran her hand across the adobe as if to comfort it. "My father painted these when my grandfather returned from the Hajj. But now the paint is flaking off." She scraped curls of dry paint off an ochre-colored camel and rubbed the residue between her fingers.

"And these?" Salma stood before a line of blue handprints.

"The hand of Fatima, to keep away the Evil Eye. My three aunts used their hands to print these when Murad was nine years old. He'd learned to recite the whole Quran so he could be circumcised. Not all boys do but our family is strict." Then, as though introducing herself through her family, Aisha added, "My father was the *omda* since the year I married. I became a widow when Murad was seven. Now, I think I'm sixty, but I don't know the year when I was born."

"You don't have a birth certificate?"

"No. I didn't need one. My father knew the year when I was born. But all my children have one," Aisha insisted, proudly. "Come on, girl, that is enough now. We must keep going. Murad is waiting for us."

"He'll meet us at the clinic, right?"

"Yes. My daughter, Soraya, and her family live above the clinic. It makes it easy for her to keep her eye on my father. He's old now but he goes to the Hoodhood Café next door every day where he smokes his sheesha and solves problems. He's a good man. Everyone in our village loves him." Salma was silent. The older woman continued. "These days many fight about water. Ten years ago, we had twice as much as we get now." The image of global warming drying up the entire country's greenery, turning it to desert, that slunk into Salma's head, stayed stuck there.

The aroma of cheese and olives mixed with smoked herring wafted from across the village square and by the time they reached the clinic, her stomach was growling. There was an enormous red crescent, the Egyptian equivalent of the Red Cross, painted on the clinic's whitewashed brick building. On its door was a handwritten sign instructing students to proceed to the rear of the building for classes in reading, writing and studies of the Quran.

Aisha rang the doorbell. Murad's sister, a woman who looked to be about forty years old, wearing a white medical coat and white *hijab* opened the door. Soraya was plump. Light-skinned, like Murad and the tufts of hair peeking out of her headscarf were jet-black like his. She wasn't wearing lipstick, but she had penciled her eyebrows to emphasize their arches and lined her intelligent eyes with thick black kohl like her mother's.

"*Alhamdu lillah.* Thank God it's you, *Amma.* Something dangerous is happening, here. Soldiers raided Kafr el Nakhil at dawn. Took seventeen men from the village; claimed they were Islamic terrorists. Bulldozed the sugar cane fields. Killed three cow. Cut off the electricity and burned-out Abu Darwish's irrigation pump. No one knows what's going on."

"Calm down, Soraya. It's just another rampage. They don't know what they're doing."

"Who's this?" Soraya stared at Salma once she calmed down enough to notice her. "What does she have to do with us?"

"The woman is injured. Your brother wants you to examine her."

"What?"

"Don't question him, girl. Do what he asks." Sometimes patriarchy had its virtues, Salma thought, hesitating on the clinic's doorstep until Aisha pushed her across the stoop. The institutional odor of urine and disinfectant immediately engulfed her. In the tiled corridor, a row of women sat shoulder to shoulder on metal chairs that lined it. Girls leaned against the wall balancing passive children, baby brothers and sisters, on their hips. Infants bawled, kids with runny noses whimpered. The silent, enduring women stared at Salma.

With her heels snapping against the floor, Soraya rushed her mother and Salma down the hall. Something in the way she averted her eyes from her patients made Salma's shoulders rise to her ears. She could have been on a dark street in a rough part of town. Why should she trust this woman? Perhaps she'd already trusted Murad too much. Suddenly, she felt trapped.

The Ehssan Clinic's administrative office was a closet-sized room with a gurney and metal stool next to a scratched-up wooden desk. Drowsy flies buzzed at the narrow window above a file cabinet against the wall.

"What's wrong with you?" Soraya had omitted even a perfunctory greeting.

"I'm sorry to trouble you, doctor," Salma said, hoping humility would diminish the woman's resentment.

"Soraya, be gentle. It's not this woman's fault. Your brother is the reason she's here."

"So, what is the—" Soraya started to ask, again, when the door swung open. A young owl-faced attendant burst into the room restraining a convulsing eight-year-old girl in her arms.

"It's an emergency, *doctora*."

"Lay her on the gurney. You," Soraya pointed at Salma. "Hold down the girl's legs. And you, Mother, turn her on her side so if she vomits, she won't choke." Salma grabbed the girl's thrashing legs, the attendant her flailing arms, and Aisha the child's head. Gaunt and hollow-cheeked, the girl was so scrawny Salma could have flipped her over by herself with only one hand.

"She's been sick for three weeks," the mother said. "I've tried everything, but the fever keeps going higher."

"What happened three weeks ago?" Soraya asked.

"The girl turned ten." To Salma, she'd looked only seven years old. "It's the summer of her circumcision. The *zaghloul* dates were ripe."

"Who did this to her?"

"My neighbor is a midwife. My daughter was fine after the cutting. The fever started the next day."

"And you waited three weeks before you brought her to me?" Soraya sounded furious. "You waited until it could be too late to save her? What's the matter with you?" Salma couldn't imagine an American doctor admonishing a patient so rudely, but here, people expected anyone with the slightest authority to push them around.

"I know it's illegal to circumcise my daughters. But the government is not above the will of Allah, even if you refuse to do what's right."

"I refuse to circumcise girls because it's wrong. Not because of the law. Show me the words in the Quran where Allah commands us to do this."

"I can't read. I'm only trying to protect my girl," the woman protested. "The sheikh says we must circumcise our girls to cleanse them, so when they're older they don't go mad." Yeah, thought Salma: so, they can't orgasm. A barbaric practice. She'd read the yearly Oxfam reports. Despite government efforts to prohibit what the West called female genital mutilation, its prevalence in the country was increasing again.

"You're an ignorant woman." Soraya's authority allowed her this outburst. "You're an idiot to follow this African tradition. It is not part of our religion." She turned to the attendant. "Bring me a drip line—with tranquilizer and antibiotics. Quick."

She stayed by the gurney stroking the girl's sweaty hair as she talked to Salma. "Children are dying every day. Unfortunately, not as fast as they're being born." At first, Salma thought this was heartless but, if she were in her place, she'd be depressed and angry, too. "Half our village is underfed and undernourished," Soraya continued. "It is brutal to be a girl. Fathers degrade them, brothers beat them, cousins rape them and their mothers have them circumcised."

"But you became a doctor," Salma objected.

"Thanks to Sheikh Nabulsi, Allah preserve him, who took care of my family after the army tortured my father to death. The sheikh is our shelter in this world."

"Yes," Aisha agreed. "He bought me an apartment in Minya so my children could go to school there. God reward the man. He did more than any father in Sidi Osman would do." Salma was shocked. These women believed the monster who wanted to kill her father was a good man. Obviously, Murad hadn't told them their sheikh now wanted to kill him, too. Salma imagined a Shakespearian play with Hani and Nabulsi as vengeful protagonists. Both convinced of their righteousness. Both denying any truth but theirs.

A loud, persistent, thumping on the front door, reverberated through the clinic and snapped her back to reality. Metal clanged against metal. Thunderous wheels crashed down the linoleum floors. The fluorescent lights over Salma's head buzzed like agitated beehives and everything seemed louder and slower. Someone yelled. Children screamed. Footsteps clapped down the corridor. The Taj had come for her. The heavy weight crushing her chest was allowing only a narrow thread of breath to reach her lungs. She coughed, expelling but not taking in air. Lightheaded, terrified, she felt her chest spasm. She couldn't breathe. She was going to die. Never see Paul again. What would her girls do without her? She grabbed Soraya's arm as she fell.

"Asthma," Soraya said, taking Salma's hands in hers. "Epinephrine. Tell the nurse to bring a syringe," she hollered to her mother. "Have you had attacks before?" Salma nodded. "Try to relax. It's the stress. Don't damage your lungs. The shot will raise your adrenaline, get more oxygen to them." Salma used her fingers to mimic the kind of inhaler Murad had for him. "Only the rich have those," Soraya laughed with a small sound at the back of her throat. Salma nodded, again. She only hoped she wouldn't get an infected needle. The country was awash in Hepatitis C. Aisha helped her daughter pull the desk chair to Salma's side to sit her up so she could breathe more easily.

"Will she be okay?" Salma asked, turning her head toward the child on the gurney.

"She is sleeping. We will keep her overnight. Her mother will stay. Now I have to check on the ambulance case."

A teenage boy entered, unbidden, before Soraya could leave. "My oldest son, Mohammed," she said, introducing the square-chinned youth with small ears, thin earlobes, and cheeks turning a circus-red. He ran his fingers through his hair, slid his hands over his shirt to smooth it out before leaning in to whisper in his mother's ear.

Concentrating on his message, Soraya first narrowed her eyes then lifted her eyebrows. "Tell your uncle I will handle it." She pressed her lips against her teeth and turned to Salma. "My brother says he has found a car. *Insha' allah*, you and my mother will leave before dawn. But we must hide you. Taj men are searching the village."

The air in the room turned thick enough to fall into. Leaning against the office wall, Salma recalled the premonition she'd had in the corridor. The odds were bad, the obstacles overwhelming. She was as responsible for Murad's safety as he was for hers. Until he could count on safe passage out of the country, she was his only protection. They had to stick together even if it meant that might be doubling their risks.

Chapter 8

October 1, 2014
9:00 pm

AFTER A QUICK DINNER, SORAYA AND HER MOTHER, with Salma between them, slipped out the clinic's back door into the thickening gloom outside and into the mosque that shared the clinic's wall. Once inside, they entered an area separated from the mosque's main hall by a filigreed wooden screen with pillows scattered at its base; a space reserved for women.

"You must hide here until Murad gets a car," Soraya said, pointing at a stack of straw pallets, her voice almost a whisper.

"Here?" Salma asked, puzzled. How was she supposed to hide under this mound?

"Behind these." Soraya and her mother pulled the pallets away from the wall. Salma snapped her mouth shut as Aisha took her hand to help climb up and over a four-foot-high stack. "I will come for you when it is time to go, my child." Noticing the concern in the old woman's face, Salma began to panic.

The two women left her boxed-in between the pile of pallets and the wall. Her throat tightened, immediately. Her breaths came out loud and fast, black spots began inking her sight. She was terrified of a panic attack that would set off an asthma attack. Her inner voice told her to close her eyes, collect herself, keep calm so she could soon be breathing normally. Its cold authority comforted her.

With her eyes closed Salma almost felt the footsteps before she heard them brushing the carpets beyond the pallets where she hid. The hairs on her neck rose; her throat filled with an emptiness she couldn't swallow.

Faltering on the verge of panic again, she listened to the voices of women she couldn't see.

"Won't they be suspicious?" a girl's soft youthful sounding voice asked. "Personally, I don't pray in the mosque at night. I pray only during Ramadan after I've broken my fast." The ticking in Salma's neck vein spread across her forehead as she waited for a response. If the girl didn't come to the mosque at night, what was she doing here, now? A voice thinned by age answered the young woman.

"It will take the imam some time to drag himself out of his bed. And more time to get here. Until then, no one will cross the threshold of this space designated for women. The *omda* asked us to stay here until his son knocks three times on the door." How ironic, Salma thought. Gender segregation was keeping her safe.

Salma missed the company of Egyptian women. Ensconced in the heart of the Hamdi household in mid-morning when the light was still soft and the heat gentle, her great-grandmother, a petite woman who smelled of fenugreek and lavender, held court. She and her female visitors gathered in tacit seclusion in rooms where no man dared enter.

As a child, Salma had sat wide-eyed and cross-legged on the carpet listening to mothers cracking salt-roasted melon seeds between their teeth; complaining about their children to other mothers, to wives about husbands and to mothers-in-law about their errant sons whom their mothers were expected to take to task.

Lounging on sofas pushed against the walls with their legs drawn under them, widows in black dresses, and matrons bulging out of their tailored suits, sipped rose water from Waterford glasses and Turkish coffee from cups trimmed with real gold. In the Hamdi house, they arranged marriages, traded in gold and jewels, and bought and sold real estate in their own names. It was there that Salma imbibed the kind of power they possessed while pretending not to understand their off-color jokes or notice the tears of laughter they dried with *eau de cologne* scented handkerchiefs. Another time, another place.

The women who met in her great-grandmother's salon had never been afraid of government officials who stole from the people, nor religious leaders, with their rules and hierarchy, who misinterpreted the Holy Quran. Sitting at their feet, Salma absorbed the message they held close to their hearts: men dominated with dogma, women cradled the soul of Islam. Rather than emphasizing the prophet Mohammed's triumphs over hostile tribes, they saw him as an example of God's message of love and compassion. If only one day, instead of analyzing Egypt's militants, Paul would take the time to understand her great grandmother's Islam. Maybe he could navigate the divide between the forces of war and those of peace embedded in all three Abrahamic traditions.

When she thought of Paul, the back of Salma's neck suddenly went cold. She was in danger, but she was not all on her own and alone. Paul didn't have anyone in Cairo. He would be all alone. What if the Taj had captured the man she loved? What would they do to him? She was helpless against the T.V. image of the journalist in an orange suit, his head tied in a black bag, that ISIS beheaded. She prayed to a god she wasn't sure existed to watch over him. It felt cheap to ask God for a favor when she wasn't sure he was real, but she didn't know any other way to plead for Paul's life. And her father's, of course.

The sound of shuffling floated over the barrier of pallets behind which she was hiding drew her from her thoughts. Soon, the apparent movement was followed by the melodious recitation of a passage from the Quran. She recognized the chapter. It was the one about the mother of Jesus—the longest *sura* in the Holy Book. "The labor pains came upon her by the trunk of a palm tree. She said, 'I wish I had died before this and been completely forgotten . . . Then she came to her people carrying him. They said, 'O Mary, you have done something terrible.'" Salma didn't have to believe the words for the evocative sounds to soothe her. They kept her company as the women continued chanting until dawn.

At dawn, Aisha brought a modest breakfast of *fuul* beans, green arugula, and fresh-baked flatbread while delivering a multi-pronged message in a long, single, breath. "My daughter sends her greetings. She could not come. The child is sicker. She said to tell you the X-rays show you are badly bruised, but your ribs are okay. Murad is getting a car. He says we must leave in a half hour."

"Where are we going?"

Aisha ignored her query. Salma scooped up a mouthful of beans with a piece of warm bread and didn't ask again.

A rooster was bugling the dawn as they left Sidi Osman in a small four-wheel drive suited for winding up the hills south of Minya. A translucent white moon was sinking, and across the valley, bars of sunlight flamed on the silhouetted hills.

Salma jumped into the front seat of the red car as though she belonged there, as though she and Murad were friends. Murad smiled. She tried to imagine what being friends with him would be like in Egypt. Where would they meet? At Starbucks in the Carrefour mall? There were sure to be people she didn't know, who knew her through her family, who would walk over to them and raise their eyebrows while they waited to be introduced to her companion. What would happen when they'd ask who his relatives were—information with which to slot him into the right social level the way Americans slot people by their occupations. They couldn't have a serious relationship; they most certainly could never marry. In fact, they couldn't even be friends.

In Egypt, she and Murad belonged to two different worlds; they'd never enjoy the egalitarian relationship they'd almost had in the States. Here, he'd be resentful when he didn't measure up to the standards of her world and, to be honest, in public, she'd be embarrassed by their social difference. Salma didn't want to think about that. Things were so much easier, more hopeful with Paul. She wondered where he was now. What was he doing? He had to be distraught. He had to be looking for her. So was her father. She was sure he'd gotten Rashid to send out soldiers. A cold finger of fear touched Salma's spine. What if Nabulsi went after him again? What if he went after Paul? She couldn't let herself go there.

She leaned forward to watch the first sliver of what would become a fierce, hot-white sun peek over the skyline before it rose into the sky. The black road was turning a charcoal grey. A flock of starlings flew overhead. She rolled down her window to better follow their flight and felt the kind of comfort only nature provides. Soothed from her core to her skin, she let the moment sink in before she glanced at Murad who flashed another matinee-idol smile and took his right hand off the wheel. Spellbound, Salma watched it hover between them and hesitate before it landed on her hand where it rested on the seat. She felt like a teenager at the movies, staring unseeingly at the screen, pretending not to notice her date had made a move on her.

It was early so there were only a few vehicles on the road, mostly trucks, and only a few cars. Aisha was napping, stretched out on the back seat. They'd been driving for an hour when they cut across the abrupt line of demarcation between the green of the irrigated land and the beige-on-beige desert reinvading it. Waves of heat rising from the ground created an illusion of rippling water in the distance. Salma stared ahead at the blacktop road coated with a faint shimmer of golden sheen. She knew sand drifting over the asphalt would make it slick and the car could slip on it as readily as on ice, but soon the pavement gave up. Surrendered. Became a trail through the gravel-strewn sand.

"Are we still going to the caves you and Rami mentioned? The ones you used to play in?" Salma asked, straightening in her seat.

"We passed them quite a way back. It's better that not even Rami knows where we hide."

Salma leaned her forehead against her window, cupped her palms to shield her eyes from the harsh light, and peered out. Sand. Sand. Sand.

"So, where are we going?" she asked.

"Have you ever been in a place where people have been praying for centuries?"

"Like a mosque or church?"

"I'm thinking of more enclosed spaces."

"For example?" Salma had no idea where this conversation was heading, but she was intrigued.

"There's a famous cave where Our Lady Maryam and Joseph stayed with Our Lord Issa when he was an infant." Salma recalled the legend— how they'd fled their home when Emperor Herod commanded all first-born males slaughtered and took shelter in an Upper Egyptian cave during their travels. "Rami and I explored caves around it but of course, we never played in that one." Murad kept his eyes on the road but looked pensive and Salma saw him swallow before he went on, "It has a special place in my heart."

"Why is that?"

"One day, when I was about ten years old, I got lost from Rami. I went looking for him on Bird Mountain and found this cave. It wasn't like any other I'd been in. Someone must have dug a pathway through the rocks to the narrow entrance that I had to crawl through. It wasn't as dark as I thought it would be inside and there was plenty of room to stand up. But there was something strange about the air. The farther in I went, the heavier it became and then it began to vibrate and vibrate, faster and faster. I felt I was walking through an invisible substance. I shivered. Yet, it wasn't cold."

"What do you think was happening?"

"Back then, I was too young to know anything about the place. If I'd been a Christian, I might have gone with my family to the June festival there."

"I've never heard of it," Salma said, and hoped Murad wouldn't comment on how little she knew of Egypt outside her upper-class Cairo.

"There is a festival every year," he continued without criticizing her. "More than two million Christians go to that mountain village surrounding the church and cave to worship Our Lady Maryam and Our Lord Issa. Think of how much psychic energy their prayers produce."

"Have you been in there since?"

"No. Not in the cave. But about fifteen years ago I went to the part that's a church with Rami who was showing a friend around."

"Really?" Salma asked in the most non-intrusive voice possible, hoping Murad would divulge more. She was encouraged when he added, "I wanted to know if *Abuna,* our father, was still the church abbot." Murad tapped a finger on the steering wheel and peeked sideways at Salma. "Actually, it was for a silly reason."

"Mmm." Salma smiled and nodded.

"I wanted to thank him," he said and the slight frown on his face dissolved.

"Thank him for what?"

"The peppermint."

"The peppermint?" Salma burst out laughing. She couldn't help herself. "You're kidding."

"Yes, peppermint. A priest or monk—they looked the same to me—found me and took me to the church when I told him I'd gotten separated from my friend and didn't know where to go."

"Had you ever been inside a church before?"

"No. When I was a kid, it was the first time for me. It's a completely different church from any I've seen since. It's carved into the mountain. The front part is held up by what are probably the original ancient Greek columns. Which makes sense. The Emperor Constantine's mother had it built—or, rather, she had it dug." Murad grinned. "Deeper into the mountain is what you call a crypt—with a picture of Sittena Maryam carrying the infant Sayedna Issa hanging on the raw rock walls."

"Was Abuna still there?"

"Yes. This time he was wearing a dark red cloak instead of a black one like the priest's. He must have been promoted. The Orthodox church has a complicated hierarchy."

"Did he recognize you?"

"Of course, not. But he remembered that years ago he'd given a young Muslim boy a peppermint and blessed him."

Salma sat silently, touched by the simple story. There was another side to the ultra-conservative Muslim, the Murad she thought she knew.

"So, we're not going to a cave near Minya," she asked, going from the sublime to the concrete.

"We're going to one above Aswan my cousin and I discovered when I visited my mother's brother one year when Eid el-Fitr was in winter, and it wasn't too hot."

About twenty minutes later Salma glanced in the side mirror and noticed a black spot on the horizon that hadn't been there earlier. "Do you think we could stop for a minute?" Although she didn't want to explain herself yet—she didn't want to sound stupid—she wanted a better look at that black spot. Murad slowed to a halt and leaned across her lap to open her door. Salma held herself back. Acknowledging his familiar gesture by touching his arm would be too intimate.

The sun was directly overhead when she stepped out. Scrub bush all around. Not an inch of shade. The hot wind blasted her with muscular strength. She thought she'd caught sight of the black spot growing larger as it advanced but she was forced to close her eyes against the glare.

Before she could fully absorb what she'd seen, Murad called out, "Sandstorm. We must get going right now." The restraint in his voice belied the look of urgency in his face. He squinted towards the horizon. "Those dunes move a mile a minute."

Soon the wind swept the desert into the sky and the sand obscured the sun. Dunes blocked the western horizon; dust clouds darkened the midday and the car began to vibrate as they drove, almost blindly, in a brown cocoon.

"Here it comes." Murad pointed to a towering wave of dust stretched across the sky. Growls and roars advanced before it. Static crackled. A savage dragon of sand devouring the world. He floored the gas pedal but there was no outrunning the storm. It swept over them like thick fog and roared like an ocean. Howling waves. Horrid wails. The sand blew sideways, striking the car, scraping off its red paint. They drove in near total darkness hoping they were heading in the right direction. Salma turned to Murad, her eyes wide, her eyebrows raised, in a silent question.

"We'll be all right." Murad patted her thigh. He kept his hand there and drove with the other hand on the steering wheel. Once more, the gesture took Salma by surprise. She hesitated. Hoping she wouldn't scare off this Murad, the one she'd once loved, she covered his hand with her own and although she kept them fixed on the road, she felt her eyes smile.

The wind dropped as abruptly as it had risen, leaving the world in an unearthly silence. Not just an absence of sound; more like an anti-sound, as though there was a hole in the air. Across the river, a row of hills rose chiseled against a stark blue sky. Domes and gables threw accents of violet shadows, dramatizing the gold light radiating off them signaling the world had returned.

They descended to a strip of green along the river and drove south to the Aswan Bridge north of its namesake city. Murad withdrew his hand from Salma's to turn to his mother. "*Amah*, the cables holding up that bridge are supposed to look like giant sails. Do they look like that to you?"

"They look more like swords to me." Salma saw what Aisha meant about the fan-shaped patterns. The industrial modernity of the steel cables jarred with the agricultural fields on the riverbanks it connected. The strings of lorries like moving blocks of apartment buildings crossing the river were scarcely pastoral.

"This president plans to revive the past president, the toppled Mubarak's, Toska project." There was no missing the derision in Murad's tone. "Reclaim five hundred and eight thousand square miles of salt saturated sand."

"Every pharaoh needs his own pyramid," Salma said, to contribute to the conversation. "Nasser had the High Dam, Sadat, crossed the Suez Canal on his Six October pontoons and Mubarak got his Toska. I wonder what this president's personal pyramid will be?"

"Well, this one's doomed. It's true that the canal from the Nile will irrigate the fields. But the salt in the soil will leach into the aquifers and there'll be a net loss of potable water." Even if she'd dared risk breaking her reconnection to Murad, there wasn't much for Salma to argue against.

"A refrigerated truck," she said, pointing out her window.

"It'll be a hundred years before one of them connects Fayoum and Cairo. Until then, I'll be buying vegetables half-cooked in transit while the wealthy…" Salma knew he was thinking of her family, as he seemed to appraise her. "They'll be buying plastic-wrapped cabbage from Holland."

"I thought I was the cynical one." Salma ignored the strained reference to her social status. Murad couldn't get past his anguish. She stuck her fists between her knees and focused her eyes on the paved road into

Aswan. How to tell him about the suspicious dot? "I'm afraid," she said. Once she admitted her fear, she couldn't keep her voice from trembling. Nor her hands. Her body tightened; her elbows pressed into her sides. Murad snapped his head around to search her face.

"You don't think I'm going to…?"

"Not afraid of you. I think someone's been following us. I thought I saw something before the sandstorm hit. It was far away but it's . . ." Salma checked her side mirror again. Whoever was tailing their car had closed the distance between them.

"The black car behind us?" A fierce glance at the rearview mirror didn't satisfy him. His neck sinews were taut when he threw his right arm across the top of Salma's seat and turned to look over his shoulder. "Damn. Why didn't you say something sooner?" He turned to ask his mother. "*Amah*, do you recognize the black car behind us?"

Swiveling around on the back seat, Aisha kneeled to stare out the window. "I'm not sure, son. My eyes are old. But I think it's one of your friends from the Taj."

"Someone in the village betrayed us." Murad kept his eyes on the road ahead. His body was rigid, his face grim and Salma sensed the tension in his jaws. Beneath his strange silence, she sensed fear that set her own heart hammering in her chest.

"The only chance we have of shaking off those dogs is in Aswan—in downtown. Once in the open desert, it will be too late."

They entered the city, and drove south along the river's west shore, past silver-studded, horse-drawn surreys lined up for tourists from the Sofitel hotel across the street. With an eye continuously checking the rearview mirror, Murad fought his way down a congested side street towards the outskirts of the *souk*, where teenage boys were kicking a scratched-up soccer ball back and forth between parked cars. The brown-spotted dog near them was devouring the contents of a bag of trash that had split open.

The *souk* itself was in full afternoon swing. The air thick with the din of vendors—men and women's voices each louder than the other— hawking everything from shaving cream and cigarettes to hand-tinted photographs of the *rayyis* and paperback copies of the Quran. Several boys dropped out of their soccer game to hold beaded keychains and necklaces to the car's windows hoping for a sale.

Salma shuddered. The black car was still visible in her side mirror. "Can we get away?" she asked, trying to contain the tremor in her voice.

"Don't worry. I know this city like the palm of my hand. Especially the downtown where my uncle lives. We'll lose them there."

Salma pressed her fingers into the ridge of bone above her eyes where a headache stirred. Fear lodged itself in her gut like a splinter as she watched Murad bite his lower lip and sweep a hand across his sweat covered brow. The area of redness around his eyes was due to more than the strain of driving. The black car had frightened him, too.

They circled three downtown roundabouts with white painted curbs before he rammed the car through a crowded intersection and into Aswan's downtown. With a hand on the steering wheel and a hand on the horn, he squeezed between a truck and bus. Other horns honked, brakes screeched, tires squealed, and several cars piled up against each other. Murad gunned the engine. Finally, they were through the downtown, through the city's outskirts, out in the open desert. They'd lost the black car. Salma gave Murad an energetic "thumbs up" and felt the heat of a blush when he responded with a victorious smile.

A mile towards the hills, the desert spread to the horizon in every direction—more monochromatic beige, on beige, on beige. It took Salma a few minutes to sort out the gradations within the narrow color range and isolate a strip of a slightly darker tone.

"There," she called out, triumphant. "A track."

Murad followed the track likely worn by smugglers crossing back and forth from Sudan, until the floor of what had been once a shallow lake became hardened gravel. He kept his hands on the steering wheel to steady the vehicle and pointed with his chin to a jagged line of limestone hills. "We're headed to that ridge."

The hills appeared to float on heat waves ascending from their base. Had Salma not encountered mirages before she would have sworn that beyond the small herd of wild camels weaving in and out of the yellow haze in front of them, a swath of water was gathered at the feet of the limestone hills.

A strong wind that seemed to come out of nowhere blasted a giant sand drift across their path and Murad had driven into it before he could stop. He gunned the motor. The engine groaned. The wheels spun in place. He floored the pedal. The tires shrieked but the car didn't budge. "*Khara!*" he cursed, jerking open his door and jumping out to get a shovel from the trunk. Salma couldn't help clear sand from under the wheels but she let air out of the tires and handed Murad the tools he needed to jack up the vehicle. They stayed stuck.

"I'm certain we can manage this," she said, encompassing the terrain with a sweep of her arm. "We'll gather rocks. Your mom can help." It took Murad and his mother two hours to pile rocks in front of the tires, with Salma only able to kick a few of the smaller ones into place.

"You drive. I'll handle the rocks that slip," Murad told her when they'd successfully positioned them. Salma felt a flutter in her chest as she got behind the wheel. No more hierarchy here. They were in it together. She turned the key and hit the gas pedal. The back end of the Jeep shimmied; the tires tried to grip. She hit the pedal, again. On the third attempt, they gained traction. The car jerked forward and broke loose in a cloud of burning rubber.

Once the sand released the car's tires, Murad took the wheel to creep up one from the line of limestone hill that rose seemingly straight up. Soon, they entered a defile where the track they drove on became a ledge along which they were forced to a crawl. The passenger side of the car where Salma was sitting balanced on the lip of a precipitous ravine. Aisha huddled as far into the corner of the back seat as she could. Salma peered down at the abyss once and then quickly squeezed her eyes shut. She felt it drawing her in and hung on to her seat. With an irrational fear of falling, she kept them shut until the car regained its normal speed.

It was evening when they stopped. They had set out before dawn. Still clutching the steering wheel, Murad rested his head on his white-knuckled hands. "*Al hamdu lillah*," he praised the Lord for his protection and let out a long breath.

"You were terrific," Salma said, wishing she could run her hand along his back—knowing she shouldn't, so didn't.

"It didn't seem as perilous when my cousins and I were kids. We discovered many caves when we were exploring around here." Salma had no experience with which to compare how Murad and his cousins played. She'd lived in a world so different from theirs.

They gathered on the ledge looking to Murad for directions. He stepped up to a gap in the cliff and shot his keychain flashlight into the opening. Suddenly, disturbed, disoriented, a colony of bats flooded out with a loud swoosh. Salma pivoted and almost tripped. The ledge was covered with jagged rock, coated with sand, hard to detect in the hillside's shadow. This was too much. She'd become a bungling idiot who couldn't keep her balance half as well as a woman more than twice her age.

"Grab only what you can easily carry," Murad told her, stacking the heavier items together: a box-full of cell phones, an extra-large battery, two crates of gallon-sized water bottles. "I'm going to bury the car at the bottom of the hill. I'll bring these in when I get back."

Still unnerved by the ride, Aisha seemed to be drifting; yet she brought in cotton pallets, a Primus burner, and several bags of groceries, insisting Salma only unload the Mylar heat blankets and pillows. Once they'd unloaded the necessities, Aisha filled a Coke can with kerosene, soaked a wick of braided cord in that and lit it. Then she dragged an abandoned plank across the cave floor to clear the center space of its bat droppings. The acid stench worsened before it diminished so Salma could finally take her hand off her mouth and nose.

The wick's flame didn't spread light far, but she saw enough to determine the cave was spacious—at least fifty square feet of it serviceable space. But cold. She helped build a meager fire and unpacked the staples: flatbread, lentils, rice, garlic, onions, dried fava beans, and stuff to cook them in. Bouillon cubes wrapped in gold tinsel, five cans of tomato paste, canola oil, salt, pepper, and cumin in brown paper packets. Apparently, Murad planned for them to hide here for several days. The tea, sugar, and metal teapot, she set by the Primus burner—an appliance, if you could call it one—long retired from urban life. Aisha pumped its tank and lit the cooking ring then filled an aluminum pot from a bottle of water Murad had left at the mouth of the cave.

"You look exhausted, Om Mohammed," Salma said, aching with fatigue. "Please let me cook."

"Do you make *adz* in your country?" What part of the query was Salma supposed to reply to? Your country? Or did she cook lentils?

"I prepare it for my girls. They love it."

"You have daughters? God preserve them. No sons?" Salma poured three handfuls of lentils into the pot without answering. Patriarchy would be rooted in this country forever. Enough, she scolded herself. There was a woman's work to be done right now: dicing onions and garlic and setting out cumin to add to the lentils. She'd show Aisha she could cook peasant style as well as anyone else.

"My daughters, Hoda and Nawal, watch cooking programs on television," she said. "They're becoming good cooks." Salma loved cooking with her older daughter who approached recipes as guidelines and never used measuring cups. Sharing the kitchen with Hoda was more of a challenge. She deliberated, calculated, and weighed even a carrot before she chopped it. They seldom cooked together because she couldn't tolerate Salma's culinary nonchalance.

Hoping Aisha, who was hovering over her as she cooked, wasn't like Hoda, she braced herself for the criticism that never came. Instead, Aisha said, "To feed her family, to feed their friends and neighbors, is the most important thing a woman can do." The statement made Salma switch gears. Feminist rhetoric be damned, she loved to cook for people—family, friends, strangers—to care for them.

After laying out three sleeping palettes, Aisha balanced a pot of water for tea on three rocks surrounding the open flame and squatted on the ground waiting for the water to boil. Salma sat cross-legged watching the smoke rise to the ceiling, adding soot to the black deposits left by previous sojourners. Christians escaping Roman persecutors, shepherds with their goats huddled around them, Bedouins on their trade routes, their camels tethered outside. Soot like this connected the centuries. Aisha interrupted Salma's musings with a welcome glass of tea that dragged her into the present where she was hunkered on a rock in a cave, hiding from killers. Trying to bring a sudden tremor in her voice under control, she raised her head to look Aisha in the face.

"I'm afraid the men from the village, the ones from the Taj, will find me. Torture me. Maybe kill me." Salma's mouth was dry, her eyes burned.

"I'm praying God protects you, my child," Aisha said without moving her attention from stirring a mound of sugar into her glass of tea.

"I have never done anything to harm them. Three days ago, I didn't even know Taj al Islam existed."

"But your father harmed the head of the Taj, badly. Sheikh Nabulsi hates him."

"Why? My father is not an evil man."

"He gave Mubarak's soldiers permission to torture the sheikh, over and over, again. Many more times than usual." Salma figured the woman didn't understand the military chain of command.

"You're wrong, Om Mohamed," she protested while yet feeling disquieted and disturbed. "My father's a doctor. He can't give orders to soldiers. He doesn't have the authority."

"You are the one who is wrong, my child. Your father has medical authority, and the legal and moral duty to prevent soldiers from torturing men like my husband to death; may the good man rest in peace." In her upset, Aisha had run out of breath. She stopped and gathered her strength to continue. "Your father signs false papers. Papers that are false medical assurance that soldiers can keep torturing men after they are already almost dead. Then he signs false official reports for victims who die anyway so the government can say they died of suicide or heart failure." Aisha's words landed between Salma's eyes like rocks from a slingshot. Her eyes narrowed, her brow contorted, and her temples throbbed, as though about to burst.

"I can't believe he did that. Even if he had, what about all the other people—from the president down? Egypt tortures people all the time. Why is the sheikh fixated on my father?" It felt as though a lump of brimstone was clogging her throat.

"It is personal, child." Aisha looked away from Salma then, silently, looked down at the ground. When she spoke again, her voice was hoarse with unshed tears. "Sheikh Nabulsi told me how your father gloated. How he smiled like a snake as the soldiers electrocuted and waterboarded him before they broke his bones. Humiliation on top of humiliation is not good for a man like Nabulsi. He remembers it with every limp."

"He personally told you my father did all that?"

"Yes," Aisha said, at this point recovered enough to raise the glass to her mouth for a defiant sip of tea.

"When?" Leaning slightly forward from where she sat on the rock, Salma reached to the ground near her feet for her own glass of tea.

"When? I'm not sure. I only know the first time he told me about being tortured was not long after Murad went to America. Eight? Maybe, nine years ago."

"Sounds like he told you more than once." Salma wondered if Aisha had known Nabulsi well enough to be talking frequently.

"It came up in our conversations."

"You talked together a lot?" Apparently, they had. How close had the two been?

"Remember what I told you, the day before yesterday when we got to the clinic?"

"You said he helped you." Salma shuddered inwardly at the duplicity of the man.

"Yes. The sheikh and my husband were in the same cell in the Mu'taqa-llat. My husband knew he would not survive so before the soldiers tortured him to death, he put me and my children in the hands of the sheikh." Salma was so irrationally annoyed at the woman for lifting the cover of the pot to check the lentils and giving them a stir that she barely listened until Aisha said, "The sheikh was good to us. We needed nothing. And he cared." The woman seemed to drift off somewhere for a moment before she continued. "After Murad left, I was alone in Minya and the sheikh needed the comfort of a woman he could trust after his wife died. It was a sad time. She'd miscarried the only child she had borne." The look she gave Salma was clearly meant to ward off the objection another woman might have expressed. "The man is only human, my child. I cooked a good lunch on Fridays when he came after the noontime prayers. He loved the food I served, and he honored me with..." Aisha stared into space, smiling a smile full of things restrained.

"He came to lunch alone, Om Mohamed?" What in the world was Murad's mother doing cooking for the man who wanted to have her son killed?

"Of course, not. A man and woman alone? That is not in our ways. He brought his sister's daughter, a quiet ten-year old girl who liked more interesting things to do than listen to grown people talk after lunch. So, I kept toys and books for her in Murad's old bedroom and she had her own special time and her own special place."

"That was kind and thoughtful," Salma said, with an artificial smile, wondering if, for once in her life, Aisha had also thought of having her own special time and place.

"She was only able to enjoy it for a year because the sheikh moved to Cairo. After that, I moved back to the village."

"That would be when he started Taj al Islam." Salma held back her sense of Aisha's loss.

"I don't know about these things, my daughter. I moved back to Sidi Osman," Aisha said, reaching for another teabag. "But why am I talking about the past when I'm worried about the present? Murad's been gone too long."

Salma was worried, too, and troubled by the black car. The vantage point from the cave's ledge was limited but she had to look for it. What if the Taj found the cave? She struggled to her feet, bracing her ribs whose injury the trip had aggravated.

As soon as she stepped out onto the ledge she leaped back, startled at a sudden, deep, and rapid *whirr-whirr* in the air. Her heart started thumping so hard it reverberated through her body. But it was only a large grey dove that exploded from behind a rock. Flexing her shoulders, Salma stretched her arms above her head until the pounding steadied, and she caught her breath.

Outside, the air was as dry as the hard ground she stood on. The sun, though still far from setting, had sunk fully behind the high desert dunes to the west. She stared towards the horizon as far as she could see and divided the terrain from the ledge to the river into visual sections. She searched each, one after the other, for a trace of the suspicious vehicle. Nothing. Surely, Murad had brought a pair of binoculars, she thought, turning to return to the cave. She'd scarcely taken a step when an unfamiliar metallic sound thrummed overhead. She shaded her eyes with her hand and squinted as she looked up. Three helicopters were circling, their blades churning the air. While she knew they were too far away to detect her, she crouched behind a boulder nonetheless with something like a scream that wanted to escape thumping in her chest.

Damn it. The Taj had followed them with a car, the government was hunting them with helicopters. A bullet of sweat ran down her spine. A swell of uneasiness made its way through the length of her body as she considered her predicament. She didn't want Nabulsi or her father to find her until she knew Murad would be safe from both.

Chapter 9

October 2, 2014
11:00 am

THE MORNING AFTER HIS VISIT TO GABBER, Paul phoned Colonel Rashid. Salma had been missing for two nights and a day, yet no one had claimed responsibility or made any demands. He'd also called his Egyptian contacts: correspondents, labor unionists, human rights activists. A few had heard of the Taj, but none could suggest a go-between for him. His sole hope was that bribing Gabber with securing an apartment for him and his family had convinced the man to turn up at noon today.

At eleven o'clock, Paul grabbed a taxi to Tahrir Square from where the cab driver swung onto Bab el Luk Street and dropped him off in the alley near Gabber's shop. Gabber was ready. In orange flip-flops, he shuffled across the concrete floor, to the old safe where he kept the shoes he wore in the 'good' part of town on its newspaper-covered top. It was also where Paul had stashed what the Mossad described as Nabulsi's personal disk; the one someone gave Abu Taleb in Yemen.

"Your secret is safe here, sir," Gabber said, slipping his flip-flops into a plastic bag and dusting off his shoes with a shirtsleeve. Likely several members of Gabber's household shared this one pair of shoes. After peering at their worn soles for a moment, he frowned, and put them on without socks. The skin around his ankles was the color of ash and the length the man was going to in order to save face, embarrassed Paul.

"We will go to Imbaba, Hays *bey*. We will meet a man I used to know," Gabber said, morosely. "That is all I can do, sir."

The two men crammed into a microbus, replete with the odor of sweat and cologne, that went down Talaat Harb Street and stopped near the Prince Restaurant. When they got off, Gabber tied the laces of his shoes together, draped them over his shoulder and replaced them with his flip-flops; he was no longer in the "good" part of town. Together they walked around the corner where the rich odor of grilled liver and vegetable tajines hung over the restaurant's outdoor tables.

Within less than a quarter mile, Talaat Harb Street devolved into the Imbaba slum—a concentration of despair spreading off the main thoroughfare like a fungus. A section of town the police avoided; an infinite maze of dirt alleys Paul would never have entered on his own. He was familiar with the district's statistics. Over two million people, an average of nine to a room, packed into tottering, mud walled, tenements controlled by drug dealers, militant Islamists, and *bultageya*—street thugs. A disgrace of a neighborhood, parts of it not ever mapped. Tangled webs of illegal electrical wires blocked its sky and the air smelled of sewage. Its pathways, too narrow for cars, were littered with plastic bottles, ripped paper, and cigarette butts floating in shallow pools of filthy water.

Two donkey-drawn rubbish carts emerged out of nowhere and three-wheeled, surrey-like, motorized *tuk-tuks* lurched around each other. Life-blood of the constipated alleys, the motorcycle rickshaws competed in blasting a cacophony of music that threatened to burst Paul's eardrums. An obese man stuffed into a green and yellow one was in peril of spilling out of its seat. Ceramic aquamarine hands of Fatima clinked on the purple top of one sloshing through muddy sewage that splattered Paul's pants.

Several elderly women squatted on the stairs, their skirts bunched between their thighs, peeling vegetables while their faded wash flapped on clotheslines overhead. Two women in black stepped from a nearby doorway and into the street with large cans of water on their heads. Goats stepped through trash to keep pace with Paul and chickens scurried at his ankles. He doubted Imbaba had ever known asphalt.

He and Gabber cut across an alley to a stall-lined one where men sold women's bras and panties dangling from hooks—an occupation that seemed incongruous in this conservative country. They passed a Voda-phone shop, a *fuul* and falafel place and yet another stall with fake leather bags. Finally, in a passage too tight for even tuk-tuks to navigate, Gabber stopped and took hold of Paul's arm.

"My friend knows the men you want, sir. One of them will meet you at his shop on the corner," he said, pointing to a cookware stall. "I'm leaving now, Hays bey. My neighbor will walk back to the main street with you. Please take care. It is dangerous to go alone." So, on the way to Gabber's friend, Paul checked each stall he passed while women and children glared at him, and men avoided his eyes. He knew he wasn't welcome in Imbaba without a local resident to vouchsafe his presence but he didn't know what kind of menace he was headed to.

Stacked five and six feet high, two columns of precariously balanced polished aluminum pots, flanked the front of the cookware stall like sentinels. Searching for its owner, Paul started to step between them. Something moved behind him. Flinging out his arms, he whirled to confront the sound. The pots rocked in place. Tumbled. Crashed to the ground. And a slender teenage girl said, "*Al salaamu aleikum,* sir. My brother, Amin, sent me with a message for you." Although she wore no makeup, the girl's face was strikingly attractive. A light-blue headscarf fell over her shoulders, and down arms. "He will meet you tonight," she added in English as flawless as her complexion. "Be at Groppi's cafe at ten but you must go alone, sir." Paul wondered how he ended up receiving a Taj message from a soft-spoken girl who addressed him as sir. Scarcely what he expected from his first contact with Nabulsi's people.

"I'll be there." Paul kept his answer short and stern and, equally efficiently, the girl turned to leave. A pair of red Nikes and peg-legged jeans peeked from the bottom of her ankle length skirt.

"Where's Salma? Why did you take her?" he asked, reaching out to grab her arm. The girl immediately placed her hand over her heart in a well-known signal that a man not touch her. Paul's shoulders tightened as he pulled away.

"All I know is that she's safe, sir," the girl reassured him.

"Why should I believe you?" She hadn't even brought proof that the Taj had Salma.

"I am a good Muslim." The statement seemed to encompass everything and, in its own way, made sense.

"At least tell me if you've seen her," he asked, agitated to the point of fretfulness.

"I take her to the toilet, sir," the girl said and left.

Pounding one fisted hand into the palm of the other, Paul stood outside the stall. He didn't know what he was waiting for until a man came out of its dark interior.

"You are Mr. Hays?" he asked, in a tone of voice that did not expect an answer. "I am Gabber's neighbor. Please. We go now." With that the man led Paul past buildings so deteriorated only twisted webs of electrical cables and leaking water pipes prevented their collapse. Then, at the point where the slums spilled them out onto Talat Harb Street, Gabber's neighbor abruptly turned and left.

It was four in the afternoon and Paul had eaten neither breakfast nor lunch. He made his way to the Prince Restaurant where in spite of the last two hours making him feel queasy, the odor of grilling meat sweetening the air made him ravenous. After the waiter took his order, Paul sat on an outdoor bench staring into space, organizing his thoughts. First, he couldn't attend to *Harper's* assignment until Salma was safely back to him. Second, while he hadn't experienced her father's duplicity himself, he knew enough about the man not to trust him. Third, he couldn't trust Nabulsi either, but at least with him matters were clear. The sheikh wanted Hani Hamdi, but he wanted the disk more. In fact, he wanted it badly enough to have Paul killed. Was a simple exchange possible? Could he negotiate Salma's freedom for the disk when he met the high-level Taj member tonight? The girl had been clear, he was to go to Groppi's patisserie alone, but he wasn't stupid. He needed protection and Rashid could arrange that. Paul had better be able to trust him.

Leaning back in his metal chair, he tried to summon the waiter standing with several men gathered around an indoor radio. Paul recognized the word "Sinai," but was too far away to hear anything else so he slouched back and just waited for his tajine of oily lamb shanks with okra and onions.

Before he'd had a chance to drain his last glass of sweetened black tea, Colonel Rashid returned his call, proposing they meet later that afternoon. Paul had not yet established where he stood in relation to the man who seemed to genuinely care about the Hamdi's, but he couldn't help wondering if Rashid's concern for Salma wasn't more personal. Be that as it may, he was happy to defer to the colonel's proposal: a show of power before negotiation. To that end, Rashid would position a squad of undercover men at the Groppi patisserie cafe to protect him and capture the Taj representative.

That night, too restless to wait for ten o'clock to meet the young girl's brother, Paul joined the pulsing mass of shoppers on the other end of Talaat Harb Street from where he'd been only a few hours earlier. The restaurant on the border of the Imbaba slums was five miles from here. Two places to eat on the same street, two worlds apart.

The Egyptian street had never been a simple thoroughfare for commerce and dwelling, it was better an extremist form of theater. Different music blared at top volume from every store, a hodge-podge of Fairouz songs in a post-modern mélange of American pop. Clusters of people strolled, chatted, and laughed in the neon-lit night. They paused before store windows to ogle flashy cell phones, gaudy high-heeled shoes, and lacy underwear. Again, a male shopkeeper hawking bras and panties from his cart and, in the very middle of the sidewalk, a man spinning a barrel of hot sugar into pink cotton candy.

Paul glanced up and down the pavement trying to spot any of Rashid's men. No one stood out. That could be good, they were well hidden; or bad, Rashid had gone back on his word. Hoping he could depend on the first option he snaked his way through the folks milling on the sidewalk, spilling into the street.

A family of five on a motor scooter made its way around pedestrians without losing speed. It's three-year-old perched on the handlebar, an infant tucked between its father's back and mother's belly, and a six-year-old clinging to the family huddle. Not one helmet. Paul turtled his head into his shoulders. This sort of fatalism could be fatal. So, could meeting Amin.

As he neared Groppi's, Paul's pulse started galloping, he couldn't seem to draw enough air into his lungs. Beads of perspiration dribbled down his ribs when he stepped between the marble pillars supporting its portico. The once pompous corner establishment faced the statue of Talaat Harb, founder of Egypt's National Bank, in the square named after him. Appropriate. Groppi's was where Harb, King Farouk, and the *ancient regime's* principal players met in the golden days of Cairo's downtown.

But Paul didn't notice the lapis lazuli blue tile of the entrance or its flower mosaics. The yellow glass Art Deco door he would normally have appreciated, barely registered on him. He drew a quick breath, prayed Rashid's men were alert and shoved the door open with hands slippery with sweat.

The large dining area was run down, its marble floor dull and cracked. Its mirrored walls so marred they'd long ceased reflecting the display cabinets across from them. A man he assumed was the young girl's uncle, the negotiator from Taj al Islam, sat in the far corner at a table facing the exit. Paul heard footsteps scrape across the marble behind him. A group of young men had followed him in.

He scoured the place for signs of the soldiers Rashid had promised, his eyes settling on an elderly waiter in a black jacket worn slick with age. No hint of salvation. There was nothing to register but the man's disheveled mustache and blank visage. Paul should never have agreed to meet the Taj here or anywhere, alone, and unarmed. He shouldn't have trusted Rashid. It was stupid. Dangerous. The guy had as much motive to eliminate Paul as to extricate him from an ambush.

He headed back to the entrance that Amin's men immediately blocked. He turned back. He had to stay calm. He had to look cool. Circling back to the display case with its selection of stale pastries, he ordered a cup of Turkish coffee from a short tight-lipped fellow with close-set eyes. Paul wondered if he'd imagined a silent nod of acknowledgment from the man. He leaned across the counter hoping he'd catch a glimpse of the soldiers that were supposed to protect him. No sign. Finally, with deliberate steps, his look unflappable, he approached the man at the corner table—the one the messenger girl referred to as her uncle, Amin.

Paul's brain stuttered for a moment; went into a sort of emergency shut down, every part of him on pause while his thoughts caught up. An image bounced around inside his skull. This was the man on the cruise boat who'd tried to kill him. He could almost see the Glock in his hand, right now. Paul's insides contracted and turned cold.

"I'm going to the toilet before I sit down," Paul said, transforming his choking into a cough and setting down his *demi-tasse* on the table across from Amin. "Watch my coffee while I'm gone." The small attempt to gain an increase in his psychological advantage worked. Amin lifted himself a few inches off his chair and looked confused.

Paul took his time finding the toilet, an excuse for more stealthy searches for the soldiers Rashid had promised. No matter how diligently he checked the corridor, he found no sign they were or had ever been there. A sensation of utter despair overcame him, rising from his legs like paralysis. He leaned against the toilet door willing himself to muster the strength he needed to return to the dining hall.

The vigor Paul had always depended on returned to his legs and his steps were forceful as he neared Amin's table. He wished he felt as strong inside, but he could feel his heart thudding against his ribs as he coughed again to clear his throat.

"I will not discuss anything with you until I have proof you have Salma. I must know she is well. All I want is to have her back with her family." He didn't know how much this man knew about Paul's relationship to her—the Taj seemed to know everything—but he wasn't going to give him more ammunition.

"That will cost them."

"How much? I'm sure Dr. Hamdi would pay."

"We don't want money, Mr. Hays. We want him." Amin's Adam's apple bobbed up and down as he spoke. "And it is not only about Hani Hamdi; it is also about you."

"What in heaven's name do you want from me?"

Ignoring Paul's question, Amin continued, "We have many sources, of low and high rank, in the police department. One recently advised us you took an article belonging to Mr. Abu Taleb. That is what we want from you."

"The policeman was a thief,"

"They all are," Amin said, and Paul had to agree. He sipped the last drop of his strong, bitter, coffee, leaving a half inch of its ultra-fine grounds on the bottom.

"He was stealing a cigarette case, a present from me to the editor." Keeping his eyes on a crescent-shaped scar on Amin's chin, he moved his cup aside and swept his hand over the worn linen tablecloth.

"We don't care about the case. You can keep it. We want the flash drive. We have reason to believe it contains confidential information."

"What makes you think that?" Paul asked, feigning a *pro forma* ignorance he knew Amin wouldn't believe.

"We suspect your friend got his hands on the disk during his visit to Yemen."

"Stealing a disk isn't the type of thing Abu Taleb would do."

"He didn't steal it, Mr. Hays. He certainly wouldn't have wanted it. It was slipped into his pocket by a traitor to the Taj. Abu Taleb didn't know he had it until he was back home." Amin's explanation rang true. "You are close to Dr. Hamdi and Colonel Rashid." The man didn't even wait for Paul's response before he added, "Did you tell them you had the disk?"

"You mean the cigarette case? Why would I do that? It's a private matter."

"Do not withhold information. It will do you no good. We know your friend had the disk that belongs to us. We heard the two of you arrange to meet so he could give it to you. It is not difficult to conclude the disk was in your cigarette case." Paul wasn't going to succeed in keeping up this charade much longer. The Taj had tapped his phone call to Abu Taleb and came to a logical conclusion. He found himself drawing back in his chair as Amin leaned forward. "Did you tell the Mossad?" Amin spat out the last word like venom.

"I did not tell anyone anything. There was no reason to do so." Paul gave each word equal emphasis. "Besides, how do I know you have Salma? How do I know she's alive?" he asked, recognizing he had tacitly admitted having the damn disk.

"Here's her bag." Amin set Salma's evening bag on the table in front of Paul. Its strap was missing, its clasp awry and someone had slashed through its beaded fabric. Paul wrapped his hands around it and felt an intense spasm of anguish.

"This is garbage," he said, forcing his voice not to break. "It tells me nothing. Worse. It tells me how violent you were with her."

"At this moment, the woman is still unharmed," Amin said.

"Just Skype her on your cell phone to assure me of that. When we know Salma will be home safe, we work out an exchange."

Amin didn't answer him but, suddenly, reached under the table. Paul jerked to the side. "Not a pistol, Mr. Hays. A detector kit," he said with a smirk, drawing out a device that looked like a laptop.

"Glad to oblige." The U.S. State Department had given Paul several polygraph tests when he'd investigated matters involving state security. Test results were not always conclusive. A trained person could get away with lies. But he wouldn't be lying. He hadn't told anyone but Salma about the disk.

Amin attached the suction pads of six sensor wires that trailed out of his equipment to Paul's forearms and fingers with purple gel. The man was a professional. Asked baseline questions: name, age, occupation, marital status. He looked up to study his face when Paul's he responded, "single," to the last one. Then he asked what Paul had gotten from Abu Taleb.

"A scan disk. Locked in a safe."

"Have you identified its contents?" Amin stared at him.

"No. But I have reason to believe that in certain hands it will destroy the Taj." Amin examined his lie detector screen and scowled. Paul knew his response would register as true. He didn't need to volunteer he received the information from an agent of the Mossad.

"Has anybody else seen it?

"No."

"Are you sure?"

"You have the answer on your screen. No one has seen the information. We're done."

Paul yanked off the sensors and reeled around, prepared for Amin's thugs to jump him. All five drew pistols. He knew they wouldn't shoot. They needed him alive. Needed Abu Taleb's disk. Still, they could torture him for the information and then execute him.

As if demonstrating the point, one of Amin's thugs slammed a knee-buckling jab to Paul's chest followed by a brutal blow to his back when he doubled over. A hot shower of pain ran from his scalp to his jaw, but he managed not to fall. That didn't last. The man grappled for his waist and crashed them both to the marble-tiled floor. The thud emptied Paul's lungs. Retching from the effort to breathe, he got to his knees. That didn't last. Two men pinned his arms behind his back and dropped on top of him. Bones collided with bones. Lights danced at the margin of his vision.

Rashid had betrayed him. He'd walked into an ambush. There were no soldiers. He'd relied on a man he'd met only twice and likely alienated the first time he did so. Rescuing Salma, the goal they shared, hadn't been reason enough for Rashid to protect him. Paul's stomach seemed to have turned to granite and time seemed to have stopped.

A rattling roar. The place rang with bullets. One struck a display case, leaving a six-point star hole in its glass. Another ricocheted off a pillar. The mirrored wall crackled, shattered into shards. They cascaded to the floor like a waterfall. Paul's ears felt they might burst. Voices were muffled. Something wet and warm clung to his cheek. It hardly mattered. Amin and his five men had gone down before the last shard struck the ground and a platoon of soldiers was in control. Rashid had Paul's back after all.

Two soldiers had already handcuffed Amin, leaving him to soak in a dark pool of his own blood. One pulled Paul to his feet, but he had to grasp the back of a chair when the room spun in place. Struggling to bring the spinning walls to a stop, he took in a lungful of air in time to see an officer talk into a shoulder mic. Suddenly, the six soldiers snapped to attention as one, clicked their heels in unison and saluted.

"Who thinks he's the boss here?" Rashid bellowed striding through Groppi's glass door. Tonight, his voice was guttural and deep, one of those voices that gave orders and demanded obedience. Paul pointed to Amin. The man's face was death-white, his mouth like a ghastly knife gash stretched in pain. Blood spurted from his upper thigh where a bullet had severed an artery. Rashid called for a cord, twisted it above the gush of pulsing blood. "You have a choice," he told him, his fingers clamped on the taut sash, "tell me where Salma is, or I let go of the tourniquet. You'll die in three minutes."

"I don't know where the woman is," Amin responded, weakened by the loss of blood.

"Then you are no use to us." Rashid began to loosen his grip.

"Call an ambulance," Amin pleaded. "I'll tell you."

"Call one." Rashid nodded to a soldier then shifted his attention back to Amin. "Where is Salma Hamdi?" he insisted, and Paul bent down to hear Amin's reply.

"Murad Ragab has her," the fading man breathed out the words "We're searching for him," he said and passed out.

Paul's shock was too great to absorb. Beset with thoughts he recognized as beneath him, he staggered to preserve his balance. Why was Salma with this guy? Was he forcing himself on her? Was she in love with him again? An image of them together flashed in his mind as he pushed past Rashid's soldiers and into the night.

Chapter 10

October 2, 2014
11:30 pm

PAUL STAGGERED INTO THE STREET WITH ITS CROWDS, its traffic, and the garish light of its store windows. Exhausted, used up; running on adrenaline, he lurched into people like a drunk. Salma was with Murad. What hold did the man have over her? Were they embracing, kissing…? He shook his head to block the lurid images of the two together, but they would not dislodge.

He hailed a passing taxi to Zamalek's Al-Jazeera Street canopied by flamboyant trees and had the driver stop at the intersection so he could walk two blocks to Hag Tarek's apartment. Red, green, and blue electric bulbs, their current "borrowed" from the streetlamps, stretched across the façades of the building. The *bawab* waved a warning. Too late. Even as he reached the front door, Paul's body went scraping across the pavement and crashed to a stop. His lungs emptied of air. Blood spewed from his nose in spurts and dripped down his jaw. He fell through time, through space. Struggled not to pass out. Who was trying to kill him? A dozen people rushed to his side. A man yelled, "The bastard on the motorcycle ran right into him. Stop the son of a bitch." Someone hollered, "Get out of the way," and strong, capable arms lifted Paul before he lost consciousness.

He came to on the Hag's sofa, its pillow soaked with blood. His brain fixated on an irrelevant detail: the first five buttons of the Hag's gallabiyah were unbuttoned and wolf-gray hairs on his chest had emerged unbound. Paul rubbed his face and groaned.

"Someone ran a motorcycle into me."

"Yes." The Hag stopped chewing his lower lip. "The *bawab* has seen the two men on the cycle before. *Bultageya.* Why would someone order thugs to attack you, Mr. Hays?"

Good question. It wasn't Rashid. If he'd wanted Paul dead, he could have had him killed at Groppi's. Hani? Perhaps. Occupied, distraught, the last thing Salma's father needed now was a journalist nosing around the acquisition of military arms. Nabulsi? More likely. He'd never let the men who'd been downed at Groppi's go unavenged, but he'd never get the disk if Paul were killed. Shivers rippled through his body. This had been a warning.

The Hag observed him from the foot of the couch. "You must remain still until the doctor comes," he said in a soft but firm voice, passing black and silver prayer beads through his fingers. "My wife is preparing mint tea."

Wishing they'd offered him a mug of strong coffee to give him the energy to sort out the new danger, Paul dozed off. He dissolved into a dream of Salma. He was waking up in her loft-bed staring up at redwood trees being fondled by the morning sun. They were both naked. She was leaning against the door jamb with a coffee cup in each hand, her body lushly Mediterranean. Her face glowed as she walked towards him, tripped on an errant shoe, dropped the cups, and burst into a frantic fit of tears. She collapsed on the carpet. Crawled on hands and knees, wailed, "Now, we'll never know our fate. There isn't any future."

He woke to the thumping of his heart. Still on the narrow sofa, now with a dreadful hollow feeling halfway down his chest.

"Please allow me to examine you," a white-gowned doctor said in a clipped British accent. "I need to rule out a serious concussion before I proceed." The dark-skinned man flashed a penlight into Paul's eyes, had him follow the arc his finger made, and palpated his scalp-wound. "I was told you were attacked. You are either extremely lucky, or you have an incredibly hard head. You only have a slight concussion, it's not problematic."

"I take it you studied in England," Paul said, with an anemic smile. "I didn't catch your name."

"Germany, too. My name is Nabil Girgis. George in English. I'm an Egyptian Christian, a Copt. Please remove your clothes."

Paul glanced at his gray-haired host, expecting the man to back away and allow him some privacy. No way. In Egypt, no one was left alone, even buck-naked. Noting his hesitation, the doctor asked for a bedsheet to hold up so Paul could disrobe.

"L-5. Pesky one," the doctor said as he pressed down on Paul's lower back. "Radiates nerve pain down the leg. Stay put for a day. Then see me for X-rays. I'll leave my card with Hag Tarek. A fine man. Good people. They'll take care of you."

Care for him they did. The *hagga* replaced the blood-stained throw with two flowered chenille blankets and a pillow while Paul limped the five steps to the chair by the Hag. A pain, like being seared by a welding-torch, shot from his lower back to mid-way down the outside of his right leg, just as the doctor had predicted.

Although it was after one in the morning, having prepared the makeshift bed, the Hagga left them to prepare tea. Paul was beyond tired. Almost killed at Groppi's. Almost killed on the street. He needed to regain control of his situation. A sweet, simple longing for Salma swept over him. Then it hit him, again. Willingly or not, she was with Murad. Tortured? Raped? Adored? He didn't think he could stand the answer to any of those questions.

He needed his phone. Without it, neither Salma nor her captors could reach him. And Rashid couldn't call with good news or bad news. Murad likely had demands of her father. Would he kill her if Hani didn't meet them? He only stopped chewing over the alternatives when the Hag handed him the phone that he'd asked him to retrieve from the back pocket of his pants and the charger from his overnight case in the bedroom.

Paul had rebooted his phone and was waiting for the Apple logo to fade when, without any warning, the floor suddenly sent shudders up his legs. The cup on the arm of his chair clinked in its saucer and the picture of the Ka'aba tilted, re-centered itself, and tilted again. Startled, he turned to the Hag for an explanation.

"*Zilzal,*" the Hag announced. Whatever it was, it was a few miles away. Two seconds later there was an explosion. There was no earthquake.

Another blast followed. Another rumble. The crack-crack of machine guns. Paul heard the all too familiar whirring, shrieking sound of bombs hurtling to the ground nearby. Less sanguine now, the older man tugged his wife to the floor as a bomb found a target closer to them and the apartment building trembled. How could a war break out with no warning?

Paul's mind needed a story to make sense of the rush of adrenaline through his body. He turned to the Hag and his wife.

"What's happening?"

"Maybe it is something related to the mosque in Sinai?" Paul remembered the man who'd left the Prince Restaurant yesterday. He could still see the disgust on his face at what he must have heard on the radio.

His phone had enough juice to access the internet where he pulled up the *Al Jazeera* news site. A post from Cairo: "Early report: Bombings in Egypt linked to Taj al Islam terrorists." Nabulsi and his Taj had declared war. That explained the *Hala Geem* emergency.

But neither the hag nor his wife had heard of the Taj and they stuck with their version of what was happening.

"You didn't hear about the trouble in Sinai?" the Hag asked. "Thirty gunmen trapped the worshipers in al-Radwa mosque yesterday. Killed three hundred and five people. Injured a thousand and fifty."

"Where is the al-Radwa mosque?"

"On the Sinai coast, on the way to el-Arish. There were thousands of Sufis, Muslims celebrating a religious occasion. Those wretched people. Completely peaceful. They do not believe in martyrdom. They only crave to be close to Allah while they are still alive on this earth." Paul knew how Muslim jihadis exploited the Sunni majority's animosity towards the Sufi sect. Sunni terrorists didn't mind blowing themselves up—taking whoever was around out with them. To perish as a martyr was a negligible price for a guaranteed seat in a heavenly afterlife.

But if bombs were exploding in Sinai, why were they dropping on Cairo? The ground shook again. The lights flickered but stayed on. "We need to find out what's happening," the hag said, ignoring the screaming and shrieking outside and turning on a small television behind a polished panel in the wooden armoire. "The government stations will have nothing. We will watch CNN International. Can you please to translate, Hays *bey*?"

The news was grim. In Alexandria, explosions reduced four-story apartments to cement blocks. With its powerful floodlights, a camera panned over walls rising from the rubble, up flights of stairs to rooms where only one wall had blown out. Beds, closets, furniture left in place like stage-sets. Through broken windows appearing on the television screen, Paul saw chair-legs, mirrors, tabletops, mattresses, and bricks.

"This appears to be a car bomb in the Sidi Bishr district." Paul translated a British journalist's breathless report. "The government is responding with tanks and water cannons. "Where are the ambulances?" the agitated reporter asked.

"The man is ignorant," the hag scoffed as bursts of detonations spaced apart continued in the distance. "No ambulances. People take care of each other. God is All Knowing and Merciful."

In Aswan, seven Nile cruise ships had exploded. The camera caught the roaring blaze against the night sky. "A group calling itself Taj el Islam is claiming credit for this massive destruction. There are reports of a full military attack across Sinai," the journalist continued. "And the entire peninsula continues to be closed to the press."

"The president lets no one in because he doesn't want the world to see how his government treats the Bedouin like rats," the hag said.

Paul had read the Amnesty International report of mass executions and razed villages. The people of Sinai were caught between the Egyptian army to its west, the Islamists in the middle, and Israeli forays over its eastern border.

As though reflecting his thoughts, the TV host shifted focus to the Ismailia Hospital. A female journalist was interviewing an elderly Bedouin woman huddled under a blanket in a dilapidated bed, who declined to give her name.

"Whichever side sees our names will kill us," she said. "The army is jailing and slaughtering our young. The terrorists hate us. The Christians hate us. They are as evil as each other. It is useless to talk about anything."

Paul could see why Aaron said Sinai would be another Afghanistan. Was Nabulsi behind this violent upheaval? Did this mean he'd forget about Salma and move on? Would he leave her to Murad until he settled the score with him, or pursue her to wreak revenge on her father? It didn't make a difference. Paul was going to save Salma, no matter what the sheikh had planned.

Part III

Government is an institution which prevents injustice other than such as it commits itself.

    —Ibn Khaldun, Prolegomena (Introduction)
      Arab sociologist historian, 1332–1406

Chapter 1

October 2, 2014
4:00 pm

THE LATE AFTERNOON SKY WAS A DEEP CONCENTRATED blue when Murad trudged back up the craggy face of the broad chasm into which he'd rolled the car. He'd been lucky. The car landed between two huge boulders so thoroughly smashed it looked like a chunk of red clay pinched by an enormous thumb and finger. His lungs rasped, he was panting, his shirtfront clung to his chest. He clasped his hands together above his head and arched his back. A vertiginous vista to his right greeted him: a monochromatic yellowish-whitish-brown expanse of sand between him and the distant Nile. Two distinct realms. In one, the hush flow of moist air over tall palm trees and green alfalfa; in the other, a barren desert, its fiercely whooshing wind and stinging sand. Like all who struggled to hold the desert at bay, it terrified him. Its rocks concealed sand vipers, venomous serpents with horny spines that protruded above each eye, and death-stalking scorpions like the one who'd poisoned Samira, his favorite cousin. It was best to stay close to his beloved river; especially in Aswan where half-submerged boulders humped like elephants ripped its waters white. In Upper Egypt, the Nile still roiled and roared with life. By the time it reached Cairo it was worn out, bored and dumpy and Murad had no truck with it.

Still near the rim of the chasm, he bent over, hands to knees until he recovered his breath. Then he scrambled to scuff away the tire marks and footprints that could betray them. When he finally headed back to the cave, Murad was satisfied they couldn't be discovered—at least not this way.

He strained his eyes to make out the plateau marking the hill he had to climb before the sun dipped behind it. Although bars of sunlight still blazed from the cliffs profiled in the distance, the evening was approaching, about to turn chilly. And the moon was new. It would not shed much light. When the inkiness of the night poured in, the landscape would look even more unfamiliar. Murad stopped on the dirt trail to take his bearings, hiking in the desert at night with no flashlight was dangerous. He heard the shrill bark of the yellow-furred foxes that came out when the sun went down. His skin prickled. Then he heard the telltale *whup-whup-whup* of a helicopter. The prickling got worse, like a swarm of locusts streaming over his body.

A shocking white light swept the terrain, bleaching it of all color. He froze against the bluff until the copter's red and white lights passed overhead. In Yemen, where there were helicopters there were drones, even when the dark made them invisible. Although he knew he wouldn't see them, he searched the sky anyway. How had the army discovered the general area of their hide-out? The military units Hani had sent were already closer than Murad had hoped.

He wasn't sure the man would really protect him. He didn't know if he could trust him, but he was sure of one thing: if the soldiers found Salma before Murad could make a deal with her father, he'd never get to make one. He'd be left to Nabulsi's mercy, of which there was none. The locusts were still creeping along Murad's skin; wasps were trapped in the veins of his forehead, buzzing and ready to sting.

Blinking away the dust on his eyelids, he struggled to go on. He licked his dry lips and swallowed to moisten his mouth. The helicopters must have scared off the desert's night animal. Murad was alone in the silent landscape that was absorbing even the crunch of his footsteps and the hiss of his ragged breath. Finally, he rounded the last rock-swell and could plant his feet on the ledge of their refuge and gave in to his exhaustion. He caught sight of Salma leaning nonchalant against the rock by the cave's entrance. Murad lost it.

"Damn it," he erupted as he neared her, his face and neck flushed and mottled.

"What's the matter?" she asked, both shocked and appalled.

"I'm breaking my back to protect you while you're going to get us killed." His blood boiled. A riptide of anger threatened to drag him into a deep sea of rage.

"What?" Salma asked, not grasping what he meant.

"Your body is sending heat waves to every drone in the sky."

"Your mother and I were worried," Salma said, calmly. "You were gone a long time."

"Go inside. You sound like a nagging housewife," Murad's sarcasm was magnified by the rawness of his nerves. Salma's eyes opened wide sheened with tears as she stared at him.

"The cave's full of smoke. My chest hurts. And I'm saving the inhalers for emergencies." She said, pulling back her shoulders, regaining her composure. But Murad's anger had already boiled over.

"You're nothing but trouble," he barked. "Why can't you manage your asthma, your ribs and whatever else is wrong with you, without doing us all in?"

"The ribs your friend cracked." Salma was snappish, accusatory.

"You'd be hanging from a ceiling hook right now if I hadn't rescued you from him."

"Hung from a ceiling hook by your people, don't forget."

Murad had never experienced Salma's rage before and had assumed she was always cold and silent when angry as she was in the States. He didn't know her eyes could be this hard, her mouth could be as thin as a cut. Shoving aside a rock, he spread his feet apart, shifted his weight onto his heels.

"*Ya* Allah, I wish we'd never met," he yelled, beating his thigh with his fist. "You shattered my heart. Now you're going to get me killed. You and your kind."

"What do you mean "your kind"?" This time, it was Salma who yelled.

"I always knew you were a rich woman, I didn't realize you were a spoiled brat." Murad's bitterness rose like bile into his mouth. "Women like you order men like me around. "Go hang up the wash. Come polish my shoes. Hurry to the market for cheese." Men like me have to go even when it's too hot for any human to be outdoors. Men like me are only drivers and houseboys for you and yours. None of you see people like us. The shit of this country doesn't touch you. You'll never have to live in the world I live in."

"That's right, I don't. I haven't." The veins in Salma's temples pulsed, she drew a fierce breath. "And you're wrong. I'm not a spoiled brat and my life isn't as rosy as you think. I'm merely an associate professor. I barely make a living wage and have two girls to put through college." She kicked at the ground. Several rocks broke loose.

"So sad. So sad," Murad mocked. "First world problems; the tough problems of the rich. Your father's a millionaire."

"You don't know my father," Salma yelled louder, Murad took a step backward. "He refused to send a single dime when my grant ran out. I cleaned people's homes to finish graduate school."

"I didn't know," Murad said, in his own defense.

"He never gave a shit." Blotches of red suppressed rage broke out on Salma's face. "Ordered me to Egypt—to live under his thumb or go to hell."

"That was after I'd left."

"Left because you couldn't own me, either. Nobody owns me. That's why I can't survive here. This country would mummify my spirit on its way back to the seventh century."

"There are those without your choices." Murad kicked at rocks again, sending clouds of dust into the air.

"You had a choice. You could have stayed in the States. I wish you had," she added almost under her breath, and he saw the tears that poked at her eyes before she looked away. He hesitated, then said quietly, not meaning to challenge her, just stating a fact.

"You could have moved back here to help your people."

"Don't you dare judge me." Salma snatched up a rock and hurled it at a scrub bush.

"I guess, you really are like the rest of your family."

"How can you say that?" Salma asked, her eyes now overflowing with tears. "We cared for each other once."

"Caring wasn't enough." A shot of indignation burned through Murad. "I wanted you to love me. You toyed with me, instead. You were—you still are—another of the damned elites, too high-class for the faceless, helpless, nobody I am. To you, I'm the kind of man your chauffeur would run down without even getting out of the car."

Salma gave an involuntary gasp, clapped her arms around herself and started shaking. When she finally spoke, she mused out loud rather than talk to Murad. "I'm ashamed of myself. I was an Egyptian mother of two and you missed your mother and sister. I must have seemed safe to you and couldn't let myself see I was taking advantage of your loneliness."

"You didn't take. . ."

"You're just being kind. You're a good man. Easy to love," Salma said, almost tenderly.

"I mean it, Salma. Although I prayed God would protect me from falling in love with you, I was weak. I should have been more careful, more vigilant. I should have accepted it wouldn't work. But, by the time I discovered the danger on your American side, I was too much in love to stop myself."

"My American side?"

"The side that goes so easily to bed with a man."

"You mean, the side who'd make love to you but wouldn't get married?"

"You know what I mean. Anyway, fate betrays us all in the end."

"Is it fate that's forcing you to betray Nabulsi?"

"Now who's unfair? I've risked my life to preserve yours. The man would have tortured you to death."

"You're holding me hostage until you can get out of the country; the one you claim I should come back to." She flung the accusation in his face. "Perhaps if you hadn't had a tantrum and left when I wouldn't marry you—or, at the time, anyone. Perhaps you wouldn't have blown-off your own life."

"The truth is cruel, my friend," Murad said, staring at his dust covered shoes. "So is life. That's my fate."

"There you go, handing over your life to fate instead of taking charge of it."

"I wish I had your certainty." Murad frowned, not just with his forehead but with his whole face. He knew at some level Salma was right. He'd always suppressed his yearnings, hoping everything would simply get better without his needing to do anything. Just like the typical peasant Nabulsi had accused him of being. Nothing but a *fallah*. Slow tears leaked from his eyes.

Salma closed the distance between them to put her hand on his arm. A sensual shudder ran across his back, to his neck, his shoulders, everywhere, as she wrapped her arms around him and leaned her head against his heart. His jaw clenched as he forced himself to clasp her wrists, separate her hands and push her away from him. He saw the color leave her cheeks, her mouth fall open, her lips quiver. His flesh felt torn where he'd pulled Salma away. Only a deep pain was left where she'd rested her head.

Salma kicked at another rock then turned away from him. When she turned back, he saw the look on her face change from hurt to anger. His mind failed to function. As though he were someone else, he heard himself say, "Don't play with me. Save that stuff for your lover." The words slung at her rang in his ears; he ached to pull back the insult but the fist in his rib cage wouldn't let him.

Salma's back was to the cave when she spun around to face him. "Comforting you is like embracing a time-bomb, listening to it tick," she said, her voice strident, her face smoldering. Then she turned away, hunched her back slightly and stumbled into the cave.

An owl glided past, the moon silvering its feathers, where Murad stood alone battling his desperate sadness. Now, he grasped what his aunt had said: the owl was a portent of death.

Chapter 2

October 2, 2014
6:30 pm

STRANGE AS IT WAS, SALMA FOUND THE DARKNESS of the cave comforting. Balanced on a rock, she watched Murad's mother chop the onion she held in the palm of her hand. Flickers of light from the small cooking fire were flickered in the razor-sharp blade of her knife as she crisscrossed the plane of the onion at *sous chef* speed. No one would guess arthritis had gnarled Aisha 's fingers.

"What's the matter?" Aisha asked. "Are you in pain? Is it your ribs?"

"My ribs don't hurt as much now," Salma answered, staring at the ground.

"So, what is wrong?"

"Murad is angry at me." Salma didn't look up. She wasn't sure she should be sharing this with his mother.

"He is anxious, my child. He is always angry when he's anxious."

"We're all anxious, Om Mohamed."

"Maybe. But my son has a particular fear."

"Do you know what that is?"

"He's afraid your father will betray him. Have him arrested. Anger spreads, you know. Maybe that's why he is angry at you."

What Aisha said made sense. The woman was right, her son had excellent grounds for his fear. Salma distrusted her father, too, but she didn't know anyone else with enough power to get Murad out of the country. In fact, she didn't know anyone who wouldn't consider him the Islamist terrorist he'd, technically, been. Throughout the world, almost every young Muslim male was painted with the same wide brush of suspicion when it came to counter terrorism.

Counter terrorism. Paul. Did she dare consider he'd help? He knew powerful people in Egypt after his stint as a foreign correspondent. Asking him to help Murad would be awkward, presumptuous. But he was a decent man who loved and trusted her. She might be able to convince him to think of Murad, not as someone who'd once been her boyfriend but as an innocent man whose life he could save. What if he refused? Would that haunt her forever? Would that tear them apart? Paul would help if she asked him to. The feeling in her gut said she shouldn't, the feeling in her heart said she had to. She couldn't let Murad be killed.

The small fire in the cave had died into a smear of gray ash before Salma fell into a fitful sleep. Her ribs stung; her body ached. The cave was now frigid, her thin pallet no cushion against the hard ground, and her filmy Mylar blanket better suited to outer space than to a cave near Aswan.

Half awake, she turned to shift the pressure from one hip to the other. A candle hovered. Confused in her drowsiness, she propped herself on her elbow. Murad was kneeling by her side.

"Forgive me, Salma. I had no right to be so angry," he whispered.

"Mmm," she mumbled, groggy and disoriented.

"I had to push you away."

She stared into the candle flame, its translucent edges flickering around the bright orange glow at its center. That Murad had given such open voice to his feelings surprised her. He always folded away when he was distressed.

"You don't have to keep pushing me away," she said as she sat up.

"I wish I didn't."

Salma heard Murad's soft but husky voice as though from a distance. Her heart seized so hard an ache rippled through her chest. Controlled by a force possessing every fiber of her being, she leaned into him and took his face in her hands. Murad's eyes blazed in the candlelight, his breathing as uneven as her own. "If you want me to stop, tell me now," she whispered.

Murad groaned low in his throat. She felt the tremor in his arms as she pressed her breasts against his chest as though fearing she could never be close enough. They kissed. His lips were as firm as she remembered but this time, tasting of sadness and fear. Their mouths held on to the words they couldn't utter as their bodies tangled together. Salma arched to meet him when she felt Murad's weight on top of her. The space around them evaporated.

"We have to stop or we'll both regret it," she said, slipping out from under him. The flare of heat from this brief contact coursed through her body but she already rued giving in to her ache for this man who drew her to him like a magnet.

Murad turned on to his side, breathless, his face and neck flushed but Salma couldn't face him. She didn't want to lose him, she wanted him in her bed. She could always draw Murad to her; even when he tried to push her away. She couldn't see how they'd be together in her real life, and she was in love with Paul. Still, she ran her hand back and forth through Murad's soft chest hair. Felt her fingers tingle. Felt her power. No wonder he accused her. He was right. She and her people were home-grown colonialists.

"If I can't be your lover, at least let me love you." Murad interrupted her self-recrimination, his voice breaking with a moan of deep injury. Salma had to muster every ounce of restraint, squeeze out every ounce of her courage, not to pull him to her, again.

"I quit being furious with you last night. In fact, you had every right to be angry with me." She clutched the metallic sheet to her chest. "But please let's not talk about love. We must change the subject. Let's talk about tomorrow."

Murad sat up. With his back against the cold rock wall, he gripped his elbows with his hands, drew up his knees and buried his head in his chest as if to choke down a sob trapped in his throat. Salma took only shallow breaths and waited while he pulled himself together.

"You saw the box of burner phones I brought," he said through lips pinched tight as though to keep them from trembling. "We'll switch them every few minutes so no one can trace us." He straightened his back and rearranged his shirt, perhaps to regain his dignity.

Last week, the fact her father hated Islamists, no matter their ilk, didn't matter to Salma. Now, everything had changed. Murad wasn't a terrorist. He was the man she'd loved in California; she was responsible for his safety. In fact, after tossing and turning for hours in the dark, Salma had obsessed about how her father would treat Murad. No, she couldn't trust him.

"Let's think about the matter of my father in a little while. I need to step out for a moment." The first sign of light slipped into the cave, dimming the light from the candle when she rose to her feet, her bladder full to bursting.

"Let me wrap this around you before you go outside." Murad dragged the Mylar sheet off her nighttime pallet. "Drones can't detect body heat through this." Despite her resolve, Salma's face turned warm with another stab of pleasure and a soft but irrepressible sob broke loose when he touched her. Determined to push through her feelings for Murad, she pulled the sheet across her chest and followed him to the cave entrance near where his mother was sleeping.

"She's leaving this morning, to her brother's house in town," Murad said as they drew near to her.

"Did you convince her we don't need a chaperone?" Salma asked, counting on her sarcasm to mask the tenderness she couldn't stop feeling for him.

"She warned me: when a man and woman are alone together, Satan is with them. And we of all people should know she was right," Murad said with a voice dulled by sad resignation.

"Love drives Satan away." Purposely flippant, Salma waved at him before she slipped outside.

When she returned Murad was standing by Aisha who was still in deep, concentrated sleep. Despite the sliver of light, soft as a feather, brushing her face, she looked older. The leathery skin over her sharp cheekbones seemed to have shrunk and wizened her face. Her ancient looking finger-nails were rough and ribbed. With her thin legs curled under the blanket, her hardened feet were exposed, their toenails tough and woody.

"Your mom might leave before we get back," Salma said as she knelt to stroke Aisha's cheek until the older woman pursed her lips, wrinkled her brow, and reluctantly awoke. She sat up slowly, her joints morning-stiff with age. Still kneeling at her side, Salma pulled out her diamond earrings. The tears in her eyes made it difficult to reattach their backs to their stems and her fingers fumbled. "We may not see each other again, Om Mohamed," she said, stunned at the sadness she felt at that thought. "Please accept these. You were right about them."

"God protect you, my daughter," Aisha said, her voice still husky with sleep. "God protect you both," she added, including Murad.

"We have to leave now, Mother," he said, patting her shoulder. "I'll see you at my uncle's, God willing. Remember what I said. Cover yourself. Pretend the Mylar sheet is an abaya. Hide behind a rock if you hear helicopters."

The smile that had skimmed his face while he talked to her, capsized when he turned to Salma. "There's no use warning her about drones. America sent the Egyptian army the most advanced ones. They fly so high, and they are so quiet, there's no escaping them. We just have to take our chances," he said as he handed her three black phones stripped to their essentials. "I checked before going to bed. There's no signal in the cave. Not even close by. It's a long hike to a spot where we'd have enough bars to call."

A slight breeze was blowing in the early morning when they set out. The sun had risen, but the crescent moon hadn't yet set. Birds whistled and cooed oblivious to the anxiety overwhelming Salma. A flutter of swifts darted across the sky. One flitted past with a startling barb of light still glowing from the sun it absorbed. Wrapped in her Mylar protection, she hiked south along the ledge alongside Murad, until the ground underfoot turned dark and crumbly. She scrambled up untrodden earth, their every step cracking open the crust that kept the wind from eroding its soil. Dust settled on her lips and eyelashes, behind her ears and between her fingers. She could hear her blood pounding as she trudged and although her ribs felt mended, her breath seemed crushed in her chest and she fretted over talking to Murad about the phone call.

"Please wait for me. I need to tell you something important." Murad leaned against the bluff to wait. Salma walked as fast as she could. When she caught up with him, she pushed against the bluff, her hand level with his shoulder, to catch her breath. "I need to tell you something," she repeated. How could she tell him they couldn't trust her father to keep his word? "I've been thinking," she said. "I'm worried. I don't think we should call my father."

"What?" Incredulous, Murad pushed away from the rock wall and turned around to face her, his eyes sharp, glittery, and intense.

"You can't trust him," Salma blurted out bluntly. "We should ask Paul to help."

Murad looked as though she'd punched him. "Your lover? You're joking." He let loose a snort. "Don't hurt me more than you already have."

"I'm serious. I can't think of anyone else. Can you?"

"If I knew anyone who could protect me from Nabulsi, don't you think I'd be dealing with them? I don't trust your father, either. Once you leave me, he'll break any promise he makes. So, I hope you stay by my side until I get out of Egypt. It's the only way to keep him honest."

"I'm not going to leave."

"I think I know your father better than you do. At some point you may have to. I don't want you killed."

"If Paul agrees to help, you can trust him. I swear. He's honest. He's a good man."

"Don't make him real—not this way." Murad straightened his back against the wall of rock in silence, his arms beside his head. "I pretend your lover doesn't exist." A web of pain-wrinkles spread across his dust-coated face then he slammed both his fists into the rock wall and bellowed. "I can't do it, Salma. I just can't do it."

"The whole thing is awkward—for both of us. I know that. I understand. There are no good choices, yet we have to make one," Salma said and waited for Murad to calm down and realize she had to ask for Paul's help. She touched his arm to get his attention then pulled back her hand, immediately. At last, he lowered his shoulders, turned, and looked past her towards the horizon.

"I guess if you trust the man, I must. After all, any promise he makes to me, he also makes to you. Let's hope he cares enough for you to stay true to his word." He slid his back down the rough rock surface and rested on his haunches. A shock of black hair fell across his forehead when he lowered his head. "I need some time, Salma," he said, his hands covering his face. "Start without me. I'll catch up."

Salma resumed the rocky trek, laden with guilt, the lump in her throat growing. Yesterday, she'd admitted to herself she'd taken advantage of Murad although she hadn't known or meant to. Today, she was about to knowingly take advantage of Paul. What kind of woman was she? But what choice did she have with Murad's life at stake?

Murad reached her, outpaced her, passed her without uttering a word and disappeared behind a boulder that almost blocked the path.

A strange sound filled the air—the sound of ocean waves flinging gravel on the shore.

"It's a damn drone!" Salma heard him yell. "Hide."

Not sure what she was searching for, she instinctively chose a spot between two boulders. The heat they emitted would mask her presence, she realized as she forced herself into the space between them, their rough surfaces abrading her arms. She could smell her desperation—like carbolic acid—in the skin between her breasts and under her arms. Murad had better be right. Mylar had better protect them from heat sensors. She hadn't brought an inhaler.

"It's gone," he hollered. "My phone's picked up four bars. Squeeze past the boulder like I did." Salma went up to the huge rock near the cliff. The space between it and the cliff-wall was narrower and longer than she'd imagined and there were other, similar passageways beyond it. "You can do it," Murad called out as though he'd picked up on her reluctance. "It's no worse than the ones we went through at the Pinnacles." Salma remembered climbing the jagged rock face there with Murad and her daughters, shimmying over boulders, pushing through fissures.

"Too tight," she called back.

"You can do it," he repeated. "I got through. You can. And hurry, the sun's getting hot."

Salma sucked in her stomach as far as she could, held her arms straight up, stepped sideways to wedge herself through three narrow crannies until the rocks finally released her into a space of blond-white ground. Murad had positioned himself in a patch of bright daylight with an arm extended overhead and was staring at his phone.

"Look, four bars," he said, giving it to Salma, pulling back his arm when hers brushed his. The sun, almost vertical in the rocky clearing, focused like a laser on her head. The surrounding stillness was stark, some big button seemed to have muted the world. Salma was punching Paul's number into the cheap, black, phone when Murad stayed her hand. "Please turn on the speaker. You're asking me to trust a man I don't know. I need at least to hear how he reacts when you ask for his help." Salma switched the phone to its speaker mode, held her breath, and punched in the number again. Paul answered on the second ring.

"It's me," she said, and pressed her palm to her heart at the two simple words connecting her to the man she loved. Her knees felt watery, her back muscles weak.

"Oh, my God, my God." Paul sounded frenzied. "Where are you? I've died a thousand deaths since you disappeared."

"I'm safe," she said, wiping away tears with her knuckles.

"I'm coming to get you, wherever you are." He sounded as though he was already grabbing the doorknob.

"First…" Salma hesitated. "I need you to do something."

"I'll do anything you want." She heard the scratchy sound as the knuckle of his forefinger rubbed across his chin which he did when he was uncertain.

"You know, of course, that someone technically kidnapped me?"

"Technically?" There was a catch in his raised voice, a tone of incredulous disbelief. "What the hell do you mean by "technically""? I know Murad Ragab kidnapped you. Where has that damn terrorist taken you?"

"He's not a terrorist and it's complicated," Salma said with a flinch and a worried glance at Murad. Then wishing there was a patch of shade to stand it, she closed her eyes against the glare reflecting off the ground and explained the situation. By the time she'd reached the point of Murad's needing to escape from the Taj he'd betrayed, her shoulders ached with tension. "He's in danger," she said in conclusion. "And I don't trust my father. He's as likely as not to hand him over to Nabulsi."

"I doubt he'd do that." Paul sounded so dismissive Salma was almost too anxious to continue. She looked down at the ground, took a deep breath, and gathered her strength.

"If my father gets involved, he'll have him killed," she insisted.

"Yes?" Paul stretched out the word to form a sarcastic question. "And…?" Murad fixed his eyes on Salma as she waited out Paul's hostile hesitation.

"Well, bottom line." She was firm. "Before Murad lets me go, he needs protection from Nabulsi."

"So, your good friend who's not a terrorist is blackmailing you."

"He's trying to negotiate. And I'm trying to help." When it came to the ask, her mouth went dry. "You know a bunch of important people who—" Murad pulled another phone from his pocket and ran a short slash of his hand across his throat. "Just a minute, Paul," Salma said, acknowledging the signal. "I'll call you right back."

Paul answered the call halfway through the second phone's first ring. "Listen. I don't care what you call it, the guy's holding you hostage."

"Sort of. But I told you, that's to protect me from the Taj. That's why Nabulsi wants to kill him. You're too decent to let that happen to a good man. We need to get him out of the country. Some place that's safe."

"I want you safe. Safe in my arms, before I turn over heaven and earth to solve the problem your friend created for himself." He sounded like he was forcing his words through gritted teeth and the emphasis on "my arms" made Salma cringe. "I don't know the man," he continued. "If I did, I doubt he and I would be friends."

"I understand, Paul. I wouldn't be asking for your help if things weren't so desperate." Salma knew she was asking for something almost impossible, but she had to. "The man's life is at stake. The longer he keeps me with him, the more likely mine will be, too. One of Nabulsi's men is bound to find us."

"That's a whole lot of stuff to throw at me at once," Paul said, somber and cold. "I feel blackmailed. You know I can't risk anything happening to you." He was silent for what seemed like forever. Sweat prickled Salma's under arms. She wanted to shout, have a tantrum, stomp her feet, and beat her hands on the ground like a toddler. Finally, Paul said, "I know a man who might be able to resettle him someplace." Her knees almost buckled with relief.

"You're a good, good, man, darling. I trust you. I love you. I-"

Murad grabbed the phone from her hand, shut it down, and pulled out another. Ignoring Salma's raised eyebrows, he read Paul's number from the first phone's screen and slowly punched it in.

"This is Murad," he said. "I assure you Salma is safe with me. We will not always have a signal, so let us set a time for your call." He paused. "You can use this number." Still looking at Salma, he nodded. "Good. Ten o'clock tonight, then. With any luck, God willing, we'll be in Aswan by then."

Chapter 3

October 3, 2014
10:00 am

BY THE TIME SALMA AND MURAD RETURNED TO THE CAVE, its early morning chill had dissipated, its interior was pleasantly warm. Parched from the sun, uncomfortable and ill at ease, they each slugged down a bottle of water without exchanging words.

"There are some lentils left," Salma said, to break the silence. "Would you like some?" Murad brought two loaves of flatbread from the cache of supplies and they ate silently, staring down at their bowls. Salma decided the best thing to do was to give each other space to reflect on what they'd decided to do. She headed to her palette for a nap.

It was mid-afternoon when she woke up with grains of sand stuck to her gummed eyelids. She found Murad outside, standing on the rim of the ledge squinting at a hawk, motionless on a current of air. At the sound of her footsteps, he turned with a flash of his wonderful smile.

"Did you get enough sleep?" he asked, apparently recovered from the awkwardness of relying on Paul's help. "Grab two bottles of water and let's go," he said still with a smile but without waiting for an answer. "It's quite a walk to Aswan but at least it's all downhill."

They must have walked for a mile when Murad stopped abruptly. "*Khara*. Shit." He pointed at a ridge to their right. "Too far away to be sure but I see uniforms. Soldiers. A dozen. They might be backtracking the route my mother took into town."

"Drones?" Salma asked.

"Probably. Small, quiet, lethal. Their heat detectors could have picked up my mother's movements."

"What about the Mylar blanket?"

"Body heat begins to leak out after a while. That's why you flatten yourself against something warm like the rock-face and hope for the best." Murad took her elbow to turn her around. "We're going back to the cave."

"But if they're backtracking your mother's route—"

"It's not the cave we need. It's the tunnel in the back. I think it leads through to the other side of the hill. If so, we can go around these guys."

Clearly, Murad wasn't certain of where the tunnel exit was—if there was an exit, thought Salma. Her stomach churning, she began the climb back. The more she thought about it the more certain she became that if they didn't risk the tunnel at least one of them would be killed. If the soldiers found them first, it would be Murad. If Nabulsi's men did, both would be dead.

The desiccated crust underfoot was rock-hard and there was neither shade nor wind for relief from the sun. Her blood rushing, her muscles aching, she hiked back to the cave as fast as she could. When she got there, she found Murad ripping up her *abaya*. Bizarre.

"What are you---?"

"We'll be crawling so I'm making pads for your arms and elbows. I'll pad your ribs, too, if I can."

"Have you ever gotten to the end of the tunnel?" Salma asked.

"To be honest, I haven't. But I've seen light from the opening and breathed fresh air."

At the thought of creeping through a dark, narrow, tunnel whose exit Murad couldn't guarantee, Salma's insides quivered. She told herself the anxiety that was making her crazy was nothing but chemicals from her amygdala ordering her brain to function. She would have to deal with whatever came up. And, come to think of it, once she stopped breathing the polluted air of Cairo, she hadn't had an asthma attack. Realizing that helped her hold herself together as she folded wide strips of black cloth into thick pads for her elbows and knees.

"We need some for your chest," Murad said, grabbing more material.

"Just a second." Salma headed to the nest of things Soraya had packed—a syringe, a vial of epinephrine, and feminine hygiene supplies—to retrieve an inhaler in case her luck didn't hold. "I need to stuff this in my bra before you wrap me up."

Murad surprised her. First, when he turned away while she reached into her bra which didn't seem necessary. Then, when he turned back and said, "You look like a caterpillar," and burst out laughing. Salma could have kissed him for keeping his sense of humor under these conditions. Instead, she grabbed two flashlights and four phones from the stash near the mouth of the cave and stood near him as he pried a boulder loose with the shovel and shimmied it aside to expose the narrow opening of a tunnel.

"We need to lay face down on our bellies to get through this passage," he said, preparing to enter headfirst. "But don't worry. Further in there's a small cave that's wider." Salma's lips felt like sandpaper when she ran her tongue over them, and took a deep, precautionary puff of her inhaler before she followed him.

Once through the opening, she was in complete darkness, in thick air that tasted of dirt. The roof of the tunnel was less than two feet above her back, so she wasn't as much crawling as shoving off with her knees, dragging herself forward, elbow by elbow, one inch by inch no faster than the caterpillar she resembled. With her vision cut off, her senses were disoriented. The directions from which intermittent clunks and thuds pierced the silence were mysterious. Were the peals echoing around her *affrits,* devils of the dark? Or worse. Soldiers closing in and nowhere for her to go. What if Murad was wrong? What if the tunnel never reached any light or air? She couldn't turn around and go back. She'd die here. Starved. Dehydrated. Suffocated. Breathing through clenched teeth, she forced herself back from the edge of panic and resumed her painful crawl.

The tunnel had steadily narrowed. Now her spine scraped against its rough limestone roof. The air she exhaled was hot. It smelled of rust. Her ribs were throbbing, her chest constricting and her inhaler out of reach. She was acknowledging her good fortune in not triggering an attack, when her body was suddenly seized with cramps. Her muscles hardened; her upper back lifted. All her weight rested on her stomach, forcing oxygen from her lungs. Again, she made herself take slow breaths in and out, coaxing air through her bronchial tubes. It was air that felt fresher, gave her hope and energized her. She stretched her arms as far forward as she could and dug her toes into the ground, pushing and pulling at the same time, hauling her body onward. One final push—like being delivered from a womb—and she landed, headfirst, into a cave like the one they'd left.

"There you are," Murad exclaimed from the shaft of weak light where he stood. "*Hamd illah bil salaama.*" Scrambling to her feet, Salma smiled at the fact he was thanking God for her safe arrival as though she were a traveler. She was so glad to see him, she almost hugged him but settled for a formal handshake that made him chuckle. There were clicking sounds crisscrossing the darkness they looked up at the cave's roof and traced the sounds to a ragged hole above them.

"Bats. Echolocation." Murad answered Salma's unasked question.

As Murad removed her knee and elbow pads, Salma peered at her guano-covered arms and legs, she moaned, "You mean, I've been crawling in bat shit?" She sounded so disgusted, they both had to laugh.

Once they set off again, they had to half-crouch up an incline until they emerged from the hill—tiny shapes in the vastness of night. Above them, the sky with only a few stars out, was like water with blue ink. The two-day old moon still a slim perfect crescent. Salma didn't know whether her tears were those of relief or exhaustion. Whoever was coming for them wasn't in this section of the desert. Feeling the world around her more than she could see it, she followed Murad through a landscape of darkness set off only by lighter darkness with feral dogs barking in the distance.

"What time is it?" she asked. The lights of Aswan had become more pronounced.

"Half-past nine."

"We've been walking for over three hours."

"Just another mile to go. There's the trail-head." The lift in Murad's voice clearly offered encouragement. Finally, the dusty trail from the desert gave way to pavement and leading to a warren of narrow streets on the outskirts of the city.

They passed two black-skinned Nubian men playing cards on a stoop. Only the flash of their ivory-white teeth and the frost-white of their eyes stood out in the night. Leafy trees appeared. Cicadas hummed like tuning forks. Coal smoke drifted through open doors and dim lights shone in the open windows of small, white-washed homes. This corner of Aswan, with its cooking-fires and the odor of fried fish, seemed like its own village to Salma.

In the sleazy section of town, she stayed close to Murad, past boarded-up houses, fenced-off lots, depressed looking nightclubs, and dilapidated coffee houses. A plump orange cat yawned on top of a car layered with dust while, here and there, an open window let out a blare of music.

A loud ringing. Salma jumped. Murad pulled out the burner phone. "That's on the Nile. Too far for Salma to walk," she heard him say. How far was too far for her to walk? How else would they meet Paul? She was afraid the blood vessels pounding in her head would explode before the call was over.

"He expects us to meet in front of the Nubian Museum," Murad told her and stomped the sidewalk at her feet. Paul was the only one who could help him, now.

"Why there?"

"Probably because it's surrounded first by open space then by a labyrinth of high-walled trenches—part of its award-winning architectural design. He must have had advice because it's also big enough for your father's soldiers to hide in. Not that I'm ungrateful, but it could easily be a trap."

"Paul would never set you up. He'd never betray you." But how could she be sure of that? At the thought he might deceive her, she felt her chest emptying like water out of a cracked vessel, escaping from inside her onto the sidewalk.

"Look at it from his point of view," Murad said. "To him, I'm a terrorist. He's got no reason to trust me. I could be bringing a brigade of terrorists to take him hostage like I took you." Salma had nothing with which to counter this concern.

"Can we take a taxi?" she settled for asking.

"Not from this neighborhood." Murad punched numbers into the phone. "But if I can get hold of my uncle, he can drive us there. Drop us off on the far side of the Archangel Michael Cathedral to be safe."

"I thought Paul said the Nubian Museum."

"Yeah," Murad said after completing his call. "The cathedral is about a quarter mile from the museum, and they share an open compound. I'd feel better if I had the chance to scout the area."

Ten minutes later, his uncle pulled up beside them in a newish Honda sedan, a traditional multicolored Aswani skullcap on his combed-flat graying hair.

"This is a bad time to ask me to help." He sounded irritated beyond reason. "Your people blew up a string of cruise ships docked on shore last night. Now I don't have a job." His brow contorted as he stretched across the passenger seat to open the door. Salma wondered if Aisha had told him her father was Hani Hamdi.

"They're not my people anymore, uncle. I quit. I left the sheikh. Now he's set his men after this woman and me."

"The government claims he's dead," his uncle said. Murad's face betrayed no emotion as he scuffed his shoes to the ground. "The president declared he'd crushed the uprising," his uncle continued. "Who knows the truth? All I know is that a car has been following me."

"I've been watching, and I didn't see one." Salma saw Murad's grip tighten on the edge of the door. "Besides, if they did follow you, it's too late to do anything. And, if they didn't follow you, we don't need to worry."

On their way to the cathedral, perhaps due to yesterday's explosions, the streets they drove through were almost empty. In the front seat, Murad fixed his eyes on the side mirror. Behind him, Salma craned her neck to look out the back window. She saw a knot of three walnut-skinned men on the sidewalk in the light of a streetlamp and a black cat with bedazzled green eyes and a nub of a tail. No one was following them.

The calm Aswan claims for itself had always seemed narcotically unreal to Salma. When she rolled down her window, she could smell the voluptuous mix of animals, earth, and plants and the headlights were picking out purple bougainvillea wiggling up white-washed walls. Once on the wide boulevard of el-Sadat Street, the sharp turns smoothed out and Salma could see the white glare of streetlamps reflecting off the car's hood, dying away to a soft shimmer then reappearing at the next light.

The municipal stadium had been darkened after the football game, some of its crowd gathered at the adjoining cafe. Past the Aswan Military Hospital, Murad's uncle overshot the turnoff to the Nubian Museum and veered left at the Hakeem Mall, towards the bluff over the Nile where the Coptic Orthodox Cathedral of the Archangel Michael stood. Murad was right; only open land separated the cathedral's massive structure from the museum's equally massive one.

"I can't wait for you," Murad's uncle said gruffly after slowing to a stop in front of the cathedral's arches washed in robin-egg blue under-lights. But the lines on his bulldog face soon softened and he offered Murad a close-mouthed grin. "There are lots of taxis around here. Take one to my house when you're done. Your mother is waiting."

No matter how intensely hot it is during the day, at night Aswan is as cold as its surrounding desert and once out of the car, puffs of Salma's breath preceded her as she walked with Murad toward the museum. An old man on a bicycle worn thin with rust pedaled past with a creaking chain and neither brakes nor lights. The two of them stepped around a boy squatting on the sidewalk engrossed in twisting squares of paper into cones for the pile of peanuts by his side. There was a tightness in his shoulders that suggested alertness, but Salma dismissed the incongruity as a sign of the anxiety that had her pulse jerking in her veins.

"Keep your eyes open. It's not safe to be so exposed," Murad said, covering his flashlight with his hand before turning it on and allowing only a thin ray of light to escape his fingers.

"Where did Paul say he'd be?" she asked, spreading the gravel on the ground with her foot.

"Close to the museum entrance." An odd choice. Perhaps not Paul's. Perhaps the Embassy had interceded. Paul had said Murad could be resettled in another country. Would the U.S. take him in? Salma caught herself imagining its happening and stopped. She didn't dare consider the implication.

A single dog, crouching, fled across the waste ground—a flat, empty, space in the middle of the compound strewn with scraps of windblown debris. Salma felt something was amiss. The night air itself seemed to quiver. She felt like a turtle whose shell was torn off. Suddenly, the pop-pop-pop of rifle shots exploded from the pitch-black dark. Salma's hands shot up, her palms spread open like flags of truce. A spotlight appeared on Murad's back.

"Move and I'll shoot you," a voice called out. She heard the click of a gun safety being released. They'd been ambushed. Her mind went numb with shock; her throat clogged with fear. What had Paul done?

"Turn to face me." A second voice, another flashlight. Murad froze. A soldier grabbed him by his upper arm. Salma wiped her face on the arm of her shirt and steadied herself against a wave of dizziness.

"What's going on?" she called out. A soldier with a marsupial face stepped into the flashlight beam.

"We are following your father's orders, Madam Hamdi." Gooseflesh pricked her neck. He was one of Hani's Presidential Guards. "We are to arrest this man and escort you to the Sofitel Hotel."

Before the monkey-faced soldier could handcuff him, Murad grasped clumps of hair near the man's scalp and brought his kneecap to the man's nose. Panting more from fear than exertion, he drove his leg into the soldier's body then threw all his strength into his fist and struck the man just below his left eye. Murad's shoulder ached with an intense throbbing that spread across his shoulders nonetheless, he took a step back and found leverage to thrust forward, again. His knee connected with the man's groin and the bastard doubled over with painful grunts. Murad's eyes narrowed as he repeatedly kicked his attack dog in the side. Near the liver. To injure him forever.

Sprawled on the sidewalk, the man grabbed a fistful of crushed cement and flung it in Murad's face forcing him to back away. Blood from his nostrils was leaking onto his camouflage fatigues but the soldier seemed to get a second breath crouched in position to attack with a solid push off the ground. With a single move, he grabbed his assault rifle, pulled himself up and slammed into Murad who was ready for him. Murad seized his wrist and smashed the rifle into the soldier's chest where it caught on his army jacket. The soldier drew back, gaining leverage to plow into Murad's chest. The two men grappled, until they fell sideways to the ground in a tangle of bloody arms and whipping fists.

From the corner of her eye, Salma caught sight of the second soldier coming to his comrade's aid. Separated from him by only a few feet, she hammered her fists into whatever patch of his flesh she could find. She'd never punched anyone before and the pain that blazed up her arm when her fist connected with his jaw, surprised her. Then, before she could land another punch, the soldier dropped her to the ground with a single swipe of his arm. He yanked her legs up. Her shirt rose to her breasts, her jeans slid down past her hips, gravel ground into her skin. She grabbed a handful of sand to throw in his face, but he pulled her to her feet before she had the chance to. Suddenly she heard Rashid shout, "Stop!" The rest of his words were lost in the roar of a descending helicopter.

Chapter 4

October 3, 2014
11:30 pm

TREES SHUDDERED IN THE DOWNWASH OF FURIOUS blasts of air. Piercing bursts of lightning white stung Salma's eyes like nettles. A helicopter sucked leaves into its vortex as its wheels met the ground. Less a dragonfly, more a dragon in desert camouflage.

It seemed hours before its side door opened and a uniformed man with large headphones jumped out. Salma hugged herself. Where was

Paul? Scanning what had become a landing pad, she stifled her sobs until she heard him call her name. The sound of his voice quickened every cell in her body. "You're here," she cried, rushing to his open arms. "You're really here. You came. You came. Thank God," she blubbered, between broken sobs.

"Of course, I came. I had no choice," Paul said, rubbing her back with long, hard strokes. "Breathe." The strain lifted from Salma's shoulders, but the turmoil in her stomach remained.

"How did you get your hands on a military helicopter? I asked you not to involve my dad," she said as soon as she'd calmed down. She didn't care if she sounded ungrateful, even critical. If he'd told her father, he'd be helping a man who both of them believed was a terrorist. Paul might as well have signed Murad's death warrant.

"I didn't talk to your dad," Paul insisted.

"Who else would let you have a military helicopter? Was it Rashid?" she asked pointing to the colonel.

"Stop." Paul raised his arm, his palm facing Salma. "You're not going to like this. I had help from the Mossad."

"Why them?" Salma pulled away, her throat aching with resentment. "You know how I feel." She swallowed hard.

"Who else could I go to? The American ambassador? He's the first person I went to when you disappeared. He categorically refused to help." Paul over-pronounced every word, letting each slice through the dry air. "The Israelis and Egyptians have a secret military agreement that made it easy for Mossad to commandeer the copter. The agent who approached me in the hotel also had a passport and identity documents faked for your friend and arranged for a family in Amman to shelter him. What more do you want?"

"Why in the world would a Mossad agent do that for Murad?"

"I made a deal. The Mossad wants whatever's on Abu Taleb's scan disk as much as the Taj does and your father should. According to them, it contains the identity of a mole in the Egyptian government. More importantly to the Mossad, the disk supposedly holds a list of Hamas targets in Israel. I guess they figure forewarned is forearmed."

Salma stared past the copter's floodlights until her eyes could focus on the trees reappearing from the darkness and saw Rashid coming out of the shadows towards them, walking with the firm purpose of someone in control.

"I'm surprised to find you here, Mr. Hays," he said, his face stretched in the grim ghost of a smile. "The average Egyptian doesn't take kindly to those with the Mossad." He pointed to where a dozen people had collected behind the low stone wall. The small crowd was quiet, as though banking on their silence to keep from being dispersed. Salma smelled the odor of cigarette smoke and recognized the man on the bicycle with the creaking chain and questions jammed her brain.

"Did you have us followed?" she asked Rashid, acting as though she was calm.

"Of course."

"So, Murad's uncle was right. He was being followed. You didn't know a helicopter would give away our position, so you followed him from his house to here."

"That's right. Once we found him, it was easy."

"How did you do that?"

"A drone picked up an image of an old woman two miles outside Aswan walking in the desert alone. No ordinary woman would do that. So, we followed her. She led us to her brother, Murad's uncle. I've had a watch on him since yesterday."

"You had drones all over the country?"

"Only from Fayoum to Aswan."

"Why Fayoum?" Salma asked then choked out the name of Murad's friend. "Rami! He wouldn't inform on us unless…What did you do to him?"

"What do you think? It didn't take too long. In the end, he had to tell us. Do you remember the saying: "The father of the child is a coward?"" Well, we picked up his children."

The cavalier way in which Rashid referred to torturing the man who'd helped her and Murad seemed menacing. Salma tried to swallow the lump in her throat, but that made her almost puke. She looked past the circle of light in search of Murad and found him leaning against a tree in the dark, handcuffed and surrounded by soldiers. Tears of bereavement welled up in her eyes and she turned to Paul for help.

"What do we do?" she asked, wiping at the streaming tears with an unsteady hand.

Paul stepped towards Rashid and pointed to Murad. "This man has to get out of Egypt," Salma felt the tension and heard the intensity in Paul's tone.

"What arrogance!" Rashid shouted. "What business do you have in the matter? Egypt and only Egypt will determine the fate of this terrorist.

He was involved in yesterday's terrorist attack." A line of fear began weaving into her spine as she stared at Murad, the slits on his knuckles still leaking blood.

"Listen, Rashid," Paul said. "This man was hiding Salma. Remember the guy at Groppi's? The one who told us Salma was with Murad, but no one knew where he had taken her? Nabulsi is desperate to find him. That means Murad is not with the Taj."

"This man was complicit. One hundred percent." Rashid wouldn't back down.

"He rescued me from the Taj," Salma objected. "He risked his life for me. If he doesn't go into hiding, Nabulsi will have him killed."

"Nabulsi's dead. The Taj is crushed." Rashid's nostrils dilated, his chest puffed out.

"That's what the president claims," Paul said, turning to face Salma and speaking loudly enough so Murad would hear him. "My sources tell me Nabulsi's alive and well."

Salma uncurled her clenched fists. And let out a massive exhalation of pent-up breath into the air, still gritty and sulfurous. Suddenly, a soldier cut across the circle of light in which she and the two men stood. Hiding his mouth behind his raised palm, he leaned in to whisper in the colonel's ear. The colonel was frowning at Salma while he listened. Dizzy, nauseous and covered in debris the copter had spread she watched Paul make his way to Murad. She felt she was going down a steep hill in a roller coaster with nowhere to stop.

The ominous thud of marching boots surged louder as they neared. A phalanx of soldiers crashed into the compound followed by Salma's father. Her neck glistened with sweat. Her shoulders shot up to her ears and she squeezed her eyes shut as though to close out the world.

"The whole country has been searching for you," her father said when he reached her. She thought she heard a slight faltering in his voice and opened her eyes. "What are you doing with this man?" he asked, standing in front of her, wide-legged and combative, pointing an aggressive finger at Murad who raised his head defiantly. "I know who you are, traitor," Hani barked. "And who your people are. Soon you will be in my prison."

"I should just shoot him," Rashid declared. Salma heard the metallic ratcheting of a bullet being forced into his pistol's killing chamber

"You'd better think twice before you do that if you still want what's on the disk," Paul spoke so calmly, they all stared at him. Salma held her breath until she saw Rashid holster his pistol and turn to Hani with an overtone of a question in his voice.

"According to 'our cousins,' there is information on the disk that may identify the spy who is helping the Islamists destroy our country." Salma knew the term "cousins" was a longtime euphemism for Israelis. The Mossad was exasperating; every time she turned around it was there. At how many levels were Rashid and her father and Paul involved with it?

Fretting, she watched her father pull Rashid a few feet away and beyond the circle of light surrounding the helicopter. Although they stood in the dark, she saw her father shake his head and stab his finger at Rashid's chest. "It makes no difference to me," he shouted loud enough for all to hear. "Do what you want with that terrorist. Give him to our cousins for all I care." Then he stepped back into the light, kicking up dust, refilling the air with a fog of detritus.

"Let's go, Salma." Hani seized her arm. She jerked out of his clutch. Breathing hard, she stood there, unsteady, as though she'd just gotten off a boat. "Move." Her father snatched her arm again. The ground beneath her seemed to revolve. Her breath kept catching in her throat, and she wondered why she hadn't triggered an asthma attack. Then a white-hot bolt of rage shot through her.

"Stop," she shouted, her heart beating so loudly her ears rang. "Don't bully me! I'm not going anywhere. I'm staying with Paul."

"Ahhh…." Her father's voice was as dry as parchment. "So, that's how it is. Turning your back on your family. Betraying your country for an American Jew." The sharp edge of his voice like a blade across her throat didn't stop Salma from releasing a barrage of grievances.

"Your country? You know nothing about your country. You have no idea how people here live." Once she'd started, she didn't hold back. "Didn't you tell me Egypt wasn't a theme park of photo-friendly antiquities waiting for my visit?" She brandished her arm towards the museum. "Well, you and your friends live in your own theme parks. Sharm el Sheikh, Starbucks, sushi restaurants, shopping malls. Whether you admit it or not, you're all afraid the people you're letting starve will attack the gated communities you hide in. Why don't you feed them instead of driving them into the arms of folks like Nabulsi?" Reaching for Murad's handcuffed wrists, she tried to calm herself despite the sick rolling of her stomach. "This man is not a terrorist. He's my friend."

It was as though Salma had flipped a switch inside her father and unplugged his power. His dark eyes went dead at their centers, and, for a split second, she saw his face crumple. Then he slipped his mask of indifference back on. She hadn't intended to hurt him so badly; she hadn't expected him to react this way.

With a deep, pained breath, Salma rubbed first her temples then her eyes and was about to go to Paul, when Murad strained against his handcuffs to hold her hand. His own were clammy and his breath was shaky, yet he was supporting her with the only gesture he could make.

"Dr. Hamdi," she heard Paul say in a steady, low-pitched voice, "if you want what is on this disk you must let me open it before I leave the country." He stepped forward silently to challenge Salma's father. "I'm leaving in the morning."

"Just give it to me," Hani said, reaching with an open hand for the disk.

"No, sir. The disk is too well protected for even your most sophisticated IT specialists."

"In that case, what makes you think you can open it?" Hani snorted and buzzed air through his lips. Without answering, Paul looked past him to Rashid.

"Do you by any chance have a laptop around here?"

"What?" Rashid scratched at his cheek with a forefinger.

"A laptop."

"Uhm. . ." His voice trailed off. His squished eyebrows formed deep frown lines over his nose. He glanced at Hani as though for permission. "There must be computers in the museum. I'll have the chief night guard let us in."

"Who is us?" Paul asked.

"You and me."

"That won't work. I need Murad's help. He must know how the Taj organizes its information. And, for personal reasons, I insist Salma come with me." Rashid glanced again at Hani whose face was still red and the tip of his nose white, but neither man challenged him.

Chapter 5

HANI'S CHAUFFEUR DROVE HIM BACK TO THE SOFITEL hotel leaving Murad to walk with Salma and Paul. The two of them in front of him, Rashid at his back, his right hand glued to his holster. Murad's face scrunched when he remembered Rashid holding a pistol to his head, ready to assassinate him.

It was less than a quarter mile from the helicopter landing to the grounds of the Nubian Museum; the dusty gravel giving way to a labyrinth of wide sandstone trenches embedded with a generous number of light fixtures. Despite the light on the meticulously maintained greenery meant to soften the starkness, it felt like a setting for a World War I movie.

The improbable group of four followed a squad of khaki clad soldiers tramping down flagstone paths with beds of deep red bougainvillea atop buttresses that rose higher than their heads. Salma stopped a few feet ahead of Murad and as he approached, he heard the bubbling of a small waterfall flowed from a concrete channel and over the sandstone trench walls. In a wave of grief, he held his breath as though to save himself from drowning. Only a few hours ago she'd been walking through the desert with him. Now she was walking with Paul. There was something graceless about being handcuffed in this alien landscape, owing his life to Salma's fiancé, wondering how long Paul would protect him if he knew how deeply Murad loved her. Perhaps the man would keep his word for now. So far, he hadn't left him alone with Rashid and his itching trigger finger. What was Rashid thinking? Why would Murad try to escape when he had no place to hide from Nabulsi?

The soldiers turned left, rounding the building to the museum's main entrance. Floodlights, spaced ten feet apart five, beamed up from the ground and rose along wall to the building's long flat roof. The night guards who pulled open the gigantic front door, saluted Rashid and let his party slip through it. In the entry hall, an imposing statue of a pharaoh Murad didn't recognize loomed over them, diminishing mere mortals as it had for five thousand years. It was gigantic. Impossible to ignore. The antechamber beyond it was so dark Murad could barely make out the flight of stairs heading down to the museum's main exhibit hall.

He turned away to look back into the vestibule where Paul and Rashid were apparently conferring while Salma stood by. He tried to catch her eye, but she was concentrating too hard on their conversation to notice him. He was embarrassed at how abandoned and forsaken he felt. The truth crept in—dark, cold, and devoid of hope. The only thing between him and death as a terrorist at Hani's hand was Nabulsi's private disk—protected by a personal password and set to self-destruct at the first unauthorized attempt to access its information. How was Paul going to open the disk if even his hacker hadn't found a way around its security?

"There must be an office around here." Paul's voice set off an eerie echo in the dark, empty building.

"To the left," Rashid said, ordering the guards to open an inconspicuous door and turn on the lights of an efficient, one-man office, with a recent model of a Dell computer on its lone desk. There was so little space that there was only room enough for three people and Rashid blocked Murad from the doorway, leaned into the room with his arms spread and hung on to the door jambs for balance.

"Hey," Paul said. "Remember? Murad comes with me." Murad swept his hand cuffed hands across his sweaty forehead

"He is under arrest."

"We've been through this before. He is my responsibility. Please uncuff him so we can get to work. Salma told me he was Nabulsi's administrative assistant. I need him to figure out the files." Rashid hesitated. Salma chimed in, "I never learned the Arabic keyboard. We'll be here forever if we have to rely on me."

"You need to discover the traitor's identity and you need to work fast. Dr. Hamdi is not a patient man." Rashid's Adam's apple bobbed up and down in his throat. "I'll be at the Sofitel waiting for you, trying to keep him calm. As for you," he snapped at Murad, "I'm taking half the squad with me. A sergeant and five soldiers will stay. I will order them to shoot you if you move more than six feet from Mr. Hays." Rashid started to leave, then spun around to Paul with an ugly twist to his mouth. "Watch yourself," he warned. "We would have been rid of this terrorist had you not interfered."

Paul took the office chair, Salma sat on the table with her legs dangling. Murad plastered himself against the wall and bent over with his hands on his knees to control his shallow breathing. Rashid and Nabulsi wanted him dead, and he was completely at Paul's mercy. The small room's walls were closing in and a crushing weight in his chest was beginning to suffocate him.

"Where do we go from here?" Salma asked.

"I'm not sure we're going anywhere," Paul grumbled, pointing his chin towards Murad as he booted up the desktop computer. "Do you have any idea what the damned password might be?" Murad shook his head and held his hands up, palms out, as though to ward off danger.

"I would guess it's in English. It's natural. Most computer commands are in English. What did the hacker who checked out the disk say? Did he try to open it?"

"Not really. But he was able to get in for a millisecond somehow without triggering the action that would wipe out the data."

"Did he find anything we can use?" Salma asked, sliding off the desk to stand behind Paul and stare at the computer screen.

"He's sure it's a fifteen-character password that starts with an A. The next character is either the number one or the letter I," Paul said, including Murad in his reply. "Does the Taj use a common algorithm?"

"The algorithms are automatically generated, and Taj has a program to decipher them. Without access to that, there is no possible way to guess what will open the disk. Frankly, I don't think it matters. Since this is the sheikh's personal—?"

"What kind of information would he keep on this?" Paul asked.

"Information he wanted to hide from others in Taj al Islam." Murad had no idea what that might be. Perhaps Nabulsi was collecting stuff to use for blackmail. His eyes darted back and forth between Salma and Paul. What if the disk didn't have what Paul thought it had? What if the "cousins" had set a trap? His nails dug into his palms; his stomach churned and cramped.

"If he didn't use a randomly generated one, what kind of password was he likely to use?" Salma asked Murad, lifting a hand off Paul's shoulders to rub the back of her neck. She looked so frustrated, Murad wished he could comfort her, but all he could do was to answer her question.

"He'd use something personal to him, one nobody would ever think of. Our chances are one in a million." He bit the inside of his thumb and scowled at Paul. "Why didn't you just give Hani the disk? Or did you think you'd hit the right password on the first try?" He felt the fear in his chest waiting to take over.

"You're forgetting I was bargaining for your life," Paul said, annoyed. "The only thing I had that Hani wanted was this disk. One chance in a million will have to do."

Murad wondered if all Jews were as optimistic as Paul. So willing to trust their own judgement. Deep inside, he couldn't imagine taking a chance like this. He'd never learned to trust that anything would turn out well.

"Stop arguing." Salma moved from the back of Paul's chair to the other side of the desk to stand by Murad. "You said the first character was an A, right?" she asked Paul.

"Right," he replied, sharply. "As I said, the hacker thought the second character was either the letter "I" or the numeral one. Remember, he had to avoid tripping the self-destruct command, so he only got a nanosecond—a blink of a glance."

"I have an idea, Murad." Salma her fingers under her chin. "Your mother told me Nabulsi used to…" She stopped midway through her sentence, looked down at the floor, then up to Murad and blushed. "Let's assume the second character is a capital 'I' not a one," she said, counting on her fingers the letters as she called out "Aisha Om Mohamed. Fourteen." She reached to twist an earring she no longer had. Murad felt a dull ache in his chest. "You're sure the hacker said fifteen characters?" she asked Paul. The air in the room had become so brittle it could snap.

"Absolutely," he insisted, pursing his lips. "Assuming he counted right." Salma counted off the letters again.

"Still fourteen," she said, picking at a cuticle. "I thought it might be your mother's name, Murad. But Aisha Om Mohamed is one character short."

"Why would the sheikh use my mother's—?"

"It's a long story. They got to know each other quite well after you left."

"What? How?" Murad's face slicked with confusion. The cogs in his brain couldn't move fast enough to take in the information or make sense of it.

"I'll tell you later. There's no time now," Salma replied. "Just believe me when I say I can see why he'd use her name on a disk he thought was private."

"Okay." It really wasn't okay, but Murad thought she might be right. "Try it with her name: the daughter of her father, Aisha Bint Ismail." Murad counted off those letters with Salma. Ten and five. Fifteen. First, they grinned then they laughed and then Salma said, "I vote we take the one in a million chance." The air was electric with nerves; yet anticipatory—like holding one's breath before a gun went off.

"We've nothing to lose," Paul said, his voice hoarse. "Rashid's not going to let us stay here till dawn."

"With due respect." Murad took the four short steps between him and them. "I'm sure I know my way around an Arabic keyboard better than either of you. If the disk doesn't erase itself, everything on it will be in Arabic." Paul stood to give him the office chair. *"Bism illah."* Murad invoked God's name as his fingers on the keyboard assumed their fateful journey. His heart all but stopped beating in the fierceness of his concentration.

"Aywaa," he pumped the air with his fist and roared a jubilant "yes." *"Alhamdu lillah,"* he praised God as he clicked the mouse. Paul clapped him on the shoulders, Salma twirled around once in the tight space. A triple row of files showed up on the screen.

After several false starts Murad found a file with the location of countrywide Taj safe houses. Three files later, he opened one labeled "other contacts" he'd passed over earlier by mistake. He ran his eyes down a list of names. As Nabulsi's assistant, he was surprised at how many he didn't recognize until he reached a name he did. Mohamed Mazen: the medical officer from Hani Hamdi's department who was simultaneously an adviser to the *rayyis* and a member of the Taj Council. Murad's insides vibrated. He'd found what he needed most. He nearly knocked over Paul when he pushed back his chair and reached across the desk to Salma. "We have something your father wouldn't want anyone to know," he said, swallowing a shout of absolute glee.

Chapter 6

THE MECHANICAL GROWL OF THE HELICOPTER ENGINE, the beating of blades, reverberated through the cabin. A galaxy of electronic devices, phosphorescent squares, and flashing red lights, put out tiny beeps. Uncomfortable in her rigid, constricting, chair, Salma squirmed and peered out her small rectangular window. At first, there was only the reflection of her own face looking back at her—an unflattering smudge of gray—then her eyes adjusted and beyond her reflection, she made out the lights of Aswan.

They were flying north to Cairo. Paul in the seat next to her, Murad in the one in front, wearing industrial-size earphones. Paul was angry. Once they'd successfully opened the disk, he'd neither looked at her nor uttered a word. His face had turned grey some time ago and now, the veins in his temples pulsed. Although they sat together, the gulf between them was so precipitous Salma felt it would take only one tiny mistake to fall in.

Her mind wandered. She found herself replaying the museum office scene and feeling the same electric thrill she'd felt when Murad recognized the name of the mole in the presidential office: Lt. Colonel Mohamed Mazen, on Taj al Islam's Supreme Council. A serious problem for Salma's father who'd seconded the man from his Department of Military Medicine to the Presidential Office where he could do the most damage.

She recalled her father mentioning the man on the drive from the airport the day she'd arrived. Mazen and Hani's time as students in the military academy had overlapped. It was natural to assume they were close. Yes, it was guilt by association but there was power in the information. Blackmail by any other words. Her father could lose everything—from his job to his life.

Salma glanced at Paul, again. He didn't look at her. Murad, she noticed, had removed his earphones. She rubbed the knuckle of a clenched fist with the index finger of the other hand and stared out the window again. They were still flying over the desert, gray and tufted with black spots where plants managed to grow. Something gnawed at her. A chill traced its icy way along her veins. Behind her back, Paul had cozied up to Israel's notorious Mossad—the one she'd been fighting for years. Could she trust what he and the Mossad had cooked up for Murad? Her doubt kept growing until it was almost physical.

"What's the plan?" she asked Paul, disquieted.

"Cairo to refuel and then Amman," Paul answered tersely, and Murad swiveled in his seat to ask,

"And...?"

"You now have a Jordanian birth certificate, identity card, and passport in your new name: Ahmed Samir. There's no changing it so I hope you like it."

"And in Jordan, what will I do?"

"It's arranged. A room with a Palestinian family and a job in their bakery."

"Do you know them?"

"Your "cousins" do," Paul said. The air in the cabin was tense and ready to snap.

"Anyone who works with the Mossad is a traitor," Murad muttered. "Collaborators, working for the Israelis." He slumped in his seat; his head disappeared behind it.

"Maybe they don't have a choice," Paul addressed the back of Murad's chair. "The rest of their family is stuck in Gaza." Salma let out a slow, restrained, breath to control the ball of anger forming in her guts, waiting to take over.

"Who in the hell came up with this plan?" Her stomach heaved unhelpfully. Paul massaged his temples.

"I was afraid you wouldn't like it, but there was nothing else to do. I had to make a deal about the disk with Aaron." Salma faced him, stiff and furious, her heart rate accelerating. Why were they using Israeli contacts? She'd spent four months in Amman running sessions to empower women in political life. She was still in touch with some of them and could—. The pilot's announcement filled the cabin before she could formulate anything concrete.

"Please be sure your seat-belts are securely fastened. We are preparing to land." The crackling of the speakers made the pilot's voice sound harsh. The throaty roar of the chopper's blades only stopped when the wheels hit the tarmac of the Almaza military airport—plunked in the middle of the residential district of Heliopolis where her cousin Mokhtar lived. Salma was thinking of the nighttime view of Cairo from his eleventh floor penthouse with its lights that spread forever. She wasn't prepared for the door opening onto flood light-illuminated Humvees surrounded by soldiers in camouflage fatigues.

While two of the soldiers refueled the aircraft, the pilot brought snacks from the commissary; tasteless soft buns with thin slices of parmesan cheese that Salma devoured during the lift off. Except for the afternoon nap in the cave, she hadn't slept in twenty-four hours. She'd crawled through a tunnel, trudged through the desert, and was jumped in the dark by soldiers. She leaned her head against the chopper's window and closed her eyes.

She couldn't sleep. The words her father said when he'd pulled her aside at the Sofitel Hotel had jolted her into a kind of numbness that kept her from responding to him at the time.

"Leave that man," he'd said. "It will never work between you. Stay in Egypt. You can be the assistant minister of health. Then, when Abdel Rasool retires, you'll be in the cabinet." Salma recognized her father had made a serious offer—one on which he could and would deliver. "Imagine the power and authority you'd have to make real change," he urged her. She could imagine it. Where would she begin? Focus on prevention: clean water, vaccinations, health education—maybe even a sexual awareness campaign? Idiotic mental ramblings. People far better qualified than she had tried and failed. And how would she handle the endemic corruption? There was no way to win in a crooked game. What a strange world she'd be living in if she accepted and. . .

She must have finally nodded off because it was the sun shining through her tiny window that woke her. They were flying over miles of tents stamped with large blue UNHCR letters of the United Nations Refugee Agency. How did a miniature, almost landlocked, seventy-five percent desert country, like Jordan, take in one point four million Syrian refugees? It already had two million Palestinian ones who now formed eighty percent of its population. Despite its unsurpassed public relations efforts, the place must be ready to explode. It wasn't the first time Salma shook her head in bewilderment about the Kingdom.

The helicopter looped east, descending into Jordan's Queen Alia airport in Amman. Unlike Cairo's Almaza, with its soldiers and Humvees, this was a commercial airport with the buzz and bustle of KLM, Misr Air, and Royal Jordanian Boeing 747s, their bright reds, blues, and greens, gleaming in the morning light.

Paul jumped out and sped ahead as soon as the pilot opened the helicopter door. Salma and Murad followed, with Murad looking desolate. His five o'clock shadow was closer to a ten, his eyes were red, and the circles below them were almost black. She had to hold herself back from taking his hand as they entered the terminal. By the time they exited, Paul was already outside, seated in a dark-blue sedan, drumming his fingers on its roof.

The sedan driver pointed to the wide-open back door and complained in an Israeli accent. "It's the middle of the morning commute. Aaron didn't figure on the traffic when he told the family we'd be there before nine." The traffic was, indeed, heavy. Twenty times heavier than eight years ago when Salma was in Jordan. It was more organized, more regimented, than Cairo's because the people of Amman mostly stayed in their lanes. Unlike Cairo's, most of Amman's apartments were new and low, except for a few skyscrapers—some still struggling to rise. The subdued glow from the polished-sandstone with which the homes on the tree-lined streets were built felt comfortable but somehow, the flavor of the other streets had changed dramatically. For the better. Warmer and livelier with one Syrian restaurant after the other.

"Where does the family live?" she asked the taciturn driver.

"Sweifeh, in the sixth." It wasn't much of an answer, but she knew Amman well enough to recognize he'd referred to the sixth of the original seven hills on which the city was built.

"That's not too far," she told Murad. "Less than a half hour away." He clasped his hands together so tightly, his fingers also lost color and Salma considered touching his arm to center him. The sense of relief flowing through her when he smiled instead of pulling away was disquieting. She didn't dare risk revisiting the psychic space joining them to each other.

The car stopped at Forn Fayez, a bakery whose window on the street displayed a myriad of baked goods. Fluffy croissants, rich chocolate chip cookies, soft pretzel *semeet*, and loaves of *shami* pita bread. Dismal as she felt about being there, Salma's mouth watered, and her stomach rumbled. At least they'd be in an Arab home where the hosts were sure to feed them.

She was right. The plump woman who opened the door of the apartment over the establishment held a plate of *kahek* shortbread in her hand.

"Ahlan wa sahlan," she greeted them, offering each a piece. Salma had a soft spot for the Palestinian accent and loved the phrase used throughout the Arab world: you are with family, be at ease. It felt more personal than *salaamu aleikum.* Murad was not at ease. He stood with his shoulder's hunched, throwing furtive glances at the doorway.

The Fayez Ziyad apartment was showy—with crocheted doilies on the back and arms of its long floral-patterned sofa and overstuffed chairs. A milk-white vase of blue and orange plastic flowers stood near a large ashtray in the middle of a coffee table covered in a plastic tablecloth that mimicked lace. The couple, in their early fifties, were gracious in their welcome, but were anxious to get back to their busy bakery. The moment Murad finished his obligatory tea, Fayez showed him to what would be his room, left his wife to tend to the guests, and went back to work.

Murad returned to the living room looking as though he'd lost all the rounds in a boxing ring. He seemed stupefied when Paul handed him an envelope "to buy clothes and toiletries." Taking it between his forefinger and thumb as though it was full of anthrax, Murad dropped it on the coffee table in disgust. "You will work in the bakery," Paul continued, unfazed. "Your cousins will send you a monthly stipend. As from today, you work for them." Salma gasped. Murad's face went as white as a death-mask.

"That'll never happen. Israel is the devil," he said in a tone more formidable than she'd ever heard him use. "I will never work for the Israeli Mossad. The worst you or they can do is kill me. I'm willing to accept that."

Salma's mouth froze open; she stood stunned, rigid as a board. Words left her. Paul had crossed a red line she only now discovered she had, and she didn't trust herself to speak to him. As though she was in command, she spun to face Fayez's wife and asked to use her phone. With her back to Paul, she waited for the woman to drag over a turquoise-colored coiled cord and called information, then dialed the number for the Ministry of Women and Children's Health.

"Please connect me to her Excellency, Minister Ghada," she said, summoning her most formal voice. "Tell her *Doctora* Salma is in Amman. We're friends," she added, responding to the secretary, and glowering at Paul.

"Ahlan, ahlan, ya habibti." Minister Ghada was her usual exuberant self. "Heba and I were talking about you just last week. She'll be as delighted as I am you're in town. Can you join us for dinner tonight?"

"Thank you. You're very kind. Unfortunately, I'm here for only a few hours. How's your daughter doing in Cambridge?"

"She loves it. As I said in my last email, she's registering for a Ph.D. in political economics." Salma waited for a second before she continued.

"Your Excellency, I need a big favor. A friend escaped from the Islamists in Egypt. He came here on false documents and needs help. I know it's a lot to ask, but can he make an appointment to meet with you? Through your secretary, of course."

"Naturally. You also have my personal cell number, dear. Give it to your friend in case he needs to reach me sooner."

"Unfortunately, I lost my phone. Would you be so kind as to give it to me again?" Salma thanked the princess, scribbled the number on a pad by the phone and slammed the receiver into its cradle. "Let's go shopping, Murad," she said, grabbing his arm and wrenching open the apartment door. "There's a coffee shop not far from the department store if you want to wait for us there," she told Paul, to be polite.

Chapter 7

October 4, 2014
12 pm

T HERE WERE MORE SALESGIRLS THAN CUSTOMERS IN THE department store. Jordan was another developing country with cheap labor and few jobs. Two slightly older than middle-aged men waddled around prayer beads dangling from their fingers, their heads down, their hands clasped behind their backs. Two slightly overweight women in loose fitting dresses, likely their wives, wandered through the store's aisles with teenage daughters in tow. When they finally stopped at the makeup and perfume counter, the men took a flight of stairs to the store's coffee shop.

Salma borrowed money from Murad, bought an inexpensive cell phone and a crossbody bag for it, and waited for him at a corner table in the same coffee shop. As soon as she'd propped her elbows on a table with a distant view of the blue-mosaic dome of the King Abdullah Mosque, a waiter took her order of coffee and a croissant. A deep sigh slipped out of her like air out of a balloon and she exhaled a long breath she didn't realize she'd been holding.

Her heart rate accelerated, again. She was furious. Too furious to think clearly. If Paul thought the Mossad would make an honest deal for Murad, he was dumber and denser than a petrified log. He'd wounded and betrayed her. It was bad enough to have recruited the Mossad to help Murad, but he'd assumed she'd go along with that. Her anger didn't assuage the pain of her broken heart. What about the years she'd spent supporting human rights for the Palestinians, arrested, imprisoned, and tortured by the Mossad while America looked on? Wouldn't that have been a hint to how she'd feel? Apparently not. He'd gotten angry at her for protecting her friend by thwarting the Mossad plan to compromise him. When all was said and done, no matter how close they'd been, no matter how in love they were, Paul didn't understand her. It was time she opened her eyes. Anyone who thought it fine for love to be blind was headed straight over the edge of a cliff.

By the time the waiter brought her order, Salma had rested her chin in her hand and was starting to calm down. Paul had done the best he could with what he'd had at hand. Who but the man who loved her would help the man she used to love? She was reaching for her coffee cup when Murad leaned over her at a perfect distance for a kiss. She moved her head away. He didn't seem surprised. Plopping his shopping bags on the floor he pulled out the chair across from her.

"Were you really talking to a Jordanian princess?" he asked, as he settled into it, acting as though she hadn't brushed his gesture away.

"Of course," Salma said. "She's the king's second cousin and his wife's good friend. She was in my workshops. I've known her for years."

"You think she'd get me into the West Bank?" He ran his fingers through his hair with its angular widow's peak, almost like a triangle in the middle of his forehead.

"I'm sure she could," Salma reassured him. "Nothing's impossible for the royal family. It controls Jordan with an iron fist."

"I know people in the West Bank who can give me a job," Murad explained. "I'd feel safer with them. I know the Mossad is everywhere but, here, I'm alone and already in their crosshairs."

"Princess Ghada can protect you, but you have to keep your head down for a while." They sat in uneasy silence and undeclared dread until the simple words rushed up Murad's throat and out his mouth and hung in the air's expectant hush.

"I don't want you to leave. I love you. Stay with me." Salma brushed imaginary crumbles off the tablecloth to avoid meeting his inexpressibly sad eyes. It felt as if a thousand buzzing flies were trapped in her chest, her head started swimming with ways to say goodbye.

"You deserve better than what I can be to you, *habibi*," she said, feeling dissociated. She fixed her eyes on a spot behind Murad's left ear to keep from falling through her own mind. "You're a wonderful man. You'll find a love who shares a full life with you." Her throat was tight, as though she'd swallowed a stone. "This isn't a farewell forever." She buried her hands in her lap and clenched them together so tightly, her fingernails left crescent-shaped imprints on her palms.

Murad's chin trembled. He stared at his cup without blinking then wiped at his nose with a paper napkin. His shoulders drooped and started gently quaking. His face blurred through the glaze of Salma's tears as she fought to keep her composure. She didn't dare love this good man too deeply. Rather than a road not taken, life with Murad would be a dead end for her.

"I have to leave now," she said. "Call the princess right away. And please write or email me. I'll worry until I hear from you." The ache of longing to stay with him reached her bone marrow the moment she turned to leave, and she couldn't swallow the lump in her throat, no matter how hard she tried.

Murad sat at the table so long he had to wave the waiter away twice. Bathed in the afternoon's natural light, he stared out the floor-to-ceiling windows at a panorama of sandstone buildings he didn't really see. He'd let Salma wound him. Again. She'd shattered his heart once before. Perhaps he wouldn't have risked his life so rashly if he hadn't been in love with her.

Still, she was firmly planted in the terrain of his heart, with him wherever he went in the world, there even when he wasn't thinking of her. Sometimes, he'd hear himself laugh in a certain way and remember working alongside her in the raised beds of her vegetable garden. Sometimes, when he was kicking rocks in the Yemeni hills out of boredom, he'd imagine he was hiking along a Santa Cruz Mountain trail with her. Mostly, he'd find himself looking deep into her eyes while they talked or grew silent together.

Yet he couldn't live forever balanced on the precarious edge of her terrains; the worlds of the rich and poor, the elites and oppressed, the free and the bound. Salma could do so because she broke rules—even rules laid down by God. Murad lived by rules etched into his soul. The ones by which his parents, grandparents and forefathers had lived. He would never be able to live with Salma.

Leaving a generous tip on the table, he collected his bags and went out in the streets of Amman. This was a world he could manage. The princess would help. He'd teach in his friend's school in the West Bank city of Ramallah. In a year, maybe two, he'd get married; have children with a woman who'd be a good mother—a woman who would understand he'd always love Salma.

The Clementina Cafe was busy, but Paul's table against a wall was relatively calm. "We can leave for the airport from here," Salma said, as she walked up to him. "I won't need a passport if the helicopter flies us back to Almaza airport."

"Would you like to eat something before we go?" Paul asked, his face blank as he rose to pull out a chair. "Their cappuccino is excellent; their croissants just so-so."

"Funny. We ordered the same things. So, no thanks. I've already eaten."

"With Murad?" Paul asked, pushing the chair into place and straightening his shoulders.

"No. He was shopping." Salma looked past him to a couple on the sidewalk eyeing his table. "People are waiting, I think we should go."

"Where is he now?" Paul asked, securing his bill and a ten-dollar note under his saucer.

"In the coffee shop. I left before he ordered." Which was true. "He'll probably have a bite before he calls Princess Ghada. He still has burner phones." How was it possible that only yesterday morning, she'd used one of them to talk to Paul? And why had things gone so wrong between the two of them when he'd tried so hard to help?

"Let's take an Uber to the airport," Paul said. A silver Honda Civic drove up, immediately and with one hand on the small of her back, Paul steered Salma to the car.

"So, how long do you plan on pretending we're not upset?" Paul asked as soon as they were seated.

"I'm not pretending. I'm tired. Too tired to make any sense." He had to know she was exhausted. She groaned with fatigue.

"I'm tired, too," Paul said. "But I'm not going to rest until we've sorted this out. Why the end run to a princess?" he asked, his face smoldering beneath his stony expression. "You humiliated me, Salma. After I did everything you asked of me, you made me feel like a fool."

"Why didn't you tell me that you made a deal with the Mossad that would force Murad to become a collaborator? Did you think he'd agree to be their operative? Did you think I'd go along with that?" Salma forced each maliciously punctuated word through teeth clenched together so hard that her temples ached.

"You ask me to save the life of a terrorist who was once your lover and then bitch about how I do it? What chutzpah. As far as I was concerned, an Islamist terrorist was holding you hostage." A flush of red surged up from Paul's neck to his forehead.

"Murad would never have harmed me. He needed protection from Nabulsi who was sure to have him killed."

"That's what you want to believe, but you know what I believe? The guy would have killed you if I hadn't found a way to meet his demands. I'm sorry you disapprove of how I did it." Paul's reddened face turned crimson. "You should have let your Princess muckety-muck handle things from the start. You shouldn't have blindsided me."

"You know," Salma looked down at her lap, "I was livid when I discovered the kind of deal you'd made with the Mossad. Now, I'm more hurt than angry."

"I'm sorry you feel that way." Paul's patently trite expression annoyed her. Wondering if he meant it to do so, she stared out the window at the traffic—cars that weren't blowing horns at each other.

"Things were good between us in the States," she continued in a carefully uncommitted tone.

"Sounds like there's a "but" after that," Paul said.

"We both lived in the same world—your world. Somehow, now that we're in my world, things have gone to hell."

"Ah, there's the "but,"" Paul pointed out.

Salma paused, reached for an earring in a bare earlobe, then dropped her hands to her lap. The Uber hit a pothole; she grabbed the hand-rest. Paul pressed his slender fingers into the skin of his forearms. She couldn't decide whether he was angry or anxious and she was too tired to have this conversation. Anyway, this wasn't the time or place.

"Okay," he said. "I'll get to the point. It's about the Mossad, isn't it?"

"In a way," she replied, hesitant. "But it's really about us."

"What's your point? I know you hate the Mossad. You disapprove of Israel. So do I."

"Yes." Salma turned to face him. "Only the depth of our disapproval is different. So is its source."

"Now, you're sounding like a sociologist."

"Don't push it, Paul. I'm too tired to be diplomatic."

"Well, don't be."

"All right, I won't." She wanted Paul to think of her as standing up for herself. "When it comes to Israel, here's how we differ." She took a deep breath and gathered her strength. "It's too late now, but it would have been totally fine with me for the British to give the Zionists Uganda, or for America to give them Florida, or if, in fact, Israel never existed." Salma checked Paul's face to gauge his reaction. He seemed to be holding himself in check, so she continued. "There's no way your disapproval of the country resembles mine. You don't like how it behaves, but you love it, nonetheless. I don't love it. It humiliates every Arab, anti-colonial, cell in my body. Here we are, planning to get married and it seems you don't know that."

"Salma, we're both too old to think people in love know each other completely. I know you well enough to respect how brave you are to marry me despite your family." After his obvious irritation, Paul's response rang so affectionately, Salma's heart skipped a beat. "We can work things out, sweetheart. I'm a Jewish American. I'm not an Israeli." Salma's eyes glimmered with watery tears. In Paul's words she heard a kindness, a kind of concern for her that was natural for him. "I can't change the world," he continued, with a confirming squeeze of her hand. "I can change myself, if you help," he added before he kissed it. All Salma could think of was how little she'd done to earn the accepting patience he was showing her. "I don't think of you as an Arab. I think of you as American with an Egyptian flavor. I can't know how you fit into your Egyptian world, but you fit perfectly well in your American one." She pulled away her hand. An almost electric shot ran through her arm when her elbow hit the armrest.

"I don't want you to think of me as being only American. That's an insult to my Egyptian identity." Her vehemence, even fierceness, surprised her. She fussed at the buckle of her seatbelt. "For all its limitations, the depth of that culture gives me strong enough roots to make the most of being American. I guess that's why most immigrants make something of themselves."

"I meant it when I asked you to help. So, tell me. I want to understand what's important to you."

Salma took a deep, nervous, breath. She didn't know if she could respond to Paul's innocent question. There were so many things she'd never shared with anyone that felt too personal, too private, to share even with him. A crack in the protective shell surrounding her inner world would leave her stripped to bare flesh, exposed to her pain. "Trust me to cherish what you say," Paul added softly. Salma took the gentleness with which he covered her hand with his as a sign he wouldn't intrude on regions of her emotional life too sensitive to unmask.

"Palm trees are important to me." She tested the waters with a safely impersonal subject. "Sounds trite, doesn't it? Even corny."

"No, it doesn't. They're icons Jung would relate to." The warmth in Paul's eyes encouraged her to go on.

"You know how you can see the top of redwoods from my bedroom skylight?" She saw him smile. "Well, as I child, when we had to go to bed before sunset, I stared at the palm fronds outside my window feathering against each other, until I fell asleep. Sometimes, I pretend they're waving in my skylight." Salma wasn't yet ready to add how now, their zaghloul dates would remind her of the little girl in the Ehssan Clinic who'd been circumcised and Soraya saying how hard Egypt's countryside was on its women.

Still, even when women were abused, despite the high price they were forced to pay, by holding their families together they kept society together. The Egyptian family was the only social institution in the country that functioned. For Paul to connect to the country's soul, to understand its culture from inside it, an Egyptian family would have to adopt him. She couldn't imagine one taking in an American Jewish man without one of their own to vouchsafe for him. She wasn't sure she could do that for Paul, but she owed him to share how she was feeling. "This week has changed my priorities. I have a more profound appreciation of how this culture defines me. How much I owe it. Don't get me wrong, half of me is as American as apple pie, but now I need to honor the half of me that's *fuul* and falafel."

"What do you think affected you so deeply?" Paul asked.

"The women. I saw them washing clothes in the river, tending their little children alongside their goats. A skeletally thin one interceded for her husband when she thought I was an aid worker who could help. I took a dried date from the handful she offered and didn't ask why she, herself, looked sick."

"Egyptians are the kindest people I know, the most generous," Paul said. "I read rural conditions are terrible—people on the verge of starvation—yet even the poorest ones offer strangers their food." Salma appreciated Paul trying to show her he could relate to what she'd said. "And, they have the best sense of humor," he added, with a smile. "I guess five thousand years of oppression will help develop one. So, whenever I think of Egypt, I think of laughter."

Salma didn't know how to segue from Paul's comments to her experience. Referring to Murad's mother was out of the question. He'd probably understand how Aisha Bint Ismail subsumed her given name and personal identity to proud motherhood, happy to be known as Om Mohamed. But why would he care that she was not like her son? Aisha didn't smile often; when she did, she beamed until her eyes vanished in the folds of her face. She wasn't as garrulous as most Egyptians, she was observant and thoughtful, instead. Yes, she'd scolded Salma over trifles, but she'd also tolerated her—surprisingly well. Aisha seemed to relate to what went on between Salma and Murad. Every Friday afternoon, she'd probably lived her own hopeless relationship with Sheikh Nabulsi.

A floodgate opened, filling Salma's mind with wave upon wave of images. She could only hold back a few of the multitude released. Children running up to her on her evening walks along the Nile Corniche and across the Giza bridge. "Welcome to Egypt," they'd call to her as though she were a foreigner. "What's your name?" they'd ask, covering their laughter with embarrassed hands when she answered in Arabic. Midway on the bridge, the lupine vendor pouring lemon juice and red pepper sauce into plastic cups filled with lupines, adding an extra spoon full for Salma with a broad-smile wink. She was thinking of the lights reflecting in the river when Paul asked, "Aren't you going to say more?"

"I was thinking," she said. She was thinking of the circle of women in Sidi Osman, cross legged on the ground, telling stories of Clever Mohamed's quest for the golden apple, stories they didn't know were Sufi parables. "I realize you know women here spend almost all their time with other women."

"Obviously," Paul said. "It goes without saying, men spend most of their time with men."

"I was thinking how the gathering of village women I saw was different from the American coffee klatches I went to when my kids were babies. I felt awkward. Every woman tended only to her own child as though it was private property. In Sidi Osman, they pass babies and toddlers from hand, to hand, to hand, cuddling them on communal laps until they fall asleep in whichever lap they land. Sort of like musical chairs."

It was too complicated to explain to Paul how Aisha and Soraya hid her in a mosque where women Salma didn't know, and would never know, protected her from the men of Taj al Islam. Images were still crowding her mind when she heard his voice trailing slowly as though his words weren't willing to leave his mouth.

"Where do we go from here?"

"It's not your fault you weren't born half and half," she said with a dry laugh.

"What do you mean?"

"It's never going to work." A shiver went through Salma's body recalling how her father had used those exact words. Her bottom lip quivered. She bit down on it to keep back her tears.

"We can make it work," Paul insisted. Salma saw a kind of sadness in his eyes she'd never seen before and turned her head away.

"I want to go home to my kids," she said in almost a whisper, willing her lips to move.

"I won't let you leave my life, easily. Not without a fight," Paul protested. The blood had drained from his stubbled face, turning it a sickly grey color. "I'll keep on pouring in love until I redeem myself for whatever crime you believe I committed." His voice broke. "Not being able to live in two worlds at the same time is not a crime."

Chapter 8

October 4, 2014
3:00 pm

SALMA RAISED HER EYES FROM HER LAP JUST as the scalloped roof of the Queen Alia terminal came into view. The air conditioning in its interior brought goosebumps to her arms; its thermostat apparently stuck on high. With Paul guiding her by the elbow through rows of rust brown chairs, they crossed the hall and followed the signs to a private exit onto the tarmac and Princess Ghada's Cessna awaiting their arrival.

When the small plane reached cruising level; Salma looked down on the airport's patch of grey buildings that were almost swallowed up by desert; marveled again at how Jordan managed to survive. Paul unbuckled his seat belt, turned to her and said above the roar of the engine, "Give us a chance to make something good happen, my love. I know we can." How could he think they could talk in the midst of this din? Besides, she couldn't handle any more emotions.

"I hope so," she sighed, both unwilling and unable to speak louder. "Still, I'm going to need some space to adjust, and I don't know if you'll be there through the changes." She covered her face with her hands and left them there for a long moment, as if to be transported. When she took them away again Paul was still there, exactly as he'd been, watching her as though his life depended on this moment.

"I can't imagine any change you'd make I wouldn't accept."

"Let's talk about this back home," she said, slipping her arm through his. "After you get back from researching that damned *Harper's* article. Now, for heaven's sake, let's give it a rest." With that, she propped her head on his shoulder and kept her eyes shut until the plane landed.

By evening, Salma stood in the Hamdi garden, alone—the enclosure resplendent in its abundance of color. Exuberant yellow chrysanthemums stood apart from the pink geraniums with their variegated leaves. Sharp-leaved oleanders watched over spike-petaled dahlias in front of them.

When her cousin dashed out to greet her, her voice was softer than the last time she had. "Thank God you're safe. We were worried to death about you," Farida said, throwing her arms around Salma who let herself lean against her.

"I have to get back to the States as soon as possible," Salma said. "My classes start the day after tomorrow. Do you think Mokhtar could get me a plane ticket on such short notice?"

"Already? You were gone all week. We haven't had a chance to visit," Farida complained. Salma dissolved into a puddle of laughter. Fighting off semi-hysterical gales, she held her stomach and doubled over, gasping for air.

Yes, she'd been gone all week. A week of harrowing car rides, desert sandstorms, hunted down by the Taj and the Egyptian army. She'd hidden first in a mosque, then in a cave, then crawled on her belly through a tunnel full of bat shit. After a unique tour of an Egypt she hadn't known existed, she'd left Murad and Paul in pain, her father furious at her and she had no idea what would happen next. Gone all week, indeed. Farida didn't know the half of it.

She was wiping off tears on the shoulder of her tee shirt—actually, Maryam's—when she heard Farida insist, "Stop laughing. Mokhtar and I think you could make peace with your father if you took some of his advice to heart. My father agrees."

"What?" Salma tried to connect the sparks swirling in her brain, only to cause a short circuit. Where did this come from?

"Listen for a moment. Both your daughters will be in college next year and your mother is close enough to keep an eye on them. Why not spend some time here?"

"What do you mean?"

"Share your skill and experience here. You could split your time. At least try it. We have some ideas you could think about."

"Yeah?"

"You could teach at the American University. Mokhtar is on the board of trustees. Perhaps you could develop a joint program between it and your university. And there are all sorts of things you could do in the Ministry of Maternal and Child Health. The minister is a good friend. I've known her for years."

Perhaps Salma could do this—go back and forth between her two worlds. Perhaps Paul would come with her. Suddenly, she was struck by the irony. In her Egyptian world, there was no getting away from her family's influence. Like it or not, here she would always be a Hamdi.

Alexandria ⊙

Suez

⊙ Cairo

Sinai
Peninsula

FAYOUM

MINYA

SIDI
OSMAN ★

Luxor ⊙

ASWAN

★ Fictitious Place

AKNOWLEDGMENTS

I wrote this book as a way of explaining the Western and Arabic cultures to each other—something I have done since childhood. I began considering the existence of two worlds when I was a seven-year-old girl growing up in Egypt. I had left a breast of chicken on my plate. My American mother said to eat my food; people all over the world were starving. My Egyptian grandmother told me to leave a nice piece of chicken on the edge of my plate for the maid. I leave you with these two world views to ponder as you read.

To write this book, I had to carve out time from a busy bi-continental life as a professor and practicing psychologist, so it took forever to finish. I've lost track of how many people read how many of its pages--I just know they're a lot. I thank every single one of them. I owe the fact I persisted to Scott Driscoll, my first creative writing teacher who became my committed advisor and stayed with me for the long haul. I wouldn't be writing if he hadn't convinced me not to drop his University of Washington class because I hadn't understood a word of the student discussion. "Don't worry," he'd told me in the corridor. "They're just MFA students one-upping each other."

My great friend, Sheryl Feldman, stands out from the crowd for having been by me from start to finish. I'm embarrassed to think of the terrible prose I asked her look at which she gracefully tackled. It was she who helped me exchange the stiff style of my academic writing to a style that I hope is more readable. I guess professors are as guilty as Master of Fine Arts students when it comes to professional jargon.

Above all, this is an effort to do what Bill, my late husband, encouraged me to do—speak truth to power. He supported my affection for the culture of the Arab world, generously.

The novel is an homage to the man I adored. It is a fictionalized story set in true circumstances.

CUNE PRESS WAS FOUNDED in 1994 to publish thoughtful writing of public importance. Our name is derived from "cuneiform." (In Latin *cuni* means "wedge.")

In the ancient Near East the development of cuneiform script—simpler and more adaptable than hieroglyphics—enabled a large class of merchants and landowners to become literate. Clay tablets inscribed with wedge-shaped stylus marks made possible a broad inter-meshing of individual efforts in trade and commerce.

Cuneiform enabled scholarship to exist, art to flower, and created what historians define as the world's first civilization. When the Phoenicians developed their sound-based alphabet, they expressed it in cuneiform.

The idea of Cune Press is the democratization of learning, the faith that rarefied ideas—pulled from dusty pedestals and displayed in the streets—can transform the lives of ordinary people. And it is the conviction that ordinary people, trusted with the most precious gifts of civilization, will give our culture elasticity and depth—a necessity if we are to survive in a time of rapid change.

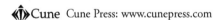 Cune Cune Press: www.cunepress.com

AMAL SEDKY WINTER IS A BI-CULTURAL, bilingual, Egyptian American woman from a prominent Egyptian family who has a foot in both worlds. Her life experience and her training and work as a psychologist enable her to compare Arab and American culture from inside and outside.

In addition to her private practice as a clinical psychologist, Amal was a court appointed evaluator, mediator and special master which led to being recruited to train mediator throughout Egypt. Having run for political office, she was also recruited to train women in various Middle Eastern countries for political empowerment. As a professor of psychology, she helped establish three graduate programs—the last being at the American University in Cairo to which she bilocated from Seattle for years.

Her lifetime of activism in support of human rights included running for political office and serving on a number of boards, including Psychologist for Social Responsibility (PsySR) and the Santa Clara County American Civil Liberties Union (ACLU).
She also served as an elected trustee of the West Valley-Mission Community College in California.

For many years Amal lived in the San Francisco Bay Area. Now she makes her home in Seattle.